THE
CRYING HEART

THE
CRYING HEART

by
Clara Bernice Miller

MOODY PRESS
CHICAGO

TO MY DEAR HUSBAND
WAYNE W. MILLER
THIS BOOK IS LOVINGLY
DEDICATED

Foreword

This is a story of my people, the Amish. And because so often others have treated them like creatures in a zoo, to be stared at for their peculiar ways and customs, I have tried, by the help of God, to set forth their life in the most natural way possible. They have the same joys and sorrows, grief and pain, doubts and fears, as is universal among mankind. Some love God and, sad to say, some don't.

To the characters of this book, horses and buggies, kerosene lamps, no telephone, and peculiar dress are just as much a part of life as radios, television, cars, and electric lights are to the average person. For that reason I have made no comment on these things, hoping the reader can take them for granted at the beginning of the story.

The characters portrayed are fictitious. The names are incidental, although they are common Amish names. It is my prayer that this book might be used to my dear Saviour's honor and glory.

CLARA BERNICE MILLER

1

MARTHA YODER picked up another sheet from the basket at her feet and gave it a hard shake, as hard, that is, as was possible for her, being in a daze. To tell the truth, Martha's mind was no more on hanging up wash than on flying. How could she concentrate on her work after such a night as last night? For Martha had had that most wonderful experience, her first date! And with such a one as Daniel Miller! Her hands were busy with the sheet and the clothespins, but her mind was going over and over the events of the night just past.

It had all started when Johnny Brenneman came in after the social sing and beckoned her to come outside. "Got a way to go home?" he asked.

"Well, I guess I can go with Mary and David," she answered. Mary was her sister and David was Mary's beau.

"Do you want another way to go?" This time teasingly.

"Oh, I don't know. Depends on who it would be with," she said guardedly.

"Well, listen, Daniel Miller would like to take you home."

Martha had opened her eyes wide. Daniel was the best-looking boy there as far as she was concerned. But after all—why, he was a good three years older than she. She had never even dreamed he had noticed her more than perhaps in the friendly greeting when they met somewhere by chance.

"I guess so," she finally answered, almost choking in excitement.

"All right, listen," he said, "if you will, you could come out with Irma and me, and he'll meet you at the gate." Irma was Johnny's girl friend.

So it had been arranged and had worked out just as planned. Of course, the usual catcalls and whistles had followed them as was customary when a new couple paired off.

Martha was so shy when she was finally alone with Daniel that she was afraid he didn't think her good company. Their talk was mostly of the young folks and social happenings. But Daniel was so easy and friendly that before she knew it, the shyness was gone. Then after a while Martha took him out to the kitchen and gave him a piece of pie. She herself didn't take any because she was afraid if she did she'd disgrace herself by being sick right before him. Then finally he looked at his watch and said, "Well, maybe I had better go; it's after twelve. Do you want to go home with me next Sunday evening?"

Martha was so thrilled that she stammered, "I—I don't care."

"All right, I'll take you home, and shall I come and get you too?"

"Well, I—I guess I can go with Mary and David again." She had been so nervous and surprised she actually did not know for sure just what she had said.

"I will get you after the sing then," David said, and he took her hand and squeezed it gently. "Good night, till then," and he closed the door gently and she heard his soft whistle as he went down the walk.

8

Martha sped upstairs and then lay awake most of the night in a daze of enchantment. When she finally fell asleep at dawn, it was only to dream of Daniel.

"Martha! Martha!" The call brought Martha to her surroundings with a jerk. Oh, my goodness, Mom probably had more wash to hang up, and here she wasn't even finished with what she had! Her quick fingers flew now as she answered, "Coming, Mom." The last pillowcase was given a final hard shake before it was pinned on the line. Picking up the basket at her feet, Martha hurried to the washhouse, where Mom was ready with more wash to hang.

"Och, what took you so long?" Mom wanted to know. "You're usually finished lots quicker than this."

"I—I was just thinking, Mom," Martha answered rather lamely.

"Ha, just thinking. I'll bet you were thinking of last night."

"Oh, Mom, how do you know? Did you hear us?" Unwittingly the truth slipped out. Not that she hadn't intended to tell Mom sometime, but after all—

"Yes, I heard you. Do you suppose I could sleep after all the noise you made?" she answered teasingly. "Who fell over a chair?"

"Chair!" echoed Martha. "No one did, that I know of."

"Someone bumped against a chair of some kind, at least it sounded like it," Mom said.

Light dawned on Martha. "Oh, Mom," she laughed, half amused, half embarrassed. "That was the little footstool. You know, the one made out of that old wooden wash machine dolly. It was standing before the couch, and I gave it a shove out of the way. Did you think someone fell over a chair?" she asked, as she laughed helplessly.

9

"Well, it sure sounded like it, and Pop thought so too. He gave me a jab with his elbow and wondered if he should go out and help you. Ha! Ha! wait till I tell him," and Mom laughed too. "Anyway, who was it that brought you home, if I may ask?"

Martha was very busy with the clothes again. "Daniel Miller," was the muffled reply.

"Daniel Miller! Well, I never! You mean Dave J.'s son?" Mom ejaculated.

Martha nodded.

"Isn't he some older than you? He's about a year younger than Mary. Why, whatever!" Mom was obviously as surprised as Martha had been last night.

"I know, Mom," Martha answered. "It surprised me too."

"Well, he's nice and friendly, I guess. From what I hear he's a good worker too. Here, why don't you finish this out here and I'll run in and get dinner. My goodness, the menfolks will be in before I have dinner ready. There's just those two other batches of clothes to finish and then it's done. I better hurry; I have that frozen steak to fry." Mom hurried out of the washhouse, leaving Martha alone with her thoughts once more.

By the time Martha had finished hanging up the wash and cleaning the washhouse, the rest of the family was already in the dining room waiting for Mom to put the finishing touches to the dinner. The men were busy reading the day's mail. Pop had the local daily and nineteen-year-old Ervin was reading a letter. Glancing over his shoulder Martha saw the address, and knew it was from someone in army camp. Twelve-year-old Rosie and eight-year-old Paul were squabbling over a monthly farm paper. Thomas, who was fourteen, was reading another.

"Quit fussing there. Who had that paper first?" Pop said to the two children. "Here, Rosie, let Paul have it. After all, you're bigger than he is. Shame on you! Come on, sit down. Mom's got dinner ready. Rosie, why don't you put water in the glasses instead of fighting like that?"

"Oh, why do I have to put water on the table all the time? I spill it anyway and then you don't like that," Rosie pouted. Rosie was much too spoiled, Martha thought, and said so lots of times. Mom brought the last of the dinner to the table.

"Come on, Rosie, do like Pop told you. Done, Martha?" Mom asked with a quick look at Martha. Martha nodded.

"Say, it says here that the age limit for boys has been put to nineteen now," Pop ejaculated. "My, if they take 'em that young, I'll have my hands full next summer."

"Why?" Mom and Martha both asked at once.

"Well, Ervin here was nineteen last week, wasn't it, Ervin?"

"Oh, my, do you really suppose he'll have to go?" Mom asked, worried.

"If they put the age limit down, I don't see how he can get out of it. I don't know if it would do any good to try for a deferment. I kind of hate to do that," he added. "Don't think it looks too good to some of our neighbors if all of us CO's* break our necks trying to get a deferment." The rest knew what he was talking about. Only last week one of their Catholic neighbors had lost a son in the thick of the battle, and the neighbor had been pretty loud in his denunciation of the lousy conscientious objectors who had got farm deferments while other people's sons had to go and fight.

*Conscientious Objectors.

11

"If Ervin is called, all I can do is let him go, I guess. It's going to take a lot of the boys around here, I'm afraid," Pop said. "Well, anyway, dinner is all ready, isn't it, Mom? Let's ask the blessing." And the family all bowed their heads while Pop asked the simple blessing.

"The letter I got here from Albert says that they got a lot of new boys from Indiana last week." After heads were raised again, Ervin imparted this information.

Mom passed the potatoes. "What else does he say?"

"Oh, just camp news," Ervin answered as he helped himself to a large piece of steak. "You know, I don't think I'd mind too much if I had to go. The way Albert writes they have lots of fun. Good experience too. Of course," hastily glancing at Mom, "I would hate to leave Pop to handle the farm alone."

"Alone? Who said alone?" Thomas said indignantly. "I can drive that tractor as well as you can. I can handle the milker just as good too!"

"I can drive tractors too," Paul put in. "Maybe we would get more of a chance if you weren't here."

"Children, children!" Mom's voice broke in. "Be quiet; don't talk like that! You would miss Ervin a lot if you had to do all he does. Do you really think, John," turning to Pop, "that Ervin will be called?"

"Yes, I do," Pop said soberly. "I wouldn't be surprised if he'd have to take his physical before the month's up. According to the news in the paper, I guess the fighting is really terrific."

"Oh, why must people always be making wars?" Mom wanted to know. "They never settle anything. Why, look at the other war. When that was over, they used to say there would be no more war. Now look at it; fighting worse than ever."

12

"I know." Pop sounded tired. "But people will be having wars and rumors of wars as long as the world stands, the Bible says."

Through all this Martha had remained silent because the horrible thought had occurred to her that Daniel Miller was nineteen too, and only several months older than Ervin. What if he had to go? "Oh silly," she thought. "After all, I've only had a date with him once, and just because he asked to come back next Sunday is no sign—" Like as not he wouldn't come back after next Sunday anyway. Maybe he wouldn't pass his physical. But still he looked as healthy as they come.

These thoughts must have shown in her face, because suddenly Mom asked, "Martha, what are you afraid of? That he'll have to go too?" She laughed at Martha's quick blush. Ervin looked at Martha and grinned. He knew what Mom meant, because he had come home last night before Daniel had left.

"Say, Pop, do you know who fell over that chair last night?" Mom was a regular tease. "Martha says she kicked the little footstool out of the way."

"So that is what it was." Pop's eyes twinkled. "Here I was thinking maybe you fell over a chair. I told Mom I thought I'd better go out and see if anyone needed help. Sounded terrible." Pop was as bad as Mom.

"Oh, she had everything under control," Ervin said. "Going on like an old hand when I came in."

"Ervin, I was not!" Martha's cheeks felt hot.

"Well, you were talking away like old pals when I saw you. He sure looked as if he enjoyed it, I must say." Ervin said.

"Is that where the pie went?" Mom wanted to know. "He must be a big eater."

13

"Surely not at that time of the night?" This from Pop.

"Oh, be quiet, all of you," Martha tried to defend herself. After all, she thought, one could take only so much! Especially when only sixteen and hoping to make a good impression on a certain someone.

But the teasing eyes of Mom and Pop twinkled at her still. Even Ervin, busy with his dessert, still had a grin on his face. Yet, through it all, Martha sensed that in the teasing looks there was love for her. This, after all, was one reason they did it. Few, except one of their own, can realize how hard it is for these sturdy, staunch people to express sentiment of any kind. So it was that Martha, not knowing how to put it in words or thoughts, knew that from them it meant parental love when they teased her.

"Well, who did she bring home anyway?" Pop asked. Then after a glance at big-eyed Rosie and Paul, he added, "I'll ask some other time. I'll get it out of Mom tonight. Rosie and Paul might be spoiled if we let them know. I think we're all through eating anyway now, aren't we? So I guess we'd better go cultivate that corn. Looks like rain."

2

THAT EVENING after the others had gone to bed, Pop opened the subject of Martha's date again. "Martha tell who brought her home?" he asked, untying his shoes. Sure felt good to take those things off, he thought, wiggling his toes.

"Yes, she did. Didn't Ervin tell you?" Mom answered.

"Yep, he told me this afternoon. So it was Dave J.'s boy? Well, I guess from what I hear he's as decent as you'd want." Pop leaned back in his chair and stretched his long legs out.

"I know," was Mom's reply, behind the daily paper. "I'm kind of surprised though. He's a couple of years older than she is." Putting the paper aside, Mom gave Pop her full attention.

"Oh, well, it's just once," Pop said. "Just like a woman, got them paired off already." His eyes twinkled at her.

"Oh, John, I have not!" Mom retorted indignantly. "I just said I was surprised because—well, because I thought he'd be 'way above her, that's all."

"I guess he's not so stuck up as some. Say, isn't he about nineteen?" His glance had fallen upon the news column that had been the center of discussion at noon.

"Yes, he is," Mom said. "He is about three or four months older than Ervin and over a year younger than Mary."

"He's liable to be called, too, then." Pop sighed rather heavily. "Sure would hate to see Ervin go, if he has to."

"Couldn't we try and get a deferment?" Mom asked.

"Yes, but I don't think I will. If the board knew we had Thomas and Paul, I don't think it would do any good," Pop said.

"Anyway, you know what the Wadells said." Mom knew what the Wadells had said. The Wadells were their Catholic neighbors, whose boy had been killed.

"But then I guess the way it is in this war, we have it better than the last one. Remember how some of our people's boys had to go?"

"Yes, I know," Mom answered. Both were silent for a few minutes as they remembered the war in their young days. Conscientious objectors who were called then had to go to regular army camps. Life had been pretty hard there.

"How about Mary's boyfriend, David? Won't he have to go?" Pop asked.

"No, he's 4-F," Mom answered.

"Mary say how long she's going to stay at the Gingerichs'?" Pop asked. Mary was working at the home of a neighboring family for the summer.

"She said till after the oats harvest. But she has the chance of a job in a few weeks at Joni Miller's. She said they want to go on a trip out west after harvest," Mom answered. "If David's still in 4-F next winter, it's possible they might get married."

"David's father isn't too good in health anyway; so I expect he will retire now that David is twenty-one." Pop used the rolled-up daily to swat at some bugs that were flying around the lamp. "Pesky things, how do they get in here?" He made another swat at the bugs.

"I know, I've thought of it too. Mary just hasn't mentioned it, but they have been going steady two years now

16

and Mary's twenty-one since last March. So I expect that is what will happen," Mom said.

Pop yawned. "Come on, let's go to bed. Still have two good days' cultivating to do yet. Got to get up early again tomorrow."

"Didn't get any rain after all," Mom remarked.

"Well, I hope it holds off till we get that corn laid by. Come on, blow out the light." Pop was already in the bedroom.

"I will. I just want to think a bit yet." Mom sat with chin in hand.

"Oh, come on, you can think tomorrow." Pop's voice was muffled by the pillow and sleep. Mom didn't answer, and soon he was asleep.

Mom, however, sat for a long time thinking. At last she sighed heavily and, blowing out the lamp, groped her way to the bedroom.

*   *   *

The next morning the family, each with Bible in hand, gathered around the breakfast table, ready for morning devotions. This family worship was such an accepted, usual thing in the lives of each of the children, it would have been impossible for them to picture family life without it. Yet, aside from that, it meant very little to them. They all knew Christ had died for the sins of everyone—Pop and Mom had seen to it that they knew—and wanted everyone to live for Him. But, except for Mary, none of them had applied it to their hearts. Both Ervin and Martha had been baptized and were members of the church. But they had yet to find that personal, living faith without which it is impossible to please God.

Pop and Mom had found it. Long ago, while traveling in a distant state, Pop had attended revival meetings and, under the plain, Spirit-filled preaching of the evangelist, had opened his heart to Christ. It was hard for Mom to give just the exact time when she first came to realize that it took more than head knowledge, but somewhere along the line she too had yielded herself to Him.

It marked them as slightly different, or peculiar. Some people said that John Yoder "thinks he's so good" and that he was "always so religious." Other people's feelings weren't unknown to Pop and, although the injustice of the words stung a bit, yet he kept on. It would take more than the slightly sneering remarks of his fellows to make him give up his religious ideas.

3

TRUE TO POP'S PREDICTION, before two weeks were up the long, official-looking envelope bearing the return address of Selective Service had come, addressed to Ervin Yoder, and within had been his notification to appear at the state induction center for his physical examination. Nor was he the only one. There were at least a dozen boys who also received their notices, among them Daniel. Many mothers and sweethearts were saddened by the thought of the impending, inevitable separation. Many of the older boys had been gone for at least eighteen months and, now that so many of the younger boys were going, their absence would be keenly felt by the young people.

Daniel had taken Martha home again the next Sunday evening and had seemed to enjoy himself—so much so that he asked to come back again the next Sunday, to which Martha was happy to consent.

Before that Sunday came, his notice too had come, and so most of their talk had been of his impending physical. "I don't know why I shouldn't pass," he told Martha. "I have always been healthy. Never was sick except for measles and mumps and such."

"Do you think you will have to go to camp then?" To Martha it was a despairing thought!

"I think I will, yes. I know we won't even try for a deferment because Father thinks it's better for the non-COs' sakes if we don't. Really, I don't mind too much.

19

'Course I hate to leave the folks and—well, you." There, he had said it!

Martha's heart felt as if it would choke her. Excitement made her stammer. "I—I—hate to see you go too. That—er—well, I don't like to see any of the boys go." Maybe she shouldn't be too personal so soon.

"But in another way I think it will be a good experience for all of us boys. You know, we tend to group all together here and sometimes I'm afraid we get too narrow in our thinking. Maybe we'll be better off if we do get some new ideas and viewpoints," Daniel said.

Martha looked at him almost with awe. He seemed so far above her in mental faculties. How did it happen he even noticed her?

"Well, I don't know too much about it," she said imidly. "I really don't know exactly what you mean. I guess you think I'm stupid—but I never thought of it that way. Maybe we are too much so."

"Oh, I didn't mean you," he assured her hastily. "But you know some people—well, they think our way of doing things is the only way."

Martha was puzzled. "Well, isn't it the best way?" she asked.

"I wouldn't say it's the best way. Oh, I know, we've all been taught so, but sometimes I think we are too narrow-minded," Daniel answered.

Martha didn't know what to make of him now.

"Oh, well, forget it for now," he said hastily with a laugh. "Anyway, if I do go, can I count on your letters?"

Again Martha's heart seemed to be choking her. "Do you really mean it?"

"Why, yes, I do." He seemed surprised at her doubt. "What makes you think I wouldn't?"

"Well, I don't know. You are so much older than I. I'm—er—surprised you even asked me for a date." Martha's words came in a rush. Suddenly she just had to plump up the sofa pillow. How she wished she could hide her face in it!

"Surprised!" Daniel echoed. "Why, I have been watching you for the last two years!" Then he too turned red because he hadn't meant to say that yet.

Martha looked at him in such amazement now that her heart didn't even make itself felt. "I never even thought you noticed me," she said.

"I did, though, Martha." He laid his hand over hers. "Do you suppose you would like to go steady with me?" His kind eyes looked right into hers. "I didn't really think I'd want to tie you down if I went away and I won't ask for that, because you might find someone while I am gone you'd like better. But for the time I am here, before I go, can I have your word to date only me?" His eyes held Martha's so that she couldn't look down at all.

"Yes, if you want me to." Now she could look down again at last. The sofa pillow needed her attention again.

"And if I go, will you write?" he asked very tenderly.

"Yes," she said ever so softly. He had to bend down to catch her reply.

"All right, I will count on it then. Say," he ejaculated, looking at his watch, "it's one o'clock already! I had better be going." He arose now.

"Don't you want anything to eat?" she asked. She didn't, but boys were always hungry.

"No, I don't tonight. It would be good, I know, but I really am not hungry. Guess I have had something better than food." He had taken her hand to help her up, and

21

when he said that, he gave it a squeeze. "If I can have a kiss, that is all I want."

Martha's heart beat loudly again—so loud that she thought he could surely hear it. But she raised her face up to him and with a tender embrace he kissed her. Then with a cheery good night he opened the door and stepped out into the soft summer darkness, leaving Martha to put her hand to her hot cheek in a daze of wonder.

4

MARTHA put the finishing touches to the cake she was frosting in elaborate swirls. "I wonder what time Mary's coming?" she asked Mom. It was Saturday evening and Mary had been planning on coming to spend the rest of the weekend at home.

"Och, I don't know; maybe not until after the chores are done. Like as not it will be late. She probably wants to help as long as she can." Mom was busy peeling early apples for sauce. "These apples are so wormy, not much good in them. Say, I wonder if Rosie has finished washing off those walks. Where is she, anyway?" Mom held the paring knife poised.

Martha looked out the window. "I don't know. The walks aren't finished yet, I don't think. She probably ran off again somewhere. Mom, you spoil her; you didn't let us do that."

"Yes, I know," Mom admitted, going to the door. "It seems to take twice as much to make her mind as it did you older ones."

"Rosie!" she called. Then in a higher voice, "Rosie!"

"Yes, I'm coming." Rosie's quick footsteps were heard from upstairs.

"Why don't you have those walks finished? Running off like that!"

"I get tired from hauling all that water," Rosie pouted. "Why can't Paul help me? He's just playing anyway."

"Well, where is he then? Tell him I said he was to help you." Mom was back at the apples again. Rosie banged the screen door shut, calling as she did so, "Paul, Paul, come here."

"What do you want?" Paul appeared at the door of the shop where he had been making a tractor. He already had two.

"Mom says you're to help me wash these walks off; so come on now." Rosie swung the broom defiantly.

"What am I supposed to do then, wash or carry water?"

"Carry water; Mom said it was too much for me." Mom hadn't said it that way, Rosie thought to herself, but it meant the same.

Mom glanced out the window. "Be sure and get them clean now," she called, "or you'll have to do it over."

"Wish Mary could come home oftener," Martha said carefully, setting the cake in the cupboard.

"Well, I guess she's kept busy over there with all those little ones to care for. Then that new baby only two months old. Guess Annie isn't too strong yet." Annie was Mrs. Gingerich.

"How long is she going to stay there?" Martha asked.

"She said a couple of Sundays ago they wanted her until oats harvest; so it will be a couple of weeks yet." Mom poured water over her apples.

"Well, I hope she comes home early tonight. I haven't had a good talk with her for a long time," Martha said wistfully as she began washing her messy baking dishes. Mary, however, did not come until everyone but Mom was in bed. Mom was studying the next day's Sunday school lesson, fanning herself with the paper while doing so. The day had been warm again and it had not cooled off yet.

Mary opened the screen door and stepped inside with her overnight case and several packages. "Everyone else in bed?" she asked, setting the case on a chair. "Probably thought I wasn't coming any more." She put the packages on the table.

"Looks like you drove to town," Mom said.

"Yes, we did. Chester wanted to take the eggs to town. He was so busy all week he couldn't take them before. He had four cases of them. Then I wanted to get some things too. I haven't been to town for over two months." Mary took off her bonnet. "It's so warm again. Are the others all asleep?" She drew out a chair and sat down.

"I don't know. I guess so, or they'd be down here if they knew you were at home." Mom laid her Sunday school lesson aside. "I suppose you have been busy all week."

"Yes, we were. We had so much canning to do, and I have been trying to get the work up to date as much as I can. Annie thinks she can get along alone in a few weeks. Honestly, I don't see how she can with all those little ones, but she thinks so."

"What are you going to do then? Will you take that job at Joni Miller's?"

"I guess so. I don't have anything else in view. I talked with Joni's Mabel last Sunday and she said they wanted someone from about the first of August until the middle of September. So I guess I'll have to work till then, Mom." Mary leaned over the table. "David would like it if we could get married sometime this fall."

"He would? Well, I'm not surprised." Mom smiled at her. "Pop and I were talking about it not too long ago.

25

He wondered if you wouldn't be doing something like that."

"David asked me last Sunday evening if I thought we could. I said I'd ask you and Pop if it suited you," Mary said.

"What will you do then—farm the homeplace?" Mom asked.

"Yes. David said his dad wants to turn the farm over to him because he isn't too well, you know," Mary answered.

"Will they put up a grandpa house next summer?"

"Yes, that's what David said. He said he wouldn't want to do anything like that if he might be called to camp, but he is 4-F, you know," Mary said.

Mom nodded. "Are you really sure now that he's the boy you want?"

"Why, of course I am, Mom." Mary seemed surprised. "Do you think I'd have gone steady all this while if I wasn't?"

"No, I didn't think so, but—well, you know, marriage is so serious, I just wanted you to be sure, that's all. You know, Pop and I have had a happy marriage and we hope our children will too."

"David is the only boy I really cared for enough to go steady with," Mary said slowly. "It is hard to talk about, but—well, you probably know how you felt about Pop. Or have you forgotten?" Mary asked teasingly.

"No, I haven't, but of course what I feel for Pop isn't the same now as it was then. It is different now; he's so much more a part of me now than he was then. Sometimes when I look back I'm ashamed how little I seemed to know about him and feel for him, compared with now."

26

Mom didn't talk like this often, Mary thought. Usually she was so jolly and teasing.

"That is the kind of marriage I want," Mary said, leaning back in her chair. The soft lamplight was shining on the glass cupboard doors. The white half curtains at the windows looked so crisp and cheerful. The big dining room seemed to speak of peace and quietness. How she hoped she could have a home like this! David would do his part, she was sure, but Mary was half scared at times that she might fail him in some way or other. She wished she could be at home all the time. Chester and Annie Gingerich were nice to work for and were good to her, but still home seemed to have a peace and quietness most certainly not found there with six youngsters to care for.

"What do you think of Martha and her young man?" Mary asked, changing the subject.

"Oh, I guess he's all right. From what we hear at least," Mom said.

"What did Pop say about him?"

"Oh, he thinks same as I do."

"I wonder if he asked her to go steady. He's taken her home the last three or four Sunday evenings, hasn't he?" Mary asked.

"Yes, he has. Sometimes I think she's too young to go steady, though. Why, she was only sixteen last April." Mom sounded a shade troubled.

"If it were some other boy it would be plenty young, but David says Daniel is as decent a boy as we have with the young folks. I wouldn't be too worried." Mary smiled at her. "Then, too, he probably will have to go to camp with all the other boys his age. I wonder if any of them have their notices yet."

"Ervin doesn't. We are looking for it any day now."

27

Mom looked tired now. After all, no mother was anxious to see her son leave, especially when none of them knew when they would be coming back or what things they would endure before they came back.

"All of those boys passed their physicals, didn't they? All of them that went with Ervin?" Mary wanted to know.

"That is what Ervin said."

"Does he seem anxious to go?" Mary asked.

"He doesn't say much now, but I don't think he cares too much, the way he talked when he got his physical notice. He doesn't realize what is coming."

Mary was silent for a moment, her eyes fixed on the table. "Of course he doesn't have a girl to leave behind, so that is probably one reason he doesn't care too much. I know I shouldn't think so, but when I see all the other girls who have had to see their boyfriends go, I am glad that David is a 4-F," she said rather guiltily.

"Doesn't his heart bother him now?" Because of rheumatic fever at twelve David had been left with a slight heart impairment.

"Not if he doesn't overdo. That is one thing I'll always be concerned about—his heart." Mary looked troubled. "I tell him to be careful and he says he does, but still—" Again Mary stared at the table.

Mom looked at the clock. "My goodness!" she exclaimed, "it's almost twelve-thirty, and here I haven't even had a bath yet. You had better go on to bed; we can talk tomorrow. Good night now," she said and closed the bathroom door.

Mary picked up her case and packages and went softly upstairs.

5

IN LESS THAN TWO MONTHS after the boys had taken their physicals, every one of them had received his notice to report at camp by the last of August. Some of them regarded it as a good chance to travel and see things; others went because they had to. Some were anxious to go, while a few who had girl friends and were more serious-minded found the thought of going harder to endure. Daniel hadn't realized how hard it would be to leave Martha behind, not knowing when he would be coming back. Now that the actual departure was at hand, he was tempted to ask her to be pledged to him alone. Hadn't he had his eyes on her, as he had told Martha, for the last two years? No other girl had ever appealed to him as she did. He was satisfied that she was the girl for him. Yet at the same time, because she was still so young, in fairness to her he didn't feel that he should make their relationship so binding. There might just be the chance that she would find someone else to care for while he was gone. Also he knew, with Ervin gone and Mary getting married and Thomas too young, to ask Martha to refrain from going with any other boy would cut her off from the young folks almost entirely. He felt that she had the right to mingle with the rest of the young folks, even if he wasn't there. So he decided to ask her, their last evening together, if she would write to him.

" 'Course I don't ask for a letter every week," he said, "but I would appreciate hearing from you every now and then." In view of his feelings he felt he was being as light about it as he could be. How he wished he could ask her to write two or three times a week! Also, to never go out with another boy! With an effort he kept those things at the back of his mind.

Martha had been heavyhearted all week at the thought of his going. Now he didn't act as if he even cared too much that he had to go, she thought. She wondered if she had done something to offend him. Maybe he thought her too young and gawky. She knew he was much smarter and—"more cultured" was the phrase she had supplied in her thoughts. She had seen that word somewhere and it had vaguely suggested Daniel. Because she felt all this and didn't know how to cope with it, Martha was extremely quiet and spoke very little on their last evening together.

Because of each one's unspoken thoughts the evening seemed to drag—this night of all nights, when they didn't know when they would see each other again.

He was going away and would learn so much more than she. He wouldn't even look at her when he came back again, she thought.

With him away, no telling who would get her when he was gone. She was so wonderful, any other boy would jump at the chance of dating her, he thought.

It was almost a relief when the clock in the dining room struck twelve and he arose to leave. But as he took her hand it was more than he could bear and he pressed it hard. "Oh, Martha, would you, could you write lots of times? And think of me even if I'm not here?

30

I—I—please don't forget me, will you?" The words rushed out, and he couldn't keep them back.

Martha looked straight at him now. It seemed to him she must see how much he cared for her. "You know I will," she said simply. "I couldn't forget you now, anyway."

"You mean you care a lot if I go then?"

"Yes, I do." Martha's eyes were downcast now and she could barely speak.

"Oh, I'm so glad!" He couldn't control himself any more. "If you care for me, would you keep yourself only for me?" Gone were his ideas about its being unfair to her to pledge her now. "Would you, please?" His heart was in his eyes.

"Yes," Martha said simply, looking right at him now. With one accord they were in each other's arms. Martha was so glad, she could hear her heart thumping like mad. Daniel laughed with the joy of it. He held her at arm's length and looked into her eyes again.

"Oh, sweetheart, you don't know how much it means, to know you'll keep yourself only for me. It makes it so much easier now, to go, I mean. I hated to make you say you'd be mine only, but I was so afraid someone else would get you. I couldn't have taken that," he said. "I thought because you were so young it would be unfair to you. You might find someone else you liked better."

"I don't think I could," Martha said. "I—well, I just don't think I will."

"Then it is not good-by, sweetheart, but only, as the Germans say, *Auf Wiedersehen*! Till we meet again," he said and pressed her to him again. This time their lips met. For a long moment he held her. Then he let her go.

"Well, I'd better be going," he said, turning toward

31

the door. "We are supposed to be at the bus depot in the morning at ten."

"Who is taking you up to the depot?" Martha asked. How she wished she could go along! Yet on second thought she realized that it was better that their good-bys were said alone.

"Brother Bill, I guess," Daniel replied. "Mom and Dad are going along too. I would have liked having you go along too, in a way, but—well, I think I would rather say good-by to you here."

"I know. I think it is best," Martha agreed.

"Then I can count on your letters? And know you are waiting for me when I get back?" Again he took her in his arms. Martha nodded. Her heart was too full of words.

"Then so long, sweetheart," he whispered and again their lips met. This time when he released her he opened the screen door and stepped outside. Then He stood on the outside and smiled at her. "If you don't want me to come back in again, you had better hook the door," he said. "I'll never get away if you don't."

Martha made a movement toward the hook.

"I guess I have the willpower now," he said and grinned. Then, with a wave of his hand, he disappeared into the darkness. Martha heard his whistle as he untied his horse. Feeling strangely sad and glad at the same time, Martha blew out the lamp and slowly went upstairs in the darkness. Up in her room through the open window she could hear the sound of buggy wheels fade away in the distance.

* * *

With so many of the boys gone, the young people's sings were considerably less lively. To Martha most of the zest was gone out of them now that Daniel wasn't there.

32

Mary had been careful in seeing that Martha missed none of the social occasions, but she and David were so wrapped up in each other that Martha found them poor company. Mary had told her of her coming marriage. Martha thought it understandable that they took small interest in the activities of the other young folks. While Martha was still at the stage where the social gatherings were of the greatest importance, Mary was ready to relinquish them forever. As Martha complained to Mom, "All Mary can talk about is getting married and furnishing houses and her hope chest and such stuff."

Mom had laughed at this. "Just wait till your turn comes. You'll be just as bad, I'll bet."

"Won't be for a long time, now," Martha said gloomily, her thoughts on faraway Daniel.

True to her promise, she had written him faithfully every week. Then, too, when Emery Bender had asked her if she would consider dating other boys now that Daniel was gone, Martha had given him a flat no. So the word got around that she was Daniel's girl and the boys left her strictly alone.

Mary and David had finally decided on Christmas as their wedding day. And as the fall deepened into early winter, plans were being intensified for that great day. Pop said the corn had to be husked first, and so Martha had gone out to help him, now that Ervin was gone. Thomas stayed home from school for two weeks. So most of it was husked by Thanksgiving. Mary had come home to help too, presumably; but, in reality, she had put in more hours sewing on her trousseau than husking corn. She had confided to Martha most of her plans, for even though there were five years between them, they were quite chummy. She had told Martha that because

33

Ervin was older, he, instead of Martha, would be a witness. "But we want you and Daniel to be waiters though," she told Martha. "Do you suppose he can get away?"

"I don't know," Martha said. "I will write and ask him. Have you written Ervin?"

"Well, I told him before he left that we were planning on getting married this fall sometime, and he said he would keep it in mind. So I haven't written yet, but I thought I would tonight. We plan to be published Sunday, you know. I better get that letter sent to Ervin today. If he can't come, we'll have to get someone else," Mary said as she put the finishing touches on her wedding dress. "Oh, isn't this a lovely shade? I just love it!" she exclaimed, holding the hanger at arm's length.

"I think it is too," Martha replied, "but not half so lovely as the one who is to wear it."

Mary looked at her lovingly. "Do you really think so, sis? Thanks for the compliment."

Martha sat down that night and wrote Daniel, telling him that Mary and David were to be published Sunday and asking if he could come home to be waiter with her. Mary at the same time wrote Ervin and asked if he could come to be one of the witnesses. "I don't care who you choose as your partner," she wrote. "You never seemed to care much for the pick of the girls we have here. But if you are a witness, you will have to have a partner. So please let us know who you want, so we can let the girl know."

After the letters were mailed, Martha waited anxiously for the replies. Meanwhile, plans were being carried out with increasing fervor at home, so much so that many a neighbor correctly guessed what was in the wind. The dining room had been freshly painted and the girls had papered their room upstairs. Also, they had cleaned and painted the spare room, which was to be Mary and David's after their marriage until they could move in with his folks.

In a way it was a relief when Sunday came and they were published. Now it made no difference if some wily old grandmother speculated as to why the Yoders were so busy cleaning everything up. Then on Monday Martha finally got her answer from Daniel. She had been watching for the mailman as she hung up the wash, and as soon as she saw him pass, she almost ran down the lane to get the mail. She waited to open it until she was in the privacy and warmth of the washhouse, where she was to clean up while Mom and Mary prepared for dinner.

"Dear Sweetheart," she read. "I got your letter in today's mail, which didn't get down to camp until tonight. One of the boys took the truck to town to get supplies and mail this afternoon. He left around two-thirty and should have been back by four, at least, but they had all sorts of tough luck, I guess. Said they had a flat and after that was fixed they got stuck in a snowbank. So it was after supper when they got here. Sure was glad to hear from you again. It gets rather lonesome here sometimes without any girls around.

"Well, I guess I can tell you that we'll be coming home for the wedding. The only thing is, we get only six days and, what with slow wartime travel, it will give us two days going and two days coming back. That will give us just barely two days there. But at least it will be long enough for the wedding. So if nothing happens, I'll see you in just a little over a week. I can hardly wait! All my love, Daniel."

Martha put the letter back into the envelope with a

thrill of excitement. It seemed too good to be true. It had been so long since she had seen him. Mentally she counted up the time. Let's see, he left in early September and this was the middle of December. Four long, lonesome months. She gave a sigh of anticipation.

*   *   *

The intervening days until the wedding passed by on work-laden wings. No one was going to be able to see anything around the John Yoder place that would cast a slur on Mom's housekeeping if she could help it. The house was swept and scrubbed from the attic to the darkest corner in the basement. The pantry and basement shelves almost creaked with the loads of cakes, pies, salads, and what not. One would have thought enough food was being prepared to feed an army.

The last day before the wedding was a flurry of odds and ends to be finished, with Martha so excited with the prospect of seeing Daniel before the day was over that she worked in confused anticipation. He and Ervin were to come to the city on the six o'clock train that evening. His brother Bill was to go for them, and they were going to come to the Yoder home just as soon as possible. Martha wished she could go along to meet them at the depot, but Daniel's folks were going, and the car would be full without her.

Martha kept a sharp lookout for the lights of a car coming down the road. She wanted to be at the door as soon as they came. Six-thirty came and went, and still they weren't there. Seven, seven-thirty, and still they hadn't come.

"I wonder what's keeping them," Mom finally said at quarter of eight. "I was waiting for them for supper, but we might just as well go ahead and eat. No sense waiting any longer."

"I'm awfully hungry," Paul complained. "You won't let me eat any cookies or such."

"Well, let's eat," Pop said, drawing up his chair. "We mustn't let Paul go hungry. Hard telling what would happen to him." He chuckled.

By now Martha was almost sick with worry. Had something terrible happened? Maybe there had been an accident or something. One heard of things like that. At that moment the headlights of a car turned into the lane.

"Here they come!" Pop said heartily. "Martha, better be ready for them." The car had stopped at the gate by now and they were all on their feet at once.

"Better take the lantern out so they can see to unload," Mom advised. Pop grabbed the lighted lantern which had been standing on the washroom floor. He turned up the wick and started for the door. As he reached for the knob, the door was opened and Ervin burst in. He was greeted by a chorus of hellos. But Martha's eyes flashed quickly behind him. Even as she was wondering, David asked, "Where's Daniel? I thought he was coming here tonight."

Ervin glanced at Martha before replying. "Daniel couldn't come."

"Couldn't come! What's happened?" the others chorused.

"He got sick the night before we were to leave," Ervin told them.

"Oh no!" Mary exclaimed, with a look at Martha.

"Yep. He didn't feel well all day Sunday, but he braced up and tried to doctor himself up so he'd be fit to come, but by that night he was raging with a fever

37

of 103. The director called the doctor and he said it was a strep throat. Said he wouldn't be fit to travel for a couple of weeks."

Martha felt all her hopes tumble around her like so many dominoes. Heartsick, she turned away, lest the others see the tears fast gathering in her eyes.

"Hmm, that's too bad," Pop said sympathetically. David and Mary exchanged dismayed looks.

"This means we'll have to look around tonight yet for another waiter boy," David said at last.

"I know. I wish I could have let you know sooner, but I figured I would get here as soon as a letter would." By this time Ervin had thrown his hat and coat across the worktable. "But let's eat before we decide anything like that. I'm starved. I haven't eaten since noon."

"Sure, sure," Pop said heartily, pulling out his chair. The others all gathered around the table again, Martha fighting a sickening lump in her throat.

"What made you so late?" Mom wanted to know, as she passed the food down the table to Ervin. "We've been waiting supper for you ever since soon after six."

"Oh, wartime travel," Ervin replied between mouthfuls of good homemade food. "You never know when you get to your destination. I don't think we made so much as one stop on time. And then it's so crowded you're lucky to get a seat. I sat on my suitcase part of the time. Say, Mom, your food sure tastes good!"

Mom looked pleased. "Think so? Well, fill up while you have the chance. Here, Martha, give him that dish of *garlrich*. You like that, don't you, Ervin?"

"Um," was all he could reply with his mouth so full. He helped himself to a liberal supply of the jelled meat delicacy.

38

"Well, who can we get in Daniel's place? Martha, do you have any other choice?" David asked, when Ervin, stuffed to the limit, finally laid down his fork.

All eyes were on Martha. Under their half-teasing, sympathetic looks Martha felt the tears come fast and hot. She blinked them back while she reached blindly into her pocket for a hanky. "I don't care who you get," she said dully, blowing her nose.

"That's a big help." Mary smiled.

They were ready now, at the close of the meal, to return thanks. While all heads were bowed, Martha bit her lip and fought to keep from crying. As soon as everyone looked up again, she left the table hurriedly. Grabbing a coat and flinging it around her shoulders, she stepped outside. Mom's and Mary's eyes followed her. After the door closed behind her, they exchanged significant glances.

"Poor thing, she'll probably go out and bawl," Mary said as she began clearing off the table. "I can't say that I blame her. It's a pretty big disappointment for her."

Mom nodded silently. She wished Martha wouldn't take things so hard. Life would be a lot easier for her if she wouldn't.

After some consultation between Mary and David it was decided that one of David's nephews, Chris Beachy, who had already been appointed for one of the hostlers, should take Daniel's place and Chris' younger brother Jonas could be hostler. But it meant making a hurried trip to the Beachy home, and David left to do that. After he had gone, Martha came in again. Anxiously Mom scanned her face. Her eyes showed redness, but she seemed composed enough. Getting a dish towel off the rack she began wiping dishes without comment, while Mary washed.

39

"How would David's nephew, Chris Beachy, suit you as a partner?" Mary asked without looking at her.

Martha bit her lips. Suit her? Of course he wouldn't! But seeing she had no choice in the matter, he was as good as anyone. He was just barely sixteen and no taller than she was. Besides, his ears stuck out so far from his head. "I guess all right," was all she said. But that night after she was in bed and the others were asleep, she wept bitter tears of disappointment and frustration.

6

A<small>T LAST THE DAY</small> of the wedding had come. It was a beautiful winter day, clear and not too cold. The family had been up since early morning getting the chores and morning work done in record time. There were many last-minute things to be done. The upstairs had to be given a final fling with the dust mop, the beds had to be made, and there were all the little extras accompanying a big wedding. The big master bedroom downstairs had been cleared a few days before to make room for the big corner table* at which the wedding party were to be seated. The partition between the bedroom and living room had been taken out and carried to the shop, so that the table ran the length and breadth of the living room and the length of the bedroom, making a table big enough for fifty people to be seated at once. Another table had been laid in the dining room where twenty more could be seated, also one in the big basement for pre-teen-age boys. And well it might, for by the time all the guests had been invited, there were at least one hundred and seventy-five people. The task of waiting on the basement table had been given to Rosie and her chum, Ellen Miller, one of David's many nieces.

*Corner table—a table set up along two sides of a large room, around the corner of which the bridal party sit during the serving of the entire meal to all the guests.

Soon after breakfast David's mother came to help get the dinner started. Not long after, Pop's oldest sister came, outwardly to help, but actually, as Martha so aptly told Mom privately, "to snoop around and see who the witnesses were going to be." It had been a hard job getting a partner for Ervin, as he himself had no choice at all, and when Mary and David had consulted him, he had absolutely refused to cooperate, saying cheerfully as he did so, "I don't care who you get, just so she isn't cross-eyed and knock-kneed."

Mary gave him a dirty look. "I have a good notion to get just such a one," she said severely. "What about Alma Bontrager?" Alma was fat and nearsighted and thirty, if she was a day.

"Suits me," Ervin said carelessly. "It is just for one day anyway."

They finally decided on one of David's many cousins, Elizabeth Shetler. A niece of his, Cora Beachy, and her boyfriend, Andy Graber, were to be the other couple. These had all spent the night at the Yoder home, and it had taken a large table at breakfast to seat them all. Mary was too excited to eat. To Martha, languishing in her disappointment, food didn't make much difference.

Shortly after eight o'clock the wedding party, composed of Mary and David, Ervin and Elizabeth, Cora and Andy, left for Joe Bontrager's, a neighboring family, where the wedding services were to be held. After they left, activity intensified at home. There were the turkeys to roast, potatoes to peel, celery to wash, cold relishes to put on. More and more women came to help, along with girls and boys who had been chosen to be waiters. At last most of the preparations had been finished, and the young folks retired upstairs, the girls all congregating in

Martha's room to dress up. Mary had chosen light blue for the waitresses, which, with the darker shade of the witness girls, had blended well with her own lovely shade of periwinkle blue.

Finally they all left for Joe's to see the actual marriage take place, each girl riding with her boy partner. Rosie and Ellen Miller went with Mom and Pop and David's folks, who, after being persuaded to go, had all piled in the big surrey.

Martha found herself self-conscious and cool with Chris. She could think of so little to say to him except for an exchange of the weather conditions. After commenting on this subject, they were both silent. Chris couldn't think of a thing to say either. He was thinking that if girls were all like this one beside him, he almost hated to grow up. Not that Martha wasn't pretty enough and all that (no wonder Daniel Miller had snapped her up right away), but if girls were all as standoffish as she was, he didn't think he'd bother with any right away. It seemed to him that even if he wasn't Daniel, Martha needn't be so stuck up with him. After all, it wasn't his fault they were in this together.

It didn't take long to make the short drive to Joe's. Joe pushed people together and set up chairs to make room for them to be seated. The minister had been more or less stalling for them and now that they were all here, he said, "If these young folks still desire to enter the bonds of holy matrimony, they may come forward to be married." Mary and David rose and stood before him while he asked them those wonderful questions of the marriage ceremony.

Mom, looking at them standing there, felt tears come to her eyes. It seemed such a short time ago since she and

43

Pop had made those same vows, and now here their oldest child was taking them herself! She breathed a prayer that God would bless their lives and make them a light in the community.

The vows were said and Mary and David took their seats again. This was the signal for all the waiters to arise and pass out of the room. They had to go back home to get the final things done before the guests came. So they hurried back to the house, with the older folks following.

Back home the activity reached a crescendo. Potatoes to be mashed, gravy to be made, turkey to be carved— all these things had to be done before the guests arrived.

One by one families started coming down the lane until the big house was crowded. Guests were seated soon after their arrival, until there was no more room at any of the tables. In the flurry of seating guests, with the waiters lined up quietly waiting for the final arrangements to be completed, Martha had a good opportunity to watch the wedding party. Mary was very lovely in her beautiful blue dress and her white shoulder cape. Her lips and cheeks were flushed with excitement, and her very carriage bespoke that untouchable something so peculiar to brides on their wedding day. David, too, looked every inch a man, with his well-groomed blond hair and his new suit. All in all they made an exceedingly handsome couple.

The table had been decorated in Mary's chosen colors of white and pink. The tall bride's cake dominated the entire table, with its pure white frosting set off with the beautiful pale pink roses on which Mary had spent so much time. Martha felt a lump in her throat again. It was all very lovely, and she had been looking forward to it so much, seeing herself in imagination with Daniel as her partner. Now not to have him here at all and to be

44

stuck with Big Ears! The thought made her taste disappointment so sharply again that she was even less civil to Chris, who in turn became more flustered and clumsy than ever.

To them had been given the task, or privilege, of waiting on the corner table. After grace was said, they were kept busy bringing in full dishes of food for the hungry diners, and carrying empty dishes out to the kitchen, where efficient cooks filled them again. There was no time for thought now, only hurried steps back and forth for more potatoes, more turkey, more gravy, to fill someone's water glass, and at last to pass the dessert. Only after that had been done was there time to relax a few moments.

At last the guests were finished and once again heads were bowed to return thanks. As soon as grace was said, the flurry of activity began again. This time the tables had to be cleared, dishes washed, and places laid for more guests.

When the time finally came for the waiters to eat, Martha and the other waitresses had very little appetite. The boys, however, filled their plates. Martha, sitting beside Chris, watched him eat with unmistakable relish. He turned red, however, and almost upset his water glass when he felt her eyes upon him.

Seeing his discomfort, Martha felt ashamed. After all, he couldn't help it if Daniel wasn't here. Besides, he was so young and obviously so ill at ease. Why, she hadn't said a kind word to him all day. After that she tried to be more courteous, with such good effect that by the end of the day he could see why Daniel Miller had grabbed her. If girls were always like this, maybe growing up wasn't so bad after all.

The day flew by as if on wings, for Mary. Before she knew it, the last guests had left, leaving behind their good wishes and presents. The two beds in the boys' room were loaded with gifts, with the overflow piled on the dressers and on the floor. There were many blankets and spreads, lovely pillowcases, and many beautiful stainless steel dishes. David had not been forgotten either. For him there were saws, hammers, wrenches, pliers, and even an anvil.

Some wag (they blamed Johnny Hochstetter, one of the waiters) had given Mary a rolling pin, with a tag attached. It said, "Now that you are married and David gets mean, use this club and hit him over the bean." This had been a source of much amusement among the boys.

All in all the day was all that Mary could ask for. The only cloud in it was when she happened to look at Martha, and saw the lack of enjoyment in her eyes. A casual observer might not have noticed it, but because Mary was such a keen judge of character, she knew that Martha's disappointment was hard to bear. Several times during the day, when she wasn't too dizzy with her own happiness, she prayed silently and secretly that God might help Martha bear up with more grace. And when Mary saw with some astonishment that at last Martha was talking and laughing with Chris and the others, she thanked God that He had answered her prayer. Martha, after her cloud of disappointment had lifted, felt more peaceful than she had for a long time.

7

E RVIN COULD STAY at home only one day. Early in the
morning following the wedding he had to return to
camp. Before going, he met Martha in the upstairs
hall and said with a grin, "Oh, yes, I almost forgot. I was
supposed to give you something." He dived into his room
and returned with a package under his arm and a smile
on his face. "Here, this is for you from the boyfriend.
Mary and David are not the only ones getting presents
around here."

"What on earth?" Martha asked, surprised, holding it
as if she might shatter it with a deep breath.

"Take it; it's all yours. I think there is a letter inside."
He turned toward the stairs. "What's the matter—afraid
it's a time bomb?" he said over his shoulder.

Martha stuck her tongue out at him and waited until
he had closed the bottom door. Where could she open it?
Not here in the hall; someone might come out of one of
the rooms any moment. She paused uncertainly before
her own bedroom door. She couldn't go in there because
Cora and Elizabeth were still there getting dressed. At
that instant she caught sight of the attic door. Just the
thing, she thought; no one would bother her there. Quickly, she tiptoed softly past her closed bedroom door and
just as softly opened the attic door. She had no more
than closed it when she heard someone, one of the boys

47

probably, clump past the closed door and stamp downstairs. She waited until she heard the bottom door close, then crept softly up the attic stairs. The light from the dormer window at the head of the stairs made it possible to read here. Seating herself on the top step, she carefully opened the package.

Sure enough, as Ervin had said, there was a sealed envelope on top. The present itself was a lovely dresser set. She was almost ashamed of the present she had sent him—only a woolen muffler and a box of homemade candy. She picked up the mirror with trembling fingers, fearful lest she might drop it. Oh, it was lovely! Such a dainty flower pattern! She put it back in the box and picked up the sealed envelope. Hurriedly she opened it and took out the card. It was a Christmas greeting, with the usual message written on such cards; but to Martha it was written for her alone. There was also a folded note, which she opened and read:

"I can't begin to tell you how sorry I am not to be there. I haven't felt too well since Saturday evening, but I was trying to fight it off. But last night I chilled all night until the boy who sleeps beside me finally went over and told the director. They took my temperature then and it was 103° and the director sent for the doctor right away. When he came he said I had a strep throat and had to stay in bed for a week at least. So there go all our hopes of seeing each other again. It would be lots harder to take if I felt better, but I'm almost too sick right now to care. I'll be too sick to enter in on any of the things going on around here. I guess I'd better quit now and give Ervin this letter. I think he is ready to go. So long, sweetheart, and think of me. Daniel."

Martha folded the note and put it and the card back in

the envelope. She picked up the mirror again, admiring the lovely spray of flowers painted on the back. Presently, directly under her, coming through the two stair wells, she heard Mom call, "Martha, Martha, aren't you coming down? Ervin is ready to go."

She jumped up hastily, almost dropping the dresser set, and looked around for a place to hide it until after the others were gone. She deposited it in an old trunk with the rug rags and softly sped downstairs. The rest were gathered in the dining room, waiting for her. Ervin was there in overcoat and hat, with suitcase in hand, ready to leave.

"What took you so long?" Mom asked rather impatiently.

Martha's eyes met Ervin's and, for a moment, she was afraid he would tell on her. He only winked at her and grinned. "She had private business probably," he said to everyone in general. "Didn't you want to tell your wandering brother good-by?"

"Yes, I do," she said, grinning back at him. He was a pretty nice brother at that, her eyes told him as he took her hand. He gave it a hard squeeze and again slyly winked at her. With her back toward the others, Martha winked back at him.

*　*　*

After the flurry of the wedding was over, life settled into its usual pace again. Mary and David stayed at home with the folks for a fortnight. Then they hitched the big team to the bobsled and piled all their wedding presents and Mary's earthly possessions in it. There would be plenty of room in the big house with David's folks, now that the last of the family had married. Most of their

49

things they put upstairs, where they would be kept until the grandpa house was built.

David's folks were very well pleased with his choice. In fact, of all the girls in the community, no other would have suited them as well as Mary. She was one of those rare people one meets occasionally who possess the priceless gift of fitting in anywhere. They were happy for her sterling Christian character and her sincere desire to be pleasing to God. They thought David had chosen well when he chose her to be his wife.

When David's oldest sister, Bertha, and her husband, Ed Beachy, decided the last of January to spend the rest of the winter in Florida, it took little to persuade the old folks to go along. There were no qualms about leaving the management of the farm to David and Mary; in fact, they did so with a sense of relief. After raising eleven children, life became less a delight than a thing to be endured.

David and Mary didn't have many regrets to see them go. In fact, Mary was secretly glad. Not that she didn't like them, she assured David, but as they couldn't afford a honeymoon, it was more like one if they were alone. To this David quite agreed!

Even after they moved to David's home, Mary still spent a day or so a week with her parents. Mom still had a quilt to make for her and her comforts to knot; so Mary went over to the quiltings and comfort knottings. All in all the winter sped by, as if on wings, Mary thought. All too soon David's folks came back from Florida, and soon afterward work was started on the grandpa house.

They had a frolic for all of David's many sisters and brothers, with all the preschool nieces and nephews, and as many of the school-age ones as were able to persuade their respective parents that going to Grandpa's was more important than going to school.

By the time the foundation was cemented, it was time to sow oats, and so the work was at a standstill for a while.

One day in early September, David's folks moved into the grandpa house. Mary was glad to be able to furnish the big house with her own things. Mom and Pop, Martha, and Thomas drove over that day in the big surrey to help her set up housekeeping. Rosie and Paul, to their great disgust, had been sent off to school.

"Go on now," Mom had said to their protests. "You can go over some Saturday."

"Don't see why we have to go to that dumb old school," Rosie complained to Paul, swinging her dinner bucket round and round. "I wish I were grown up. Grownups get to have all the fun."

"Ha, you wouldn't like to be grown up and have to do all the work grownups do," Paul said, his eyes on a late summer butterfly. "Say, isn't that a beaut?" he exclaimed, pointing to the butterfly. The butterfly swooped and fluttered over them. Paul made a wild pass with his dinner bucket and, to his great delight, hit it squarely; but in the process, his dinner bucket came open, scattering the contents over the road. The two gasped in dismay and stood staring at the sandwiches, cookies, and apple that were to have been his lunch.

"Oh, Rosie, what will I do now?" he said in a choked voice.

"You can eat mine," Rosie said quickly. She could find a way out of most scrapes. "Quick! there goes the bell. Here, put those things in your bucket and we'll put it under the culvert till tonight." After they had done so, they raced down the road to the schoolhouse.

Over at Mary's house, there was much friendly joshing and teasing. David's father asked Martha, with a wink at Pop, if she was the reason paper was so hard to get. Martha, not knowing what he meant, wondered why she should be to blame.

"You write so many letters, that is why," he informed her. "You and all the others like you. Yes sir, that's the reason; all these girls writing to their beaus, no wonder paper is hard to get." Martha made a face at him, and the others laughed at her.

Mary and David hadn't invested very much money in furniture, and so it didn't take long until everything was in place. With the wedding presents and other new things from Mary's dowry, the house looked cheerful and bright by the time everything was in order. Loving hands washed the dishes from assorted boxes and baskets and carefully put them into the big glass cupboards.

Thomas, who was a practical joker, with a bit of help from Martha, put a table leaf into the bed in the downstairs bedroom. He went around afterward looking all innocence, wishing secretly that he could be there when it was found. He would have been disappointed, because Mary found it before she undressed. She and David guessed correctly who had done it.

8

MARTHA AND DANIEL exchanged letters faithfully after he went to camp and, for Martha, a letter from him was the high spot of the week. After Mary and David were married, she had no way of joining the young folks' gatherings, as Thomas was considered too young to go. Consequently most Sunday evenings were spent at home, and so she had plenty of time to write long letters to Daniel. At first his letters were full of routine camp news and so on, but later the quality of their contents changed. Not that he didn't tell her how much he missed her and all that, but there seemed to be something bothering him. More and more he wrote of values and ideas, rather than just people and happenings.

"Have you ever wondered what your goal in life is to be?" he wrote once. "Haven't you ever had the feeling that there is more to living than following in the steps of our fathers and grandfathers? Doesn't it ever seem to you that life is just a gamble? Heads you win and tails you lose, as the gamblers say. Sometimes it does to me. There seems to be something, some empty space in me, that's not satisfied. I have been thinking (we have lots of time for that). Perhaps it's because I long to see home folks and you again, but I don't know if that is all it is. Please don't misunderstand me; I like you as much as ever, more so, but there is something else. Sometimes at night when all the others are sleeping, I lie awake and I seem to hear a voice saying, 'Come!' But where and what is it? I wish I knew. I only know that I can't be satisfied until I do know. I wish it would be soon, because sometimes it almost makes me crazy, what with being homesick for you.

"A little bird told us that we twelve boys from home might be due to leave by the last of September; so I sure hope to see you by then. I would like so much to see you again. You have heard the saying, 'Absence makes the heart grow fonder.' Well, it surely has in my case! I hope it has in yours too. So long, sweetheart, and think of me lots. Daniel."

Martha hardly knew what to make of letters like this. She had accepted the life she knew for its face values. One was born, grew up, married (if one had the opportunity), had children, and grew old. Those were the things going on all around her, and for her there had never been any question of their changing. As for a goal in life—well, for her, as far as she knew, it was probably getting married, and having a homelife like Mom and Pop.

Small wonder, with Daniel writing letters like this, that she was vaguely troubled. It seemed to her that it only pointed up all the more that Daniel was much more gifted than she was. For the first time since they had been going steady, she began seriously to consider whether she would be able to cope with his seemingly higher mental capacity well enough to be a companion to him for life. Of course with each letter he always assured her that she wasn't to think he didn't like her. He always seemed anxious to get that across.

Then one day in mid-September she received another letter from him which for a time quieted all the misgivings she harbored. "Hurrah, sweetheart," she read, "get set for the wonderful news! I'm due for a leave on the twentieth, and don't think I won't be seeing you as soon as I can after that! Just think, fifteen wonderful days with you, I hope. The rest of the boys are coming too, but, except for Ervin, I hope you don't look at them twice. But, oh, I've been wanting to see you for so long! Don't you dare to break my heart by turning me down! Seriously now, we are leaving soon after midnight on the twentieth; we looked up the timetables three weeks ago and know them by heart. We arrive home early the morning of the twenty-second. I have written my folks too, and I suppose Ervin will let your folks know. I hope you are there to meet me at the station; if not, I will be seeing you sometime that day or evening, if I can wait that long. We will have until October third to spend with home folks. So just hope with me that we'll have good luck and won't be caught in these wartime transportation snarls. I won't write again before I see you, so am sending lots and lots of love. Daniel."

Oh, she was glad! It shone in her face, and her steps seemed to have wings. She fairly radiated good will, not even bopping Rosie when she teased her unmercifully. Usually when Rosie teased, Martha felt it her right to pinch her or something like that. Even Pop noticed the change and tormented her about being careful lest she float away on wings before Daniel got hold of her. She was as lighthearted as a bubble!

To Martha's disappointment she found she couldn't go along to the station to meet Daniel after all. Because of gas rationing, only two cars could be spared to go for the boys, and it would take all the room available to bring all twelve of them home from the station.

It was evening before Daniel got over to see her. For one thing, the train was so crowded that the boys took turns standing, and Daniel stood for the last hour before reaching home. Before that he hadn't been able to sleep because of a couple of drunks who had been singing and carrying on most of the night. When he reached home, he went right to bed and slept until afternoon; so it wasn't until after supper that he finally arrived. Martha was waiting for him in the big dining room. She saw the lights of the buggy turn into the lane and come swiftly up to the tie rack. She waited until she heard his brisk, quick steps coming up the walk. Then because she wanted to meet him alone, she quickly stepped outside. At sight of her, he held out his arms and said in a wonderfully glad voice, "Oh, sweetheart!" She met him at the top porch steps with a force that would have unbalanced a less sturdy man.

"Oh, sweetheart!" he repeated in an exultant voice. He looked down at her in his arms with a joyous smile. "I have been looking forward to this for so long," he said with a break in his voice. He held her at arm's length. By the soft light from the window he could see her plainly. "You look just like I pictured you," he told her fondly.

Martha was looking at him with a glad light in her eyes. "You look wonderful to me, too," she said softly, "except you look—well, bigger."

"You are beautiful, simply beautiful; that is all I can say." He drew her close again. All at once he laughed softly. "Will you look at that?" he asked, releasing her and turning her around to the window. Paul was inside, his face pressed against the glass, trying to see them.

"Oh, the little stinker," Martha said in exasperation.

"Just wait till I catch him alone. We might just as well go in." He reached around her, opened the door, and followed her inside.

The family were all glad to see him. Ervin and he clasped hands and clapped each other on the back as if they hadn't seen each other for a long time. Ervin had spent most of the day sleeping too; now he was as carefree and teasing as ever.

"I see you can still walk," he said to Daniel. "At least she didn't knock you completely off your feet."

"Oh, Ervin!" Martha said, blushing. They wanted to know all about his trip. Ervin, as usual, had been cheerfully noncommittal. Soon they were laughing at his account of their encounter with the two drunks, with Ervin supplying a word now and then. Before they knew it, the clock struck nine. Mom jumped up and shoved Paul and Rosie off to bed, despite their protests.

"Go on now," she told them, "it's high time you were in bed. I can't get Rosie up in the morning as it is." Besides, she knew that Martha and Daniel wanted to be alone. One by one the others left for bed, too, until finally they were alone.

For a long moment they looked at each other across the room. To him, she seemed the loveliest girl he had ever seen. Her cheeks were flushed a delicate pink and her red lips were curved in a lovely smile. To her, he was the handsomest man she had ever seen. He seemed so much bigger than he was a year ago and his shoulders so broad!

He crossed the room and seated himself at her side on the sofa. Again they looked at each other a moment in silence. A tender smile was on his face and complete adoration in hers. He took her hand and kissed it. "Still my girl?" he asked, keeping her hand in his.

Martha nodded, her eyes never leaving his face.

"Do you want to keep it that way?" he asked, smiling down at her.

Martha nodded again.

"Thank you," he said simply. "I used to imagine this so often when I was away. I was afraid that with me away you would find someone else. I don't know what I would do if that should happen on top of this other thing." He bit his lip after he said that. He hadn't intended to say anything about it now.

"What other thing?" Martha asked.

"Oh, nothing," he answered, just a wee bit shortly. "Let's forget I said it and just enjoy ourselves. We haven't seen each other for so long."

Again Martha was vaguely troubled. What was wrong with him? She couldn't figure it out.

9

WITH ALL THE BOYS AT HOME, events perked up considerably among the young folks. Besides the Sunday evening sings, social occasions were planned on the slightest pretext. So Martha and Daniel were caught up in a whirl of activities. Several birthdays were celebrated, besides popcorn huskings, cane strippings, and so on. Even if there was nothing going on, Daniel dropped in about every evening the first week until Mom put her foot down and said that Martha had to go to bed early for a change. She told Daniel that Martha was so sleepy in the daytime, she couldn't even think.

"It's a fact," she said with a twinkle in her eyes. "Today she was supposed to clean out the wall cupboards, and do you know what she did? She absentmindedly cleaned the bottom of the worktable instead."

"What was wrong with that?" Daniel asked, with an amused smile.

"Why, she cleaned that yesterday," Mom laughed. "Then today she did it all over again!"

Daniel stopped coming so often, but even so they were together as often as opportunity presented itself. The first week he seemed gay, almost deliberately so. But gradually that spirit was replaced by a strange moodiness. He would sit beside Martha for long minutes staring into space and ignoring her completely. Then all at once he would come to with a start and usually laugh, halfhearted-ly. When Martha wanted to know what was wrong, he'd only say evasively, "Just thinking, that's all," and change the subject.

Because of Daniel's increasing moodiness, Martha began to dread being alone with him. She began to wonder if perhaps their relationship should be broken off, if neither one of them was getting any enjoyment out of it. Yet each time they parted, he assured her over and over that it wasn't her fault. She wasn't to think that it was anything she had done. Usually he would end up by saying lightly, "It is nothing; let's forget it."

Because of all this Martha was considerably less happy being with him than she had imagined she would be. It was almost a relief that the end of his leave was drawing near. The last evening Mary and David had invited the whole family and Daniel over for oyster stew. Martha told Daniel not to come for her, as she could just as well ride over with Ervin and save him the bother. In reality, she was beginning to feel so uncomfortable in his presence that she dreaded being with him more than necessary.

When they were all gathered around the table spread out in Mary's big dining room, there was much visiting and teasing. Ervin had one of his rare streaks of talkative-ness, clowning and teasing all evening, keeping everyone laughing most of the time. None of the others seemed to notice that Martha and Daniel were more quiet than usual, or if they did, they thought it was because of their coming separation. It was still early when Daniel asked her if she was ready to go. She nodded without speaking and, with a heavy sense of dread, went to get her wraps.

"Going already?" Mary asked in disappointment, when they came to say good-by. "Why, I thought you'd stay a while yet. David got a new carom board last week and he was going to get you to play."

Martha looked up at Daniel with a questioning look. "I'm sorry to disappoint him," he said, making an effort at lightness. "But I would like to talk to Martha. I won't have much longer to do that, you know."

So good-bys were said all around and everyone came out to wish Daniel well.

"Don't keep him dangling," Ervin said to Martha. "Tell him either yes or no." Martha smiled vacantly. It didn't seem to make any difference how they teased her any more—not when she had such a burden on her heart.

When they finally stepped outside, Pop called after them, "God bless you!"

Daniel gave a sudden start but managed to say simply, "Thanks."

As soon as they were alone, all his forced gaiety was gone. He was silent after he helped her into the buggy and untied the horse, until they were well down the road. When they came to the corner where they usually turned off for home, he drove right on past. "Where are you going?" Martha asked in surprise. She looked at him sharply and was almost shocked at what she saw. By the light of the dashboard his face looked haggard.

He looked down at her without a smile and said, "I want to drive around a bit before I go back inside. I just had to get out of that house."

"Why, what is wrong?" she asked. Her voice was sharp.

"Martha, do I look like a crazy man?" he asked miserably.

"I have never seen one, but you have me wondering." She was in earnest. "What is wrong? I must know."

They came to a crossroads and Daniel drove over the

61

culvert without replying. Then he wrapped the reins around the whip socket and turned to her. "I wish I knew," he answered with utmost misery in his voice. "I don't blame you for wondering if I am crazy. I'm beginning to think I am."

Martha was silent. There seemed nothing to say to that. Finally she asked, her voice still sharp, "Is it because you have done something you shouldn't have?"

He leaned against the side of the buggy with his arm over his face. "I can't think of anything now. Oh, I suppose I have done the usual things most boys do, but nothing very bad."

"Is God speaking to you then?" Martha asked less sharply. Worry was replaced by pity now. He looked so wretched!

At that he lifted his head sharply and looked her full in the face. "What makes you think that?" he asked. It was his turn to be sharp now.

"Oh, well, I just thought it might be that," Martha said hastily. He had never talked to her like this before.

"Well, I'm beginning to think that is what it is," he said at last, leaning back against the seat. "But what does He want? Where is He? What does He want me to do?"

Martha was silent, and he went on. "When I came home, I was determined I was going to get this out of my mind. I wasn't going to let it bother me and spoil my leave. I was going to enjoy myself with you and see if I couldn't forget the whole thing. But I can't; it's bigger than I am."

"Is that why you were so gay last week?" she asked.

"Did you notice that?" he asked with a faint smile. "I thought I was fooling you."

"You didn't, though," she answered. "I noticed it right away."

"I may have acted gay, but I sure haven't been in my heart. Anything but that," he told her.

"Why don't you talk with Bishop Fred about it?" Martha asked.

"I thought of it, but I didn't know what to say. What would he have thought if I'd come up to him and told that I was being bothered with something but didn't know what it was? He'd have thought I was crazy for sure. Besides, it is too late now," he answered.

They sat in silence for a while, each with his own thoughts. After a few moments he cleared his throat and said, "Before I came home, I had myself believing that it was because I was homesick for you. I thought it would surely blow over after I had been with you a while. But it hasn't; in fact, it is worse than ever. I haven't slept more than an hour or so every night since I came home. That was one reason why I came over every night last week, because I thought if I were out late enough I might be able to sleep better. Oh, it helped some, but that finally caught up with me."

"I'm sorry Mom said what she did," Martha said.

"Oh, that was all right. After she said that, I realized it was true. You needed your sleep even if I couldn't get any," he said. He seemed less agitated now.

"If I can't help you in your trouble, maybe we'd better quit," Martha said with an effort.

She was totally unprepared for his reaction. He sat bolt upright with a jerk and said in a shocked voice, "O Martha, no! Don't make me go through that!" He grabbed her by the shoulders in a hard, viselike grip. "Please say you don't mean that, please!" He gave her a shake.

Martha had never seen him so anguished before. She reached up mechanically to loosen his hold on her shoulders. He was gripping her so hard it hurt.

"All right, I won't," she said. "I'm sorry I said it."

He let go of her shoulders now. "Thank you," he said simply. "If there is one thing I've been counting on all this while, it was knowing I still had you. It has helped me more than you will ever realize."

He unwrapped the reins and backed out of the drive. Martha was silent until they had gone some distance down the road. "I hope you find your way out of this soon," she said with genuine sympathy. Her heart ached for him.

Daniel smiled at her faintly, "Thanks, I do too." He slapped the reins across the back of the horse sharply and the horse broke into a trot.

"Do your folks realize that something is bothering you?" Martha asked.

"They haven't said anything. I think they thought the reason I was so quiet was because I was losing so much sleep seeing you. Anyway, that is what Dad teased me about," he answered.

"Why didn't you talk to him about it?"

"Same reason I didn't say anything to Bishop Fred, I guess," he said.

"How does it happen you tell me about it then?" she asked.

He slowed the horse down to a walk. "Martha, it is hard to tell you what you have come to mean to me. Of course, when I had the first date with you, I realized that you were the girl for me. I think I told you that I'd been watching you for two years before I ever dated you. Now, since I have been gone I realize it more than I

64

ever did. I think of it like this, usually: myself as one half of a circle and you as the other half of the same circle. Does this sound silly to you?" He searched her face earnestly.

Martha looked at him almost with awe. She had never realized he thought of her like this! "No, it doesn't sound silly," she said quietly. All at once he had her in his arms, dropping the reins over the dashboard in the process.

"I love you," he said softly. "I never told you that before; it was always, 'I like you.' But right now I am telling you that I love you. I have been thinking that in my heart for a long time, though," he smiled at her tenderly.

"I love you, too," Martha said with a tremulous smile.

He picked up the reins again but kept her in his arms. "That was one reason why I counted on you through all this, because I knew that we belonged together," he said.

"I almost failed you though," she said with an inner pang of sympathy for him.

"I can't say I blame you at that. I don't know how I would act if I were in your place."

"Oh, I sure hope you find your way out of this trouble before too long," she said.

"It seems to me that I must. It has been building up so much more the last week," he said. He sounded very tired. He released her and gave the horse another sharp slap with the reins. "I'd better get you home and get home myself, I suppose. We are to be at the station at three-thirty tomorrow morning," he said.

"You're going up to the station the same way you got home, aren't you?" she asked.

"Yes, that is what was planned. We are all supposed to make our good-bys at home. This gas-rationing business makes it hard to get around."

Two cars were to take all of the boys back to the station. Ervin had already told them at home, but Martha wanted to be sure. Daniel hadn't mentioned anything about her going along.

They were at her lane now and the horse turned in of his own accord. They were silent until they stopped in front of the tie rack. Daniel made no move to get out. "Why don't we say good-by out here?" he asked abruptly. "Please don't be offended, but I don't think I'll come in tonight. Besides, it is probably about eleven anyway."

He took out his watch and snapped on the dome light. Now she saw that he looked worn and tired. "It is all right," she assured him. "I hope you can sleep tonight."

"Thanks, I hope so too," he said. Martha moved as if to get out. As she did so, he took her in his arms once more. This time their lips met.

"Good-by, my darling," he whispered. "And thanks again for loving me." All at once Martha found herself sobbing on his shoulder.

"I wish you didn't have to go. Not with you feeling as you do."

"I know, I know," he replied, suddenly wretched again. With a sigh of despair he released her and Martha slowly got out of the buggy. With a tired gesture, he waved at her, then picked up the reins and clicked sharply to the horse. Martha stood at the gate and watched until he was out of sound. Then, with an unbearable ache, she slowly went up the walk to the house.

10

MARTHA HAD NEVER REALIZED that one could have such an ache in one's heart and still act as if nothing were wrong. None of the others seemed to notice that anything was unusual after Daniel left, or if they did, they thought it was because of his departure. After he had been gone two days, she received a card from him which had been sent en route, but after that she had no word from him for almost two weeks. Life could go on, though, she found. Cornhusking had started and Martha went out to help Pop. Thomas was out of school now, which helped to get the job done faster. Martha found it soothing to her troubled heart to be out under the blue October skies. The weather was fair most of the time—beautiful Indian summer weather.

Sometimes she husked with Pop and sometimes with Thomas, but with neither was she very talkative. As Thomas was quiet by nature, he didn't mind. But Pop was more garrulous. He tried to open conversations, only to have Martha answer absently or not at all. Finally he asked her, "What's troubling you? Did your boyfriend quit you?"

Martha looked up with a start. She hadn't heard a word until he said, boyfriend. "No, it's not that," she replied, busying herself with an ear of corn.

"You didn't get into trouble, did you?" This time his voice was so sharp Martha looked at him in surprise. Pop had never talked to her like that before. At first the realization of what he meant didn't penetrate and she looked puzzled. When it finally dawned on her, she almost laughed in dismay. Did Pop think she didn't have any higher principles than that?

She shook her head at him with an indignant, "No! Do you think I'd do that?"

Pop sighed and turned to husk another ear of corn. "Well, I hoped you'd have higher principles than that," he said. "If Daniel didn't quit you, what is wrong? How come you are so quiet?"

Martha was tempted to tell him. Perhaps if she told someone, the burden wouldn't be so heavy. She almost opened her mouth to do so when the thought struck her that she would be betraying Daniel's confidence in her.

"Because," was the only answer she would give him as she turned to shuck another ear. And that was all he could get out of her.

The next day she got another letter from Daniel. No one went for the mail at noon; so Rosie and Paul picked it up on their way home from school. They usually husked corn until dusk, and Martha helped with the milking so that they wouldn't be too late for supper. It wasn't until they were seated at the supper table that she knew she had a letter. Then it was because Rosie told her in a bored voice that Daniel had sent a letter again.

"Doing that again," she said with a sniff. Martha ignored it. But by the look on her face Mom saw that something was wrong. Usually Martha had jumped at a letter from Daniel, not waiting a minute before reading it. But now she made no move to pick it up. In fact, she let it lie on the cupboard until after the dishes were washed. Then, picking it up and bidding the others good night, she went upstairs.

She found herself trembling so violently when she was finally alone in her room that she could hardly light the lamp. Something seemed to tell her that this letter would be momentous. With trembling fingers she tore it open, drawing a chair close to the dresser as she did so. By the soft light she read:

"Martha Darling, Glory hallelujah; it's over now! I suppose you are wondering what I'm raving about; so I'll begin at the beginning. Well, after I left home, I was still as miserable as ever. During the time en route I guess I fooled the other fellows because no one said anything about it. I guess the others were all feeling pretty blue themselves, and they didn't think I was acting peculiar. But, except for that card I sent you, I just couldn't bring myself to write you anything. The only thing I knew, you already knew, and there seemed no point in writing you that. Besides, I hated myself for making you so miserable. I began to feel I was a rotter and the most selfish thing on earth not to release you from our relationship when you asked me to. And yet I was so thankful you stuck by me.

"I guess about that time the other fellows noticed something was wrong, because they began to tease me about losing my girl and so on. I'm very glad they were wrong! But anyway, even Ervin gave me a wide berth, I was so grumpy and grouchy. All in all I was miserable and made everyone else so. It was still the same, just as if someone were calling me and I couldn't find out who. You had mentioned that maybe God was talking to me and I began to be certain that was my trouble. But I couldn't seem to get anywhere by praying; God seemed far away. I had just about decided to talk to the director about it when word got around that we were to have a speaker with a special message for us. So I decided to wait until then and see if I could get anything from that. But it wasn't going to be until the next evening, and all the night before I was almost beside myself. I couldn't sleep or eat, I was in such misery.

"Finally evening came and we all met in the dining hall. I was one of the first ones there and the director introduced me to the speaker. He seemed to have eyes like an Xray. I think he saw at once that there was something wrong with me, but we didn't get a chance to be alone. I would have unburdened the whole thing to him if we had.

"When he began preaching, it was just as if we two were alone in the room. I don't remember all he said, but the gist of it was about yielding our lives to Christ. He told us that we were all there (in camp) because of an obligation to our government. But he asked if any of us realized that he had a far greater obligation to God. He said that we were in CPS* because we were called
*Civilian Public Service.

to go and that when we had received the call, we had dropped everything and gone, whether we wanted to or not. Christ was calling all of us too, and did we answer when He called? Did we drop everything as we had done when we received our notices, or did we ignore the call?

"He said things would probably have been made pretty hot for us if we hadn't responded to the government's call, and in the Judgment things would be plenty hot for us too, if we ignored God's call. Then he said that perhaps we were being called by God and didn't know it, and when he said that, something clicked in my heart.

70

He asked us then in such a kind way to open our hearts and heed Christ's call just as we had the government's. He told us that when we heeded the government's call, every one of us knew we would not get any reward; but he said if we heeded God's call, there would be glory for our reward. Right then and there I told God to come into my heart and use me for His honor and glory. Such a wonderful peace flooded my soul as I never dreamed possible! I told God to use me wherever and however He wanted to, and I meant it. I still do.

"The speaker was available after the service for spiritual counseling, but I hurried out of the dining hall as soon as the benediction was said, because I wanted to be alone with this wonderful thing. When I got out, even the stars were smiling at me, and the first thing that came to my mind was that verse in the Nineteenth Psalm which we had in devotions a few days before: 'The heavens declare the glory of God; and the firmament sheweth his handiwork.'

"Well, anyway, I spent the next hour or so walking out there and just thanking God for finally revealing Himself to me. When I did go in, everyone else was in bed, as far as I could see, and I was rather glad, because I wanted to be alone with my precious Lord just then. Here is the funny part of it: I slept like a log for the first time in months. I never felt better than I did this morning. Devotions really mean something, too. Before this I just couldn't understand the meaning of the Scriptures, but this morning the director read the Twenty-third Psalm and I can tell you, that is mine now!

"So this evening I just had to tell you all about it. I knew you were probably worried and heavyhearted, and I would like to ease your burden. Don't worry about me, because it is all right now! I thank God from the bottom of my heart for such a sweetheart as you. I just pray that I might always be true to you.

"I haven't had a chance to talk with Ervin about this yet, but I sure would like to. Johnny Brenneman, too, for that matter, as we three have been pals all through camp.

"I think it is probably late and time for lights out; so I will close now, and I wish for you the grace of God. Please pray for me, that I might always be pleasing to my precious Lord. I realize that only as I am fully yielded to Him can I get the most out of life. Write soon, darling. Daniel."

When Martha finished reading the letter, her emotions were mixed. She was glad that Daniel had finally found relief. But she was more puzzled than ever. What did he mean by saying that about yielding to Christ? Of course she knew that Christ had died on the cross for the sins of everybody, because she had heard the preachers say so lots of times. And wasn't she yielded to Christ by not doing bad things and by living a quiet life? But what did he mean about being used to God's honor and glory? She just couldn't understand it. She seemed to be just as troubled as before.

For a long time she sat staring at the rug, rousing at last when she heard Thomas come upstairs. She finally undressed and, blowing out the light, crawled into bed. She was tired in body and soul!

11

MOM WAS PLAINLY WORRIED about Martha now. After the letter from Daniel, she thought maybe he had asked to stop writing. But when another letter came before Martha even got the first one answered, she knew that wasn't it. She finally confided her worries to Pop and found out he was just as troubled about it as she. Pop told her about the conversation in the cornfield.

"Just seems like something is troubling her," he said. "I can talk to her and she doesn't even seem to hear me."

"Maybe she has some spiritual problem," Mom said.

"Well, it might be, but she sure doesn't want to talk about it. Can't get a word out of her," Pop replied in a concerned voice. His children's welfare was close to his heart. He had always had a real faith in God and he thought he had taught his children the same. For a while they sat in silence.

At last Mom said softly, "Why don't we pray about it?" So they knelt down by the bed and confided their fears to God. When they arose, they both felt better.

Cornhusking was finally finished, and Mom and Martha hurried to get the house cleaned and the yard raked before winter set in. Martha found hard, invigorating work the best thing to help her keep some measure of calmness. She knew what Daniel was talking about, when he told her the last night of his leave that he had to get out of the house, because she felt the same way. A weight seemed to be pressing on top of her when she was inside, and she couldn't explain it.

Christmas finally came and a few days afterward Mary presented the folks with their first grandchild, a little boy whom they called John Lowell. David promptly shortened it to Johnny. The folks were quite excited and pleased about it, much to the wry amusement of David's folks. After their already large clan of almost sixty grandchildren, one more didn't mean much.

Martha went over to help until Mary was strong enough to do the work herself. She found something satisfying in caring for the tiny creature. From the first he seemed to have a decided will of his own, letting his wants be known by a loud, healthy wail. They were all agreed that he looked just like David, although Mom insisted he had Pop's eyes (which goes to show how grandmothers are). His eyes were expressionless as yet.

More boys were called for service and the group of young folks dwindled still more. Thomas was finally judged old enough, and he obligingly took Martha whenever a social occasion arose. But it was rather dull with so many gone.

"No one is left but the simmies,*" Elizabeth Shetler so
*Young boys just beginning to date.
aptly put it one night when she, Cora Beachy, Susan Gingerich, and Martha were together.

"Some people like simmies," Martha said, raising her eyebrows at twenty-year-old Susan, who, for want of anyone better, had been dating sixteen-year-old Chester Miller.

Susan laughed good-humoredly. "Well, it is better than sitting at home all the time." They couldn't make her mad teasing her about it.

Daniel continued to write Martha puzzling letters. He repeated over and over about being so happy to be yielded to Christ and serving Him and things like that. At Christmas he sent her a beautiful white Bible with some of the verses underscored. But Martha couldn't seem to apply them to herself. For one thing, she didn't understand what they meant; for example, this one from Isaiah: "All we like sheep have gone astray; we have turned every one to his own way." And in the same book was another one where Daniel had written "my favorite" in the margin: "Thou wilt keep him in perfect peace, whose mind is stayed on thee: because he trusteth in thee."

She tried praying about it, but she couldn't get anything out of that either; God didn't even seem to be listening. Some of her bewilderment got into her letters to Daniel. She asked him, "How can you know whether you are yielded to Christ? Isn't just living a quiet life and not doing things you shouldn't and so on the same as being yielded? I try to understand the things you write about, but I just can't. I read those verses you underscored in the Bible, but I can't get anything out of them. Oh, I know Jesus died on the cross for the sins of the world, but how can I apply it to myself, as you say? I wish I could, as it seems so important to you. Maybe if you prayed for me, it would help."

When Daniel received letters like that, he was burdened afresh. Was he to be denied fellowship with her because she couldn't understand him? And especially now when he was so happy in the Lord? It made him live in an almost continual state of reliance on God, praying always that Martha would be able to understand and turn her life over to God, too.

He finally confided his fears to Ervin. Ervin, to Daniel's great delight, had given himself to Christ the same evening he had. So in their spare time they were together more than ever, comparing notes on Bible study and just generally discussing the things of the Lord.

It was the evening after Daniel had received Martha's letter when they were together once more, reading the Bible. They had been reading chapter fourteen of the Gospel of John that evening. They had read only a few verses when all at once Daniel burst out, "Ervin, I'm worried about Martha."

Ervin looked up startled. "Why, what is wrong?" he asked.

"Well, I have written her everything about my experience since I gave myself to God, and she just can't seem to see into it."

Ervin was silent for a moment. Finally he said, "Can you blame her?"

"Why do you say that?" Daniel asked, plainly surprised. He didn't expect Ervin to talk like that.

"Well, what I mean is that she can't understand it any better than we could have, say, six months ago. Do you think you would have? If someone had asked you whether God had control of your life a year ago, I bet you would have thought whoever asked was crazy. I know I would have."

It was Daniel's turn to be silent as he contemplated that. It was true, as Ervin had said. Only six months ago he wouldn't have known what it meant any more than Martha did now. "What do you think we can do about her?" he asked at last.

"You have written her, and that is about all I know to do right now," Ervin replied. "Anyway, we had better go on with our reading; it's not too long till it will be time for lights out. You read the next verse now."

" 'And whatsoever ye shall ask in my name, that will I do, that the Father may be glorified in the Son,' " Daniel read from John 14:13. Almost at once a glorious light dawned on him. "O Ervin, do you realize what that means?" he asked in a glad voice.

Ervin stared at him. All at once he smiled. "Yes, I do. That seems to be the answer to our problem, doesn't it?"

"Well, come on, let's ask Him for help for Martha then," Daniel said joyously, and they knelt down to ask God in His wonderful love and mercy to reveal Himself to her.

*   *   *

Winter was almost over once again. The snow had melted, to be replaced by soft oozy mud and cold little puddles everywhere. Martha was glad—glad because once more she could work outside as soon as it dried up. The prospect of being outdoors was much more inviting than being cooped inside all the time with such puzzling thoughts. But before the outside work began, Mary decided to make a quilt for Johnny's crib. He had long outgrown the bassinet, and they had been forced to borrow a bed from one of David's older sisters.

Pop hitched Gertie, the family driving horse, into a single buggy, and Mom and Martha went over to help Mary quilt. Mom was still troubled about Martha, because, try as she might, she couldn't get her to unburden herself. True, she had always been more quiet and reserved than Mary, but it made Mom's heart ache to see her become more so. Mary had always confided to her before her marriage. She still did, for that matter, although Mom had enough sense to realize that David should be her main confidant now.

She hoped that she could get Martha to talk today when they made this trip alone. But she was at a loss to know how to begin. She wondered if it would be better to throw some hints, or if she should plunge right in. Finally, concern became too much for her and she blurted out, "Martha, what is troubling you?" There it was said at last, come what may.

Martha looked at her quickly, rather startled to see Mom's eyes full of loving concern riveted on her. "Why do you ask?" she inquired listlessly.

"Well, because it hurts me to see you so troubled, that's why!" Mom said in a concerned voice.

Martha sighed heavily. How could she tell her? She cleared her throat and burst out, "Mom, what does it mean to say that you are yielded to Christ?"

So that was it! Then Pop and she had been right in their surmise. "Why, to be ready to do His will, I believe," she answered carefully. If she could only say the right thing now!

"Daniel has been writing so much about it ever since he has been back in camp, and I can't understand it. He says he has done that and is happier than he ever was before. He says that he is ready to do anything or go anywhere God wants him to and I believe it. But how does that apply to me?" It was a relief to talk to someone about it.

Mom prayed inwardly for guidance. She did want to help her daughter! "Well, it would mean just like Daniel says, I guess, to be ready to serve the Lord at any time," she said carefully.

"Are you yielded to Him?" Martha asked abruptly.

78

"I want to be—yes. As far as I know, I try to be," Mom answered.

"Since when have you felt that way?" Martha asked.

"Well, before you were born I realized that God must work in me. Before that I knew that we must ask Him to lead us, but never the way I did then."

"I know, but did you do as Daniel keeps saying, just give your life to Him and let Him use you as He wanted?" Martha asked again.

"Yes, I did," Mom said simply.

Martha was silent for a few minutes and then asked, "Why didn't you ever say anything to me about it before, then?"

"Why, I thought we did try to. At least, Pop and I have always tried to live for God and maybe we just thought that living it in our everyday life would mean more to our children than a lot of words."

Martha was silent again while she pondered Mom's reply. It was true, Mom and Pop had always lived a faithful, Christian life, but as far as she could see, she was doing the same.

They arrived at Mary's and the conversation ended. Mom just hoped that what she had said made sense to Martha. She hoped for a chance to talk to Mary about it, but no opportunity arose during the day, as Mary had also invited David's mother to help. Much as Mom hoped for it, there just didn't seem to be a time to be alone with Mary long enough to get started. She would have to tell Pop about it that evening when they were alone.

When they got home that evening, there was a letter from Daniel again. Martha put it in the cupboard until after supper was over and the dishes were done. She did hope that it wouldn't be another of those hard-to-understand ones.

Finally she was alone in her room, and she opened the letter almost wistfully. As she did so, a small tract fell to the floor. She stooped down to pick it up and read, "Does It Seem Hard to Understand?" on the outside. Surprised, she opened it and read: "Does it seem hard to understand how Christ's death on the cross is your atonement? Does it seem hard to understand how you can give your life to God? Does it seem hard to understand how God can forgive your sins if you believe that Christ's blood was shed for you? It need not be. 'If thou shalt confess with thy mouth the Lord Jesus, and shalt believe in thine heart that God hath raised him from the dead, thou shalt be saved' (Romans 10:9). If you realize this, believe it with your heart, then tell Him so. and ask Him to come into your life by faith."

All at once a great light seemed to break into her soul. "I know now!" she said aloud. Then with tears in her eyes she knelt by her chair and quietly and humbly told God that she wasn't worthy to have Him, but would He please come into her heart and use her for His honor? As she did so, the burden of the last few months was gone. In its place was a great, deep peace. She got up from her knees and took the folded letter out of the envelope and read: "Martha sweet, here I am again. Maybe you get tired of my saying the same thing over and over, but to me it is worth repeating. It's just that I am still so happy in the Lord and can't thank Him enough that He loved unworthy me enough to reveal Himself to me. All those weeks of agony before I gave my life to Him seem as nothing now. I know now that was the only way He could get me to listen. I know now that I was nothing but a sinner, like everyone else, even if I had told you that I was no worse than anyone else. But I realize now that I have that sinful human nature as bad as the worst sinner. God has shown me so many things through the Bible the last months. Some of those chapters seem to have been written for me alone. I hope and pray so much that He will come to you, too. You say it's hard to understand and I suppose I don't explain it right. I am sending a little tract that may be more clear than I can make it. My prayers are always with you, that God will help you understand."

The rest was routine camp news and Martha laid the letter down without finishing it. Her lips curved into a wonderful smile. Wouldn't he be overjoyed at what she was going to write him? She reached into her dresser drawer and took out pen and paper.

12

MARTHA'S LETTER reached Daniel right at the time he needed it most. For the first time in his new spiritual life he was discouraged. The joy that was in his heart and that radiated out to others had been so lasting and sweet that so far he hadn't experienced discouragement. Daniel's conversion had been a real one; he had kept nothing back. There had been a genuine yielding and a sincere desire to be pleasing to God in all things. Because of this, and because of above-average mental faculties coupled with a deep desire to know the will of God, he had spent much time studying the Bible, both alone and with Ervin. He had grown spiritually by leaps and bounds, so that he had a clearer insight into the Scriptures than Ervin. Because of all this, he had so far escaped that insidious discouragement that often overtakes young Christians. But when week after week went by, and finally lengthened into months, and still Martha couldn't seem to see the light, it began to wear him down. At first, when she hadn't been able to understand, he had believed, in simple faith, that if he could only explain it more clearly, she would be able to understand. When that didn't work, he resorted to earnest, fervent prayer, especially after Ervin and he had had that talk about John 14:13.

But now it seemed to him that he had prayed for her for so long, and with such fervent desire, that she should be yielded to God. Wasn't God going to answer his prayer? It seemed to him that He must, because didn't He mean what was written in John 14:13? Or in Matthew 7:7: "Ask, and it shall be given you"?

The day when Martha's answer finally came had been one of those days when everything seems to go wrong. There had been exasperating days out on the project, and on the way home the gas line on the government truck seemed to have water in it, making it cough and sputter. Then, as the last straw, within a mile of camp, one of the tires had gone flat and, when they wanted to put on the spare, they found it flat, too, necessitating a walk back to camp to get it repaired.

By the time he had repaired the flat and taken it out to the truck again, and driven back to camp, it was past suppertime. He ate a rather cheerless supper alone and decided to go right to bed. Nothing was going on that night, and Ervin had been sick the last day or so with a heavy cold; so that ruled out Bible study. But when he got over to the dorm, he found his mail lying on his bed. He glanced through it quickly, hoping for a letter from Martha, yet at the same time almost dreading it. If only she could understand! He prayed a little prayer that her letter might be good news.

"Please God, help her to understand," he prayed as he tore open the envelope and began to read.

"Dearest Daniel, I can understand it all now. I can't see how I could have thought it hard to understand. But that little tract you sent made it all sound plain and easy! I did just like it said and asked God to come into my heart and use me for His honor and glory like you have been saying, and He did! Oh, I am so glad! I thought I'd write and tell you right away because I knew you would want to know. Forgive me for being dumb for so long; I can see now that it is easy. I guess I was trying to make a hard thing out if it.

"Please keep on praying for me, that I might see more clearly and yield myself fully to Christ at all times. I can't help but thank God over and over again that I am privileged to go steady with such a wonderful boy as you. I just hope that I can keep up with you, and that I will never do anything to make you ashamed of me. I'll try and pray for you, too, that you will be doing God's will always. Your loving sweetheart, Martha."

Daniel thought he would burst with the glory of it! Oh, this was wonderful, and he had to be alone right now to thank God for it. But where could he go? It was too public in the dorm; so he hurried outside. He stole around the corner and started toward one of the sheds, but thought that might be locked. It didn't really matter; he could talk to God right here. He lifted up his face toward the sky and took a deep breath of happiness.

"O God," he prayed. "O Father in Heaven, how can I thank you enough? I just can't, I know, but I am so glad, Father."

Words failed then, but his heart was pouring out things too deep for words. For a long time he stayed thus in silent adoration. At last he seemed to have poured out his heart in full. Softly he went back inside and found most of the others in bed. He wondered if Ervin would be asleep. He stood for a moment debating whether he wanted to go over to the infirmary and tell him, but finally decided against it. He could tell him tomorrow. Tonight it was just between God and him. He undressed and crawled into bed, lying in silent praise and thanksgiving for a long time. The last thing he could remember seeing before he finally went to sleep was Martha's face with a soft, shining brightness on it.

* * *

Letters from Daniel were a constant source of joy for Martha now. No longer did she open his letters with nervous apprehension. On the contrary she could hardly wait to open them and see what new thing he would share with her. He had advised her to start daily Bible reading in the Gospel of John, remembering how it had helped him, and this she did faithfully, finding new truths every time she read. Some of those verses seemed to lift her off her feet, they were so wonderful. When she read the third chapter of John, it seemed to have been written for her alone. And the sheer love and mercy of God revealed in verse sixteen: "For God so loved the world, that he gave his only begotten Son, that whosoever believeth in him should not perish, but have everlasting life," made her weep in deepest praise and thanksgiving.

The family noticed the difference almost at once, but because of her natural reserve it was a little hard for them to approach her. Even Rosie remarked that Martha seemed to be like a bird, always flying around and singing. And truly she was. Those songs sung so lightly in the Sunday evening sings took on new meaning. Instead of singing them for the beauty of the music, as she had always done before, they were sung for the message in the words. Mom and Pop talked about it together one evening a few weeks after Martha's conversion.

"She seems so different," Mom said. "She used to act as if something was troubling her all the time. But now she's always singing and laughing."

"Hasn't she said what happened yet?" Pop asked.

"Oh, she lets remarks drop every now and then, but

that's all," Mom answered. "But she seems happier than I've ever seen her before."

"Maybe she's done what she told you Daniel was wanting her to do—taken Christ into her heart," Pop said hopefully.

"Well, I think that's it, by the way she talks. John, maybe we don't make Christ plain enough for our children to understand," Mom said abruptly.

Pop was silent for a moment as he thought that over. "Sometimes I'm afraid we don't," he said at last slowly. "I have been thinking about what you said Martha told you a few weeks ago, and I got to thinking like you say. We don't make it plain enough."

"We have always told them that Christ died for our sins, though," Mom said thoughtfully.

"Yes, I know, but did we ever make it plain that it's a personal affair?" Pop asked. "Sometimes I'm afraid we take too much for granted. We read from the Bible and have our morning prayer, but I'm beginning to wonder if that is enough; especially so the last few weeks."

Mom was silent for a few moments, then said, "But Mary gave herself to the Lord a long time ago. I know that because she told me. How does it happen that she was able to understand?"

"I don't know why," Pop answered. "I'm just glad she did. And Ervin, too, for that matter. If Martha has done that now, I just don't know how to thank God enough."

"But we still have three more to go," Mom said soberly.

"I know," Pop said, "and I'm praying that God will help us make the way to Him simple enough so that they can understand."

"Now we've got a grandchild to show the way, too,"

Mom said with a chuckle. "That Johnny! Pulls himself up in his crib already and he's barely six months old!"

Pop's face lighted up. "Isn't he some boy, though? He seems to know me already."

The next day Mom finally had the coveted opportunity to talk with Martha. The two women were up in the attic doing the semiannual cleaning. Martha was singing softly to herself one of the old familiar hymns. It seemed to Mom that she had never seen her so quietly peaceful.

"Happy, Martha?" she asked.

Martha looked up quickly from the seeds she was sorting. "Oh, yes!" she said radiantly.

"What's the secret?" Mom asked lightly.

"Oh, Mom," Martha said happily, "I wish I could tell you how different life looks. I used to dread the future, but now—well, everything is different," she said lamely, at a loss for words.

"Why?" Mom asked quietly.

Martha sat back on her heels, and her eyes held Mom's. "Do you remember what we talked about when we went over to Mary's the other week?" she asked earnestly.

"Yes, I do," Mom said.

"Well, that evening I had another letter from Daniel and he sent a little tract with it. I don't remember all it said, but it was something about taking Christ as our Saviour and giving our life to Him. Daniel had been writing the same thing, but I just couldn't seem to understand. But when I read that tract—well, it seemed so clear and simple and I did just what it said. It's made the biggest difference in my life," she concluded.

Mom felt the tears well up in her eyes. She dropped the box of soap she had lifted and wiped her eyes with the corner of her apron. "Oh, Martha," she said humbly, "you don't know how happy that makes me!"

All at once emotion overwhelmed her. Martha got up swiftly and stepped lightly across the boxes at her feet. Mother and daughter were in each other's arms. They remained so for a few silent, precious moments. It was as if the old attic were holy ground sanctified by the godly joy of the two women.

13

IN DANIEL'S NEXT LETTER he mentioned the fact that transfers to eastern mental hospitals were available.

"The director called us all together after supper tonight and gave us the details," he wrote. "Ervin and I talked it over afterward and prayed about it together and we both have decided to apply for a transfer. We hope to be able to go to the same place because we've seen this thing through together so far and I hope we can continue. Have I ever told you what a wonderful brother you have? It must be something that runs in the family—wonderful brother, wonderful sister. Well, anyway, I sure thank God for both of you. I know Christ is my main center now, but earthly friends mean a lot, too.

"I read a saying once where some famous soldier or someone said something like this to his sweetheart: 'I could not love thee half so much, loved I not honor more.' Well, I will put it like this: 'I could not love thee half so much, loved I not Jesus more.' I've found that this is true. I used to think when you were just my sweetheart that I loved you. But since you are also my sister in Christ—well, words just fail. The realization that we are now one in Christ outshines everything else.

"As I said, Ervin surely has been a big help ever since we started camp life together. For that reason we hope to be able to be transferred to the same hospital if we can. So pray for us that if it's the Lord's will for it to be so, we can be together in this next phase of camp life."

A week or so later Martha received another letter from Daniel.

"Praise God from whom all blessings flow," he wrote. "Our transfer has been okayed, and Ervin and I get to stay together. We are to report at an Ohio mental hospital on June 25. But here is where some good news comes in. We leave here June 1; so we can have all that time in between with home folks! It thrills me through and through to realize that my Saviour has so kindly brought this to pass. He is all-sufficient, I know, but earthly loved ones are dear to my heart, too. So here's hoping to see you in about two weeks. I can hardly wait!"

Needless to say, the news thrilled Martha, too. Little shivers of joy tingled through her whenever she thought about it, which was often. The last few days before Daniel's furlough seemed to drag on lagging feet. Finally, however, the day came when they went to meet the boys at the depot.

Martha's heart beat faster when she saw her lover again. He was bigger and handsomer than ever. Because of natural, inbred reserve, neither of them dared to display any affection under the curious eyes of onlookers, but even so, much was said without words, by the pressure of his hand on hers when they shook hands, or their eyes when they met, as they often did. It wasn't until that evening, when they were finally alone again, that he dared embrace her. Looking into her eyes he laughed a deep laugh of loving joy.

"More wonderful than ever," he said lightly, lest his voice break. Martha could only smile tenderly as she looked up at him. He released her and with one accord they sat down on the couch behind them. He took her hand in his.

90

"How's everything going?" he asked gently. "I mean with you and God."

"Good so far," Martha replied.

"Is it all I said it would be?" he asked.

"Yes, it is," she answered. "In fact, I don't think you told the half of it."

"It's great to have Him as your Lord and Master, isn't it?" he asked.

"Yes, it is," she agreed. "I'm so sorry I couldn't see it sooner."

"I was so glad when you wrote me that you'd taken Him in your heart. I almost burst. I had to get alone somewhere and thank Him over and over," Daniel said, still serious. "I had prayed so much for you, and—well, when you couldn't seem to understand, I just didn't know what to do," he finished.

"I'm sorry," Martha said quietly. "I tried hard to understand what you were talking about, but I just couldn't for so long. Then that evening when I read the tract you sent, it was just as if a light had gone on in my soul. It all seemed so simple and easy. I just asked God right then to come into my heart and take full control, and He did."

Their eyes met and held again for a long moment. All at once Daniel said, "Why don't we kneel and thank the Lord together?"

She nodded and they knelt together in front of the couch. Daniel began to pray, and it seemed to Martha that she had never heard anyone pray as he did.

"Our dear Father in Heaven," he prayed, "we come before Thee with hearts that are bursting with thanksgiving and praise. We do thank Thee so much for answered prayers! And, Father, I can't thank you enough for this girl beside me. When I realize that you had it planned before the world was made, that man should not live alone, and that Thou hast given me this wonderful girl to love and to cherish, Father, I must just thank you over and over. Help me to be worthy of her. Help me that I might always treat her as Thou dost the church, Thy Bride. In Jesus' name we ask. Amen."

He arose and reached down to help her to her feet. He held her hand in his and looked deep into her eyes.

"Martha, it seems settled already, but you will marry me, won't you?" he asked tenderly. "I could have written you and asked, but I wanted to see you personally when I asked you."

Martha was far removed from the shy girl she had been when he had the first date with her. Even so, she was so overwhelmed she could barely stammer. "Y-yes, I will," she said, and felt her face grow hot.

He sat down and pulled her down beside him. "Thank you," he said. "I've been imagining this for quite a long time." He smiled at her. "But you will be willing to wait for a while yet, won't you?" He was serious again. "Because I would rather have my term behind me before I get married. Oh, I know lots of the men get married while they're away. But I'd rather have something saved up to start out with before we get married. You understand, don't you?"

Martha nodded. She felt the same way. Besides, just the realization that Daniel wanted to marry her was enough to treasure for now. She could plan and look forward and warm her heart with it for quite a while.

The days sped swiftly by after that. As on Daniel's other leave, social events were planned in honor of the visitors. Many of the older boys, tired of waiting so long, had married and taken their brides with them wherever they chanced to be. In two years familiar faces had departed, only to be replaced by newer and younger ones. Martha, thanks to Thomas, had been more or less with the young folks, but to Daniel, after his long absence, it seemed to be an entirely unfamiliar group. Then, too, so many of them, boys especially, seemed so empty-headed and carelessly lighthearted. Few of them seemed to have any thought of the future beyond either dreading or looking forward to their term of service, according to individual temperament.

Ervin seemed to notice it, too. He asked Thomas one day, after a particularly frivolous evening, "Don't you fellows ever have any serious thoughts?"

"What's wrong now?" Thomas asked good-humoredly.

"I suppose I think of it more, but don't you ever realize 'life is real, and life is earnest'?" he asked.

"Who says I don't?" Thomas asked, still unruffled.

"Well, you don't act like it at least. Life seems to be one long picnic. Don't you realize that God wants to be the master in your life?"

"Oh, there's plenty of time for that," Thomas said. "We're young only once. Let's enjoy it while we can, you know."

"Enjoy it!" Ervin exploded. "The only joy worth having is the joy of the Lord."

"Oh, I don't know," Thomas replied, still carelessly. It seemed impossible to arouse him. "Lots of fun in living yet."

"Oh, fun!" said Ervin. "I'm not talking about fun; I'm talking about joy."

"What's the difference?" Thomas asked.

93

"Joy of the Lord is lasting; fun of the world certainly isn't," Ervin answered.

"Well, now, you know, I just never thought of it like that," Thomas said thoughtfully. At least his armor of lightness seemed to be pierced. But when Ervin wanted to talk of it further, he only changed the subject. Try as he would, Ervin didn't seem to be able to approach him after that.

After the leave was over, life settled back into the same pace again—busy summer days filled with hard physical labor. Often at the end of the day Martha was so tired from the canning or the hoeing in the garden that she was sorely tempted to go right to bed and skip daily Bible reading. But whenever she came to that point, she remembered Daniel's admonition not to neglect it, if she could possibly help it.

"It is very important that you get in the habit of doing that," he had told her, "even if you can't read more than a verse or so a day."

She did her best to keep it up, and found she was rewarded in doing so. The sublime beauty of the words and the love of God expressed in the messages fed the deepest desire of her soul.

Letters from Daniel helped, too. He always shared some thought that had come to mean much to him. As a result of all this, there was a steady spiritual growth, not the spectacular growth Daniel had experienced, but a growing realization every day of what God meant to her.

So the days passed swiftly, all things considered, and in August the world went wild over V-J Day. Such rejoicing! And yet it was only the joy of the world, with no lasting source. At what cost victory! The greatest weapon of destruction known to man! And with what futile results!

Thoughts like these were on the minds of most thinking people, but among those of Martha's community, there was also the hope that conscription would end now and the boys would be coming home soon.

Daniel didn't sound so optimistic in his letters.

"I don't suppose I will be out of this before late winter at the best," he wrote. "Most of the boys here feel the same way. Those who are older and have been in longer will get out first, of course. But, except for missing you, there is really not too much of a desire to get out, on my part. I definitely feel that the Lord has led me here, and I find the work very satisfying. To see some of these poor people who have been bound by Satan, some for quite a while—to see them respond to plain love is really marvelous. Poor men! Some of them have had quite a life. I suppose you could find all kinds of sin represented here—in the lives of the inmates, that is—but yet God loves them just as much as He does you and me. Christ's blood was shed for them just as much as for anyone else. I pray that my life will count for Christ enough so that some of these sin-blighted souls will see His beauty in me.

"Another reason I am thankful to God for leading me here is because of the fine bunch of boys who make up the rest of the group. Some are married and have their wives here; a few have children. But anyway we surely have times of Christian fellowship together. They have Sunday school every Sunday and I enjoy that. I don't get off every Sunday, though, as we take turns working. So although I'm not there every time, I sure love it when I am there. Then, too, there is a little mission on the other side of the city and most of us go over there Sunday evenings. So all in all, I find this a very profitable experience, and hope to be here for a few months yet, at least."

Martha thanked God for the letters and for Daniel's happiness, and submitted to things as they were. She continued to read the Word and meditate upon it in her everyday tasks. Fall passed by on rapid, work-laden wings, what with canning a bountiful harvest and getting the house cleaned.

Before they knew it, cornhusking time was upon them. Once again Martha went out in the fields to help. But she was far from being quiet and troubled now. In fact, she bubbled over with inner joy. Pop found her an ideal companion. Many were the discussions they had over some point of Scripture, Martha divulging something she had found, with Pop confirming it. In fact, she astounded him with her spiritual perception. Usually she quoted Daniel's letters, bringing out some point he had mentioned. Pop got to looking forward· to husking with her. Whenever she happened to husk with Thomas, he found the day long without her stimulating conversation.

Not so with Thomas. Martha could get nowhere with him beyond the ordinary everyday events. As Ervin had noticed, he seemed to have no thought higher than a good time. Whenever Martha mentioned the fact that he owed his Saviour something, he would put her off lightly. "Not now," he would say. "Plenty of time for that later on."

Ervin wrote more often now and, wonder of wonders, it seemed he had finally found a girl! In one of his rare letters to Martha (usually he let Daniel write her about him and contented himself with writing the folks a postcard about every other week), he had told her.

"At last I've found a girl I can look at twice," he wrote. "Aside from my sisters, girls have been girls, as far as I'm concerned. But one of the boys, Bill Weaver, had his sister here to visit a few times. Her name is Alice ˙and she's the most wonderful girl I have ever met. The second time she was here I managed to get a talk with her alone, and the more I talked with her, the more I was convinced she is the girl for me. I think it's mutual, because she said I could come see her sometime—after I had asked her, of course. So I am hoping the next time Bill gets a week-end leave, I'll be able to manage one, too, so he can take me under his wing. They aren't quite the same affiliation, but if we belong together, that can be changed, I'm sure."

Daniel wrote about it later.

"It amuses me to hear him rave about her. Bill and he went over there over the weekend, and that is all he talks about. To hear him, she's the most wonderful girl ever. I told him she was all right for him, but that she couldn't be the most wonderful girl, as you were that. He allowed that for a sister you were okay, but that she was something else. It was all in fun, of course, and we had a lot of enjoyment over it; but seriously, she is a lovely girl. I'm glad he has found someone at last. I hope she will be as much a joy and inspiration to him as you have been to me.

"I will have to tell you of the new experience I had Sunday. Ervin missed out on this. But, anyway, in the afternoon about six of us took some of those salvation tracts the church puts out monthly, and went over to the slum district and passed them out. Some of the people refused them, but the majority took them. A few even expressed joy in them and said they liked to read that kind of literature. We never did anything like it before, but I hope we do it regularly now. We could take in different parts of the city every time. That way we might be able to cover the whole city at least once.

"I realize more and more that there are many souls who

97

need Christ; especially since I have been here in the hospital. So many people without Him! Even when one tells them of Him, many are indifferent. But the knowledge of my Lord and Saviour grows more precious to me day by day. Then, too, another great blessing is the knowledge that you, too, are walking with God. God grant that I might always be true to you!"

14

CHRISTMAS CAME and just as quickly was gone. In honor of little Johnny's birthday, Mary invited the family over for dinner the Sunday following. The guest of honor romped and played placidly all day, taking all attention as a matter of course. He could walk now, on wobbly legs that betrayed him more often than not, making him sit down with a resounding bump, a source of much amusement to Rosie and Paul. He would sit for a moment, regarding them with eyes of hurt astonishment, and then lurch to his feet again.

Rosie delighted in him. Like most girls her age, she adored babies. Mary found her a willing baby-sitter if the need arose. She had grown into a tall, pretty girl by now—too pretty for her own good, Martha thought, because she was inclined to be vain of her appearance. She was as strong-willed as ever, though. Many were the sighs she caused Mom, and many were the prayers uttered on her behalf. Mom used to wonder why she was so different from Mary and Martha, who, aside from the common childish outbursts, had never shown such willful disobedience as Rosie sometimes displayed. For the sake of peace in the family, Mom let her have her own way many a time.

Martha had talked to Rosie once or twice about taking Christ into her heart, but she gave no response. So, as with Thomas, she could only pray that somehow God would reveal Himself to them in His own good time.

In February, Johnny's parents gave him a sister. They named her Elizabeth after Mom, but, as David said, that was too big a name for such a little girl, and so they called her Bethy. Martha went over to help take care of her. She found Mary a wonderful help in spiritual matters. They would have some of the most stimulating conversations. Martha was glad for Mary's companionship again. She thought wistfully at times of how nice it would be to have a sister her age with whom she could chum. She almost envied some of the girls who had sisters almost their own age.

Ervin wrote Martha again, telling of another visit to Alice Weaver's community. "This is the third time I have been there," he wrote, "and each time I enjoy it more. Alice's folks are nice. They have a large family, all of whom are married except Bill and Alice. Bill has a girl friend at home, and he has been going home at least once a month. The first time I was there, Alice kindly invited me to come home with Bill any time I could, and I'm not one to turn down an invitation like that! The next time I asked her if she would consider going steady with me, and what do you know, she said she would! Really, my heart was in my mouth when I asked her, but she graciously put it back in the right place. There is only one thing I regret about going over to Alice's community. That is, I miss out on helping our boys pass out those salvation tracts. I did get to go once and surely enjoyed it. Daniel was leader that time, and I'm telling you, he really has something. He was asked some of the trickiest questions and not once was he stumped. One old fellow asked him if he thought he could go around and convert sinners like them. He said it in a sneering, hateful way, and Daniel answered just as friendly as you please, that no, he didn't think so at all, but that God could. He quoted II Peter 3:9: 'The Lord is not slack concerning his promise, as some men count slackness; but is longsuffering to usward, not willing that any should perish, but that all should come to repentance.' The old man didn't know what to say for a moment, and Daniel prayed with him before we left. Here's praying that the Word sown might take root.

"Daniel is a wonderful boy. You can sure thank the Lord for the privilege of being his best girl. He seems to have a certain something about him that not everyone has. He can do just about anything with those poor fellows in his ward. Honestly, I have seen some of them behave like animals and, when he comes around, they straighten up and don't seem like the same beings. It is because he gives each one a sample of his personal love for Christ. Once or twice I've barged in on him when he was having private devotions and, honestly, his face just glowed. He puts me to shame with his persistent witness for Christ. He can talk to anyone about his soul. When I try it, I get to stammering and stuttering and I don't suppose I get it plain enough for anyone to make sense out of it.

"But with all this he is still every inch a man. He is the best table tennis player in the hospital and about the strongest boy I have ever wrestled with. He has a sense of humor, too. Always seems to have a store of good clean jokes, ready to tell at appropriate occasions. I said clean jokes. Some of the paid attendants used to tell some of the dirtiest stories when we first came here. Daniel soon stopped them. Not by what he said, but by the look he gave them and by refusing to laugh; also by the fact that he changed the subject to spiritual matters. It was enough to make them stop peddling their dirty jokes when he was around. I started out writing the praises of Alice and end up writing the praises of Daniel. Well, it should be sweet music to you. Don't know how it happens that I get the urge to write you so often lately. You know that is usually not my way. Must be that since I've found a girl, I must confide in a sister.

"By the way, how are Johnny and Bethy? I have been thinking of sending them a present. God bless you, Ervin."

15

E RVIN?"

"Hmm?"

"I can't get that old man out of my mind."

"What old man?"

"You know, the one that talked so nasty to us when we gave him a tract last Sunday."

Ervin laid down the hometown weekly he had been devouring, and looked at Daniel curiously. "The one you quoted II Peter 3:9 to?"

"Yes," Daniel said earnestly. "Remember how he was bluffed after I said that? And how he shook when we had prayer for him?"

Ervin nodded.

"Well, the Lord has laid him on my heart so heavily the last two or three days that I would like to go see him again."

"You mean tonight?" Ervin asked.

"Why not? It's early yet, only seven-thirty," Daniel answered with a glance at his watch.

"I guess we could. Do you remember where he lived?"

"It was quite a way, but I would recognize the place when I saw it, I know."

"How shall we go—call a taxi? They are pretty hard to get, you know."

"Well, we can try, at least. If the Lord wants me to go and talk to him, He will make a way to go, I'm sure," Daniel sounded confident.

"Okay then, let's go." Ervin wasn't going to be put to shame for spiritual slothfulness if he could help it. Besides, this should be good.

They slipped on their jackets. "What should we take along?" Ervin asked.

"Bibles, I guess. I've got mine in my hip pocket. Oh, yes, and this." *This* was a soul-winner's guide.

They started downstairs. "That is a pretty spooky part of the city to be out in at night, isn't it?" Ervin asked.

"I know, and if the Lord hadn't been talking to me so loudly about this man, I wouldn't choose to go. But I know He wants me to." He stopped short and faced Ervin. "Are you afraid to go?" he asked searchingly. "Because if you are, you needn't come along."

"Of course I'm not afraid!" Ervin retorted indignantly. "Besides, I'm on my way already. Come on, I'm even ahead of you." With a teasing grin Ervin bounded ahead to the door.

"Good old Ervin," Daniel said approvingly. "I knew you wouldn't let me down."

They stopped at the telephone booth at the corner. Daniel leafed through the book and found the number of a cab company. Keeping his finger on it, he got his billfold out of his jacket pocket. "No, you don't," Ervin said quickly. "I got mine out while you were looking for the number. This one is on me." He inserted the coin in the slot and dialed the number Daniel pointed out to him.

He got no satisfaction from that cab company, however. "What now? They say their cabs are all busy," he said turning to Daniel.

"There are other companies. Here, let's try this one," Daniel said, pointing to another number. "Shall I try it?"

He took the receiver down and reached for a coin he

had placed on the ledge. He wasn't quick enough, though. "Didn't I say this was on me?" Ervin said with mock severity, as he inserted his coin in the slot.

Daniel smiled without answering because at the other end of the line he heard a bored voice say, "Checker Cab Company."

Daniel asked for a cab and gave the address. He was informed that there was one in the vicinity that would be notified and would be there soon. Thanking them, Daniel hung up and relayed the information to Ervin. Then, closing the door of the booth, they stepped outside into the early spring darkness to wait.

"By the way, I was going to ask you, how come you carry your Bible in your hip pocket? Don't you know that is the easiest pocket to be picked?" Ervin asked.

"Sure I do," Daniel answered nonchalantly. "That is why I carry it there. Let someone pick it; I can always buy a new Bible. It may be the only one the poor soul has ever seen. I always keep a salvation tract in it, too; so if anyone should swipe it, he can at least find the way to God through it."

Ervin shook his head in amazement. "Whoever would have thought of it, but you! Beats me."

"Oh, I don't know if it will work," Daniel answered. "Just another way to maybe reach some soul for Christ. Here comes our cab."

The taxi stopped at the curb and they got in. "Where to?" asked the gruff-looking driver. Daniel gave the address. The driver turned around and regarded them in suspicious surprise. "What did you say?" he asked.

Daniel repeated the address slowly, thinking he might not have said it plainly enough.

"That's kind of a rotten place to be in at night," the

driver said as he started up. "What are you going to do—go slumming? Because I thought you guys didn't go in for such stuff."

"No, we are going on an errand for the Lord," Daniel replied pleasantly.

"The Lord who?" asked the cabby, again in a suspicious voice. Plainly he didn't know what to make of them. Ervin laughed to himself.

"The Lord Jesus Christ," Daniel answered.

"What's He got to do with it?" the cabby asked, threading his way expertly through the heavy after-dinner traffic. "People in a hurry to get to the theater, or the dance, or what not," Ervin thought to himself.

"Don't you know anything about Jesus Christ?" Daniel asked, leaning forward in his seat.

"A good swear word, that is about all," the cabby answered. "Do you know anything about Him?" he asked Daniel in return.

Daniel had his Bible out by now. He held it up so that the cabby could see it in the rearview mirror. "Do you know what this is?" he asked earnestly.

The cabby turned around and glanced at the Bible, narrowly missing a panel truck as he did so. Ervin caught his breath. He surely hoped the Lord was with them tonight. They needed Him, that was certain, in traffic like this!

"It's a book of some kind," the cabby said. For the first time a note of uncertainty was in his voice.

"It is the best Book in the world," said Daniel solemnly. "It happens to be the Bible. It tells me in here that all men are sinners, and are going to Hell unless they ask the Lord Jesus Christ to come into their hearts. Did you know that?" he asked the cabby gravely.

The cabby shook his head. "You must be one of those religious guys," he said. Again there was a note of uncertainty in his voice.

"Not religious," said Daniel pleasantly. "Only a sinner saved by grace."

"What are you talking about?" asked the cabby. Desperation was showing in his voice. He'd never heard anyone talk like this before. Maybe they were escaped inmates of the hospital, instead of attendants, as he had thought! But no, they had dark hats and dark jackets, the way those boys dressed. Maybe some guy knocked some of those CO boys down and made off with their clothes, he thought crazily. Ervin was amused, the poor man's thoughts showed so plainly on his face.

"Haven't you ever heard that God made man perfect in the first place, and that He put him in the Garden of Eden, and he disobeyed God?" Daniel asked. He felt a surge of urgency. Silently he prayed, "Please let me explain to him, Father. I might never see him again."

"You mean that apple stuff that Eve was supposed to have eaten?" he asked in amazement. "Sure, I've heard jokes about that. You mean it's real?" Ervin watched the lighted windows fly past and prayed that Daniel might be given the right words to say. A man's soul was at stake.

"Yes, it is," Daniel said. "About the apple we aren't told; the Bible says it was fruit of the tree. But it is true that God made man perfect in the beginning. Then He put them in the Garden of Eden. Adam and Eve disobeyed God by listening to the devil and ate the fruit of the tree of knowledge of good and evil. Because of that they had to be put out of the garden. And because of their sin, they could have no more fellowship with God, as He hates sin and cannot stay where it is.

"But because He loved Adam and Eve and all the human race that was to be, God had prepared His Son, the Lord Jesus Christ I told you about, to die for the sin not only of Adam and Eve but of everyone who was ever going to be. Now, all man has to do is to believe what I have told you, and to be sorry for his sins, and to ask Jesus to come into his heart and take over."

"And will He then?" asked the cabby breathlessly. Perhaps this was what he needed. It would be the answer to a lot of the questions troubling him lately—questions like why there were so many wicked people in the world, and why man was on this earth anyway, and who was responsible for the whole mess.

"Yes, He will," Daniel assured him. He quoted the beautiful key verse of the Bible: "For God so loved the world, that he gave his only begotten Son, that whosoever believeth in him should not perish, but have everlasting life."

They were at their destination at last. The streets were lined with dilapidated buildings on either side, and the characters shuffling along on the sidewalk didn't exactly look companionable.

"Where do you want to get off?" the cabby asked. "You didn't answer my question of how you happen to be going down here," he added curiously.

"Because I want to talk to a man about the same thing I was telling you," Daniel said.

"You don't say!" ejaculated the cabby. "Did he send for you?"

"No, but God sent us," said Ervin.

"You mean God told you the address and everything?" asked the cabby, more amazed than ever.

"Oh, no," said Daniel, amused. "We were down here

the other Sunday, this boy and some others, and gave out these tracts." He dropped one over the back of the seat.

"Here is the place!" exclaimed Ervin. "I remember that sign over there." He was pointing at a sign across the street which read, "Al's Beer" in sloppy letters, obviously done by a novice at painting. It was lit up by a streetlamp a few doors down.

The cabby drew up to the curb. "Do you fellows want me to pick you up again?" he asked. Maybe God had sent them, as the big fellow said, but it was plain that they needed someone to look out for them down in this dump!

"Why, yes, that would be nice," said Daniel, pleasantly surprised. "But I don't know how long it will take."

They got out and Ervin paid him. Daniel glanced around. Men peered at them from doorways with drunken, bleary eyes. A woman's shrill laughter was heard next door.

"Here come those Jesus guys again," she screamed. "What are they trying to do—convert us? Or join us, maybe?" Having her call them Jesus guys didn't hurt Daniel, but her obviously sinful state did. He pretended not to hear the loud guffaws that followed her sneering jokes, praying at the same time that God would show her the light.

The cabby pocketed his fare, then said, "I'll cruise around, and come back every twenty or thirty minutes, until you come out again. Sure this is the right place?" he asked with a doubtful look.

Daniel assured him that it was, and they turned to go. The cabby glared at the nearest bum and started slowly up the street. He surely would feel awful if something happened to them, nice fellows like that. After a turn around the block, he parked the cab opposite the place where the boys had gotten out and decided to wait for them. Let the boss say what he would, he wasn't taking any chances. He picked up the tract Daniel had given him and began to read.

* * *

After the cab was gone, the two boys looked at each other. "It was up a flight of steps, wasn't it?" asked Ervin.

"Yes, it was. Here they are," said Daniel, pointing to a rickety stairs two doors down from the beer sign. They climbed the steps slowly. At the head of the steps one dim bulb glowed, giving out a ghostly yellow light. At the head of the stairway they stopped. Again they looked at each other.

"Which door, do you remember?" asked Daniel. Unconsciously he lowered his voice. He suspected there probably were listening ears behind those doors.

"Let's see, seems to me it was about the next to the last one down, wasn't it?" asked Ervin, peering down the dimly lighted hall. They made their way down the hall softly, half expecting someone to open a door and stop them.

"O Father," Daniel prayed silently, "keep Thy hand over us from now on as Thou hast so far." At last they came to the door designated by Ervin, and Daniel reached up and knocked.

"Who's there?" asked a gruff voice within.

"It's those men who told you about Jesus the other Sunday," answered Daniel. Confidence and trust were in his voice. Ervin marveled once more at the childlike faith Daniel possessed. He seemed so sure God had led

110

them here. He prayed that God would grant him wisdom and give him the knowledge to say the right thing.

The door opened just enough for two bleary eyes to peer through. Suspicion fairly crackled. "What do you want?"

"We came because God sent us," Daniel said.

The door opened wider, revealing a haggard, unshaven man, possibly in his early sixties. "How do you know He sent you?" the man asked.

"Because He has made me think of you continually for the last three days. I kept praying about you and finally I knew God wanted me to come see you," Daniel said simply. "I brought him along, too," with a nod at Ervin.

The man regarded them in silence a moment, then said, perhaps a shade less gruffly, "Well, come on in then." He stepped back to let them in, closing the door after them and locking it. He made no move to do anything further, continuing to regard them with suspicion.

Daniel reached into his hip pocket and took out his Bible. Then he took out the tract he carried there and showed it to the man. "Did you read the other one I gave you?" he asked.

The man nodded. Ervin was surveying the room, trying to do so without being too open about it. What he saw wasn't much: an old table in one corner; two or three chairs, one without a back, the others with most of the back slats missing; a ramshackle bed with a tattered cover. There was no window and the air was foul. A single bulb was all that lighted the room.

"Do you realize that what it says is true?" asked Daniel.

"What if I do?" the man said. The gruffness was gone. Instead he seemed uncertain.

"Listen. If you read it, and know it to be true, won't you ask God to forgive you, and won't you take Jesus as the way out?" Daniel pleaded, love in his voice.

The man stood with his back against the door, regarding his tattered shoe tips. Wetting his lips he said with an effort, "I'm so sinful, God couldn't do anything for me."

"I'm sorry to contradict you, but that is not true. God tells us in the Bible, 'Come now, and let us reason together, saith the Lord: though your sins be as scarlet, they shall be as white as snow; though they be red like crimson, they shall be as wool.' "

The man looked up to find Daniel's kindly eyes piercing him through. All at once emotion welled up and he began to cry. "Is it really true then? Will God forgive me? I'm an awful sinner, you know," he sobbed.

"My friend, God is ready to forgive anyone who comes to Him. He tells us here that Christ Jesus came into the world to save sinners. Do you want to be forgiven?" Daniel asked.

"Yes, I do. I've been in a terrible misery the last few days. I want to have peace in my heart," the man said. The sobs had subsided a bit.

"Why don't you tell God so?" Daniel asked.

"You mean here, without going to church or anything?" he asked in amazement.

"This is as good a place as any. Just bow your head and ask God to forgive you. He will do it," Daniel assured him.

"O God," began the man in a broken voice, "I'm an awful sinner, but I want to be forgiven. I've stolen, and lied, and gambled, and sworn, and made fun of you, and gotten drunk, and smoked, and run around with women, and—and I'm so sinful. But, God, I am so sick and tired of my sins and being such an awful man. I'd like to be right with you and live for you." He stopped and looked at Daniel.

"Do you believe God heard you?" Daniel asked.

The man nodded, his tear-stained eyes never leaving Daniel's face.

"Then thank God for hearing you and saving you," said Daniel kindly.

"Thank you, God, for hearing me and saving me. Now please come into my heart and make me a better kind of man." He looked at Daniel again, and Ervin saw the biggest change come over him. "He has saved me!" the man exclaimed with a joyous light in his eyes.

Daniel reached over and took the man's hand, gripping it hard. For the first time during the interview his voice shook a little. "God bless you!" he said. "I am so glad for you."

All at once the man seemed to remember his manners. "Here, sit down, why don't you?" he said, reaching for one of the ramshackle chairs. He went across the room and got another chair for Ervin. They seated themselves, Ervin mentally holding his breath when the chair he had been given gave an alarming squeak. "To think that God sent you right at the time I needed you most!" he exclaimed. "I was so down and out and miserable, I was about ready to kill myself."

"God works in marvelous ways," Daniel assured him. "More than we can understand, but He is working just the same."

"Did you come all the way down here, this time of the day, just because of a hunch?" the man asked, wondering.

"Not a hunch," Daniel corrected him. "God sent us

113

down here. As I told you before, you've been on my heart the last few days; so tonight I asked my friend here to come with me to see you," he explained.

"Well, I am sure glad you did," the man said. "I can't thank you enough."

"May I ask what your name is?" asked Daniel pleasantly.

"Oh, sure, sure," the man said. "My name is John Glaspy. Came here forty years ago. My folks were farmers and I hated the farm. Wanted to try city life. I have tried it all right, pah!" He almost spat his contempt of it.

"Well, let us introduce ourselves. My name is Daniel Miller and this is my friend, Ervin Yoder. We work out at the state hospital."

Ervin nodded pleasantly when John acknowledged the introduction. "Were you ever married, John?" he asked.

"Yes, I have been married twice. My first wife died after we had been married ten years. She was a good woman and life wasn't so bad then. After she died, I got to drinking too much. Then about five years later I got married again. My next wife—I can't blame her now, but she was harder to get along with and we fought lots. I can see now that I just aggravated her. She finally up and left me; haven't heard of her for a long time," he finished.

"John, now that you've given your life to God, you will want to know more about Him, won't you?" asked Daniel.

"I sure would like to," said John.

"I am going to give you my Bible and let you read it for a few days. Do you suppose you could find your way over to the mission on Tenth Street on Sunday evening?" Daniel asked.

"I think so," John answered.

"All right, you keep this Bible until then and I will

114

have another one for you by that time. You can read anywhere you want to, but I would read the Gospel of John first. Then God will lead you on where He wants you, if you let Him."

John took the proffered Bible. "This is sure nice of you," he said. "First you come and tell me I need to be saved, and then you come and tell me how to be saved, and now you give me your Bible."

"Well, we are just so glad you have turned to God. I certainly have prayed for you," Daniel said. "Why don't we have a word of prayer now, and then we had better go."

John assented. They bowed their heads and Daniel prayed.

"Father, we come before Thee now with thankful and joyous hearts, knowing that Thou art more glad than we, because another soul has been born into Thy kingdom. We thank Thee so much for answered prayer. Most of all, we thank Thee that Thou hast loved us enough to send Thine only beloved Son to die for us on the cross. And now, Lord, guide this newborn soul aright, and lead him into Thy Word. Show him how to live for Thee, Father. Help him to be a witness for Thee, and we ask for Thy continued care over us, Father. In Jesus' name we pray. Amen."

After they had prayed, Daniel and Ervin got up to go. John was profuse with his thanks. "I just can't get over it. You guys came over here just for me."

"God sent Jesus down here to earth just for us," Daniel replied. "If He did that, we can do no less than we have done tonight. And besides, no telling what would have happened if we hadn't come."

"I had just about decided to kill myself," John said.

115

"I was so tired of myself and of my sins, I didn't know what to do."

"We will have to go now," Daniel said. "It's getting late and the cab driver said he would wait for us. God bless you now."

Daniel and Ervin both shook his hand. Ervin said, "I would like to say, 'God bless you,' too. I am glad I didn't try to talk Daniel out of coming down here tonight."

"You know you couldn't have," Daniel said. "You knew God was talking to me." The two boys smiled at each other. John could see that this was no run-of-the-mill friendship.

"By the way, is there anything you need in the way of food?" asked Ervin, turning to John.

"No, thanks, I don't have much money, but I don't need much either. The rent isn't much up here," John assured them.

"Do you have a job?" Ervin asked.

"I do odd jobs around the neighborhood. I don't get much pay, but like I say, it doesn't take much."

The two boys finally took their leave, assuring John that they would pray for him. They made their way downstairs again. "I wonder where our cab driver is?" Ervin said amusedly. "Bet he got tired of waiting. Didn't seem anxious to spend any time down here as it was."

"That's what you think," chuckled Daniel. "Do you see what I see?" he said, motioning across the street toward the waiting cab.

"Well, what do you know!" Ervin exclaimed.

"Didn't I say the Lord would take care of us?"

At sight of them the cabby started up and drew over into the street. He stopped and the two boys got in. "Any

116

luck?" asked the cabby. "In another five minutes I would have called a cop."

"There was no cause to worry," Daniel assured him. "The Lord had everything under control."

"You don't say!" said the cabby. "Never saw anyone with the nerve you have. Why, sitting out here and waiting for you gave me a ringside seat for three fights. Sure would hate to live in this neighborhood!"

"You asked if we had any luck," Daniel said. "I would say that the Lord saved another soul from Hell."

"What do you mean?" asked the driver as he picked his way in and out of the traffic.

"Did you read the tract I gave you?" asked Daniel.

"Yes, I did, but what does that have to do with it?"

"Didn't it tell you that to be saved one must be sorry for his sins and ask God to forgive him?" Daniel asked.

"Yes, it said something like that," the cabby answered.

"You see, God had been convicting this man we went to see, and when I asked him if he wanted to take God at His word and be forgiven, he said yes. He didn't right away, because the devil was telling him he was too sinful, but when I told him that no one was too sinful, he finally came to God and asked to be forgiven."

The cabby was silent for a few moments. Ervin could see that he was mentally digesting what Daniel had told him. At last he said with an effort, "I'd like to try the same thing."

"Do you really mean it?" asked Daniel. He almost jumped over the front seat in excitement.

"Yes, I do," said the cabby. "I'm so sick and tired of life and living, I don't know what to do sometimes. All the wickedness in the world, and people living in sin and not caring."

"Could you park for a minute? I'd like to have your full attention if I may," Daniel said.

The cabby drew up beside the curb. They were in a quieter part of the city. "Now you realize that you are a sinner and that to be right with God you must tell Him so, don't you?"

"Yes."

"Well, why don't you tell Him so?"

"O God," the cabby prayed, "I am a sinner, I know, but I'm so tired of my life. Please forgive me for all the bad things I've done and please do like this tract says, come into my heart, because Jesus died for me, too, same as for these nice boys here. Make me fit to be called yours."

"Amen!" echoed Daniel fervently.

The cabby turned around and looked at him. "Is it really that simple?" he asked wonderingly.

"Yes, it is," Daniel assured him. "It doesn't take a lot of words when one is sincere."

"Why haven't I ever heard of it before?"

"I can't tell you that," said Daniel. "Maybe God had to let you wait until now so you would accept it. Would you have listened if someone had told you sooner?"

"I don't know; probably not," admitted the cabby soberly. "But I do know that I have been dissatisfied with my life for a long time now."

"The main thing is that you have given your heart to the Lord. Now that you have done that, you will want to know all about Him. Do you have a Bible?"

"No, I don't."

"Well, I would give you mine, but I gave it to John."

"John?" echoed the cabby.

"The man we went to see, John Glaspy. But I would

118

advise you to get yourself a Bible and start reading it. I can think of no other way that would help you more. Ask God to show you the things He wants you to know, and He will show you."

"Thanks," said the cabby. "Sure am glad I picked you guys up tonight. I haven't felt so peaceful for a long time." He started the cab again. "Shouldn't I join a church now? What kind should I join?"

"Well, I wouldn't want to tell you that. I would rather think you should pray to God to lead you to the church He wants you to be with. I will, however, invite you to come over to our mission on Sunday evening."

"Is that where you go?"

"On Sunday evening, most of the time. Sunday mornings we have services for all the CO guys who work in the hospital."

"How many are there of you, anyway?" asked the cabby.

"Let me see, about twenty-five or so, I think. Two of them got their release last month; so that leaves some less at Sunday school. Both of them are married and their wives worked there, too."

"Do you boys get paid big wages there?"

Daniel smiled. "No, we don't get any wages."

"What!" exclaimed the cabby in amazement. "How come you don't get paid? I wouldn't work in there without wages."

"Well, you see, we think our witness means so much more, and speaks so much louder, if we don't work for wages," Daniel explained.

"That is a new one on me!" said the cabby. "How do you boys keep going then?"

"We get our room and board furnished by the hospital

119

and our home congregation sends us a small allowance each month. Then we can work on our off hours if we want to. So you see we aren't so bad off," Daniel concluded cheerfully.

"You act as if you knew something about us," broke in Ervin, speaking for the first time. "How does that happen?"

"My wife's uncle is in that hospital. Been in there for five years, at least. She goes to visit him every now and then. I never go; I couldn't stand going in there and seeing all those batty people."

Daniel and Ervin exchanged amused grins. "I look at it this way," said Daniel, serious again. "I think of them as people for whom Christ died, just the same as He did for you and me. Then, too, I don't suppose we look any better in God's sight at times than those poor people. A lot of them are in there because of sin, really. Makes one rather sad at times."

By this time they were in sight of the big hospital. Ervin looked at his watch and saw that it was ten o'clock —two hours since Daniel had interrupted his reading. The momentous events that had happened since then! He breathed a prayer of thanks to God for His infinite love and care.

"By the way, what's your name?" Daniel asked the cabby.

"Dick Simms," he answered.

"Are you glad you have given your heart to the Lord?"

"I sure am!" Dick said fervently.

"Let's have a word of prayer before we go; then you can tell God so."

The three men bowed their heads and Dick prayed first. "Dear God, I am so glad that you have shown me the way out of my sinfulness tonight. I'm so thankful that you put me in contact with these boys. Help me to live for you and be a witness the way these boys are." He stopped and, after a moment's silence, Daniel prayed.

"Our wonderful Father in Heaven, we come before Thee with hearts that are overflowing with joy and thankfulness tonight. And we realize, Lord, that our joy is as nothing compared with Thine, because Thou lovest us so much more than we can realize, and because it is not Thy will that one soul should be lost. So, Father, we just commit this man into Thy hands, knowing that Thou wilt take full care of him. Please, Father, grant us strength and wisdom to witness for Thee. Help us also to use every opportunity to be doing Thy work. In Jesus' name, Amen."

After the prayer, the boys got out of the cab. Ervin got out his billfold to pay their fare. When Dick saw what he was doing, he said emphatically, "Oh, no, you don't. I won't take any pay from you. I should pay you after what you have done for me tonight. This ride is strictly on me!"

The boys looked at each other and Ervin raised his eyebrows in perplexity. He tried to proffer a dollar, but Dick shook his head. "No, I mean it! I won't let you pay. What you have done for me is worth a lot more than your fare is."

Ervin finally pocketed his billfold and resolved mentally to put the amount in the Sunday school offering. So with handshakes all around and hearty good nights, the boys took their leave. Dick watched until they were inside the door, and then he slowly drove off into the darkness.

16

DANIEL WROTE TO MARTHA, giving her a full report of the evening. A week later he wrote and told her that both men had been at the mission services Sunday evening.

"I was glad to see them. Funny how the common bond of Christ in our hearts melts all barriers. But the Apostle Paul told us, 'For by one Spirit are we all baptized into one body, whether we be Jews or Gentiles, whether we be bond or free; and have been all made to drink into one Spirit' (I Corinthians 12:13). John was shaved and clean and looked an entirely different soul, as he was, too. Dick Simms had his wife with him, an ordinary enough woman as far as looks are concerned, but entirely special to God, I am sure. She seemed to take a genuine interest in the services. Here's hoping that God will bring her to Him, too.

"I had gotten a Bible for John and marked some verses I thought were most important for him right now, and you should have seen him. He was like a child with a toy. I could see that he had been reading mine meanwhile, because there were a few smudges in it that hadn't been there before; but, bless his heart, I'll treasure them.

"Pastor Grabes of the mission made the men feel welcome, and invited them back next Sunday. I feel like a mother hen with her chicks, but is it any wonder? The whole experience has taught me that when the Lord speaks, it is best to answer. The opportunity might never come the second time."

Martha, reading these lines, felt an admiration akin to worship in her heart as far as Daniel was concerned; especially so because, compared with what she was doing for Christ, Daniel's ability to talk to anyone of the ways of the Lord was almost a miracle. She did so want to live for Christ and shine with a radiant inner glow for Him, but her efforts seemed futile and puny. Like Ervin, she found it hard to witness to just anyone about his soul; and to be engaged to someone who could do, seemingly without effort, what she couldn't do, even with prayer and force of will power, was enough to make her put Daniel on a pedestal and regard him with awe. Not that Martha realized what she was doing, so subtle are the workings of self, but with every letter from Daniel describing his work, or from Ervin singing some fresh praise of Daniel, the stem on the pedestal got a little higher. The only result any of this had on her direct consciousness at first was the necessity of exerting a little more will power in Bible reading, and the vague realization that she wasn't getting as much out of it as before.

More and more of the boys in the hospital were getting their discharges and Daniel and Ervin were expecting theirs any day. They looked forward to their release with mixed feelings. They were discussing it one evening after three boys had left that day, permanently discharged.

"I will miss the other boys," Ervin said. "This kind of work isn't exactly what I've imagined my lifework to be, but I'm really glad I have had it."

"I know. I feel the same way," said Daniel. "In fact, I wouldn't trade it for any amount of money. For one thing, just the knowledge that I found the Lord while in camp is enough to make it worthwhile to have been here."

"Same here. Really, I have wondered sometimes if I would have given my life to God if I had stayed at home for the past three years."

"I know what you mean. I've been wondering the same thing," Daniel said as he threaded a needle. He was trying to mend a hole in the heel of one of his socks. Of neccessity they had to do their own mending. "This is one of the jobs I'll be glad to be done with," he said with a rueful laugh.

"Mending and patching? That is a job. Those boys who had their wives here were lucky; they got it done automatically."

"Seriously, though, there are a lot of things I have learned the last three years that I hope will make me a better Christian," Daniel said after a pause. "Just the experience of mixing with others from so many different groups has helped me a lot. You know how we used to be, or how so many of the home folks still are; most of them think their way of doing things and looking at life is the only right way. I don't like to say it, but it is true."

"I know," Ervin agreed. "I have been so glad for the many fine Christian boys we have met. I know now that our group doesn't have a monopoly on God the way I used to believe."

They sat in silence for a while. Daniel still wrestled with the heel of his sock. How did women get the hang of it? He had seen his mother do it lots of times at home and she never had the exasperation he did. He guessed it was because God had made it that way.

"What are you going to do when you do get out?" Ervin asked abruptly.

"Go home, I guess, and get a job and save up money

124

to get married. What will you do—same thing?" Daniel grinned at him.

"I think I will get a job and save up money, but for a different reason."

Daniel looked at him, rather surprised. "What's on your mind now?"

"Well, I don't think I will go home and settle down at farming. Farming is all right, and whoever wants to do it is welcome. I wouldn't belittle it. But I don't think the Lord wants me to do it."

"What does He want you to do?"

"Well, I have prayed about it quite a lot and the clearest idea I have so far is to go to school for a couple of years. I rather think I will try to teach school then."

"You will! Well, good for you!"

"You approve of it then?" Ervin asked. For some reason it mattered a lot if Daniel thought he was doing the right thing.

"I certainly do. I think it is a good idea. I have prayed about my future, too, or rather ours, because Martha is just as involved, but the only answer has been to go back home and, as far as I know, settle down there. I don't mind farming; in fact, I rather look forward to it again."

"Then another thing, you and Martha are engaged, and have that settled. Alice and I aren't yet," Ervin said after a pause.

Daniel grinned at him. "What's wrong? Afraid she won't have you?" he teased.

"I sure hope she will have me! You know, it's funny, but I used to laugh at all you lovesick boys, always writing to your girls, or looking for a letter, or talking about them, or making those little mats in camp with their names on them. I thought you were silly," Ervin confessed.

125

"You are just as bad now yourself," Daniel said wickedly. "If I remember right, you wrote her last night and got a letter from her today. I wouldn't be surprised if you write again tonight. Who is lovesick now?"

"I know, I know. You needn't rub it in! By the way, when did you write Martha last?" Ervin could be just as teasing. "Didn't you write last night, too? Maybe you didn't get a letter today, but you probably will tomorrow."

They looked at each other and grinned; it was nice to be pals!

Sure enough, one day in early June, Daniel and Ervin received their notices of discharge. Daniel met Mr. Dale, the administrator of the hospital, the same day in the main hall. After a pleasant greeting the administrator said, "Are you busy right now, Daniel?"

"I was on my way to the basement for therapy supplies, sir."

"Do you have to be right back?" asked Mr. Dale.

"Well, not right away," Daniel answered, rather puzzled. He wondered what Mr. Dale wanted.

"I would like to talk with you a few minutes, please. Can you come to the office now?"

Daniel nodded. Mr. Dale turned and went toward his office, and Daniel followed slowly. He was at a loss to know what to make of the whole thing. Had he done something wrong? He searched his mind frantically, trying to think what it could be. Mr. Dale looked pleasant enough, though. He cleared his throat and, turning to Daniel, said, "Well, Daniel, I guess you will be leaving us before long."

"Yes, sir, I expect I will."

"I will be sorry to see you go. I have appreciated your work here very much. I have watched you quite a lot the

126

last months and I admire the way you handle the men in your ward. In fact, I would be glad to offer you a permanent position here."

Daniel was definitely taken aback. "Thank you, sir, but really I never gave it any thought."

"No, I don't suppose you did. What are your plans after leaving here, may I ask?"

"Well, I thought I'd go home and get a job for a while, then settle down there and farm," Daniel said.

"Do you like farming?"

"Yes, I do."

"Do you miss it?"

"Yes, sir, sort of. I always like to work with the soil at home. Then, too, I like being outdoors."

"Yes, I can imagine you would. I suppose it was pretty hard on you to be cooped up inside, here in the hospital," said Mr. Dale with a smile.

"Well, I wouldn't want to say that, sir. I certainly am glad for the experience I have had here. I know it has broadened my viewpoint considerably. It has also helped me to realize more fully what the Lord has done for me, sir."

Mr. Dale's eyebrows went up. "I don't quite follow you. What do you mean when you say, 'what the Lord has done' for you?"

"Well, sir, when I look at those poor people, who so often act like animals (you know they do)—when I look at them and see how unloving and unlovable they are from a human standpoint, and realize that Christ loves them, too, it makes me love Christ all the more," Daniel finished earnestly.

Mr. Dale was silent a moment. He absently fingered

the paperweight on his desk. Finally he said, "Is that the secret of your life? I have wondered what it was that could make you handle those men in your ward, who as you say, act like animals sometimes."

"Yes, sir, it is. I can't help but love them, because I know that Christ loves them, too. It makes all the difference in the world. I know I couldn't love them if I didn't have Christ in my heart."

"What do you mean by having Christ in your heart?"

"Well, sir, I turned to God and told Him to take control of my life and to use me to His glory. When I did that, I died to my own nature and desires. So now I can say with the Apostle Paul, 'I am crucified with Christ: nevertheless I live; yet not I, but Christ liveth in me.' "

Again Mr. Dale toyed with the paperweight in silence. After a moment he said, "Well! If that is what makes you able to take life's jolts and not fuss the way most people do, and if it makes you love those—those human animals—then all I can say is, you really have something—something we all should have."

"We can all have it," Daniel said softly. He was so glad for this chance to witness to Mr. Dale. If only the things he said would stick! Not because he said them, but because God's power would be shown.

Mr. Dale was silent again. All the while Daniel was sending an unspoken prayer to God. "Please, Father, give me the words to say."

Finally Mr. Dale cleared his throat. "Daniel, I—I admire your motives, certainly. I just wanted to give you an official word of appreciation on behalf of the hospital." He pushed back his chair and got up. Then reaching out his hand to Daniel, he continued, "So I would like to say, thanks a lot for the fine service you have given here the past year. I wish everyone who worked here would do as well."

"Thank you, sir," Daniel answered, slightly embarrassed. He turned to leave.

"You said something about going home and settling down, Daniel. I suppose you have the girl picked out?" said Mr. Dale with a smile.

Daniel met his eyes and blushed slightly. "Yes, I do, sir."

"Someone who has been true to you all the while you were here?" asked Mr. Dale, again with a twinkle in his eye.

"Yes, she has, sir. We started going steady before I left for camp."

"I see. Your childhood sweetheart, then?"

"Well, I guess that is what you would say. Not exactly childhood, though."

"Does she live in your home community?"

"Yes, she does," Daniel answered. "Ervin Yoder that works here—you know him—is her brother."

"That is nice, and I noticed you two seemed to be special pals. Is that why?"

"Well, it's not the only reason, sir. It helps of course, but we would be close friends anyway," Daniel told him.

"I certainly wish you luck in life, Daniel. Good morning, now. I think I am due for a conference in a few minutes." Mr. Dale glanced at his watch, then started up the hall. Daniel went the opposite direction, silently praying again that God would somehow help Mr. Dale understand what he had been trying to tell him.

17

IT WAS LATE IN JUNE when Daniel and Ervin left for home, officially discharged from Civilian Public Service. There were only a handful left at the hospital. Bill Weaver was still there, but he was expecting to be discharged in the near future. He had also confided to Ervin his intentions of getting married soon after his discharge, and had already asked him to be one of the groomsmen. Ervin rather wished the marriage would take place before they left for home, when he considered his pocketbook, but was cheered at the thought that it would give him a chance to see Alice in late summer. He had been thinking it would be quite a while before he could do that again. He still hadn't asked her to marry him, mostly because his voice failed him whenever he thought of it in her presence. Maybe he would have to wait until he got home and then write and ask her, he thought hopefully. That way it wouldn't be quite so nerve-racking.

It was good to be home again, to be back with home folks and catch up on local affairs. To be part of the young folks was a change, too, after missing that for so long. For Daniel, the best thing was to be with Martha again. He had been homesick for her so often! Now to enjoy her companionship again! Best of all, to discuss the things of the Lord with her, always finding her an eager and attentive listener.

He found a job with a carpenter gang, busy once more

now that controls and rationing were over. The pay was better than he had dared hope for while still in service. So by careful calculation and saving, he wondered if they could get married by fall.

He confided his thoughts to Martha one Sunday evening. "Martha, do you suppose we could get married by fall?" he asked.

Martha looked at him hopefully. "Do you want to?"

"Don't you?"

"Yes, I do," she replied frankly. "If we can afford to, that is. I thought you decided we might have to wait until spring, at least."

"I know I did, but I have been figuring up that if I save as much as I can, and then maybe keep on at carpenter work through the winter, we might get married this fall. That is, if you still care to have me." He smiled tenderly at her.

"Maybe I will reconsider and turn you down," she teased.

He caught her hand quickly. "You wouldn't do anything like that to me now, would you? What have you been doing, two-timing me and finding someone you like better?" he asked in mock severity.

"Like Irma?" she asked. Irma had promised to be faithful to Johnny Brenneman during his stay in service, but the loneliness had gotten the best of her. It had been discovered that she was keeping company with another boy secretly. Needless to say, her name had become a byword among the young folks. Johnny, thoroughly disgusted, had left for the west to spend the summer.

They gazed fondly at each other for a moment. Finally she asked, "Seriously, though, do you really want to?"

"Yes, I want to, Martha. We have been going steady

131

for—let's see—at least three years. I would like very much to be married to you and settle down."

Martha nodded. "I agree. It has been too long, but I just thought you said you wanted enough money to get started good first."

"I think we can make it if we don't try to get everything right away. I will probably have to get everything second-hand, but that doesn't bother me. I don't think we have to have everything new to be pleasing to God. In fact, I think it will please Him more if we can be content with just a little." Martha nodded agreement and Daniel continued. "Another reason I would like to get married is because I don't feel at home with the young folks any more. I suppose it is because I have been gone so long, and they have changed hands, so to speak, and—well, it just doesn't seem the same any more."

"I suppose it would be so," Martha assented. "But I was here all the time and I am beginning to feel the same way. So many of the older ones have married and settled down, I feel we should, too. Then there is quite a bunch of simmies coming up."

"I've noticed that. Many of them seem so light-minded and indifferent to spiritual things. I noticed it last year on my furlough. What makes them so? Or is it just me?" Daniel asked.

"I think some of it is because of the uncertainty of the times we are living in," Martha pondered.

"That is probably part of it. I heard one of the younger boys say that he was going to have a good time while he could; he didn't know how soon he'd have to be leaving for service."

"That is what Thomas says," Martha reflected. "He says that if they are going to keep on with conscription

132

the way it seems now, he will have to go before long, and then he would miss out on so many things. He says he might just as well enjoy life now; that there is plenty of time to be serious later on."

There was a pause while Daniel gazed at the floor in deep thought. "But surely some of them are concerned with higher values than that, aren't they? Some surely realize that life is more than 'eat, drink, and be merry.' "

"Well, there are you and Ervin and me, at least. Then I know that some of them are thinking, at least some of the girls. There are lots of those who don't like the way some of the boys act; I have heard them say so."

"I wonder if any would be interested in a young people's meeting or something like that during the week— something on the order of the midweek meetings we had at the hospital, where we could get together and study the Bible and sing some special songs and then have prayer for all at the end," Daniel mused.

"I am sure some of them might. It's a fine idea, but where would we meet? In some home?" Martha asked.

"That would have to be the place. I wonder if we could get it started. I wish we could." He sat up straight. "Let's try it."

Martha considered a moment. "We could probably have it here. I don't think the folks would care. In fact, they might be glad to have the young folks do this, instead of attending some of the wild parties that have been going on."

"Maybe we could get something started here. You ask your folks, will you? And if they don't object, maybe we can have one in the near future. Also ask them what they think of our getting married by fall, will you?"

"Yes, I certainly will. I'll let you know as soon as I

find out. But I know they won't have any objections about us. They like you a lot, Daniel. Just anything you say goes with them." Martha smiled at him.

"It does? Well, I hope it is always going to be like that. I would hate to ever spoil their trust in me." Daniel looked gravely at her with wordless love. God grant they might never fail each other!

* * *

Mom and Pop had no objections to their getting married. As Martha had said, they had a high regard for Daniel and anything he said was all right with them, mostly because he never did anything unseemly. Of course, there were times when Mom thought Martha was too young, but it made all the difference in the world that she was marrying Daniel. To no other boy that she knew of could Mom have relinquished her daughter so readily. Even David, much as they had grown to love him, had not the high regard and esteem Daniel had with them.

Partly because of Daniel, they readily consented to have a young people's meeting at their home. As Martha had predicted, they would much rather provide a place for that than for one of the wild parties which were beginning to be common among the young folks.

So a young people's meeting was duly announced, and to Daniel and Martha's surprise quite a number attended. Daniel, who was chosen leader by common consent, used for his theme Ecclesiastes 12:1: "Remember now thy Creator in the days of thy youth."

He capably conducted the open discussion period, asking thought-provoking questions that neither Martha nor Ervin would have thought of. Thomas, sitting on the outskirts of the group, was outwardly noncommittal, but in-

134

wardly more uncomfortable than he had ever been. Why must Daniel disturb his careless indifference, anyway? What business was it of his if he chose to have a good time while he could? The time was coming quickly enough when life would be serious. Maybe in a year from now he would be in some outlandish hospital, and then look what he would miss! No fun anywhere!

Thomas wasn't the only boy, or girl for that matter, who had uncomfortable thoughts. Some were realizing that their life, which they had always before considered their own and no one else's business, might after all be God's concern. These found satisfaction in the meeting, something their souls craved. To them, it was all the more special because it was only for the young folks. They dared voice their opinions here, which wasn't the case in Sunday school, where the discussions were for the married men mostly. So when, after the closing song, Daniel asked the group if they would like to have another meeting in the near future, more than half of them assented.

"Does anyone care to open his home for us to meet in?" Daniel asked. There was a pause while each one considered. Finally one of the older girls, Miriam Hershberger, timidly said that they could probably meet at her house.

"Fine!" Daniel said. "Now, how soon would we care to have another meeting—next week? Or should we wait a week?" Again there was a pause. Then one of the boys suggested they wait a week. Daniel assented, knowing that with something new it was best to go slow. So it was agreed that in two weeks they would meet at Miriam's house.

"Shall we choose someone to be our leader?" Daniel asked. "My leading tonight was just temporary; I will gladly turn it over to someone else." But no. one else seemed to feel capable. So, by common consent, Daniel was again chosen to be the leader. Martha, sitting in the back of the room, felt that Daniel was the only one among the entire group who would know the first thing about such work. Not even Ervin would qualify because he was too shy to be a public speaker. Again admiration bordering on worship surged through her. Was there ever a boy like Daniel? She doubted it.

*   *   *

Because of the increasing amount of canning, and because she wasn't feeling well, Mary asked Mom if Martha could come over and help her for a while. "Do you think you can spare her, or will you need her at home the rest of the summer if she gets married this fall?" Mary asked.

Mom considered for a moment. Then she said, "No, I won't need her. In fact, I think it's best if she does help you. That way Rosie won't be relying on her all the time. I really think she should be with you."

So Martha went over to help Mary for the rest of the season. After consulting with Mom and Pop and considering her own wishes, she and Daniel finally decided to be married the first week in October. Martha loved the month of October. To her it was the most beautiful season of the year, with the turning of the leaves and the blue October sky. So it was decided that she stay at Mary's until the week she was to be published, which would avert suspicion and still give her time to do her sewing.

The two sisters found much joy in being together again. They were in perfect agreement in spiritual matters. David, too, was spiritually awake, and they had the

136

most satisfying conversations. Especially satisfying were the morning devotions, which were kept as informal as possible.

The young people's meetings were a source of inspiration, too. Martha enjoyed them very much. Daniel was a talented and capable leader, able to draw the shyest into the discussion. More than once Martha felt adoration surge through her when she listened to him. She was sure no one else could do as well.

* * *

In late August, Ervin left for the east to be groomsman at Bill Weaver's wedding. Alice was as glad to see him as he was to see her. She was secretly expecting him to propose, but to her disappointment, he said not a word about it. She consoled herself, however, by the fact that he seemed to enjoy her presence as much as ever.

Ervin would have liked to propose, but whenever he thought of it in her presence he got flustered and embarrassed, and talked about anything else except that. He was more resolved than ever to write and ask her. He still felt that wouldn't be as nerve-racking as proposing in her presence. He confided to her Martha and Daniel's plans to marry in October, however, and asked her to come out and visit the folks then. To this, Alice gladly consented.

After Ervin returned home, he started his freshman year in the local parochial high school. It made him feel self-conscious to be in the same class with fourteen-year-olds, but under the circumstances it was the best he could do.

One evening in early September, Daniel came for Martha to take her to the young people's meeting. He was driving a handsome sorrel filly, as skittish and high-strung

137

as she was handsome. Martha had been sitting on the porch swing waiting for him. It had been a warm day for September, and she and Mary had been canning tomatoes all day. Now she was glad for a chance to sit in the coolness of the evening after the hot, steamy kitchen.

Daniel drove up to the gate and called, "How do you like my horse? Isn't she a dandy?"

Martha walked out to the gate, eyeing the horse with distrust. "She is beautiful, but is she safe to drive? She looks awfully wild to me," she said. The filly was pawing the ground, impatient to be on her way. It took all of Daniel's efforts to hold her.

"Would you rather not go with her then?" Daniel asked.

"Oh, yes, I will go with you, but are you sure you can handle her?" Martha asked doubtfully.

"Come on, then, I've been driving her in the breaking cart for two weeks now," Daniel said, his arms pulling back on the reins firmly.

Martha got into the buggy and Daniel clicked to the filly sharply. She reared, causing Martha to gasp in alarm. Then with a bound she was off, with a speed that to Martha was the next thing to running away. Daniel seemed not to be afraid, however, and guided her with a sure hand. After the first burst of speed, she quieted down and Martha dared breathe normally again.

"Isn't she a beauty, though?" Daniel asked again, when he was sure that he had everything under control.

"Beauty is only skin deep," Martha commented wryly. "I would rather have a safe horse than a beautiful one."

"Oh, she will be safe when she gets over the first scare," Daniel assured her. "When Dad gave her to me, he said I could have her if I broke her. I have been working on

138

her for two or three weeks. If you think she is wild now, you should have seen her when I started."

Martha didn't have time to make any comment, because the filly saw something flapping beside the road—an old paper sack someone had dropped. With a wild lunge she bounded to the opposite side of the road. Martha gasped again and Daniel concentrated all his efforts on the filly until he had her quieted down again.

"You know, I have been giving her lessons, but she's been giving me some, too."

"What do you mean?" Martha asked doubtfully. She wondered what a wild thing like this filly could teach anyone except to give her a wide berth.

"Well, just like that paper sack. It couldn't hurt her, but she almost went wild about it. How many Christians act the same way when God presents something unusual to them! They act as if it were going to get them, just as this filly did. Then, too, I have been hitching her to Dad's old Molly, the slowest old horse you ever saw. Molly wasn't good-looking to begin with, and she acts as if she knew it and had given up hope a long time ago. She waddles along, content to get one foot in front of the other, and nothing ever disturbs her," Daniel said.

Martha smiled and asked, amused, "What lesson is there in that?"

"How many people act the same way? Just as if all they cared about was to somehow stumble through life with the least possible effort. Nothing ever arouses them; all they care about is to live undisturbed and half asleep, just like Molly. Why, you just can't hurry her!"

Martha was silent for a moment as she pondered this. "I guess that is true," she assented. "But you said the colt had taught you the lesson."

"She did. She is just the opposite; she gets stirred up at the least little thing, just the way some Christians do when God disciplines them. Like this colt, if they see even a suggestion of something scary, they think it is going to get them, and they start crying for God to have pity on them—they are perishing."

Again Martha smiled. "I would rather have her safe and gentle anyway," she said.

"Well, I know, but just consider this. Won't it be a beautiful sight, with all the verve and zip she has, when she is finally subdued enough for a woman to drive? Think of how she will be—spirited, yet under control; lively, yet gentle; quick to go, but just as quick to obey the command to stop. To me that gives a beautiful picture of a Christian—full of fire for the Lord, yet at the same time every thought under His control; quick to do His will, both in doing, and in waiting and letting Him do. Why, it even gave me the theme for tonight's lesson."

"It did!" Martha exclaimed.

"It is in Psalm 32:9: 'Be ye not as the horse, or as the mule, which have no understanding: whose mouth must be held in with bit and bridle, lest they come near unto thee.' It is a perfect theme, it seems to me, for young folks—not to be so high-strung and hard to handle that God has to use hard reins to hold them back. And I'll bet this colt thinks that a bit is awfully hard, especially when she wants to go and I want to keep her from going. Just the way God has to do sometimes to Christians."

Martha could see the truth of his words. Admiration surged over her afresh. Who else but Daniel would have thought of such a thing!

"Don't you have a name for her?" she asked. "I notice you just call her the colt."

140

"No, I haven't picked a name yet. I was going to give you the honor of naming her," Daniel smiled at her.

Martha lifted her eyebrows in mock astonishment. "Well, in the light of your words, maybe we can call her Dynamite. That is full of zip, but does a lot of good if controlled." She said it just for fun.

"Dynamite," Daniel mused. "Say, I think you have something there. I would like that name."

"Oh, silly!" Martha said laughingly. "I would rather have a prettier name than that. Why don't we call her Star or Lady or something like that?"

"Star would be nice. We will call her that."

So it was settled and Star, entirely unaware of her name, was trotting quietly now. They were almost at their destination.

"I almost forgot with our talk about Star, but there is a visiting preacher at ———— church now and I would like to hear him some evening," Daniel announced. "Which evening would it suit you best?"

Martha considered. "I don't care; I suppose we could go tomorrow night, as far as I know. Have you heard him before, or how does it happen you know of him? Who is he?"

Daniel named a well-known evangelist and said, "One of the boys in the hospital was from his congregation and he bragged about him a lot; so I would like to hear him if I can."

Martha consented, and they decided to go the next evening. When Daniel called for her he was again driving Star. She wasn't quite so skittish; in fact, she seemed rather quiet. David, coming in from late haying, stopped to have a few words with Daniel.

141

"Some horse you have there," he commented. "Is she yours?"

"Isn't she a beauty, though? Dad raised her and gave her to me. He said if I broke her, I could have her."

David stood and admired her. "Is she about broke?" he asked.

"Just about. I told Dad he could use her to haul in hay today, and she has quieted down some."

Martha came out then and, after a few parting words to David, they left. Star seemed more subdued and more willing to trot quietly. "Just about ready for you to drive," Daniel assured her. "Got to have a family driver ready if we get married in a few weeks."

Martha smiled at him. "Not much of a family yet," she said teasingly.

"Let's see, how long is it before we are published? Next Sunday?"

"Yes," Martha said happily. It seemed so long since they started going steady. Three long years. Three years of waiting and writing!

"Our courtship has been mostly by correspondence," Daniel said. "But that way we didn't have a chance to get tired of each other's presence." He looked at her with a grin. Once more admiration bordering on worship surged through Martha. How wonderful he was!

They found the church crowded almost to capacity when they finally arrived. Many of their own young folks were there, because the speaker had special appeal to them. Most of his messages were spiced with timely words they understood. His message for the evening was on idolatry. At first Martha thought it beside the point to preach a sermon on such a subject in this community. Wasn't this a Christian community? Why, no one would

142

dream of worshiping idols, she was sure. But as he unfolded the Scriptures and explained his text, Martha began to see that it was only too possible to worship idols even here in this Christian community.

"Some people wouldn't dream of bowing to an idol," the preacher said. "But, nevertheless, they are caught worshiping something else besides God. At least their worship is divided. Perhaps they worship their own opinions; perhaps it is their wealth. It may be they worship their reputation, evidenced by the fact that they would rather have praise of men than praise of God. Young men may worship their sweethearts, or girls their boyfriends."

At these words, a terrible burning sensation shot through Martha. She glanced up quickly at Daniel, sitting beside her so strong and handsome, drinking in every word the preacher said. She worship Daniel? Almost angrily she pushed the thought from her. Oh, don't be silly!

18

ON THE LAST MONDAY before Martha and Daniel's publication, Mary and Martha did a huge washing, mostly because Mary wished to have everything clean before Martha left on Wednesday morning for home. Martha was going to work on her wedding dress the few remaining days. After they were published, there would be little time for that, what with getting the house ready for a wedding and all. As they worked, they discussed local events they had heard over Sunday.

"Did you hear that Joe Yoder's Annie had another operation?" Martha asked.

"Yes, isn't that too bad! How many has she had already—six or seven, isn't it?" Mary said sympathetically.

"Something like that, I think. Why must that poor woman suffer so? Her husband treats her like a slave; and she's had twelve or fourteen children and lost about four of those, and now this yet," Martha said.

"I know, she seems to be having more than her share of sorrows, one would think. And yet, through it all, I know she has a faith in God that would put some of us to shame," Mary said as she hung up one of Bethy's little dresses. "Sometimes she makes me ashamed of myself, Martha. Here I don't like it if my children are so close together, and fret because I don't feel well, but compared to her troubles, mine aren't worth mentioning."

Martha was silent for a moment, then said, "You don't

144

suppose she was a wild girl when she was young, or something like that, that God is punishing her, do you?"

"Martha, do you know what you remind me of?" Mary asked wryly.

"No, what?"

"Do you remember our devotions the other morning, when we read about Jesus healing the man born blind? Remember how the people who brought him to Jesus asked who had sinned, the man or his parents, that he was born blind?"

"What then?" asked Martha, interested at once. Mary's comparisons were usually good.

"Well, Jesus told them that neither of them had, but it was so that the glory of God could be made known."

"What does that have to do with Joe Yoder's Annie?"

"Why, just because she's had a hard life doesn't mean that she sinned, but more so the glory of God can be shown through her. Who knows, perhaps in glory she will shine brighter than many of us who have gone through less."

Martha pondered this for a moment. It seemed a difficult thing to understand. "Is that why God calls on some people to suffer terrible things here on earth, so their glory will be so much more? Why can't we have that glory without such suffering?"

"I can't tell you that, sis. All I know is that the other day I read a verse in II Corinthians, the fourth chapter, I forget which verse, but it said this: 'For our light affliction, which is but for a moment, worketh for us a far more exceeding and eternal weight of glory.' That seems to tie in pretty well with our discussion, doesn't it?"

"Yes, it does," Martha agreed. "But it says, 'our light

145

affliction.' I'll bet Annie doesn't think her afflictions are light. I'll bet nobody does when he is going through them."

"That is all too true, but it reminds me of another verse—isn't it in Hebrews, where it says, 'Now no chastening for the present seemeth to be joyous, but grievous: nevertheless afterward it yieldeth the peaceable fruit of righteousness unto them which are exercised thereby.' "

Again Martha pondered this. Finally she said, "Well, that gives me a new idea about suffering, Mary. I never thought that our afflictions would be turned into glory for the Lord and glory for us. But I can't say, even at that, that I would welcome suffering."

"I know what you mean; I feel the same way. And yet, if it is my Lord's will, I want to be decently submissive, at least, even if I wouldn't welcome it."

They were finished hanging up the wet wash, and Martha picked up the basket to take it back to the washhouse. "Would you clean up, Martha?" Mary asked. "I'll go in and start dinner. I hear Bethy crying anyway."

"Sure, go ahead; I will finish here," Martha assured her.

"I'll let you sleep a little longer after dinner," Mary teased. "Just think, only a few more days and you won't be losing sleep running around. You will be an old married woman by then. Then just wait a few years and you will be losing sleep because of a baby, the way I do."

"Oh, go along with you," Martha said, laughing. "Don't discourage me before I get started."

*   *   *

Martha yawned. She had slept for quite a while after dinner and still felt groggy. She picked up the clothespin bag and went outside to get the wash off the line. It was a lovely September afternoon. The countryside seemed steeped in peace and contentment. The cornfields were beginning to lose their summer dress of green and were turning to a tawny, golden ripeness. She was looking forward to husking corn again this fall. She and Daniel had planned to stay with her folks for the winter, and while Daniel was working on carpenter jobs, Martha was going to finish her dowry. If they couldn't find a farm to rent, they intended to rent a house and Daniel would keep on with the carpenter trade for another year. With these thoughts in mind, Martha brought in the dry clothes. Once inside, she found Mary ready to help fold. Martha got out the ironing board and lighted the iron. As she did so, she noticed a buggy drive into the lane. It was a strange buggy and she wondered who it was.

Mary saw it too. "Who could that be?" she asked Martha.

By this time the buggy had stopped and they recognized the driver. It was Dan Graber, the man for whom Daniel's carpenter gang was putting up a hog house. He came slowly up the walk toward the front porch and Mary went to the door to meet him. "Hello," she said pleasantly, opening the door.

He stepped into the dining room and, when he saw Martha, he stopped. Then, moistening his lips and glancing from Mary to Martha, he spoke. "I—I—came over to tell—tell you something." He stopped. Martha and Mary looked at each other. What did he mean? He began again. "Something I wish I didn't have to tell you." They were more puzzled and, seeing their bewilderment, he continued: "This noon when the carpenter gang ate their lunch, they noticed Daniel didn't come to join them. They thought it was peculiar, because no one knew that he was leaving, and he was around just before they quit work. One of the men went out to the barn to see if he could find him—and—and—" Again he stopped, as if words failed him.

"What then?" Martha's voice was sharp with fear. Had something happened?

"They found him lying behind that sorrel colt of his," he said quietly.

"Is he badly hurt?" Again her voice was sharp. "Oh, please, God, no!"

Mr. Graber glanced desperately from Martha to Mary. At last he said gravely, "Daniel is dead, Martha."

The room spun and spun and Martha grabbed for something—anything. The effort to hold on was too much, however, and she let go and sank into utter darkness.

* * *

Martha wasn't the first one to find out that one could go on living even if one's heart was dead with grief. Everyone was kind and considerate and very sympathetic. The few days before the funeral were a hazy dullness to her, with nothing in sharp focus.

Daniel's death was a shock to the entire community. Everyone had come to respect him for his fine character and his consistent Christian life. To be sure, there were a few who had looked askance at the young people's meetings he had been leading, but respect for his death kept them silent. Martha was the object of special pity when the community learned about their intended publication on the following Sunday. Scores of people called at the home of Daniel's folks to extend their sympathy.

No one knew the full details of his tragic death. Star was quietly munching hay when he was found at her heels. Had he not exercised sufficient caution in going into

148

her stall? He uttered only a few groans and was dead before the doctor arrived.

Daniel's death was an eye-opener to many of the young boys, but to Thomas especially. Hadn't he always felt that there was plenty of time to be serious about God? Perhaps, after all, it would be better to yield to God in one's youth, as Daniel had said at the first meeting. He realized all too well that if he were called as suddenly as Daniel, he would have nothing to show to God for his salvation. He had never asked God to come into his life and take full control, as Martha had been wanting him to do. But, on the other hand, his flesh argued, must it be done now? Couldn't he wait just a little longer? But suppose something should happen to him? Suppose? Oh, just wait a while! So ran his thoughts the few days before the funeral.

To Ervin, the loss of Daniel was a staggering blow. Daniel dead? He couldn't believe it was true! He felt almost as if a physical prop had been knocked out from under him. Daniel, who had always been such a wonderful help, a true friend in time of need! Their friendship had been very deep the last year. He called Alice and, in a choking voice, told her the sad news.

"Oh, Ervin, not Daniel!" her shocked voice came over the wire.

"Yes, it is true," he assured her sadly. "We can't believe it has happened ourselves."

There was a pause. "How is Martha taking it?" she asked, her voice thick with sympathy.

Ervin almost broke down, and swallowed hard several times. Martha was his favorite sister. "She is pretty quiet about it now, but I think she is so dull with shock that she really doesn't realize what is going on," he said.

"Poor girl, I imagine the worst will come later," Alice answered, still rather thickly.

"I'm afraid so," he agreed. "Alice, do you think you could come out? You were coming out in a week or so anyway, and—and—I wish you would come."

"I surely will! I'll tell Mother and Dad, and we will make arrangements as soon as we can. When is the funeral?"

"Thursday afternoon," he answered, feeling strangely comforted. It helped to know she was coming.

"I will be there just as soon as I can, Ervin. I'll try and be there by tomorrow evening, at least," she assured him.

"All right, darling." The word slipped out before he knew it. He had never called her that before. "I will be looking for you. Good-by till then."

"Good-by," her voice echoed over the wire. He hung up and, despite the grief in his heart, he was thrilled to know that he would be seeing her again in such a short while.

True to her word, Alice was there by Wednesday evening. Ervin and one of Daniel's married brothers went up to meet her at the depot. They were there in plenty of time, and Ervin got out and paced up and down the cindered yard. At last the train came, whistling and roaring to a stop. The lovely fall day was almost closing, with the last rays of the sun glinting through the tall trees on the other side of the street.

At that moment Alice appeared on the steps and Ervin's heart skipped a beat. The evening sun caught the gold in her hair and she looked like an angel standing there. He took a step forward and at that moment the sun slid farther down. Now that she was no longer blinded by it, she caught sight of him. "Oh, Ervin!" she cried gladly. She was loaded down with bags, and he took them gently from her and set them at his feet. Their hands met and clasped. It was all his natural reserve would let him do in public. Their eyes held for a long time and they were unaware of the throng around them. Finally he felt some-one at his elbow; it was Daniel's brother. With a start Ervin turned around and blushed. He had forgotten where he was.

* * *

Hundreds of people attended the funeral. Luckily, the lovely fall weather continued and the overflow could sit outside. Daniel's relatives were many and filled up the house. Bishop Fred had been chosen to preach the fu-neral sermon. Martha, with grief-dulled ears, heard his words only dimly. She seemed to be utterly without feel-ing. Not that she didn't speak when spoken to, or break down and cry when someone pressed her hand and whis-pered sympathetic words. But it was as if the Martha that could be seen and the real Martha were two differ-ent persons.

Bishop Fred spoke of Daniel's fine example of living a God-fearing, consistent life even when away from home. "It reminds me of Joseph," he said. "When he was sold into slavery in Egypt, did he decide to break loose and lead a life of sin? No, he kept on leading the same godly life he had been living at home. The thing that kept Jo-seph pure, when in faraway Egypt, was the same thing that kept him pure at home. It was the faith in him that made the difference. This young man here, from the testi-mony of others, had Christ in him, keeping him pure and free from sin. We are sorry to see some young men make the sad mistake of leading a life of shame and sin when

151

they are away from home, as this young man was. They seem to think that if Father and Mother aren't there, they can live as they please. But they forget that Someone else can see them—Someone far more important than parents. Doesn't it make you sad? They do themselves so much harm by their loose living."

Thomas almost shuddered when he heard these words. Wasn't that what he had been planning to do? Hadn't he decided that if he ever got away from home and away from under Mom and Pop's thumb, he was going to have a grand, good time? His conscience poked a knowing finger at him. "Shame on you," it said. "Haven't you ever given God's reckoning a thought?" For the first time in his life he uttered a voluntary prayer. "O God," he prayed, "help me to live for You!"

Ervin, sitting between Martha and Alice just back of the coffin, cried out in silent grief, "Father, why did you take the best one? Why couldn't it have been someone else—someone not half as fine as Daniel?" But even as he prayed, he was almost ashamed of himself. Who else, of all the young folks, was better prepared and more willing to meet his Saviour than Daniel? But again—perhaps because Martha, so numb with grief, was sitting beside him—he cried from the depths of his heart, "But why? Why did it have to be Daniel?" Emotion overwhelmed him again and he bent down and cried in a fresh torrent of grief. Alice, sensing his sorrow, reached out her hand and touched his arm. Blindly he caught her hand (for once his natural reserve left him) and squeezed it so hard it hurt her.

When it was over and the last of the sympathetic helpers were gone, Ervin spoke his final words of sympathy to Daniel's parents and numerous brothers and sisters.

He and Alice were waiting for Martha to pack her bag to go home. Alice was going to stay over the weekend and this was the first time she was going to his home. For the sake of staying with Martha, and because of his own deep attachment to Daniel, he had brought Alice straight to Daniel's home after her coming. Martha, of course, had come over the first evening of Daniel's death and stayed since then. She appeared now, looking pale. Ervin, taking her bag from her, met her eyes. They seemed to be bottomless wells of grief. It almost frightened him and he quickly looked away.

"Ready to go?" he asked Martha quietly. She nodded wordlessly. He turned to Alice at his side. "You have your bags in the car already, don't you?"

"Yes, I do," she replied, smiling at him. Momentarily he almost forgot his grief while he feasted his eyes on her.

"Come on, then, let's go." He stepped aside for the girls to precede him out the door. Without a backward look, Martha went down the walk and out to the car. The blessed dullness of shock was wearing off and she was almost at the breaking point. She was silent all the way home except for noncommittal answers to the questions Alice asked. Much as Ervin loved Alice, he wished she would let Martha alone. Because he and Martha were so alike in temperament, he realized more than anyone the strain she was under. His own heart seemed momentarily to be wept dry, but he was too weary of spirit to care. The most important thing for the present was to get a good night's sleep.

*   *   *

It was Sunday evening, the last night Alice would be there. Ervin had taken her to the Sunday evening sing

(Martha hadn't cared to go), and now they were slowly making their way home again. Even though their being together had been impelled by deep sorrow, it had been wonderfully satisfying. Mom and Pop had been all that Ervin could wish for in gracious hospitality. They had put forth every effort to make Alice's visit pleasant. Even Martha had borne up well after her first evening at home, and helped to make the stay pleasant. Alice couldn't help admiring her, when she considered the experience Martha had gone through, because not once after that first evening did she break down. Poor Martha! Time enough for the floodgates to break through and the depths to be plumbed! Time, and to spare, for darkness and the ashes of disappointment!

They were at home now and he got out of the car to open the door for her. As she alighted, he caught her to him. It was the first time he had dared do such a thing. Alice reached up and laid her hands on his shoulders. By the soft light he could see her eyes. Never had she seemed so sweet and appealing. All at once his silly notion of proposing by letter was gone. Instead, he said softly, without a trace of a stammer or stutter, "You will marry me, won't you? Please say yes!"

The look she gave him made his head spin and it was his answer even before she whispered ever so softly, "Yes, I will."

19

AFTER THE NUMBNESS of shock was gone, in the first few weeks following Daniel's death, it seemed to Martha that she was in a well of grief. She wept at times until she was sick, subsiding for a time only to be caught in a fresh torrent in a day or so. The family looked on in helpless sympathy. What else, after all, could they do? Sometimes at night Mom would awaken from a troubled, restless sleep, to hear Martha crying in anguished grief. At such times, with her own heart almost breaking, she would get up and softly wander around the house, whispering inarticulate prayers and crying to herself. When Martha's sobs subsided after a while, Mom would go back to bed. Or it might be that Martha was doing some task around the house when she would burst into grief. At such times she would stand with bowed head and weep until she was exhausted. If Mom heard her, she would steal up softly and put her arms around her and hold her until the storm was over.

But as the fall changed to winter, the tenor of Martha's feeling changed. Whereas at first it had been pure grief, gradually resentment set in. Why did God have to take Daniel? Why couldn't it have been someone else? What had she done to deserve such sorrow? At such times she thought she would go crazy with grief. Daytime was bad, but the nights were pure torture. There wasn't enough work to keep her busy, and so she had too much time to sit and brood. Actually, Mom and Rosie could have done all the work without Martha's help, but out of respect for her grief, Mom thought it best to keep her at home.

Because of Mary's continued poor health, they started to do her washing and ironing, but even so there was too much idle time for Martha. She would sit and stare into space, arousing only when spoken to. It began to worry Mom, and one evening she confided her fears to Pop.

"I don't know what to do with Martha," she began unhappily. "I pity her too much to think of her working out, but I don't like the way she sits and broods all the time."

"Doesn't she seem to be getting any better?" Pop asked, troubled.

"No, she doesn't. In fact, the last few weeks it seems to be worse than before. Sometimes the look in her eyes makes me shiver, it is so—well, so scary," Mom said.

"She helps you with the work, though, doesn't she? I mean, she doesn't sit idle all the time, does she?"

"Oh, yes, she helps me all right, but we don't have enough to keep us all busy, and it gives her too much time to sit and think. Keeping busy would be the best thing she could do."

Pop was silent for a moment. "It almost makes me cry, too, to think of the whole thing," he said at last. "I don't want to question the wisdom of God, but I can't help wondering why He took Daniel. It seems to me that the church needs young men like him pretty badly, and now to have him taken away all at once—" His voice trailed into silence.

"I know," Mom said with a sigh. "I feel the same way. Maybe we thought too much of him; but it seems to me he was about the finest Christian I ever knew."

156

She was silent for a moment. At last she said, "Maybe that's why God called him. Who else would be better prepared to go than he?"

"That is true," Pop admitted. "But still, it hurts me to have to see Martha go through this. Seems like the only thing we can do to help her is pray for her." Mom got up and wandered around the room aimlessly, straightening a cushion here, a curtain there. She came back to her chair and sat down. Pop's eyes followed her. "Do you suppose she could have a breakdown of some kind?" he asked anxiously.

"That is what bothers me," Mom admitted. "She doesn't eat anything to speak of, and I don't think she gets too much sleep, as often as I hear her crying in the night."

"One thing that helps her, though, is that she is still young. Young people can get over grief better than an older person can," Pop said hopefully.

"I'm not so sure about that," Mom contradicted him. "Martha always was one to take things hard. Not that she ever said much, but you can see it."

"Why don't we pray about it now?" Pop asked.

"Yes, let's do. I have to have God's help; I can't go on alone."

So together they knelt and Pop prayed in a troubled voice at first. As he continued to pray, however, he gained hope and assurance and his voice became more peaceful.

"Our dear Father in Heaven, we come before Thee with sorrow in our hearts—sorrow because our child must sorrow. Father, we cannot understand why Thou hast taken Daniel from us, but we know that our loss is really his gain. But please, Father, help Martha to bear her grief and to look to Thee for her strength and help. Father, we just ask Thee to help her to be able to submit to this as Thy will, and to grow in Thy grace. But, Father, we would appreciate it so much if something could be done to help her realize that others have sorrow and troubles, and that keeping busy would be one of the best things for her now. So, Father, we ask that Thou wouldst show us something in the near future that could give her work to do, something that would help her take her mind off her grief. These things we ask in Jesus' name, who taught us to pray. Amen."

After he had finished, they rose to their feet and looked at each other. Mom gave him a tremulous, teary smile. He reached over and took her hand. "It's about as hard on you as it is on Martha," he said anxiously. "If you don't watch out, you will have a breakdown too."

"Oh, John," she said, breaking into tears, "it cuts me through like a knife to see her; I can't help it. I'd rather go through something like this myself than have her."

"I know, I know," Pop said heavily, reaching out and drawing her sobbing figure to him. They clung together for a time, their tears flowing freely. At last Mom released herself and, blowing her nose, said in a matter-of-fact way, "Well, come on, let's go to bed; I am tired."

The very next day David came over with the news that Mary was sick in bed. "Doctor says it is virus pneumonia," he informed them in an anxious voice. "She has an awful cough and she just can't seem to get over it. Then, in her condition, it is just that much harder on her. I wonder if Martha could come over and help us?"

Mom looked at Martha in silent entreaty. "Do you think you want to go?"

Martha shrugged her shoulders. "I don't care," she murmured indifferently.

158

Mom and David exchanged glances. "Will you get ready then?"

Martha nodded. Wearily she went about getting her things ready. If she must exist somewhere, one place was as good as another.

She found Mary in a serious condition. It was alarming to hear her fits of coughing. She shouldn't have been doing her own work for quite a while, but she hated the thought of a hired girl, choosing rather to manage as best she could with David's help. After the folks started doing her washings and ironings, her hopes were high for a quick recovery, but such was not the case. Instead, she gradually became worse, until finally the doctor ordered her to bed.

Martha found no idle time here. There was washing and ironing, baking, cleaning, sewing, and, besides all else, the care of Mary and the children. Not that Mary called for much, but Bethy was teething and consequently fretful. Johnny was—well, lively, to say the least. Was there a cake on the worktable, frosted and cooling? Johnny found it and sampled it. Was there a pan of water in the sink? Johnny found it and poured the contents on the floor and on himself. Was the cupboard door unlatched? Naturally Johnny found that, too, and either mixed the contents together or scattered pots and pans all over the house, depending on which cupboard it happened to be. More than once he tried Martha's patience to the limit. But if nothing else, he helped her to think of other things besides the loss of Daniel.

Mary was feverish off and on, and the anxiety over her helped Martha, too. Mary was expecting another baby in March and that made it all the worse. So, for the time being, Martha worked in the evening until she was tired enough to go to bed and sleep. True, there were still nights when she lay awake staring into the darkness, her mind going over the details of Daniel's death, and finally cried until she slept. But, at least, there was no time to sit and brood over her grief in the daytime.

On the last day of February, Mary's baby came, prematurely, mostly because of Mary's condition. It was a boy, and David chose to name him Philip. So now Martha had more work to do. From the beginning he was a good baby, something they were all thankful for. David said that it was enough to walk the floor with Bethy, without having another one to keep them awake nights.

They hoped that Mary would be able to regain her health, now that the baby was there, but they were to be disappointed. The coughing was as bad as before and her strength did not return. One night after a coughing fit had left her weak and exhausted, David asked in alarm, "Mary, what is the matter with you? You have me worried."

Mary looked at him with anguished eyes, saying, "I wish I knew. I am worried, too."

"What did the doctor say the last time he was here?" David asked.

"Not much," she replied weakly. "He was in such a hurry, he didn't stay long. He looked at the baby and that was about all."

"Well, I am going down to the office tomorrow and tell him to come out here and look after you. I think you have dragged around with this long enough. I think it is high time you got over it!" David said decidedly. He stood beside the bed regarding her with serious eyes. He didn't dare tell her how worried he was. But something had to be done. Why, she had been sick most of the winter!

"Dear heavenly Father," he prayed silently, "if it be Thy will, please bring back my darling's health!"

A fretful wail from Bethy made him turn to her crib. She was crying and throwing herself around in the manner so common to her at night. He picked her up and talked to her in soothing tones until she was quiet again.

Mary watched him with loving eyes. How good he was, and how kind and tender to the children! She thanked God so much for him. This burden of ill health, for the last year, would have been so much harder to bear if he hadn't been so sympathetic and helpful. Their married life had been very happy and satisfying so far. The thought of Joe Yoder and Annie flashed through her mind and she was almost guilty with her happy married life. Annie had gone through so much! And with so few words of kindness from the one who should have been kind above all others. Why must some husbands be so mean to their wives?

David's threat wasn't an idle one. The next day he went down to the doctor's office and told him in polite but no uncertain tones that he felt that Mary was in a serious condition. "Something definitely is wrong with her," he said decidedly. "She should be getting her strength back. Why, she has been dragging around for the last three or four months with that cough!"

The doctor considered for a moment. "Does she have any fever during the day?" he asked.

"I wouldn't know about that. She never complains if she does," David answered. The doctor promised to be out that day and thoroughly examine her.

True to his promise, he came that afternoon. David couldn't complain of lack of interest on the doctor's part now. On the contrary, he examined her more thoroughly than he ever had before. His face became grave before he was through, and David, watching him, became more worried than ever. At last the doctor straightened up and absentmindedly gazed out the window for a while. Mary and David regarded him questioningly. He finally gave them his attention again, looking from Mary to David and then back to Mary.

"Stay in bed for the time being," he told her. "I would like to talk with you, David, for a minute, please."

Worried and mystified, David led the way into the kitchen. Martha was there, ironing in the mechanical way so peculiar to her since Daniel's death.

The doctor greeted her and turned to David with a serious face. David almost dreaded hearing his words. For some unexplained reason he sensed they would be upsetting. "I hate to have to tell you this, and I hope I'm mistaken, but I am awfully afraid your wife has TB," he said kindly.

David's heart skipped a beat. No wonder he had been dreading the doctor's words. "Oh, please, not really!" he said in dismay.

"It's tough, I know," the doctor said sympathetically. "As I say, I hope I am mistaken, but she really has all the symptoms: fever, that cough over a prolonged period of time, and loss of weight. I think she said she weighs ten pounds less than she did right after the baby was born. All this makes me afraid that is what it is."

"Isn't there anything you can give her that will cure it?" David asked.

"I am afraid not, David. The cure is usually a long, slow process. It will mean complete bed rest in the state sanatorium. I still say that I might be mistaken; I sincerely hope I am. I would like to send some specimens to the state laboratories and see what they say about it before I tell you for sure."

David stared out the window. Finally he turned to the doctor again and asked in a dull voice, "If Mary does have it, does that mean she will have to go to the sanatorium?"

"I'm afraid so, yes. Some cases can be treated at home, but I wouldn't advise you to attempt it for her. For one thing, it is contagious, and it would be too much of a risk with the children."

"How long would she have to be away?"

"Well—just a rough guess, I would say a year at least; more likely—"

"A year!" broke in David, in consternation. "Do you really mean it?"

The doctor reached out and put his hand on David's shoulder. "I am sorry, David. I realize it sounds like a long time, but as I said, TB takes a long time to cure. It may even take longer than a year. I hope not, but count on at least that long and very likely longer."

David's heart was a dead weight in his chest. He stuck his hands in his pockets and stalked over to the window, gazing with unseeing eyes over the cold, wet landscape. March was like a roaring lion these days. After a long, silent interval he turned to the doctor again. "I suppose Mary will have to be told?" he asked lifelessly.

"I am afraid so, yes. Do you want me to tell her?"

"No, I can," David said. "How soon will you get the report from the laboratory?"

"If I send it in today, I should hear by the end of the week. If they confirm my suspicions, I will make arrangements right away for her to be admitted to the sanatorium,

David. In the meantime, try to keep the children away from her, especially the baby. Does she nurse him?"

David nodded.

"Well, that will have to be stopped. He will have to be put on the bottle. I will give you a formula."

"Give it to her," David said, motioning to Martha, who had been listening to the conversation with amazement and alarm.

The doctor handed her the slip of paper. "Would you be able to stay on if Mary has to go?" he asked kindly.

"I suppose so; I haven't any other plans," Martha replied spiritlessly.

"You folks sure have had your share of tough luck in the last few months," he said. "Too bad about Daniel, Martha. He was a fine man."

Martha swallowed the unbearable ache in her throat and turned away almost rudely. She busied herself at the stove and, with her back turned, managed a muffled, "Thank you." Tears started to flow freely and she fiercely crumpled the slip of paper with the written formula on it. She heard the doctor talking to David again.

"I will get those specimens now before I go and, as I said, I will let you know what they say as soon as I find out. In the meantime, keep your chin up, David."

David nodded mutely. He dreaded facing Mary again. As he led the way back into the bedroom, Mary looked up in quick suspicion. Something was wrong, she could see by the look on David's face. He refused to meet her eyes, however, and busied himself with baby Philip.

The doctor finally left with professional cheerfulness, and no sooner had the door closed behind him than Mary turned to David and asked in an anxious voice, "What did the doctor say it is, David? It is something serious, isn't it?"

David didn't answer for a moment. How could he tell her?

"Isn't it?" she repeated, catching hold of his sleeve.

With a sigh David sat down on the edge of the bed. There was no use in keeping anything from her; she would guess it all anyway. He took her hand in his and squeezed it hard.

"Yes, it is serious," he finally admitted.

"What is it? Tell me, please," she pleaded, giving his hand a shake.

"He's afraid it is TB," he said at last.

"TB!" Mary echoed in alarm. "Does he think I have TB?"

David nodded. She needed a strong man to encourage her now, but he felt like crying. "What will I have to do now?" she asked.

With an effort David met her eyes. "You will have to spend some time in a sanatorium," he said.

"Oh, David, not that. Tell me it's not true!" She was crying now.

"Oh, darling, I'm afraid it is." He was almost crying himself. He caught her in his arms and held her tight. How could he ever let her go?

For a few moments they stayed so, Mary crying and he close to tears. At last Mary pulled away and said, "Was he really sure that that is what it is?"

"He said he might be mistaken; that is why he wanted those specimens. But he was pretty sure it is."

"Then if he isn't sure, I'm not going to believe it," Mary said resolutely. "I will wait to be discouraged till I know for sure."

She had no more than said it when a spasm of coughing seized her. She coughed and coughed until she was too weak to hold up her head. David watched her in agony. There was so little he could do for her. After the spasm was over, she made a feeble effort to spit into the napkin David handed her. At the same moment they saw that the napkin was tinged with a pale reddish sputum. They looked at each other in silent dismay. They both knew that spitting blood was another symptom of TB.

20

THE NEXT FEW DAYS were miserable ones for Mary, alternating between desperate hope and dreadful calamity. Her married life had been so happy and satisfying. Her heart cried out in grief and disappointment. How could she go and leave David and her darlings? And Baby Philip only three weeks old! She found no comfort in praying, because she was too distraught to trust. Whenever she tried it, her heart was so choked with despair and desperation that she couldn't seem to get through to God.

As for David, it seemed to him that it was the hardest thing ever asked of him, to have Mary go away. He felt as if a great weight were hanging over his head, ready to fall and crush their home to pieces. True, it was for Mary's welfare, but to have her away from home for perhaps a year and maybe longer was unbearable. He finally retreated to the haymow, where he wept and prayed until his heart was emptied and released of its utter despair. As he lay on the dusty hay in the gloom of the mow, a verse of Scripture flashed through his mind: "Though he slay me, yet will I trust in him." Where was that verse found? Oh, yes, Job had said it.

David got to his feet resolutely. If Job could trust the Lord under the calamities he had gone through, then, by the grace of God, David Miller could, too! He went down the ladder and stood for a moment in the feed alley. Finally he bowed his head and closed his tear-weary eyes.

"Thank you, Father," was all he whispered, but it was enough. With a peaceful heart he began to give the horses their daily measure of hay.

On the following Monday the doctor came again with the news that the state laboratory had confirmed his suspicions, and that Mary definitely had tuberculosis. He had already made the arrangements for her to enter the sanatorium by the first week of April. In a way it was a relief to know the worst at last, thought Mary wearily. Her heart had been wavering between hope and despair so often the last few days.

The doctor looked at her in kindly sympathy. "I know it will be hard not to, but try not to worry too much," he told her. "You will get better much sooner if you don't worry."

Mary looked at him as if he were crazy. "I wonder what you think I am made of," she commented wryly. "Here I am leaving a baby four weeks old and two other small children, and you tell me not to worry!"

The doctor smiled. "It sounds difficult, I know, but really you are leaving them in good hands. I meant what I said; tuberculosis can be cured quicker if the patient has peace of mind. Worrying is the worst thing you can do. Don't you have any faith in God?"

Mary looked at him sharply. "Of course I do!" she assured him impatiently.

"Then you'd better exercise it. Leave these things in His hands; He can take better care of them than you can."

Mary blushed at the rebuke. It was needed, though, she admitted to herself. But not to worry about leaving her three children seemed impossible.

David's folks received the news with genuine sympathy.

They had grown sincerely fond of Mary since her marriage. But because of old age and feeble health there seemed to be so little they could do to help her, as far as practical help was concerned.

When Mom heard the bad news, she thought her strength would give out under this additional blow. First Martha, now Mary! She offered to take baby Philip and care for him. "It will make that much less work for Martha," she told Mary. "Not that Martha couldn't take care of him, but I thought I could do that much. Rosie will be pleased to have a baby to take care of."

Mary consented, but not without inward pain. Baby Philip was four weeks old and she had tended him only a few times. She remembered the joy and pleasure she had had in Bethy and Johnny when they were that age. And now she was to be denied him! No telling when she would be able to take care of him again. He wouldn't even know her as mother when she got back. Bethy and Johnny would grow completely away from her. She tried to push such thoughts to the back of her mind, remembering the doctor's words.

The day for her admittance arrived all too soon. Mary left the house with a heavy heart after the last good-bys. She'd cried so often the last few days that there were no tears now. She leaned against David all the way to the hospital, storing his blessed closeness in her heart for future loneliness. He kept his arm around her in tender protection. They spoke little. Each heart was too heavy for words.

When she was admitted at last and there was no more to be done, David went home with a heavy sense of loss. He said nothing to the driver, a kindly old man who made his living driving the Amish people to and fro. The driver, out of respect for David's feelings, spoke nothing either. He thought it was too bad about this young couple. They obviously enjoyed each other's presence so much it was torture for them to be parted. He wished it were still so with himself and his wife. He sighed, wondering when his wife had last been sorry to see him leave home. She never seemed glad to see him come back, either.

*   *   *

Martha found much to do after Mary's departure. There was the yard to be raked, and the garden to be made. There was the house to be cleaned and the raspberries to trim. Mary had wanted a new strawberry patch, and so there was that to be done. And besides, there were Bethy and Johnny to take care of. Bethy was fairly well adjusted to her by now; she had taken her mother's absence more lightly than Martha dared hope she would. Besides, she was such a sweet, gentle child that caring for her was more of a pleasure than a duty. But not so Johnny! From the start he resented Martha, perhaps in some vague, childish way blaming her for Mary's absence. Mary was a good mother, loving but firm, gentle yet consistent. Besides, she had the patience with him that only a mother can have, while Martha's patience was exhausted with him time after time. He was mischievous, lively, and curious. He got into the hen house and broke the eggs. He played with the garden hoe and mislaid it in the weeds of the back orchard. He sneaked upstairs when Martha was outdoors and helped himself to her things, tearing her books, spilling a bottle of ink over her white shoulder cape. When Martha found him that time, he was lying on the couch, asleep, with the empty ink bottle clutched in his ink-stained hands. A quick investigation was all she needed to confirm her suspicions, and what she found made her more angry at him than she had ever been. She rudely shook him awake and demanded in a harsh voice, "Why did you make such a mess, you naughty boy? Why did you?"

He regarded her sleepily for a moment in silence before comprehension dawned. Then he dropped his eyes to the empty ink bottle in his hands, in sullen defiance. "Why did you?" she repeated angrily, giving him another shake. He refused to answer. She picked him up and spanked him soundly. He screamed and kicked in retaliation. Then, giving him another shake, she set him on a chair forcefully.

"I don't like you!" he screamed. "I want my mamma. I wish you would go away; I want Mamma." He huddled there, sobbing, the picture of dejection. At first Martha was too angry to care. But gradually her anger wore off, to be replaced by pity. He was still sobbing and sniffling a few minutes later when she went over to him and picked him up. At first he resisted, but seeing that she wasn't angry any more, he let her rock him. He sobbed again in a pitiful voice, "I want my mamma."

Martha's heart contracted. "I know you do. I wish she were here and—I wish Daniel were here, too!" She began sobbing, mingling her tears with Johnny's.

For perhaps the thousandth time since Daniel's death she asked the aimless question: Why? Why had God taken Daniel? Why did she have to go through something like this? What had she done to deserve such treatment? Why? Where was God? Most of the cards she had received after Daniel's death had assured her that God was standing by, ready to comfort her. But where was He? He seemed utterly indifferent to her sorrow. Did He purposely inflict His children with some grievous pain and then stand back

171

and watch them suffer, His ears deaf to their cries and His eyes blind to their plight? At least God had never seemed as remote and uncaring as now.

She remembered the sweet fellowship she'd had with Him in the first months of her yielding to Him, and her soul longed for such comfort again. But she seemed unable to break through her high wall of grief and despair to get to Him. For a long time she sat, rocking Johnny and staring into space, until his sobs subsided and he slept again. At last she got up and laid him gently on the couch, then busied herself about the kitchen, getting dinner ready in record time.

21

MARY MADE NO PROGRESS at all the first two months she was at the sanatorium. However, her condition didn't get worse. But her family doctor's admonition went unheeded. She lay and worried about her family constantly. Was baby Philip doing well? Was he keeping Mom awake nights? Was Bethy still teething? Had she forgotten her? And Johnny, what was he doing? Was he into some mischief? She was afraid Martha couldn't be as patient with him as a mother would be. True, he was always into a scrape of some kind, but she had noticed, even before she got sick, that Martha was usually quite short with him. Such thoughts troubled her constantly and in consequence she was nervous and emotionally exhausted. She didn't realize what an influence this had on her condition until the day after a checkup, when the doctor asked her searchingly, "Are you worrying about something?"

"Well, maybe I am," she answered, ashamed. Her family doctor's words flashed through her mind: "Have you no faith in God?"

"Your family, perhaps?" he asked kindly.

"Yes," she answered shortly.

"Who is staying with them, now that you are away?"

"My sister," she said.

"Does she seem to be handling them all right? Or maybe she is having trouble."

"No, no trouble," Mary said, totally ashamed of herself now. He seemed to put it in an entirely different light.

"Are they all in good health? Your baby, let's see, how old is it now?"

"Just about three months," she answered. "A boy, named Philip."

"And is he growing? Doing fine?"

"Yes, he is. At least my husband says he is," she assured him.

"Well, Mrs. Miller, if your children are all right, and your sister seems to be handling everything well, just what is your trouble? We have given you everything we can think of and you have had complete bed rest, but you aren't a bit better than you were when you came. I think you probably spend all your time worrying about the family. Am I right?" His eyes pierced her through. Mary had the grace to blush. She dropped her eyes before his and bit her lip.

"The cure of tuberculosis depends a lot on the patient's peace of mind," he told her gravely. "It is just as important as rest and medicine. So, if you love your family and want to get back to them as quickly as possible, you will have to stop this worrying. I mean it. Have you no faith in God?"

Mary started. The same words her doctor at home had asked her! "I thought so," she said. She was almost too ashamed to speak.

"Well, you should use it, Mrs. Miller. Leave your worries in His hands. He can do a better job of watching over your family than you can." He smiled gently.

"Thank you," she murmured in a low voice.

"That is all for now; I will see you in a day or so," and with a cheery wave he left the room.

Mary's mind was in a turmoil. She could feel God's loving eyes on her in grave rebuke. She hid her face in her hands. "Have you no faith in God?" The question echoed and reechoed in her mind. "Have you no faith in God? Then use it!" Mary recognized the voice so full of loving rebuke. No one else but her heavenly Father talked to her like that.

"I thought I did," she answered dreamily.

"You don't act like it. Here I have given you two months to commit yourself to Me, and you have failed, so far that even others notice it."

"But my darling babies, Father," Mary protested frantically. "Do you think it is easy to give up my darlings to others?"

"Why not give them to Me? I love them more than you ever can. Didn't I say, 'Suffer little children to come unto me'?"

"O Father, it's so hard, so difficult. I love them so! I miss them so!" Mary was sobbing piteously.

"Nothing is too difficult if you ask Me for grace. Come, try it. Take My yoke upon you, and learn of Me. I will give you rest—not of the soul only, but also rest for that poor sick body of yours."

Mary sobbed for a long time. The voice of God let her sob. Then it spoke again.

"Are you willing? Willing to turn everything over to Me? You will never start getting well until you do."

"Yes, Lord," she finally answered, weak and spent. "I am sorry, Lord. Take everything—my husband, my babies, and most of all myself. Do with us what is pleasing in Thy sight."

"You will never regret it," was the tender answer. "Go in peace now and rest assured I am taking care of everything."

A strange, wonderful peace came into Mary's heart.

The loving, tender arms of God seemed to enfold her in a warm embrace. For the first time since she had found out about her illness, Mary was quiet and peaceful. If God was taking care of David and the children, there was no need for her to worry about them. A tender smile broke out on her face, lighting it up with a heavenly glow. After a while she went to sleep.

In the weeks that followed, Mary found a more wonderful communion with God than she had ever experienced before. Now that her mind wasn't occupied with ceaseless, senseless worrying about her loved ones, it could be used to channel deeper, spiritual discernments to her. The hours she spent in meditation over some portion of Scripture had a healing effect, not only on her soul and spirit but also on her weak, sick body.

There were other results, too. The nurses saw that she was different. Many of them found in her inspiration and encouragement. They regarded her with special kindness, not only because of her spiritual qualities but also because she was so uncomplaining, and satisfied with so little care.

Then, too, Mary had to admit that being in the sanatorium wasn't as bad as she had expected it to be. Of course, she couldn't see the children, but as the hospital was only a half-hour's drive from home, David could come to see her at least every Sunday. He rarely missed coming, and it was the highlight of the week for both of them.

One Sunday in late July he came, and Mary's quick eyes noticed the look of care on his face. For one moment pain shot through her. The desire to be at home and help him carry his load was so acute it almost took her breath away. She sent a silent plea to Heaven for grace, for David and herself.

After the first tender greeting, he sat down rather heavily beside the bed. It was so wonderful to see him again! Their eyes met and they smiled, full of love and concern for each other.

"How are things going?" Mary broke the silence.

"About as usual, I guess," he answered.

"Are the children all right?"

"Yes, they are fine."

"Baby Philip growing?"

"Like a weed. Your mom says he tries to sit up already," he told her proudly.

"What about Bethy. Does she talk?"

"You ought to hear her. She jabbers away all the time. Just like a woman." For a moment the look of care left his face as he grinned at her. She smiled back, happy to see his humorous spark once more.

"What about Johnny? Is he still into everything?"

The look of care came over his face again like a cloud, and he sighed heavily before answering. "I'm afraid so," he said at last.

"What has he been doing now?" Mary asked quickly.

"About as usual."

"Tell me what is wrong," she demanded.

He looked at her and smiled faintly. How did she know something was wrong? Those quick eyes of hers, nothing escaped them. "Who told you something was wrong?" he asked, trying to stall her off.

"I can see by the look on your face," she told him. "What is it? Did he ruin something?"

"Yes, I'm afraid so. Not of ours, which is the worst thing about it."

"Of Martha's?"

"Yes, he went up to her room again yesterday, after I have repeatedly told him not to, and took the scissors and cut slits in her good black dress."

"Oh, no!" Mary said in a shocked voice.

"Martha, of course, was very angry with him. I can't blame her much, when I look at her side of it, but—" His voice trailed off into silence.

"What then?"

"Mary, I hate to talk like this about your sister but, after all, it's our boy!" he burst out.

"What did she do?" Mary asked anxiously.

"Well, in polite terms, I suppose you could say we had words over it. She got pretty angry about it and said I let him do as he pleased and spoiled him, and so on," he said drearily. "As the crowning point she said she wished she didn't have to take care of our ornery little brats, and that if she had to do a mother's job, she wished, for goodness sake, she had her own home and her own husband, meaning Daniel, of course."

"Oh, David, this is terrible!" Mary said in a heartbroken voice.

"I know. I feel the same way. I know he is mischievous and into everything. But he is our boy and she doesn't have to talk like that. Besides, I can't help it if Daniel was killed. For her sake I wish he were living, so she could have the joy of married life; but she doesn't have to take it out on poor Johnny." Mary covered her face with her hands. She felt like crying aloud. "Now I've gone and made you feel bad about it," David said in a contrite voice. "I wish those eyes of yours weren't so sharp. Telling you about this was the last thing I wanted to do. Now you will just lie and worry about it."

178

"What did you do then?" she asked, recovering a little.

"I told her she didn't have to act as if she were the only one who had troubles, that other people had them and didn't act as if it were a personal insult. I said that if she acted like that it was no wonder God took Daniel away from her, that she wasn't fit to be the wife of such a fine boy."

"Oh, David, you shouldn't have said that!"

"I know," he said miserably. "I hate it now. If she feels as bad about it as I do, I pity her."

"Why don't you apologize?"

"This morning I was still too mad about it, and then after the sermon Bishop Fred gave us, I knew I was just as much in the wrong as she, but I didn't get a chance to talk with her. She took the children over to your folks after dinner. So now I guess I will have to apologize tonight."

Mary was silent. If only she could be at home and take care of her children herself. But God seemed to have other plans for her now. She sighed deeply and sent a silent plea heavenward for help to resist the temptation to worry herself sick about this. Something told her that if she let this get the best of her, gone would be the sweet communion with her heavenly Father. And that was so sweet that the thought of losing it made her shrink. With an effort she committed the whole thing to Him who loved David, Martha, and the children far more than she did. With that the peace and sweetness of God's presence came back again, stronger than ever.

David, watching her, saw it too. One moment her face looked drawn and worried; the next it was as if her features had melted into an entirely different mold. The furrows in her forehead vanished; her lips, which had been tense

179

and tight, now relaxed, and a faint smile was on them. Someone had helped her, that was sure. He regarded her with tender awe. She opened her eyes to meet his; the smile on her lips lighted her face completely.

"Is it all right now?" he asked softly. She nodded, wordlessly. He reached over and took her hand in his. "You don't worry so much any more, do you?"

"Not any more," she said simply. "God showed me how silly it was. Not only that, but a very poor light for Him. Even the doctor noticed my distrust in God."

"He did? What did he say about it?" David asked interestedly.

Mary told him of the doctor's interview with her on that memorable day—the day when she handed her loved ones over to God and had received in return the peace that passeth understanding. David was silent for a while after she had finished. He was strongly reminded of his own experience in the haymow, the day before Mary's departure. Then, too, he had resolved to trust God in everything. But how soon one forgot! He had been too homesick for Mary and so dispirited and blue the last week that it was no wonder Martha and he had clashed. From the bottom of his heart he pitied Martha. Daniel was gone from her forever in this life, whereas he still had Mary even if she couldn't be at home. At the thought he squeezed Mary's hand.

"What did Bishop Fred preach about?" Mary asked abruptly, changing the subject.

David sat up and released her hand. "Well, it was pretty good, just what I needed. I can't recall it word for word, but he talked about how self-pity causes so much trouble for most of us. That made me squirm because I knew I had been guilty of that. Then he said that if we would

180

only look ahead to our eternal future more, instead of pitying ourselves so much, many of our problems would disappear. He said that our heavenly Father loved us too much to make us suffer just for the fun of it, but that everything was for our souls' eternal glory."

" 'For our light affliction, which is but for a moment, worketh for us a far more exceeding and eternal weight of glory,' " Mary quoted softly.

"Exactly! That was just the verse he used. Then, too, he said that helping others who were in trouble was a good way of forgetting our own troubles. I guess that is another thing wrong with me: I was so wrapped up in my troubles, I couldn't sympathize with Martha in hers. Although if I do say so, I think Martha is in the same boat," he concluded candidly.

Mary smiled faintly. Most assuredly that was true.

"Martha started out so well, I guess we thought she was beyond reproach," he went on after a moment. "I never dreamed that anything could ever sway her, but I can't recall when we last discussed spiritual things. In fact, most of the time we don't talk much of anything. We are both blue and homesick, I guess," he concluded.

Mary's heart ached afresh. God was good and loving and it was all for their eternal glory, she knew, but she surely hoped it would be His will for her to be well before long.

"Then, Mary," David broke in on her thoughts hesitantly, "Bishop Fred told the church that he was considering having an assistant ordained by fall. He said, as we all know, that Brother Joe is getting old and since Brother Dan's death last winter, he felt we should have another minister."

"He did?" Mary asked interestedly. "Well, it is true. He really should have more help."

"I know. But, Mary," and at this his voice dropped lower—so low that she had to listen carefully to catch the next words—"I think it is going to be me."

"You!" Mary exclaimed.

He nodded without looking at her. "I know it might sound funny, but when he was talking, something shot through me right then. I knew right away that it was God, letting me know that it was to be me."

"Oh, David, sweetheart!" Mary's voice was filled with emotion. She reached out and took his hand, and tears came to her eyes.

He leaned abruptly over the side of the bed and buried his face in his hands. "Mary, I dread it!" he almost wailed. "You know why."

Yes, Mary knew why. Being a minister wouldn't be an easy job. True, Bishop Fred had keen spiritual insight, but the majority of the members didn't. There was growing opposition to men who, like David, had caught a glimpse of the glory of God. Most of them preferred to sleep in the traditions of the fathers, instead of serving a living Christ. The young people's meetings that had been so hopefully started had been discouraged and finally squelched completely, much to the disappointment of Mary and David. They felt that such a movement would have been profitable for the good of the church, but their feelings in the matter weren't shared by everyone. With a sigh Mary reached up and ruffled the wavy hair on the bent head before her.

"Please, God, grant him courage and power," she prayed silently.

22

MARTHA GAVE the porch swing another shove and swung slowly in the soft dusk. She had been canning peaches all day, and it felt good to be outside tonight. Bethy was already asleep and Johnny was out in the hayfield with David, who, with the help of Bishop Fred, was putting up the last cutting of hay. She could hear them now, coming down the lane with another load. Unconsciously she sighed, dreading to move because she was so tired, but there was some ice cream in the kerosene refrigerator she was going to serve when they were finished.

Since Johnny's episode with her black dress and the subsequent clash between herself and David, he had been taking Johnny with him wherever he could. She felt a tinge of guilt because really there were times when it was almost dangerous to have him with David, but at least he wasn't into some scrape or bothering her. Bishop Fred's sermon, that had made such an impression on David, had cut deep into her, too. She felt the rebuke keenly, but she seemed unable to quit pitying herself. It seemed to her that no one she knew had ever been called upon to go through the same suffering she had. And it all seemed so uncalled-for. Who else among the young folks had been so richly blessed with talents and leadership abilities as Daniel? Who had been more dedicated to Christ, or more willing to forsake all and follow Him?

For him to be so suddenly snatched away in the bloom of youth was still unthinkable.

She had accepted David's apology rather stiffly, and had asked him for forgiveness in turn. David had forgiven her wholeheartedly and made every effort to make things easier for her, such as taking Johnny with him everywhere he went. Martha had been truly ashamed of her part in the matter and had asked God for forgiveness. But as far as peace was concerned—inward peace, that is—she just didn't have it. Yet, she wanted to have it. This burden of grief, mingled with self-pity and resentment, that she had been carrying around with her ever since Daniel's death, was heavy. At times she thought she would suffocate. Was there no relief? No comfort to be had? Or must she resign herself to living with it throughout the dreary, endless years of her life?

She heard the men come in now. Evidently they were not going to unload until morning. She got up and went into the kitchen to get the ice cream ready for them. Might just as well take it outside and eat it, she thought. The kitchen was so hot from the day's canning. She set the dishes of ice cream on a tray, along with cake and a pitcher of cold water and glasses, and carried it out to the men on the porch.

"Ice cream!" Bishop Fred exclaimed, smiling, when she offered it to him. "After a hot day like this, I never turn that down."

Martha smiled back in return. It was impossible to be stiff with him. He was so vitally interested in everything and everyone, it always caused one to respond. They talked of community events as they ate, Martha adding a remark now and then. After they were finished, David said to

Johnny, who had been sitting quietly beside him all the while, "Young man, it is your bedtime; do you know it?"

Johnny looked up at him and grinned. He liked Daddy so much! A lot better than bossy old Martha! It was so much fun to be with him that he forgot all about getting into mischief. He got up obediently from the steps and started for the kitchen. Martha half rose to follow him, to get him ready for bed, but David was already up. "Don't get up," he told her. "I'll get him ready for bed. I know you have been busy all day."

Martha protested halfheartedly, but he drowned out her protests and she sank back on the porch swing again. It was nice to stay out here in the darkness, with the lamp from the kitchen window making squares of light on the porch. The stars were out already, and Martha loved their cheery twinkle. Bishop Fred made no move to leave, seeming content to rest a while. They sat for a while in silence, each with his own separate thoughts. Martha was thinking that if God made the stars to twinkle so cheerfully, then surely He must be concerned with the welfare of His children. And Bishop Fred was wondering how to approach this girl, who was wearing her grief as unbecomingly as one wears an ugly garment. He had been wanting to talk with her for some time, and he wasn't going to let the opportunity slip by. He sent a plea to Heaven for wisdom.

"Well, Martha, how are things going?" he asked abruptly.

Martha looked up, half startled. She had been so busy with her thoughts, she had almost forgotten he was there. "Oh, about as usual," she said hesitantly.

"Is that good or bad?" he asked kindly.

"I guess not so good."

185

"Isn't it any easier to bear yet?" he asked.

Martha stared at the squares of light on the porch floor. "No, it isn't," she said at last, slowly.

"Do you ask God to help you bear it?" he wanted to know.

Martha wished she wouldn't have to answer. "God doesn't hear me when I pray," she said dully.

"He doesn't? Well, now I wonder why not." If she felt that way, no wonder her grief was so heavy to carry.

"I have prayed to Him, but it is just as hard to bear as ever. So I don't think He hears me; at least, praying never helps."

Bishop Fred's heart ached for her. Loss of Daniel was hard, he believed that, but it sounded to him as if she suffered from a greater loss than that. "Have you felt this way ever since Daniel's death?" he asked. "Or perhaps even before that?"

"No, not exactly before he was killed, but—" Her voice trailed off. At that moment something flashed through Martha's mind—something that had been buried way back, deep in her mind. What was it that preacher had said, just the week before Daniel's death? Memory surged through her, causing her to cringe as if someone had hit her. "Some girls worship their boyfriends." The words had burned her very soul, and what had been her subsequent reaction?

Martha's mind was in such a turmoil it made her feel sick. Incidents flashed across her memory as if projected on a screen. Her mouth felt dry and she ran her tongue desperately across her lips. All those times she had regarded Daniel with awe akin to worship—his letters telling of witnessing, the times he had explained some new

186

truth to her, the young people's meetings he had led. She closed her eyes in agony of remembrance.

Bishop Fred's voice came to her, seemingly from a great distance. With an effort she brought her mind back to the present. "Is there something else between you and God?" he was asking seriously.

In the pale light Martha could see his face raised to hers. She felt, rather than saw, his eyes piercing her through. Only her acute agony of soul made her answer. "Yes," she said miserably, burying her face in her hands.

"Martha, you and Daniel weren't guilty of impurity, were you?" he asked, his voice more grave and intense than she had ever heard it before.

Martha looked up quickly, not realizing what he meant at first. When she did, she said indignantly, "Of course not!"

His relief was so great he didn't mind being snapped at. "I certainly didn't really believe that of you. I am sorry I hurt your feelings, Martha. But if it isn't that, what is your trouble?"

Again Martha's lips were dry and she ran her tongue across them. How could she tell him? This good man of God would probably be just as shocked as he was at the suspicion of her purity. He would probably never be guilty of such a thing. Idol worship, that preacher had called it. "Thou shalt have no other gods before me." Martha cringed in guilt again. And yet, half angrily she tried to push it away from her. What had started all this anyway? Why did Bishop Fred have to be sticking his nose in her affairs?

"I can't tell you," she said rudely.

"I am sorry if I have offended you, Martha," he said, quietly and kindly. "I don't want to make it any harder

187

for you than it is already. But your sorrow has been heavy on my heart this long while. A true believer always suffers with another's sorrow. You must realize, I am sure, that your experience has made others sympathize with you. I am sure some of them suffer just about as much, because of it, as you do. Your folks, for instance."

His words brought tears to Martha's eyes. She thought of the times Mom had held her as she cried her heart out after it had happened; of Pop's miserable eyes, sympathizing with her every time she met them; of David's kindness, when he had almost as much to be sorrowful about as she had.

Bishop Fred rose to go. It was plain that he had said enough and yet there was one more thing. "Have you stopped reading your Bible?" he asked kindly. He didn't want to offend her again.

Martha was almost too ashamed to answer. It had been a long time since she had done more than study her Sunday school lesson. But his words, so kindly spoken, demanded an answer. With an effort she said dully, "Yes."

"Won't you please start doing that again?" No word of reproof or rebuke. His kindness did what a rebuke never would have done. "Won't you?" he repeated.

She nodded without speaking. He towered above her and she got up from the swing. Inside she could hear David pulling a chair away from his desk. She wondered idly why he hadn't come out again after putting Johnny to bed.

Bishop Fred held out his hand and Martha took it. "Good night, Martha," he said. "Rest assured that we are praying for you."

"Thank you," she said simply. "I need and appreciate that."

"And you will start reading your Bible again?"

"Yes."

"That is good," he said warmly and turned to go. "Good night," he repeated. "And I am sorry if I offended you."

Martha nodded, forgetting he could not see her. She remained standing there until he was gone, then, picking up the tray with the empty dishes, went into the kitchen. She avoided the living room, feeling she couldn't talk with David with this feeling in her heart. So she went upstairs without saying good night to him.

David had stayed inside purposely, hoping that Bishop Fred could help her in some way. He had known that the bishop was wanting to talk with her. He had questioned David concerning her and, from his remarks, David had gathered that he realized she was rather difficult to get along with at times. So tonight instead of going outside he had stayed inside and read, praying silently that God would give Bishop Fred wisdom to say the right words.

Alone upstairs, Martha sat down by the window without bothering to light the lamp. The soft night breeze blew faintly across her cheeks, hot with emotion. All the memories came back with full force, now that she was alone. How often had she worshiped Daniel, feeling he was the most wonderful person she had ever known or heard of! And how often had she regarded him in almost the same light as God! But he had been wonderful! No one else could hold a candle to him. And why had God taken him away from her? In desperation she got up and lit the lamp. As she glanced about the room, her eyes rested on her Bible lying on the dresser. She picked it up and leafed through it, remembering with fresh longing the time when it had been meat and drink to her. Bishop

189

Fred had wanted her to read it regularly again. She laid it down. As she did so, it fell open to Exodus 20. The words that met her eyes were, "Thou shalt have no other gods before me." Martha gasped. Her heart was a dead weight within her, and her hand went to her mouth. Then, with an effort she reached down and slammed the Book shut. She hadn't worshiped Daniel! Besides, even if she had, wasn't he worthy of it? She blew out the light and threw herself across the bed, to lie there and stare into the darkness, her mind in a turmoil. Still fully clothed she dropped into a troubled sleep.

The next few days were miserable ones for Martha. At times she was ready to admit that she had made a god of Daniel. Anything, just to be rid of this burden of misery. And yet every time she was on the verge of admitting it, she drew back. Daniel had been a wonderful man. No one else was like him, at least no one she knew. He had been the finest Christian she had ever met, and others said so, too. The letters Ervin used to write to her had been full of the praises of Daniel. And the letters of condolence had been full of praise. So why shouldn't she have a high regard for him? Yet after all, he was just human. It was possible to hold men in too high regard. In a dim way she realized this. Yet always she refused to admit openly, even to herself, that she had been giving Daniel worship—worship that belonged only to God.

David noticed that something more than usual was wrong. She had less to say than ever, rarely speaking unless he asked her a direct question. Although he pitied her from the bottom of his heart, her silence only intensified his longing for Mary's companionship. He so longed for her presence at home again! It made him ready to cry at times, seeing Martha so silent and heavyhearted, it would a husband-to-be? I've been married only four years and it would be a lot harder to give up David now than it would have been when we first married," Mary said earnestly.

"I don't care. I wanted Daniel for my husband!" Martha was crying now. She groped in her purse for a handkerchief.

"Martha, I can't say I blame you. I might be just as bad in your case, but it seems to me that you are just thinking of yourself in this. Can you honestly say, after searching your heart, that you would want Daniel to leave the glory above, even if it were possible, and come down to this world of pain and woe again? Would you really deprive him of his actual presence with the Lord just so you could have him for your own selfish interests? True, you would have served the Lord together, but you can still do that alone. I don't think you are giving God a chance to reveal Himself to you through this, Martha. All you do is wish Daniel back. Back! To nothing but what this world has to offer. Exchange the bliss of Heaven for this! Think, Martha!"

Martha's mind was in a quandary. It was actually the first time she had thought of it in that light. She sat in troubled silence.

"Yesterday my roommate had her radio turned on," Mary continued. "She is down in therapy now, a wonderful Christian lady—another of those blessings. Anyway, she had her radio going, and they were singing some beautiful song—something about 'out of the ivory palaces into a world of woe.' I knew it was about our dear Saviour, but those words fit Daniel, too. Would you want him to leave those ivory palaces and come down into this world of woe again? If you were unselfish, I don't think you

194

coupled with his own lonesomeness for Mary. More than once it drove him to the haymow to fall full length on the soft hay and pray brokenly for grace to endure. He knew God didn't send these things to His children just because He got pleasure out of watching them suffer, but couldn't it be made a little easier at times? Every time such a suggestion crossed his mind, he asked God quickly to forgive him for such thoughts.

He continued visiting Mary every Sunday—more often if he could get away from his work at home. He usually offered to take Martha along. Sometimes she accepted; sometimes not, preferring to stay at home and care for the children so that either Mom and Pop or David's folks could go along. Besides, she knew that Mary and David enjoyed being alone together. When she did go with him, she found an excuse to leave them for a time so that they could talk alone. And so when she had an opportunity to go with a neighbor who wanted to visit a relative in the same hospital, the week following her talk with Bishop Fred, she accepted. That way she could stay at home on Sunday and take care of the children. Besides, Bethy needed a new bonnet and winter coat and she wanted to consult Mary about it.

She found Mary sitting beside her bed with an open book in her lap. She looked up when she heard Martha and said gladly, "Well, hi! This is an unexpected pleasure. How does it happen I see you today?"

Martha explained about the neighbor. Mary listened with interest. When Martha was finished, she said, "I will have to go over and visit her—if they will let me, that is."

"I see you are dressed. Does that mean you can be up and around?" Martha asked.

191

"A few hours a day. My, it seems good to get out of that bed!"

"Does the doctor think you are improving as fast as can be expected?"

"I think he does, yes. At least, I don't suppose he would let me get up if he didn't think so."

"Do you still cough so much?" Martha asked, looking at her with interest. "You look a lot better, that's for sure."

"Well, thanks, I feel better, too. I don't cough at all any more. That is another blessing. The Lord has been giving me one after another. Blessings, I mean," she explained.

Martha turned her eyes away from her. She would just as soon not talk about the Lord's blessings. "What are you reading?" she asked, indicating the book in Mary's lap. Better change the subject, she thought. Mary had eyes like a hawk.

"Oh, this is another of the Lord's blessings," Mary said, holding it up. "You know, every now and then I get hold of a book that is a milestone in my life. This is one of them."

"Why, what's it about?" Martha asked, interested again. Maybe it was what she needed.

"The ministry of suffering," Mary told her earnestly. "Aside from the Bible, nothing else has helped me accept this—this sickness of mine—as much as this book has. As I said, it is a milestone in my life. I wish you could read it; I am sure it would help you, too."

"Oh, Mary, don't begin on that subject!" Martha protested, feeling a quick nausea. She didn't want to be raked across the coals again.

"Why not? I can't think of anything that would help

192

you more. It would give you a new insight into your problem."

"The one who wrote it probably never had any trouble in this life. Those are always the ones who can give advice to others," Martha said bitterly.

"On the contrary, she did. In fact, it makes me ashamed of myself for being so soft about my own troubles. Really, the book would help you a lot. I know it would."

"What did she go through that was so unusual?"

"Well, she lost her husband first."

"I did, too; at least, he was going to be my husband," Martha interrupted, in a tone of self-defense.

"Yes, but she had a large family to support, and besides, she wasn't well. Then in quick succession she lost her mother, who had been very close to her, and soon after that her only sister was killed. You still have Mom and Pop, and us. Not that we are so much," she concluded gravely.

Martha was silent for a moment. Yes, she had Mom and Pop, and Mary, also Ervin. And even Bishop Fred was concerned about her. He had set up a chain reaction in her that was tearing her apart, but Martha was honest enough to admit that it wasn't his fault.

"How long was she married before her husband was killed?" she asked after a pause.

"I think she said about fifteen years."

"Well, she had him that long at least. Daniel was killed before we could even be married," Martha said thickly. If Mary was going to start this, she would have her crying all over the place. "Maybe if I could have had him fifteen years, I could resign myself to it, too."

"What makes you think it would be any easier to up a dear husband after fifteen years of marriage

193

would. I don't like to hurt you, Martha; I love you. But I think you are going to miss the blessing the Lord has for you in this entirely, if you don't watch out."

"Blessing!" echoed Martha thickly. "How can there be a blessing in this?"

"There is, though," Mary assured her stoutly. "You know the saying, 'Every cloud has a silver lining.' Well, that is definitely true. Paul was saying the same thing when he said in II Corinthians 4, 'For our light affliction, which is but for a moment, worketh for us a far more exceeding and eternal weight of glory.' "

Again Martha thought that perhaps Mary was right; maybe she had been thinking only of herself. Yet she couldn't help it. She missed Daniel so much. She had loved him so—too much, a subconscious voice told her. Martha flinched.

Again Mary broke into her thoughts. "I don't know the reason God saw fit to remove Daniel from this world. Certainly, looking at it from our human viewpoint, one would think that he was needed here. It is true he had leadership abilities and talents out of the ordinary. There's no question about it; he was a sincere, dedicated Christian. But there must be some great blessing in store for you in this, Martha. It is just like the lady in this book says: the greater the trial, the greater the blessing. So please don't botch it, Martha. Reach out and grab it!"

Martha fiddled with the handle of her purse, avoiding Mary's eyes. "How can I do that?" she asked huskily after a minute.

"Tell God that you know you have been selfish in this. He will gladly forgive. And if there is anything else, tell Him that, too. You might just as well; He knows all about it anyway," Mary concluded.

Her words pierced Martha's heart afresh. So God knew that she had been—well, idolizing Daniel. Her cheeks felt hot and her heart was racing within her. She still avoided Mary's eyes, feeling sure Mary would see the truth at once if she looked at her. She was saved from replying by the appearance of the neighbor, who was ready to go. Martha got up quickly with a sense of relief. She had about all she could take of this sort of thing for the time being. She wanted to be alone for a while. After a few words of good-by they left. Not until she was home did Martha remember that she hadn't mentioned a thing about Bethy's new bonnet and coat.

Alone in her room that night Martha sat beside her dresser in the soft glow of the lamp. The words Mary had spoken that day came back with new force, now that she hadn't the distractions of daily cares. Mary had told her she was going to miss the blessing of this entirely if she didn't watch out. Funny, but it had never dawned on her before that there was any blessing connected with this. At least the heavy burden of grief, resentment, self-pity and, lately, of guilt, had never, even in a dim way, suggested a blessing.

Then, too, Mary had said that she should confess to God that she had been selfish in this; and if there was anything else, she should tell Him that too. Martha groaned out loud and stood up. The very atmosphere of the room seemed saturated with guilt. She couldn't stand this; it was suffocating her. But where else could she go? A verse from the Book of Psalms flashed through her mind: "Whither shall I flee from thy presence?" Yes, where? There was no place. She was pacing around the room now. She must get rid of this. All at once her eyes fell on her Bible, half hidden under another book. She had promised Bishop Fred that she would read it daily, and she hadn't. Not after that first evening when she had read that verse in Exodus 20: "Thou shalt have no other gods before me."

Martha was past arguing with herself now. She stopped before the dresser and reached for the Bible. Aimlessly she opened it, hoping for something to help her, yet at the same time dreading to open it. She saw these words: "Have mercy upon me, O God, according to thy loving-kindness; according unto the multitude of thy tender mercies blot out my transgressions. Wash me throughly from mine iniquity, and cleanse me from my sin."

This was what she needed—and wanted too, with all her heart. She read on: "For I acknowledge my transgressions; and my sin is ever before me." Tears were starting to flow now. She blinked her eyes and continued: "Against thee, thee only, have I sinned, and done this evil in thy sight: that thou mightest be justified when thou speakest, and be clear when thou judgest."

This was all so true. She couldn't blink back the tears any more. They came in a flood, as if some dam had been broken. But she wanted to read more. With an effort she read through her tears: "Behold, I was shapen in iniquity; and in sin did my mother conceive me. Behold, thou desirest truth in the inward parts: and in the hidden part thou shalt make me to know wisdom."

How true! God wanted to have her very secret heart, and fill it with His truth and wisdom. Martha stooped over the dresser and buried her face in her arms. "O God," she prayed brokenly, through sobs, "I know I have sinned. I know I have made an idol of Daniel. Lord, please forgive!"

She gave herself wholly over to weeping now. All the

tears she had shed since Daniel's death were not like this. Those had brought no relief, but these—well, it was as if they were a cleansing stream, washing out her very soul. For a long time she sobbed, every sob making her cleaner. At last she stopped, with peace greater than she had ever known before in her heart. It was the same peace that had been David's in the haymow so long ago when Mary had gone to the hospital; also Mary's, after that talk with the doctor.

Martha picked up the Bible again and read on: "Purge me with hyssop, and I shall be clean: wash me, and I shall be whiter than snow."

"Yes, Lord," she breathed. "Oh, do that to me."

"Make me to hear joy and gladness; that the bones which thou hast broken may rejoice." Joy and gladness! How long was it since she had had that!

"Hide thy face from my sins, and blot out all mine iniquities. Create in me a clean heart, O God; and renew a right spirit within me." Right spirit! Yea, Lord, who needed it more than she did? She was so tired of the spirit of grief and resentment.

"Cast me not away from thy presence; and take not thy holy spirit from me. Restore unto me the joy of thy salvation; and uphold me with thy free spirit." There it was. Joy again! And free spirit! Free from sorrow, guilt, resentment, bitterness, and self-pity. Oh, glory!

"Then will I teach transgressors thy ways; and sinners shall be converted unto thee." Yea, Lord, that was her desire. Daniel had done that, she thought, remembering John Glaspy and the taxicab driver.

"Deliver me from bloodguiltiness, O God, thou God of my salvation: and my tongue shall sing aloud of thy righteousness. O Lord, open thou my lips; and my mouth shall shew forth thy praise. For thou desirest not sacrifice; else would I give it: thou delightest not in burnt offering. The sacrifices of God are a broken spirit: a broken and a contrite heart, O God, thou wilt not despise."

A broken and contrite heart! Well, Lord, that was hers now. She shut the Bible and sat down on the edge of the bed. How wonderful to know that a broken spirit was acceptable to God, she thought. Oh, wasn't God wonderful—so tender, and full of mercy!

23

NOW THAT SHE was no longer chained with the shackles of grief and bitterness, Martha began to take notice of those closest to her. Johnny was perhaps the first to profit by her changed condition. Not that she wasn't tried to the limit of her patience at times, but still, she wasn't as demanding and bossy as before. He responded at once, of course. He still loved to be with David, but he made considerably less fuss if necessity required his staying with her.

Then, too, she regarded Mom with new tenderness. Her heart was pierced at her careworn face and stooped back. Funny she hadn't noticed it before, but Mom's face was much more wrinkled than it had been. Pop, too, for that matter. Thomas, praise the Lord, confided to her the next time she was alone with him that he, too, had accepted the Lord as his Saviour soon after Daniel's death.

"Daniel had a lot to do with it," he told her seriously. "After he was killed, I began to see that if I should have to die, I would be lost. So I thought I had better give myself to God while I still had the chance. I'm so glad now I did," he confided simply. Martha cried with joy about that when she was alone again.

Paul, solemn and quiet, had grown. The last Martha had actually noticed him, he had been just a baby, it seemed to her. Here he was as tall as she. But it was Rosie who really made her open her eyes. Rosie was sixteen and fully grown! And such a beauty! Red, red lips and the pinkest of cheeks, with eyes dark blue and clear. Slightly haughty, though, Martha saw with a pang. Clearly Rosie needed Christ in her heart. From the teasing, half-envious remarks of some of the other girls, Martha gathered that Rosie was giving the boys quite a time. Evidently she was considered the supreme date and she knew it. But she was Rosie of the strong will, Martha found out one day when she was home. It made her heart ache to hear the insolent way Rosie sassed Mom. She prayed much for her after that—prayed that Rosie might in some way come to know Christ as Saviour and Lord of her life.

When fall communion came, David's prediction to Mary came true. Nor were others surprised when the lot fell on him. Bishop Fred, especially, was grateful to have him for his assistant. They had been working together as neighbors for the last five years and he knew him as a sincere, conscientious Christian. Too many of the people in the church were worldly and indifferent to the true spiritual things, and so David was especially appreciated by Bishop Fred.

Then came the memorable Thanksgiving Day when Mary, who had improved beyond their wildest hopes, could come home to spend the day with them. It was for only a day and a half, but it was good to have her home. She could hardly take her eyes off the children. Johnny was four now and a big boy in his eyes. He wasn't too big to climb into her lap to be cuddled, though, when it wasn't full of Bethy and Philip, that is. Bethy was such a dear, dainty little lady! She had to grow used to her mother again, much to Mary's inner pain. Except for seeing Mary a few times through the window, this was the first time since her departure that they had been together. It didn't take long to make up, however. Here was someone who would hold her all the time, Bethy found out. Martha didn't have time, but this new mommy person did. She quietly profited by it, being on Mary's lap most of their waking hours during the short time Mary was at home. Philip she hadn't seen since she had gone to the hospital. Then he was a baby four weeks old. Now he was sturdy and square, with a calm level gaze for her. Mom and Rosie had done a good job of taking care of him. He accepted his mother without fuss, sitting quietly on her lap as long as she cared to hold him.

The time for her return to the hospital came all too quickly. It was hard to give up her dear children after seeing them once more. But one thing made it a little easier—the thought of being with them at Christmas. She consoled Johnny with that fact when he burst into tears at her departure. He pestered David and Martha after that by asking them, half a dozen times a day, if tomorrow would be Christmas. So with many a backward look and waving of good-bys from Johnny and Bethy, Mary went back to the hospital. David sat with his arm around her all the way back, and Mary relaxed against his comforting shoulder.

Then came Christmas, and Mary was at home once more. She could stay three days this time and she lived them to the full. She went to church on Christmas Day and heard David preach his first sermon. Tears rolled down her cheeks as she listened to him tell, in an unsteady, halting way, what Christ's birth meant to the world. She prayed silently through her tears that God would use him to His honor and glory, and make him strong in the Lord.

After the services were over, how good it was to greet

old friends once more! They flocked around, anxious to tell her how glad they were to see her, and how much they had missed her. In the next two days Mary and David held a veritable open house for the many people who came—kind friends who wanted to share their good fortune.

All too quickly the three days were up and Mary had to go back to the hospital. Both Bethy and Johnny burst into wild sobs at her going and refused to be comforted; rather, they cried themselves to sleep. Martha cried a little too, seeing their tear-stained eyes when she checked up on them after they were asleep. She hoped Mary could come home for good before too long.

After the excitement of Christmas was over, life settled down into the winter routine, with sewing to be done, butchering, and an occasional quilting bee to relieve the monotony of regular work.

Friends, besides the family, noticed the change in Martha. Since Daniel's death she had spoken rarely unless spoken to. Few had seen her smile, either. She had given up all contact with the young folks, finding no pleasure in their company. They seemed to her so silly and careless, giving no thought beyond having a good time. They weren't all like that but, with her perverted outlook on life, they appeared so.

Now that she had peace in her heart once more, she could look at her old friends in a different light. Most of them were married and many of them were already proud parents. Martha duly exclaimed over their offspring, keeping her inner pain at what was being denied her to herself. Not that there weren't still times when she missed Daniel. Once in church she looked up to see Daniel's younger brother, who bore a close resemblance to him, sitting a

203

few rows in front of her, and the way he was holding his head made him seem so like Daniel that she gasped. For a moment she thought she would cry aloud, but she bit her lips and buried her face in Bethy's soft hair so quickly that Bethy looked up, puzzled at her action. She heard nothing of the service for a while, fighting within herself for control. She had to cry in silent agony to God for grace to keep from crying out loud. It came finally, leaving her spent emotionally, but peaceful within. She didn't dare look in the direction of Daniel's brother again, keeping her eyes on the floor until the services were over. She breathed a sigh of relief when the young boys filed out after church. Only then did she look up.

* * *

Mary continued to make good progress in regaining her health, and during the late winter and early spring she came home every weekend. Bethy and Johnny looked forward to it, often making Martha impatient because they asked so often if tomorrow were Sunday.

Mary looked forward to Sundays, too. She enjoyed especially those Sundays when David preached. He was getting better every time, his voice no longer halting and unsteady but stronger and surer, as he told of the love of God. He did not hesitate to tell the people not to trust in the traditions of the fathers, but to trust in the finished work of Christ. Bishop Fred prayed much for him, knowing that his messages were sorely needed. It made him sigh, though, as he realized that such preaching would make David enemies. His own heart had long been burdened for his people, realizing that many of them were smug and complacent in their traditions and heritage, rather than humbly trusting in Christ.

Winter passed and spring came, bringing with it field

work and garden work. The days passed quickly for Martha, with housecleaning and everything else. Besides, the last time Mary was home she told them the good news that if she kept on improving as she had been, she could come home to stay by the first of June, going back only for an occasional checkup. So they all hoped and prayed that her progress would continue, each for his own separate reasons. David, of course, prayed most, because it would mean so much if she could be home with him all the time. Martha saw that for the sake of the children it would be best if Mary were constantly there. Her weekly visits were regarded by them in the light of a holiday, with discipline rather lax; it often took a day or two to get back into routine after Mary's return to the hospital.

Mom wanted her back because her heart had been so heavy with burdens since Daniel's death that it seemed to cause actual physical pain at times. Besides, lately she hadn't been feeling well at all, with a strange pain in her stomach. She hadn't told anyone about it, though, not even Pop. He had enough troubles, she thought. For one thing, Thomas was leaving for his term of service soon after the first of June, and that would leave Pop and Paul to handle the farm alone. Paul was only fourteen and frail, and Pop was getting more stooped every day. She counted his years in her mind—she never could remember his age—and realized with a sharp pang that he was close to his middle fifties. No wonder he couldn't work as much as before. Thinking of it, neither could she.

Rosie was the one who caused her the most sighs. After a flurry of dates with a different boy every week, she had finally settled on one, Joe Beachy, who was almost twenty. She had been going steady with him ever since Christmas.

Mom didn't object to his age; it was just that Rosie was so self-willed and provoking. She was too big to spank any more, not that Mom didn't feel like doing it lots of times. Something or someone else was going to have to tame her down. With the temperament she had, it made Mom shudder to think of some of the knocks she would undoubtedly get from life. One couldn't make a face at life without getting a slap in the face in retaliation. About the only thing Mom could do for her was commit her to God, praying that in His own good time He would cause Rosie to commit herself to His will.

* * *

Mary came home in June to stay. Oh, it was good to be home! The first night she couldn't sleep for thankfulness. Of course she had had many unforgettable experiences in the last years—things for which she wouldn't exchange any amount of health. Her roommate, for instance, who, as she had told Martha, was a blessing of the Lord. Theirs had been a friendship that was to last by correspondence until broken by the death of one. Then her fellowship with God in Christ as Saviour had been so rich and sweet! Surely she wouldn't have had that at home with all the cares of wife and mother. Now that it was over and she was at home again, she prayed that never would she have to go through anything like that again.

She still kept Martha to help her. The doctor had told her to go easy on the work, conserving her strength as much as possible. It made no difference to Martha. One place was just as good as another, and she was quite attached to the children, Bethy especially. It didn't take that young lady long, however, to transfer all her affections, and Mary wept for joy when Bethy accepted her so completely once more.

The summer flew by for them all, with no break in their orderly routine until Ervin, who had by now taken two years of high school, announced that he intended to get married by fall. It hadn't been easy going to school with others almost ten years younger than he. So when he found out about special tests that could be taken for college entrance, he availed himself of them and, to his great delight, passed with flying colors. In the fall he would be leaving for the eastern church college, which happily was situated in Alice's home community. They had been engaged now for two years and were anxious to get married. He would work when he wasn't in school, and Alice planned to keep her job. By living in a trailer on her folks' vacant lot, they could manage, they thought. Mom shook her head when she heard of it.

"What is wrong with that?" Ervin wanted to know, rather impatient at her disapproval.

"Ervin, a woman's place is in the home," Mom answered positively. "A wife has no business to neglect her home and get outside work."

"But, Mom, Alice will have nothing but the trailer to take care of and that won't take much time. Besides, we both have to work to make ends meet."

"Then you have no business getting married," Mom stated emphatically.

"Well, maybe we don't, but we are tired waiting. After all, we have been going steady for over three years and engaged for two."

"I know, but one more year wouldn't hurt you. I know yours is the modern way, but—"

Nothing could change his plans, and Mom admitted to herself that, after all, at twenty-five, he ought to know his own mind. So she said nothing further about it and they went ahead with their plans.

In October they all went east for the wedding. It was on a lovely fall day and Alice had chosen the tawny fall colors as her bridal colors. Everyone had to admit that she was a beautiful bride, with her pink cheeks and her blue, blue eyes. Even Mom conceded that maybe it was going to be all right, after all. Alice seemed to have a level head on her shoulders for all her beauty. Besides, Ervin had a sound, solid background and certainly should be able to make a happy home. Above all, they were both sincere, dedicated Christians, which was really the main thing.

Martha rejoiced to see them both so happy. Only at the last, when the preacher pronounced them husband and wife, did a wave of emotion engulf her. One day—a long time ago, it seemed to her—she, too, had been going to take this solemn step. There was no bitterness in her heart any more, only sorrow for a very loved one gone. But someday they would be together in glory, and, as she thought of that, it didn't hurt as much. She dried her eyes and afterward could smile again, a poignantly beautiful smile. More than one person was struck by this beautiful sister of Ervin's with her clear eyes that seemed to have depths in them that were unfathomable. Martha had no idea of that certain thing which radiated from her personality. Yet few could look at her without noting it. The radiance of the grace of suffering, a more experienced one would have called it.

They spent a happy, busy week there, helping Ervin and Alice get the trailer located and straightened up. They enjoyed the Weavers' kind hospitality, and the day for their departure came all too soon. It was with many good-bys and much waving of the hands that they finally left.

24

ONCE AGAIN winter was upon them. Christmas came and went without anything out of the ordinary happening to ruffle the calm round of life. Toward the last of January, David's aged mother passed away. She hadn't been especially sick, but a gradual decline had been noticeable for some time. Mary grieved for her sincerely, knowing that she had been all a mother-in-law should be. True, she had all the quirks of character so common to elderly people, but, as a whole, their relationship had worked out well. After her death, David's equally aged father went to stay with David's oldest sister, who had a houseful of girls and could take care of him better than Mary could with her small ones.

One day a few weeks afterward, Martha, looking up from the worktable where she was rolling out piecrusts, saw Mom drive up. As she watched her come up the walk, she was struck anew by how much she had aged in the last year. Quickly she wiped her floury hands and went to open the door.

"Getting stiffer every day," Mom complained mildly by way of greeting. "Guess I am getting old for sure."

"Oh, Mom!" Martha said in quick alarm. "You look as if you were sick."

The sound of voices brought the children running from the living room to see who was there. As soon as they saw who it was, they were upon her with cries of, "Grandma! Grandma!"

"Oh, my, don't push me over," she protested good-humoredly. "Let me get my breath and sit down first."

Martha pushed a chair behind her and she sat down heavily. Mary, leading Philip by the hand, came from the bedroom to see what caused the commotion. It was impossible to visit until the children each had a piece of candy from Grandma's spacious pocket. After that she patted Bethy on the cheek, tweaked Johnny's ear, and gave Philip a sound kiss.

"Now go on and play," she said with good-natured authority. "Grandma wants to talk to Mommy and Martha."

"Go on." Mary verified the command, seeing that Mom had something serious on her mind. They went, and Mom sent a loving look in their direction. How sweet they were! Most wonderful grandchildren anyone could have. Of course, she was prejudiced.

Then she turned to Mary and Martha and said without preamble, "Rosie wants to get married."

"Rosie!" Mary and Martha said in chorus. They stared at her dumbfounded.

"Why, Mom, Rosie is only seventeen years old!" Mary was the first to recover.

"I know, I know, but you can't tell her that," Mom said wretchedly. Then all at once she did something that they had very seldom seen her do before. She buried her face in her arms on the kitchen table and cried. Mary and Martha looked at each other, genuinely alarmed. This time Martha was the first to recover. She reached over and enfolded Mom in her arms, remembering with a pang how often Mom had done the same for her.

They stayed so for a moment, with Mom still sobbing and Mary standing by, helpless to stop her. The children came into the kitchen and stared at them with big round eyes. This was something terrible to their childish hearts. All at once Bethy broke into loud wails herself, the sound of which caused Mom to stop. She pulled away from Martha and blew her nose loudly; then with a half sob and half laugh she stepped over and took Bethy into her arms.

"Grandma scare you?" she asked through her tears. "Here, take another piece of candy." She reached into her pocket for a handful. "I don't know what ails me, crying like a baby," she said shamefacedly to no one in particular.

"When does Rosie want to get married?" Mary asked, seeing Mom had partly regained her composure. "Next June?"

"Next June!" echoed Mom. "If she'd only wait that long. No, she wants to be married just as soon as we can get ready."

"What is her hurry?" Martha asked.

"I don't know what." Mom was still dejected about it, but some of the overwhelming heaviness had left her. "Oh, I know Joe is old enough," she resumed. "He is twenty-one and I guess he is pushing pretty hard. Besides, from what Rosie says, he is hoping that if he gets married he won't have to go away for his alternate service. She has been hinting at it for a couple of weeks, ever since Christmas, for a fact, but last night she came right out and said plainly that they were planning on it."

"What does Pop say about it?" Mary asked.

"He doesn't know what to say. It surprised him quite a lot, I guess. I didn't think she was serious about getting married; so I didn't even mention it to him. I see now that I should have, but I was hoping all along she didn't mean it."

"Well, maybe marriage would be the thing to tame her down," Martha observed, cutting the dough off the edge of a pie shell.

"Maybe, but with the temperament she has, I am afraid she is in for a big surprise. I declare, I tried my best to bring her up to obedience and fear of the Lord, but sometimes it doesn't look as if I had made a dent on her. I gave her twice as many spankings as all the rest of you put together. You know that," Mom concluded.

They both knew that. Pictures flashed across Martha's mind of Rosie, petulant and pretty, defying Mom ever since she was old enough to talk; getting her own way, by fair means or foul, regardless of whose feelings were hurt in the process. In fact, Joe had been going with another girl until Rosie's debut among the young folks. Then he had dropped her like a hot potato and started dancing attendance on Rosie. Rosie had walked off with him, proudly triumphant, not even giving a thought for his poor, wretched, former girl friend. Such was Rosie.

Mary brought the ironing board from the pantry and started ironing. Laying one of Bethy's dresses across the board, she asked, "What will they do after they are married? Do they have that figured out, too?"

"She said they wanted to rent a farm somewhere, but where they will get one so close to the first of March is beyond me. Last night Pop and I were both so shocked we couldn't even think, but this morning Pop told me that he had thought it over, and if they were going ahead and getting married anyway—why, maybe we could put up a grandpa house and have them farm the homeplace."

"What!" Mary exclaimed. "Why so?"

"Pop is just getting to the place where he can't work so hard any more, and what with Thomas gone and Paul

213

not being too strong, he has had more than he could handle the last year. In fact, he said that Paul told him he would like to go to high school and then later on to college and be a teacher like Ervin. Paul does seem too light for heavy farm work," Mom explained. She had entirely regained her composure by now. She still held Bethy on her lap and, as she talked, she stroked her hair gently. "So I came over this morning to tell you girls about it. I guess we will have to be making plans for this wedding. I guess I will have to have Martha at home for a few weeks, Mary. I would try to do it with Rosie's help, but I'm afraid I can't depend on her; and then, too, I haven't been feeling well myself lately."

"How big a wedding does she want?" Martha asked as she slid the last pie shell into the oven. "I suppose an awfully big one."

"Yes, she does. She said last night that both she and Joe wanted all the uncles and aunts on both sides and all the young folks. No, a small wedding just wouldn't do for her."

"When is it to be?" Mary asked, putting the finishing touches on the little dress.

"They want to be published a week after this Sunday. That would make the wedding by the last of February. Last night when she told me, I just wasn't going to give in, but that is just the way it always goes with her. She just insists on her own way in everything." Mom gave a heavy sigh. "But I guess the Lord knows how to deal with her; I'm sure I don't."

So Rosie and Joe were married. Rosie insisted on her own way in everything. There must be a huge wedding; no less than two hundred invited guests would do. Rosie insisted on pink dresses for the table waitresses, an unheard-of color in the church for that purpose. She insisted, too, on the lightest of blue for a wedding dress, also unheard of. Likewise she insisted on Mom's coming to the ceremony to see her married, also unheard of. There was one thing to which she had to give in, and then it wasn't to Mom that she did it. That was the corner table. Rosie didn't want one; they were old-fashioned, she said. Mom demurred, feeling that there were enough breaches of convention as it was. But Rosie insisted quite loudly, and Mom was about ready to give in when help came from an unexpected source—no less than Joe.

"Why must I have a corner table? They are the silliest things I ever heard of. Other churches don't have them," Rosie said.

"Oh, Rosie, what is wrong with that? You are getting your own way in everything else, but I am not giving in to that," Mom said emphatically.

"I don't care. I don't want a corner table! I am not going to have one, either!" Just then Joe stepped in.

"Rosie," said Joe, "if your mother thinks you are to have a corner table, then we will have one. I like those best myself."

That was all, but it was enough. Rosie still looked petulant. Mom stared at Joe in open-mouthed wonder. Then she went into the bedroom and, shutting the door, stood with her back to it for a moment. All at once the humor of the situation struck her and she broke into silent laughter. Maybe Rosie had found her match at last!

25

A S SPRING CAME ON, Mom and Pop started planning for the grandpa house. It was evident to all that, for the sake of harmony, Rosie should be mistress of her own house as soon as possible; so just as soon as the carpenters could begin work on the house, it was started. By the end of June the basement had been finished and the frame put up. By the end of July the plasterers had finished. Martha came over and helped Mom with the painting and varnishing and, by the last of August, Mom and Pop moved out of the old house that had been their home for the last twenty-five years. The new house wasn't quite finished, but Rosie was so anxious to have her own things established that to put off moving seemed unwise.

Rosie reveled in getting her own furniture set up. If Mom had in times past despaired of ever teaching Rosie the know-how of good housekeeping, her mind could rest now. Rosie turned out to be a wonderful housekeeper. She seemed to have a natural flair for home decoration and even the most finicky of housekeepers couldn't have found fault with her. Besides all this, Rosie was joyously looking forward to being a mother.

Rosie loved babies, whatever else her faults. The care of Baby Philip while Mary was in the hospital had been mostly in her hands, and she had loved it. So now that she had a home of her own, she wanted babies—lots and lots of them. A big family wouldn't be a burden for her; in fact, she looked forward to it. She couldn't keep it secret;

216

she told everyone. It tickled Mom to see her, so eager and sure of her good fortune. But whether Rosie ever stopped to thank God for her happy lot was open to question. Rosie was all-sufficient unto herself, but many were the prayers offered by Mom and Martha that she would open her heart to Christ.

Mom kept Martha for a few days a week even after they were moved, because that old nagging pain, which had bothered her for a year, took a turn for the worse. In fact, it got so bad that Mom was forced to tell Pop about it. He listened sympathetically in silence as she told him.

"It has been bothering me for a year. I didn't think it worth mentioning before, as long as it wasn't getting worse, but I'm afraid I will have to do something about it before long," she finished miserably. She hated the idea of going to a doctor, or of being sick, for that matter.

Pop was worried. Mom so seldom complained that when she did, it was usually serious. "Best see a doctor as soon as you can," he said. "Even if it's not serious, it is best to know what it is. Don't you think so?"

Mom didn't answer; maybe if she tried to ignore the pain it would go away. So she pushed the idea of going to the doctor out of her mind. Besides, she was too busy. It was time to get at all the fall work in earnest before winter set in. The evenings were already getting chilly. As if that was all the incentive she needed, she pushed on and worked twice as hard. The new house must be entirely painted before cold weather set in. Then there were dozens of cupboards to arrange, besides the attic of the old house to be cleaned. Rosie wanted to use it for her own storage, and the accumulated junk of years

217

had to be disposed of. She would go to the doctor when fall work was over.

But one night she reached the limit of her endurance. She woke up from an uneasy sleep with pain rising in waves over her. She groaned, tossed, and turned, trying to find a position that would help. Finally a terrible pain wrenched through her, causing her to cry out and wake Pop.

"Huh, what's wrong?" he asked. Mom gasped. "What is the matter?" he asked again.

"Oh, John, I am having terrible pains." She was crying now—short little whimpers reminding him of a hurt pup.

He got out of bed, felt his way through the dark, and lit the lamp. At sight of her pain-racked face, his heart turned to water. "Oh, Mom, what is the matter? Mom, what is it?" his voice was anxious with fear.

Mom could only shake her head. She lay curled up tight, and pitiful moans escaped from her pinched lips. Pop hesitated no longer. She needed a doctor and in a hurry, too. He reached for his trousers hanging on the foot of the bed.

"Listen, Mom, I am going after a doctor. Can you hear me?"

A slight nod told him she did. He pulled up his suspenders and reached under the bed for his shoes. It didn't take him long to dress, although he broke a shoestring in his nervous haste. "I'll call Martha to stay with you while I call the doctor."

A groan and slight nod told him she understood. He fumbled his way out into the kitchen, grumbling about not being able to find his way in this new house. He lit another lamp and hurried upstairs to Martha's room.

"Martha," he called urgently as he opened the door. "Martha, come, wake up. Mom's awful sick!"

His clumping steps on the stairs had half awakened Martha already. She sat up in bed and regarded him questioningly. "Mom is awful sick," he repeated. "Come down and stay with her while I go get the doctor."

Martha got up and slipped hurriedly into her housecoat. "What's wrong with her?" she asked in alarm.

"I don't know," he replied, turning to go when he saw that she was up. "She woke up a few minutes ago and was in awful pain." He was halfway down the stairs by now. The door banged after Pop as Martha came into the kitchen. She could see the light of his lantern through the window as he started hurriedly down the lane. He was going to the home of a neighbor, to call the doctor on the telephone.

She went into the bedroom and found Mom still curled up in pain and still moaning. Martha's heart contracted in fear when she saw her drawn face and her ashy gray lips. Mom's forehead felt clammy wet under her hand. What was the matter? "O God," she prayed, "please don't let it be bad!" She wasn't much of a nurse, but there was surely something she could do to help. Getting a wet cloth from the bathroom, she wiped Mom's face. It seemed a long time since Pop had left. Martha was almost beside herself with anxiety, but reason told her he was probably only at the neighbor's home by now. Mom moved a little and moaned again. She turned her head from side to side, trying to find relief. If only Pop would hurry!

After what seemed ages but in reality was only fifteen minutes, Pop returned. He stopped at the gate, trying to decide whether to go over and wake Rosie and Joe, but because of Rosie's condition, he decided against it. Besides, there was nothing to do until the doctor came.

He found Martha sitting beside Mom's bed, wiping her face with the washcloth. As he came into the room, she looked up and asked, "Is he coming soon?"

"He said he would be here in fifteen minutes," he answered in undertones. "How is she?"

"The same as she was when you left," Martha said anxiously. She noticed again the lines so deeply etched on Mom's face. Pain made every one of them noticeable. Only a few short years ago, Mom's face was as fresh and plump as a girl's! The cares of life over the last few years certainly had robbed her of her youth. The last weeks she looked sick, but Martha's anxious inquiries only brought forth evasive answers. Nothing was wrong—nothing that work wouldn't cure.

Pop came around to the foot of the bed and, gripping the bedpost with both hands, regarded Mom with anxious eyes. He hoped nothing was seriously wrong. They had shared the joys and sorrows of life together for the last thirty years and, as he looked back, they were very happy ones. Why didn't the doctor come? Surely he had time by now.

Martha looked at him. "Shouldn't the doctor be here by now?" she asked. "Surely it's been fifteen minutes and more."

"I think so, too," Pop answered. He went into the living room and peered out the window. There were no headlights yet. A groan from Mom brought him back into the bedroom. Martha tenderly wiped her face again.

"What could be the matter?" she asked in dismay. "Oh, please, God, don't let it be serious!" she prayed.

220

"Must be what she was telling me about a few weeks back," Pop said anxiously.

"What was that?" Martha asked in surprise. "Was she complaining about something bothering her?"

Pop nodded. "Didn't she say anything to you about it? She told me she had been having pains in her stomach and that they had been getting worse. I wanted her to see a doctor then."

"Well, she didn't tell me," Martha said in a hurt voice. "I thought she didn't seem to feel well, but I couldn't get anything out of her. She would just laugh and tell me I was imagining things. If I had known, I sure wouldn't have let her help with all the heavy work we have had the last few days."

Pop didn't reply because he saw the lights of a car shining in the yard.

"Here comes the doctor," he said, with relief in his voice. Just then he heard the clock on the kitchen wall strike three. Only a short hour ago he was asleep and, as far as he knew, everything was all right. How quickly things could change.

The doctor came up the walk briskly. Pop marveled that even at this hour he could be so cheerful. "Well, John, what seems to be the trouble?" he asked.

"I don't know," Pop said in a worried voice as he led the way into the bedroom. "She woke up about half an hour ago and had terrible pains. Wasn't even able to talk much."

The doctor regarded her intently, but she gave no sign of recognition. He took her pulse in silence and listened to her heart for a moment. Straightening up, he said, "Her heart seems to be all right. Has she been complaining lately?"

Pop told him of the pain in her stomach. "She said it had bothered her for a year or so. I wanted her to come see you then, but—well, I didn't push her to go and so she didn't," he concluded lamely. If only he had made her go! Maybe this could have been avoided.

"That could mean more than one thing," the doctor said gravely. He was busy now, preparing to give her a hypo. "I'm going to give her a shot and then see how she is by morning. If she is no better by seven or eight, let me know. I'm afraid she will have to go to the hospital if she isn't."

Pop's heart sank as he heard that. He knew the doctor must really think it serious. Martha felt the same way. "Oh, please, God, not that!" she pleaded.

At that moment Joe came in to see what was going on. He and Rosie had been awakened by the light of the doctor's car shining in their window.

"Go see what's wrong over at the folks," Rosie had insisted. "A car just drove in and it is all lit up over there. Maybe someone is sick."

Joe came into the living room in time to hear the doctor say to Pop and Martha, "So you keep an eye on her and let me know just as soon as you can see a change in her. She may be better in an hour or so. I hope so."

Joe's eyes took in the scene. Plainly Mom was sick. She was lying in bed, white and still, and Pop and Martha were huddled together dejectedly at the foot of the bed, anxiety in their eyes. The doctor was putting his things back into the satchel. Joe looked from one to the other. Mom was seriously sick by the looks of things.

The doctor greeted him pleasantly. "What's wrong?" Joe asked, unable to suppress his curiosity any longer.

"She seems to be quite sick," the doctor told him with

professional cheerfulness. "I have given her something to calm her, but she is not out of danger yet."

Pop accompanied the doctor as he left the house. "Let me know, no later than eight at least," the doctor said, "and if she is no better, I will be right out and we will see about taking her to the hospital."

Joe lagged behind and asked Martha in a wondering voice, "What happened? What is wrong with Mom?"

Martha told him what had happened. "How did you find out something was wrong?" she asked.

"Rosie woke me and said a car had driven in and that it was all lit up over here. She made me come over and see what had happened," Joe explained.

When Pop returned, he asked in a low voice, "How is she now?" It was as if he were afraid loud talking would wake her up to more pain. Mom seemed to be resting quietly now. There was no sign that she heard them as she lay there with her eyes closed.

Pop sighed deeply. Somehow he felt that it wasn't over yet. He stood for a moment looking at Mom, oblivious of the others. At last he roused himself and spoke heavily. "You two might just as well go back to bed. I will bring in my rocking chair and watch her the rest of the night. Nothing else to do, I guess."

"What time is it?" Joe asked, suppressing a yawn. As if in answer to his query the clock on the wall struck the half hour. Three-thirty!

"Well, I had better be going back," he said. "Let us know how she is as soon as you can."

After Joe had gone, Martha looked at Pop with indecision. He was already carrying his old hickory rocker into the bedroom.

"I don't think I will go upstairs, Pop," Martha said

223

finally. "I couldn't sleep anyway. I can lie down on the couch."

"Well, just as you wish." Pop seemed relieved to have her close. It gave him a sense of comfort to have someone else share his vigil.

Martha got a quilt from the closet and dozed fitfully on the couch the few remaining hours of the night. The lamp had been left burning in the bedroom, and by its dim light she could see Pop sitting in the old rocker. One time she saw him with his face buried in his hands as if he were crying and she longed to go and comfort him. About that time he straightened up and she again fell into a slumber. Another time she awoke to see him kneeling beside the rocker. Martha started to get up, but the sound must have disturbed him, for he arose and sat down. The next time she awoke, it was to see Paul, who had slept through most of the night's excitement, standing beside the couch. In the dim light from the window he looked very young and white.

"What's wrong, Martha?" he asked fearfully. "Is Mom sick? I heard a car drive away last night and then I heard talking and I wondered what it was. What is it?" Martha sat up. Where was Pop? Oh, there he was, still sitting in the rocker, but asleep. "What is it?" Paul repeated insistently.

"Mom is sick," Martha told him.

"What is wrong with her? When did she get sick?" The questions tumbled out in his eagerness to know.

"Last night about three o'clock. We don't know what is wrong with her. The doctor didn't either."

"Is she better now?" His voice was troubled and his thin face was white and anxious.

"I don't know. The doctor gave her a hypo so she could rest, and we are to see how she is this morning."

Martha got up and drew her housecoat around her. The sound of their voices had roused Pop and he sat up and rubbed his eyes. Martha entered the bedroom, followed by Paul, and they all looked at Mom with anxious eyes. She still seemed to be asleep. Ever so gently Pop picked up her hand and felt her pulse. That roused her and she moaned softly, turning her head from side to side. Their eyes were fastened upon her as if trying to make her respond. At last she opened her eyes and looked around. Again she moaned softly.

"How do you feel, Mom?" Pop's voice ended on a high questioning note.

Mom turned her head at the sound of his voice. "What's wrong with me?" she asked in a thick, dazed voice. Why did she feel so weak and spent?

"You are sick, Mom," Pop told her gently.

"Did you call the doctor?" It all seemed so faint and far away—like a bad dream.

"Yes, we did. You had an awful pain in your stomach, remember?"

Yes, she remembered now; it had been terrible. The pain was still there—a dull, steady ache now; no longer knife-sharp.

The sound of the kitchen door reached their ears, and Martha went out to see who was there. It was Rosie, looking beautiful and worried. She had come over to see how Mom was.

"How is she?" she asked as soon as she saw Martha.

"She is awake now. She doesn't seem to be quite as sick as she was last night." Martha's reply was low. Rosie followed her into the bedroom. Mom looked up, curious to see who had come in. Her eyes looked questioningly at Rosie. How did she happen to know she was sick?

"What shall we tell the doctor? Shall we say you feel the same or better?" Pop asked gently. He wished so much he could say better, but he was afraid she was not.

Mom considered a moment. The pain wasn't so sharp any more, but it was still there; so something must be wrong yet.

"You can say I still have pain, but no so bad any more," Mom finally answered in a weak voice.

Pop sighed and left to call the doctor, as it was already past seven. While he was gone, Martha got breakfast ready and packed Paul's lunch for school. He was a freshman in high school now, the same parochial school Ervin had attended.

When Martha met Pop at the door upon his return, he was blowing his nose violently. She had the feeling that he wanted to cry, and she could sympathize with him.

Neither she nor Pop was hungry, although Pop made a pretense of eating. Paul, however, with a half-grown boy's appetite, made up for both of them. As Martha watched him devour two eggs and a large dish of cereal, plus innumerable slices of bread liberally covered with Mom's good butter and fresh grape jelly, she wondered idly where he put it. He was thin as a rail for all his eating. She was glad to see him eat, however, even though the thought of food made her sick.

26

WHEN THE DOCTOR came again, he asked innumerable questions and poked and prodded Mom until she winced in pain. At last he said seriously, "Well, John I think she had better go to the hospital. This could be just about anything. So to make sure, she had better be under observation for a few days."

Pop sighed heavily. He knew that was what the doctor was going to say. While Martha packed a few things in a bag, and Joe was dispatched to tell David and Mary, Pop went for someone to take them to the hospital. Paul had already left for school, with a last-minute admonition to let him know as soon as they found out what was wrong.

At the hospital they examined Mom thoroughly. The pain was always there, however, constantly reminding her that something was wrong. One of the family stayed with her all the time, partly because of the doctor's orders, and partly because they dreaded the idea of leaving her alone. Most of the time either Martha or Pop stayed, although Rosie and Joe did share a night vigil.

After Mom had been in the hospital about a week, and after consultation with other doctors, it was decided to operate. One evening, as the doctor was making his late rounds, he spoke a few words with both Mom and Pop, then turning to Pop he said pleasantly, "John, could I have a few words with you?"

Pop nodded and followed him as he left the room.

He wondered if the doctors had finally discovered what was wrong. Visiting hours were over and the halls were deserted, except for the aides and nurses, who were making their last-minute rounds. There were a few others, however, who, like Pop, were watching over loved ones in danger. Pop's heart went out to them; he knew how they felt. He even nodded to one who looked up as he passed the door. Kindred cares made them friendly, even if unknown to each other.

"John, we have finally decided to operate on your wife," the doctor said at last. "We think we know what her trouble is, but of course we could be mistaken; we hope so. With your consent, we will operate about day after tomorrow. It is up to you to tell us to go ahead."

Pop was silent for a moment. Should he ask what was wrong? He wanted to know, but at the same time he dreaded hearing the answer. Finally he asked in a husky voice, "What do you think her trouble is?"

The doctor cleared his throat before replying. It was always hard to tell loved ones these things. He glanced idly up the hall and then back to Pop. "John, I hate to have to tell you and I hope we are mistaken, but I am awfully afraid your wife has cancer," he said gravely, but kindly.

Pop felt as if someone had knocked him breathless. For some reason, that was what he had been afraid of ever since the beginning of Mom's illness.

"I am sorry, John," the doctor continued. "I realize it is quite a shock to be told this. I still say I might be mistaken; I surely hope so. But perhaps if you consent to an operation, her life can be spared for quite a while. That is something to hope for anyhow."

Pop lifted a silent prayer heavenward for strength, both

for himself and for Mom. Then, raising his eyes, he said quietly, "Go ahead and operate. You know best."

"Thank you, John. We will go ahead with our plans then."

"What about her? Should she be told?" Pop asked bluntly. "Would it be the best thing for Mom if she knew?"

The doctor met his eyes again. "No, John, I don't think so. Not before the operation. We will just tell her about operating and as little about it as we can get by with until afterward. We can tell her then."

Pop agreed and started up the hall. There would be plenty of time to tell her afterward. Feeling as he did, however, he dreaded going back to her room right away. Women's eyes were so sharp, they usually knew the minute something was wrong.

All of the lights were out in the patients' rooms now except the dim night lights in those rooms where there was an especially sick patient. As Pop passed the room where the man had nodded to him, he saw him sitting with a hand shading his eyes and a book lying face down on his lap. Pop paused, his heart touched by the man's attitude of dejection. Maybe there was something he could say to help. Sensing someone's presence in the doorway, the man took his hand away from his eyes and looked up.

"Hello," Pop said, half embarrassed now that he had stopped. The man returned his greeting pleasantly enough. Encouraged, Pop continued. "That your wife?" nodding toward the woman on the bed, who appeared to be sleeping.

The man nodded and Pop asked kindly, "Is she very sick?"

"Yes, she is." A shadow seemed to cross his face and

229

Pop, seeing it, felt a pang of sympathy. Mutual anxiety made him talkative.

"I know how that is," he told him earnestly. "My wife is very sick, too."

"Oh, I am sorry," the man said politely. "I hope she is better soon."

"Thanks," Pop replied simply. "I hope yours is, too."

He turned to go, now that the flush of the impulse to talk had faded. "Good night," he said over his shoulder, as he started up the hall. He had better be getting back to Mom.

To his relief, Mom was already under the influence of her nightly sedative and was sleeping quietly. Pop dropped into the chair beside her bed and picked up his Bible. He had brought it with him to read through the lonely night hours. Its words comforted him as nothing else could. He had selected many of the comfort verses a previous night and shaded them with a pencil. He glanced over at Mom, who lay so still on the high hospital bed. Then opening his Bible at random and leafing through its pages, his eyes fell on these words from the Book of Proverbs: "Whoso findeth a wife findeth a good thing."

How true! He looked back over the years to the time when Mom had been a pert young bride. It seemed to him now that he had been a thoughtless ungrateful young wretch. Mom had meant to him then only one hundredth of what she did now. They had grown up together; had been schoolmates, although he was two years older than she. Their courtship hadn't been hindered; in fact, they had the blessing of their parents.

As he looked back now, pictures flashed through his mind: of Mom, proud and happy as a young bride and mistress of her own home; somewhat like Rosie, he thought. Then her cup of joy was full as she looked forward to the arrival of her first baby. That joy soon turned to sorrow, however, when the baby boy, too weak and frail, died soon after birth. He remembered how Mom cried and cried, and he, a bewildered young husband, was unable to comfort her. Later she looked forward happily to the arrival of her second child, although she was somewhat fearful until it was over and Mary, strong and healthy, was placed in her arms. In time they were blessed with another child, Ervin, married now and looking forward to being a father himself soon. Then came Martha, who had gone through a great sorrow already. He wondered what God had in store for her. It must be something special, he thought. Later Thomas came to join the family. He was now grown and working in a large Midwestern city hospital.

He mused on dreamily. After Thomas there was a span of five years before Rosie was born. During those years he had grown accustomed to seeing Mom without a baby on her lap, and Mom had been content and happy with the children she had. The first inkling that another baby was on the way, however, had not been unpleasant to her. Rosie was self-willed from the beginning and, as the years went by, Pop noticed how often she tried Mom's patience to the limit. Now Rosie was married—hardly more than a child herself—and looking forward to being a mother. He certainly hoped it would teach her a few lessons, like giving in to others and showing consideration for other people. He sighed. Like Mom, he too had prayed often that Rosie might come to the source of true happiness. Had they failed in some way? Had they hidden the light of life under a bushel of conventions, traditions, and the daily cares of life?

Thomas, too, had been utterly unconcerned about the ways of Christ in his youth. True, he had joined church and had conformed to the regulations of the church as far as outward appearances were concerned, but he had been perverse for a long time. Then Pop remembered that fall, so long ago it seemed, when Martha had been weighted down with conviction and indecision. Hadn't they been explaining the way of salvation clearly enough to their children? Had they been giving the impression that to be baptized and become a member of the church was all that was needed? It had taken Daniel's instruction and pleading to make Martha see the light, and Pop was thankful that her eyes had been opened at last. At that time he was ashamed before God as he realized that he had not carried out his responsibilities, and he rededicated his own heart to God, to be used for His service. Since then Pop had had a closer walk with God than ever before.

Paul, frail and weak, was their last child. Mom had nursed him to health, although Paul would never be strong. He had been Pop's baby, really. It was Pop who carried him over the farm, even before he could walk. Then after he began to toddle, seldom did Pop make a trip away from home without Paul's little figure on the seat beside him. It was Pop who had the patience to answer all of his childish questions. Mom, usually busy and impatient, although good-humored, didn't always find time for the small questioner. At such times Paul would ply Pop with his eager questions.

Now, all too soon, Paul was a freshman in high school. The thirst for knowledge, manifested in those childish questions, had turned him into a bookworm. At an early age Paul had discovered the magic world of books and always, when time permitted, he was engrossed in one. It had seemed heartless to Pop to choke that unquenchable thirst for knowledge by making Paul a farmhand. Therefore he made his decision to send Paul to high school, even though for his people it was an unheard-of thing. True, Ervin had gone to high school, but Ervin had paid his own expenses and had changed his church affiliation.

Pop sighed, longingly. His own people were dear to his heart, but why must they be so stiff-necked? Must everything be done as the fathers had done it? After all, the fathers were only people, and subject to failure. Not for anything would he consider leaving the church, but that didn't mean he agreed with everything that was going on in it.

A slight movement from the bed brought his musings to an end. He sat upright with a jerk. How long had he been sitting here? He fumbled around and drew out his heavy, old-fashioned watch. It was one-thirty. He had been so occupied with his thoughts that it didn't seem as though he had been sitting here that long. He laid the Bible on the bedside table and arose stiffly. Funny how a man got so stiff as he got older! Time was when he had been as agile as a spring chicken.

Mom was turning her head from side to side, in a way peculiar to her when she didn't feel well. He watched her anxiously, hoping she would sleep on. He was afraid if she awoke, she would want to know what the doctor had said, and he dreaded telling her.

She opened her eyes and looked around the room. Seeing Pop, she asked in a voice thick with sleep, "What time is it?" The constant sedatives kept her only half conscious, even in her waking hours.

"One-thirty," Pop answered gently. She lay with her

233

eyes closed for a minute and he thought she was going back to sleep. Then she opened them again, and tried to sit up. Pop reached out his hand, not knowing whether to help her up or push her back.

"I would like a drink," she said. Pop helped her and she took a few swallows. "Tastes awful," she said. "I wish I had a drink of good water from home. Why don't you bring some for me if I am going to be here for a while?"

She lay back on the pillow and was silent for a moment, although her eyes were open. "I had the funniest dream," she said in a musing voice. "I dreamed we were still building the new house, but couldn't get it finished. Every time we asked the carpenters to come and work, they said they had to make a coffin—that it was needed more than the house."

Her words froze Pop to his seat. Did she realize what she was saying? He gripped the arms of the chair in consternation. Did she know what was wrong with her? Had something been revealing to her things to come?

"But it was just a dream," she said, laughing. At that Pop relaxed slowly. If she thought it was just a dream, then far be it from him to frighten her. "But please, God," he prayed silently, "please don't take her away from me yet! How can I get along without her?"

Again Mom lay silent for a while, with her eyes closed. Pop watched her with loving, anxious eyes and wished she would go back to sleep. He wondered if he should call the nurse to give her another sedative, but decided not to as long as she didn't seem to be in pain.

"Did the doctor say anything special to you?" she asked abruptly. He cleared his throat and prayed silently.

"He said you needed an operation," he said finally.

"When?"

"Day after tomorrow."

"Is it a serious operation?"

"Serious enough," he replied.

Mom turned her head and gazed at the ceiling. "I was expecting that," she said calmly enough. Then she closed her eyes and said nothing more about it. Pop finally relaxed again and for long moments both were silent and motionless. In fact, Pop almost dropped off to sleep, to be aroused by a slight movement from the bed, accompanied by a deep sigh. The sigh echoed and reechoed in the depths of his heart.

27

MARTHA CAME early the next morning to take Pop's place, and he was glad to go home and get some sleep. They exchanged a few words in the hall so that Mom wouldn't hear them.

"How does she seem this morning?" Martha asked anxiously.

"About the same," Pop answered. "I talked with the doctor last night and he says she'll have to have an operation." Pop fiddled with his watch chain without meeting her eyes.

"When?"

"Tomorrow," he said, trying to evade any more questions.

Martha saw that he was worn out; so she turned to go up the hall. Pop roused himself and asked how long she planned to stay.

"Until this afternoon," Martha said, turning to face him. "Are you coming again tonight? Mary and David said they could come tonight if you wanted to sleep."

After thinking it over, Pop replied, "They can come late tonight. I'll come back this afternoon and then you can go home again. All right?"

Martha nodded, and Pop turned and walked down the hall to the elevator. He found the neighbor, who had brought Martha, waiting for him in the lobby. After a few words of greeting, they stepped out into the crisp October air. The fresh air was like a stimulant to Pop, cooped up as he had been in the stuffy hospital all night. He breathed deeply, savoring its freshness.

Their conversation on the way home was on desultory topics: the weather, cornhusking, and the corn crop itself. Pop found a certain rest of spirit in these commonplace things. No special thought, no strained moments were required. As they drove in the lane, the neighbor turned to him and asked how Mom was. They had been neighbors for ten years and, even if they were of different church affiliations, their friendship was genuine and solid. Pop appreciated his friend's concern, but he was beginning to dread the question.

He answered hesitantly, "About as well as can be expected. The doctor is going to operate tomorrow."

"John, I sure am sorry to hear that. Do they know what her trouble is?" He little realized the pain his question caused.

Pop sighed. What could he say? If it was best for Mom not to know, should he tell everyone else? They stopped in front of the gate now, and Pop got out of the car, glad to be home. The neighbor asked no more questions and Pop was relieved. After making arrangements to take him to the hospital in the afternoon, the neighbor left. Pop opened the gate and started slowly, wearily, up the walk to the house. At the steps he turned and gazed out over the landscape, bright in the hazy fall sunshine. The cornfields lay tawny and ripe, ample evidence of another good crop. The bright green of the alfalfa was slowly turning dark, showing signs of frost. It was the first year, for forty years at least, that had not found him in the cornfield, husking the rich golden ears. He had always enjoyed it. On crisp, cold mornings, the *bang, bang* of the corn in the empty wagon box had been music to his ears.

Those had been days of meditation, of quiet musings, or sometimes of good talks shared with one of his children. He had especially enjoyed the times when Martha had been his helper, finding in her nature resources so like his own. But all of his children had helped with the husking at one time or another.

Now that was over. Joe, like so many of the younger generation, looked with scorn upon shucking corn by hand. He made it plain that he wouldn't be caught at that back-breaking job. A picker was the thing for him. Even now Pop caught the distant roar of one going through the fields. Joe was exchanging work with a neighbor—unloading corn for him—and in return the neighbor was to pick Joe's corn. Pop sighed as he turned to go into the house. These things were bound to come; you couldn't expect the younger generation to be content with old standards. It was the age-old problem of the elder giving way to the younger.

He found the kitchen bright and tidy and Paul sitting at the table reading while waiting for the school bus. Paul looked up quickly from his book and met Pop's tired eyes.

"How is she?" he asked anxiously. His thin boyish face was strained. This illness of Mom's was beginning to tell on all of them. Besides, Paul was too young to be admitted to the hospital as a visitor and he hadn't seen Mom since she left home.

"About the same," Pop said as he sat down at the table. "Anything to eat around here?" he asked, rubbing his hand across his forehead.

"There should be." Paul got up and closed his book. "We ate a long time ago. Martha wanted to before she

238

left." He opened the cupboard door and got a box of cereal.

"Oh, that is enough," Pop assured him. "I don't want much—just a little before I go to sleep."

Paul went to the refrigerator and got the milk. As he did so, Pop noticed his thin, stooped shoulders. "Listen, boy," he said good-naturedly, "you read too much. You sit over a book so much you are getting stooped over before you're old. You'll have to watch that or I will have to put you to farming again."

Paul grinned. "Pop, you know I am not a farmer. Besides, I try to work after school as much as I can. I fixed fence for Joe last night."

Pop was putting heaping spoonfuls of sugar over his cereal. He liked it very sweet; it gave a man lots of energy. He thought of the times Mom had teased him about it in an amused, exasperated way. She always said he would end up with diabetes.

"Which fence?" Pop asked. With Mom sick he hadn't been looking after things as he usually did.

"The one down in the slough field. The cows broke a post down trying to get into the cornfield. Joe wants to get that field picked this week if he can. Says the cows need the pasture," Paul explained.

He was standing by the kitchen window now, watching for the school bus. It was time for it any minute. At that moment he heard it rumbling down the road. He quickly slipped into his coat, grabbed his lunch pail and his ever-present armful of books, and started out the door. "Good-by, Pop," he called and slammed the door behind him.

"Can't that boy watch out? He will break the glass in that door yet," Pop said impatiently, his words echoing through the empty house. He had finished eating now, and was ready for some sleep. He had dozed a little last night, but not enough to feel refreshed. The tiredness he felt creeping over him now was nothing compared to those times when he had worked hard all day long. This was fatigue not only of the body but of the soul and spirit as well. The words of the doctor echoed and re-echoed in his mind.

"I'm awfully afraid your wife has cancer."

Pop dropped wearily into his old hickory rocker and sat there with his chin in his hands, the picture of dejection. The stillness of the house was unbroken except for the tick of the clock in the kitchen, and the faint sputtering of the oil burner by his side. His spirit was too tired even to pray, although the silent cry of his soul was one unbroken prayer. Must Mom be taken from him? Or was he looking at the dark side of the picture without considering a very possible recovery? He hoped with all his heart that the doctor was wrong. He rubbed his eyes as he considered the events of the past night. At last he pulled off his shoes wearily and stumbled to bed.

At noon he was awakened by Rosie, who came over to invite him to her house for dinner. Pop wasn't much of a cook, she knew, and would probably appreciate a good hot meal. He could sleep again after dinner. Besides, she wanted to know how Mom was. When he had come home, she had been busy in the milkhouse and so had missed talking with him.

"Pop, wake up, and come on over to our house and eat dinner. Do you hear?"

He mumbled sleepily and Rosie repeated her invitation. Leaning on one elbow, he rubbed his eyes. Was it already dinnertime? He had only now dropped off to sleep!

"All right," he mumbled drowsily. "Go on over; I'm coming."

So Rosie went over to her own kitchen, cheerful and bright, to put the finishing touches to the dinner. Joe was already there, reading the daily paper. As Rosie passed behind his chair, she rubbed her hand over his cheek. Still reading his paper, he reached up and caught her hand, brushing it with his lips. Such things made her heart contract. She loved him dearly! As passionately as her strong nature insisted on its own way, so passionately did she love Joe. She put her arms around him and kissed the top of his head. Joe laid his paper down and pulled her around to his lap. Cradling her there for a moment he looked into her eyes. A beautiful girl, this wife of his! She needed a strong man to handle her, of course, but so far he didn't regret his choice. Now that they were expecting their first child, her beauty was intensified. None of that ill health so common to expectant women for her! She looked the picture of health with her pink cheeks and blue eyes. He kissed her tenderly, and she responded with a soft laugh.

"You had better let me down before I break you down," she said. "Besides, Pop will be coming soon."

Joe grinned and released her. "Go along with you then," he said. "Bothering a man when he is reading in peace and quiet!"

Rosie ruffled his well-combed hair and turned to the stove. She wanted dinner to be perfect, for Joe's sake and also to show Pop how good a cook she was. That Mom had doubts as to Rosie's ability to cook a full meal was well known to her; so she had worked hard at being a

241

good cook after her marriage. The delicious aroma of fried chicken floating through the house smelled every bit as good as any Mom had ever cooked. Rosie looked fondly around the kitchen. All the old furniture had been moved out and in its place were a new kitchen table and chairs and a lovely oil stove and refrigerator. With crisp white curtains at the window over the sink, it was a kitchen to make any bride's heart beat faster. She had worked hard to achieve a cheerful effect. In fact, she had remade the curtains twice before she was satisfied with them. All through the house the same fastidiousness could be observed. Rosie reveled in housekeeping.

Pop's footsteps sounded on the porch just as Rosie put the last of the food on the table. Sleep had refreshed him, although his eyes still had a discouraged look. It was lost on Rosie and Joe, however, absorbed as they were with each other. Joe greeted him pleasantly and motioned him to a chair at the table.

After Joe asked the blessing, Rosie inquired about Mom.

"She is about the same," Pop answered evasively, helping himself to the mashed potatoes. He used to have a big appetite, but the last few days food tasted flat.

"Do the doctors know what her trouble is yet?"

There it came again. How much should he tell them when they asked? It hardly seemed fair to Mom to tell others when she didn't know about it herself. He deliberated while putting gravy on his potatoes. "Well, I guess they have an idea," he said at last. "At least they are going to operate tomorrow."

"They are!" Rosie exclaimed. She looked at Pop searchingly. For the first time she noticed the deep lines in his face and was alarmed. Why, Pop looked positively old! Funny she had never noticed that before!

"When did you find out?" she asked.

Pop was busy buttering a piece of bread and kept his eyes on it as he answered. "Last night. I talked with the doctor when he made his rounds. He said if it was all right with me, they would operate tomorrow."

"Can they help her?"

Pop wished with all his heart he knew; wished he could tell everyone who asked that everything was going to be all right after the operation. He wished he had faith in it himself. "They think so," he replied. "They wouldn't operate if they didn't."

Seeing that he was reluctant to talk about it, Rosie asked no more questions. They ate in silence, Pop too occupied with his thoughts to make conversation. Toward the end of the meal he managed to ask Joe about the fence that had been mended and how the corn was doing.

"Bet I get eighty bushels an acre from that south field," Joe told him proudly. He loved farming as much as Rosie loved housekeeping.

Pop was glad Joe took an interest in the farm. It made it easier to hand the responsibility of it over to him when he saw that it would be in efficient hands.

"Yep, a really good crop this year. It should be enough to give me a big shove upward. Not bad for a start." Joe said it almost boastfully.

For some reason his words jarred Pop a little. It was as if Joe were taking all the credit for this year's good crop. Pop didn't like that attitude. Due credit should be given to the Lord. Weren't the times and seasons in His hands as were all good things? Pop decided to give Joe a gentle rebuke.

"Yes, it is good," he agreed quietly. "But we must remember that without God's great goodness we wouldn't have anything."

"Oh, sure, sure," Joe replied carelessly. "But being a good farmer is a big help."

Pop said nothing further. After all, if Joe couldn't see his debt to God any more than that, it would do no good to reprove him. They were finished with their meal now and, after returning thanks again, Joe pushed back his chair.

"Out to the cornfield for me. We finished Bill's field this morning and he is coming over to pick the south field this afternoon. I'd like to get that out this week if we can."

"Paul said you needed the pasture," Pop said understandingly.

"Yes, I do," Joe said. "I don't want to start feeding hay unless I have to, and now that the alfalfa has frozen, I don't like to pasture it."

"Getting time to have the corn out anyway," Pop observed, looking at the calendar on the wall above the kitchen table. "October is almost over."

"Yep, time sure flies," Joe said, his hand on the doorknob. Now that they were living alone, he rarely left the house for his work without giving Rosie a kiss, but with Pop here he decided against it. Instead, he contented himself with a kiss blown toward her while Pop was looking at the calendar. Rosie responded with uplifted eyebrows and a wonderful smile. The sound of the door as Joe left brought Pop back to the present. He had been counting the days since Mom had gotten sick. It had been over a week now, but it seemed much longer.

"Did Joe get our mail, too?" he asked, noticing the paper lying on the cupboard.

"Why, yes, didn't you see it?" Rosie asked in indifferent surprise. "I laid it on the kitchen table when I came over to wake you for dinner." She was slowly clearing the table now. Being a good cook made her eat too much, and eating too much in her condition made her sleepy and lazy. She wished she were finished with the dishes so that she could take a nap.

"Well, I guess I will go over home again," Pop said. "I will try to sleep some more, then go back to the hospital about four o'clock."

"I thought I would go along," Rosie said, "but I don't think I can stay as long as you do. Do you suppose I could go up with you and visit Mom a little and then come back with Martha?"

"I don't see why not," Pop replied. And so it was arranged.

Back at the little house, Pop picked up the mail Rosie had brought over. There were a number of cards for Mom, some advertisements, and the daily paper. Taking the cards into the living room, he sat down in the rocker and proceeded to open them. They were from friends, relatives, and neighbors, all wishing Mom a speedy recovery. Some had words of Scripture in them, which helped more than he could say. He bowed his head in silent prayer, thanking God for friends who cared, and asking Him to bless these kind ones for their concern.

There were a card and a letter from Thomas, and Pop read them eagerly. He was well and busy, and sorry to hear of Mom's illness. He hoped and prayed she would soon be better. He would try to get a weekend off before long and come home. Meanwhile they were to take care of themselves. That was all. Pop wished Thomas were more of a letter writer. His letters were always terse little notes, with no more in them than this one.

He picked up a big letter from Ervin and Alice and tore it open. There was a card for Mom with a letter, and then a small envelope which told Pop by its very size what it contained. Eagerly he opened it. Yes, he had another grandson, James Ervin. A pleased smile broke out on his face. Mom would be very happy to know this.

28

THE OPERATION was scheduled for nine o'clock the next morning, but long before that Mom was under the influence of sedatives—too much so to talk. Pop's vigil of the evening before had ended at midnight, when Mary and David had come to relieve him. He had spent the rest of the night in fits of restless sleep, ended completely with the first streaks of the fall's late dawn. He was at the hospital again by eight, skipping breakfast entirely.

He found Mom drowsy and unable to comprehend what he said. After a few attempts he gave up trying to make her understand and waited in dejected silence until the stretcher came to take her to the operating room. He was alone, as Martha had stayed at home to take care of Mary's little ones while Mary and David slept. They were all coming up at noon. Pop dreaded the idea of the long wait alone, but Paul was too young to be admitted, Joe too busy picking corn, and Rosie had to cook for the men. So he had been left without the comforting presence of any of the family.

After Mom disappeared behind the big double doors of the operating room, Pop wandered aimlessly down the long hall. Nurses and aides were busy, coming and going on swift, silent feet, bathing a patient here, making beds there. He felt out of place in the midst of so much feminine activity. Finally he went back to Mom's room and picked up his hat. Might just as well go out for a bit of fresh air, he thought. The odor of ether was already strong in the halls, and it made him feel light-headed.

He went across the street to a short-order place and ordered a cup of coffee, a roll, and a dish of cereal. While waiting for his order, his eyes roamed over the room. It was a small place—room for only two dozen customers at the most. At this hour it was almost empty, as breakfast was over and it was too early for the morning coffee break. The waitress was a brisk, elderly lady. As she talked to the cook in the back, Pop looked at her, almost without seeing her. His gaze shifted to the window, to the huge building of brick and stone that was Mercy Hospital. He could see the entrance from where he was seated, and noted that someone was coming or going constantly. He wondered how many of them were like him, heavyhearted because of some loved one who was sick, perhaps even in danger of death. God pity them, he thought. He was brought back to his surroundings by the waitress, who was placing his order before him.

"Do you have someone sick over there?" she asked kindly.

"My wife," Pop said quietly, pouring the cream into his coffee.

"Well, that is too bad," she sympathized. "What seems to be her trouble?"

That question again! Pop felt that courtesy demanded an answer, but what should he say? "Well—they aren't too sure," he replied evasively. "They are operating on her right now."

"Well, I sure hope she gets better soon," the lady said in friendly sincerity.

"Thanks," Pop said gratefully. He marveled at how the kind words of total strangers could help.

248

After eating, he felt much better and made his way back to the hospital. The big clock on the wall of the lobby said ten o'clock and Pop marveled that time could go so slowly. It seemed hours since Mom had been taken to the operating room. Picking up a newspaper from one of the tables, he tucked it under his arm as he waited for the elevator. He hoped the operation would soon be over.

There was a small lobby outside the operating room, where many an anxious person had waited long weary hours. Pop found it occupied with a young couple, worried and distraught in appearance. The man nodded to Pop and lighted a cigarette. Pop unfolded the newspaper and started to read. Perhaps if he started at the front and read the whole thing through, Mom would be out by the time he had finished. So he read in minute detail, slowly and deliberately. He even read the sports page, although he knew nothing whatever about sports. He read the classified ads, some of them twice.

When he finished and looked at his watch, he thought it must have stopped. He held it to his ear, but the steady ticking told him it was running. He sighed and put it back in his pocket. As he glanced at the young couple across from him, the man looked at him and smiled faintly.

"Time sure goes slow when you are waiting," he observed.

"Doesn't it though!" the man answered fervently.

"Have you got someone in there?" Pop asked, nodding in the direction of the operating rooms.

"Our boy," the man replied. He seemed glad to have someone to talk to.

"Anything serious?" Pop asked in friendly interest.

249

"Bad enough. He broke his leg last spring and it just won't heal. This is the second operation he's gone through since then," the man informed him.

"Well, that is too bad," Pop said in genuine sympathy. So many people in trouble! So many hearts burdened! "How old is he?" he asked, wanting to keep up the conversation.

"Eleven," the man answered, stubbing out his cigarette in the ash tray beside him. "He is the only child we have. Who have you got in there?" he asked Pop. He didn't seem quite so nervous now that he had someone to talk to.

"My wife."

"That is too bad." The man looked at his own wife and smiled. At least he was sharing a vigil with his wife, not waiting endless hours for her.

"What's your wife's trouble?" The wife spoke up for the first time.

Pop was tired of evading that question. After all, he would probably never meet these people outside the hospital again. "Cancer," he said quietly.

The woman spoke in a quick, troubled voice. "I'm sorry. I mean, I shouldn't have asked."

"It's all right," Pop assured her earnestly. "You couldn't have known, of course."

"Well, surely she can be helped," the woman said, trying to think of something comforting to say. "I mean, they can do such wonderful things nowadays."

"I hope so." Pop met her eyes, then looked down at his hands. "But sometimes I'm afraid." He stopped. The man and woman were silent. What could one say? After a moment Pop spoke again. "But whether the Lord will be so good as to give her her health back, or if He will

250

call her home, I don't know. She would be better off at home with the Lord, but—" Again he stopped. "Yes, she would be," his heart was crying silently, "but what about me? What will I do if she dies? God, have you thought about that?"

The couple looked at each other self-consciously. Simple faith like this was out of their line. The man cleared his throat, then said in an embarrassed voice, "Well, I guess one would be better off if life were all over but—well, most people don't think of those things if they can help it."

Pop nodded. How right the man was! Only the bare essential facts made them think of an afterlife. But what had he said—about being better off dead? Pop felt he had better make his meaning clear.

"I said my wife would be better off if she died, but I am sorry to say that many people wouldn't be," he said gravely.

"I don't quite get your meaning," the man said nervously. He ran his hand through his hair with a jerky motion.

"What I mean is that my wife has taken Christ as her personal Saviour, and if she dies, God tells me in His Word that she will go to Heaven. But that is the only way she will get there!"

The man shook his head, perplexity written on his face. He exchanged a quick nervous look with his wife. He wondered if this was a religious crank and if they had better go.

Pop, seeing that his reply had cast doubts in the man's mind about his sanity, hastened to assure him. "Oh, don't think I am crazy," he said quickly. "All I have been telling you is in the Bible. Do you read it?"

"Well, no, we don't." The man was ill at ease before

him. "We just don't seem to be very religious. I know you people are, but—" Again he trailed off into nervous silence. He wished he could light a cigarette again, but with this man talking about God, he felt he shouldn't.

"Here's a little book I would like to give you," Pop said, holding a tract out to the man. "It tells you what I was talking about in better words than I can. Won't you please take it and read it?" The man reached out slowly and took the proffered tract. He turned it around and read the title, "The Way to Life."

Just then the big operating room doors opened, and a stretcher was wheeled through them. All three were on their feet instantly. It was the eleven-year-old boy, and Pop sank back in his chair, sick with disappointment. The parents were by the side of their boy at once, the woman laughing and crying at the same time. There was no sign of recognition on the boy's face, but Pop heard the nurse say, "We will take him back to his room and he will come around before too long." Her voice grew fainter as she pushed the stretcher up the hall. The woman left without a backward look, but the man turned back to Pop.

"Thanks for everything," he said simply. "I will read the booklet you gave me."

"You do that," Pop answered, thankful, at least, that it hadn't been given back to him. "I sure hope your boy recovers now."

"Thank you. I hope your wife is okay, too." The man turned and left, leaving Pop alone once more. He listened to the sound of their foosteps becoming less audible in the distance. Then he pulled out his watch again. Mom had been in there two hours now. How much longer would it be? He wondered when the others would come. Probably not until after dinner. He glanced around the little waiting room. There wasn't much to see: a few chairs, a table with magazines, and that was all. Getting up, he wandered over to the window. There were cars coming and going, people hurrying along with brisk steps, dogs wandering about, looking for a bit of adventure. Most of the trees now stood half naked, their branches reaching to the sky like so many arms outstretched toward heaven. The hospital was situated on a hill, and the streets stretched down to the river in the distance. The sky was overcast, and Pop wondered if it was going to rain. He hoped Joe would get that field of corn picked today. Tomorrow was Sunday and the last day of October. The days faded into each other up here; they were all so much alike that one almost lost track of them. Watching, waiting, eating odd meals, sleeping in snatches—that was all life consisted of for Pop.

He sighed and turned from the window. He hated the idea of waiting here alone. Maybe he could go outside for a walk again. He had almost decided to go when the thought struck him that maybe Mom would be brought out and he wouldn't be here. He hesitated. If only someone would come out of those big mysterious doors and tell him that Mom was all right—that she was going to be just fine! But no one came. Wearily he picked up his hat and started down the hall. If Mom was out of the operating room on his return, it would be a welcome surprise; if not, there would be more weary waiting.

The brisk air made him gasp when the glass door of the lobby swung shut behind him. He had to step lively to keep from getting chilled. There was even a faint suggestion of snow in the air, just enough to give him the delightful anticipation of it. He quickened his pace and walked down the street with brisk, sure strides.

While walking he lost track of the time and must have been gone an hour before he thought of turning back. He was downtown by now, and more tired than he cared to admit. Slowly he retraced his steps and was very glad to turn the corner and see the large building rise up before him. As he entered the lobby he glanced at the big clock again. Twelve-thirty! He hastened over to the elevator, hoping against hope that the operation was over. There was another man in the small waiting room now, a complete stranger to him. Pop hesitated on seeing him, then asked in a breathless voice, "Have you been here long?"

"About an hour," he answered, glancing at his wristwatch.

"Has anyone come out of there?" Pop pointed toward the big doors.

"Not since I have been here," the man said. "You have someone in there?"

"My wife," Pop said listlessly, dropping into a chair. "She has been there since nine o'clock this morning."

"That's too bad," the man spoke softly.

Pop settled back and closed his eyes. Martha and the others weren't here yet either. "Dear heavenly Father, how long will she be in there?" he prayed silently. "It must be awfully serious if it takes this long."

He sat for a long time, his head back and his eyes closed. Finally the big doors swung open and a stretcher was wheeled out. Pop was on his feet in an instant and at the side of the stretcher. He almost cried with relief when he saw Mom's unconscious face. The rise and fall of her chest told him she was breathing. The nurse in attendance looked at Pop with professional interest.

"Is this your wife?" she asked.

Pop nodded. The lump in his throat wouldn't let him talk.

"We will take her back to her room and let her recover. She will be coming out of it before long."

Just then the door swung open again, and the doctor, seeing Pop, called out, "John, I would like to talk with you." He sounded tired.

Pop walked slowly toward him, not without a longing backward look at Mom, who was being wheeled quietly up the hall. The doctor held the big door open, and Pop stepped into the sacred precinct. It looked just like the hall outside, he noted in surprise. There were doors leading here and there, and Pop knew that somewhere behind one of them, Mom had spent the last three and a half hours. He followed the doctor into a little private office, and the doctor closed the door after him and motioned him to a chair. He dropped into one himself and faced Pop, distress written plainly on his face.

"John, I wish with all my heart I had better news for you," he began hesitantly. "But I am afraid it isn't encouraging. It was cancer, all right. We did what we could, but I doubt if it did any good. The thing was too far advanced already." He ran his fingers through his hair wearily.

Pop sat very still, with the foolish notion that if he moved, he would scream. The room seemed to be going around. At last he ran his tongue over his dry lips and asked, "Will she die?"

The doctor propped his elbows on the desk and buried

his face in his hands. "I am afraid it is not cured, any-way," he said dejectedly through his fingers. These things almost made him wish he were a ditchdigger.

"How long?" Pop asked, meaning how long might she live.

"Six months, a year at the most."

For a while they sat in silence, the doctor with his dejected thoughts and Pop too stunned to think. At last the doctor continued, "We will keep her here until the effect of the operation wears off; then I would advise you to take her home and take care of her there. There is no use making needless expense for you."

Pop nodded, barely hearing him. His mind was going in circles, trying to grab a fragment of hope. "Could any other doctor help her?" he asked after a moment.

"Frankly no, John. You could find so-called specialists who would make wild claims, of course, but don't listen to them. Your wife has had some of the best cancer specialists, and they say the same. Two of them looked in on this case this morning, in fact. So I wouldn't advise you to spend time and money looking for relief. There's just nothing more to be done."

As the doctor spoke these words, all hope fled from Pop's heart forever. Then and there he gave in to the inevitable. "Thy will, not mine, O Father," he prayed in silent submission. "But, oh, how can I live without her?"

"Believe me, I am sorry, John. Before the operation, after we were pretty sure she had cancer, I felt quite confident that we could help her. But the operation showed us we couldn't. As I said, it was too far advanced."

Pop was looking down at the floor. He felt too utterly

dejected to look the doctor in the eye. "Shall I tell her?" he roused himself to ask.

"That is just as you wish," the doctor said. He was toying with a pen, keeping his eyes on that. "If you think she would rather know, then tell her. You know her temperament better than I do."

Pop nodded, and, knowing Mom, he decided she would rather be told. But not now, his heart cried out. Wait until she comes home.

"I will do all I can to make her last days as bearable as I can, John. She will have all the medicines at our disposal for this. Even so, I must warn you, she will have some very bad days."

Pop nodded dully. He was well aware of that. One of the elders of the church had died of cancer two years ago—a slow, painful death.

The doctor arose, and Pop got stiffly to his feet, too. It surprised him to find strength in his legs. Then another thought came to him and he almost dropped down again. "How can I meet her, knowing this?" he cried in agony. The doctor put a kindly hand on his elbow.

"She will be too much under the influence of drugs to more than notice you for the next few days. By then you will have gotten a grip on yourself."

Pop nodded, relieved. The doctor opened the door of the small office and waited until Pop passed through. "Did you think she was never going to get out of here?" he asked kindly, as he closed the door and followed Pop down the hall to the big double doors leading to the main corridor.

Pop smiled thinly. "Yes, I did," he admitted.

"We had her in a recovery room for about an hour

257

before we took her out. We wanted to be sure everything was all right."

They were at the doors now, and the doctor pushed them open with his shoulder, allowing Pop to pass through. The doors swung shut behind them and they were out in the hall, the small waiting room before them. It was full of people, and, seeing that, the doctor took his leave, bidding Pop a kindly good-by. After he had gone, Pop started slowly up the hall to Mom's room.

29

TEN DAYS AFTER the operation Mom was home again. It was good to be at home! Her soft bed felt like the finest of down after the hard hospital bed. And how things had changed since that pain-filled night only three short weeks ago! Here it was almost the middle of November and only a few weeks until Thanksgiving. The early frost had long since stolen away the lovely green grass and leaves, leaving the trees mostly bare, and the grass sere and brown. The corn was picked and the yard raked. Winter was just around the corner, to be sure.

Not once since the operation had Mom bothered to ask what it revealed. It was a relief to Pop, who lived in dread lest she ask and he would have to tell her. The idea of lying to her was unthinkable; so the truth would have to be told. At times his conscience bothered him and he felt he should tell her. But each time he thought desperately, "Not now! Not yet! There is plenty of time."

Mom was, of course, confined to her bedroom, but made no more trouble than was necessary. Nevertheless everyone was conscious of her illness. Martha stopped helping Mary, now that she was needed at home. Pop willingly did all he could. It helped just to have him sit in the bedroom and entertain Mom.

None of the family, except Pop, really knew about her condition. Martha opened the subject one time, but soon discovered that he was reluctant to talk about it. To the great delight of all, however, Mom seemed to be making some progress, and by Thanksgiving was able to walk to the kitchen for dinner. The afternoon brought a houseful of callers; so she stayed up. Among others who called were David and Mary, who of course brought the children along. Mom was so glad to see them that she insisted on holding either Philip or Bethy all afternoon. Seeing that she was almost her old self again, Pop hoped—a wild, desperate hope—that the doctor was mistaken after all, and that she was going to be all right. The evening brought a letdown, however, for after the callers were gone, she was so tired that it took both Pop and Martha to get her to bed; and once there she sighed—a long-drawn-out sigh.

"I'm so glad they all left," she murmured, meaning the callers. "They made me so tired, even if I was glad to see them."

"Why didn't you tell us?" Pop asked in tender solicitude. "We would have been glad to put you back to bed. We don't want you overdoing yourself."

"I didn't want to make any bother," she said. "I make you all so much the way it is."

"Oh, Mom," Pop protested, "you know you don't!" He almost said they might not have the chance much longer.

Just then Martha came in with a cup of steaming broth and a slice of toast for Mom's supper. When she had finished eating, Pop carried her tray out to the kitchen, where Martha had supper ready for the rest of the family. Later, when Pop went into the bedroom, he found her fast asleep.

As the Christmas season approached, Mom was seized with an irresistible longing to have the whole family together again. True, they had all been together at Ervin and Alice's wedding a little over a year ago, but she

260

wanted them all around her this year for Christmas. Then, too, she wanted to see her new grandson, James Ervin.

Thomas' letters were short and sketchy, revealing very little. He had not been able to come home for a weekend, as he had hoped to do, and they were all disappointed. He still had another six months to serve of his two-year term. What his plans were after that was unknown to them. They wondered if he knew himself. He had been writing to a girl from home, Lydia Schrock, ever since his departure, and so chances were he might get married soon after his discharge.

Of course, Mom had the others around her and she thanked God every day for them. Martha was there, taking loving care of her constantly, and Rosie and Mary were apt to drop in any minute of the day, often bringing some delicacy to tempt her waning appetite. Paul, the baby of them all, grown thin and tall, had formed the habit of coming into her bedroom every evening, to share the day's school news with her. She treasured all these things in her heart, finding in them more than compensation for her constant weakness and dull pain.

That she had pain could not be denied, although she admitted it to no one but herself. If the others asked, she gave them a light, evasive answer. No use making them worry over her more than necessary, she thought. Besides, it made her nervous to have people so concerned about her. Hitherto, she had been the one concerned about the others. Mom, not realizing it, was a good example of the Scripture which says, "He that is greatest among you shall be your servant."

Pop wrote to Ervin and Thomas, asking them, begging them, if at all possible, to come home for Christmas.

261

Some of his personal urgency must have been conveyed to both of them, because they wrote back and assured him they would certainly be there, barring sickness or accident,

The family plunged into preparations for the coming holidays immediately. Mom sent Pop on innumerable shopping trips. She wanted to get every one of them a gift. It wasn't hard to choose for the grandchildren: a wagon for Johnny, a doll buggy for Bethy, a noisy little train for Philip, a beautiful crib blanket fortified with some rattles for James Ervin, and that was done. The men weren't hard to buy for either; Mom decided on white shirts for each of them. But it was hard to decide what to buy for the girls. They had all the houseware they needed, those who were keeping house; and towels—they had all they needed of those. She finally decided on dress material; what woman couldn't use another dress? But Pop gave up now, protesting that he didn't know dress material from gunnysack material, and so Mom called in the faithful neighbor lady for help. One day when Martha had gone to town to do her own Christmas shopping, the neighbor came and Mom confided her preferences to her. The lady was happy to be of some help and vowed to do her best. A few days later she sent Mom a note, enclosing a sample of the material purchased—a lovely dark blue. The neighbor would cut the material in proper lengths and wrap it.

Mom looked forward to the holidays with all the anticipation of a child. She urged Martha to bake cookies and to make candy: the dark chocolate fudge, thick with nuts, which was Ervin's favorite, and the creamy white divinity so loved by Thomas. Pop helped with the candymaking, licking the spoon for reward. Martha kept a plateful on the library table for pre-Christmas sampling, finding it empty every evening after Paul went to bed.

The last few days were filled with activity. Rosie helped Martha dress a plump young turkey, purchased from the neighbor who raised them. They baked the family's favorite pies, mince and raisin. Pop laid in a store of nuts and candies, also a bushel of apples and a crate of oranges, in anticipation of callers over the holidays. And at last came the day before Christmas, with Thomas arriving in the morning and Ervin and Alice and James at noon. Ervin and Alice had driven the twelve hundred miles in their car, with baby James in a basket in the back seat. They were tired from driving and happy to be home at last.

Mom was so glad to see them that she laughed and cried at the same time. She was able to be up and around part of the day, and was sitting in the rocker in the living room when they came. She fell on Ervin's neck with a glad cry, and Ervin's arms went convulsively around her. She looked so white and thin! So many lines in her face! He held her away and looked at her with a lump in his throat.

"What have you been doing to yourself?" he demanded in loving tones. "Why, you are wasting away to a shadow!"

"Doing to myself," Mom echoed happily, still clutching his hand tightly. "Why, I'm being so lazy I am ashamed of myself. But where is that baby? I didn't want to see you just to talk about myself."

Ervin picked up the basket from the chair where he had put it at sight of Mom. Alice reached over quickly and picked up the tiny bundle possessively, her face the picture of tender motherlove. Rosie, looking on, felt a stab of jealous anticipation. In a few short weeks, she too would be a mother.

Alice handed little James over to Mom for inspection and Mom reached out eagerly and took him into her arms, sinking back into her chair to exclaim and croon over him. He opened his eyes wide and looked at her.

"Oh, isn't he the sweetest thing!" she exclaimed, forgetting that she had said the same thing about all the others. It was decided that he had Ervin's nose and Pop's chin, with Alice's looks across the eyes. All at once, as if resentful of being criticized, he broke into loud wails.

"He didn't like to have it said he looked like everyone else," Pop said, chuckling.

Before they knew it, the day was over. They retired rather early, because the travelers were tired from driving the night before. The home folks were tired, too, a happy fatigue from all the preparations of the preceding days. Besides, they wanted to get up early the next morning and get ready for church. Ervin looked forward to seeing his old friends once more and Thomas to seeing his chums. Thomas had left in the evening to see Lydia, first getting an invitation from Martha for Lydia to be there for the next day's festivities. Martha laughed good-naturedly at him when she extended the invitation. She was not above a bit of teasing. Although there was no special one for her any more, it didn't make her unresponsive to the love lives of others.

The next day was perfect, clear and cold, with a light blanket of snow on the ground. There was a pleasant rush in the morning to get breakfast over, with Mom reveling in it. Doors opened and banged shut. There were quick footsteps all through the house. Thomas and Ervin made innumerable trips upstairs.

At last they were ready to go, all except Pop, who was staying at home with Mom, and Rosie, who wasn't going any more, because the baby was due before long. Rosie was going to watch the turkey in the oven and set the tables while the others were gone. The potatoes were peeled and soaking in cold water, and the dressing was mixed and ready for last-minute baking. Dinner would be on the table soon after they returned from church.

David preached the sermon that morning, and how Ervin did enjoy it! It was the first time he had heard him preach, and he bowed his head and prayed silently that David might truly be used of the Lord in his home congregation; and that these people might serve the Lord instead of the traditions of dead forefathers. After the services, many old friends and acquaintances came to shake hands and exchange a few words with Ervin, most of them extending an invitation to visit them.

When they got home, the delicious aroma of turkey made their mouths water as soon as they opened the door. The men retired to the living room to talk while the women got dinner on the table. Mom had Pop pull her rocker into the big kitchen, where she could watch the activity freely. She held little James as much as she could, with Bethy a shy onlooker. Philip refused to be held, preferring to scatter the contents of the toy box all over the living room floor.

At last dinner was ready and, after the hushed moment when Pop asked the blessing, they all did justice to the good meal before them. Even Mom ate considerably more than she usually did. Occasionally, while the others were eating, she leaned back and regarded them all in grateful appreciation. They were all there with her: Mary and David with Philip between them and Johnny and Bethy at their sides. Johnny was a big boy now, almost ready to start to school. Bethy was still a dainty little lady, although no longer a baby. And Philip was solid and calm.

Next to them were Alice and Ervin. How glad Mom was to see them again! Alice was as beautiful as ever, although a little inclined to plumpness. Farther up was Thomas, with Joe beside him. To the left of Pop was Paul, and Mom smiled in fond amusement as her eyes fell on his heaping plate. The boy seemed to live to eat. To Mom's right was Rosie, looking prettier than ever. Mom caught her exchanging glances with Joe across the table more than once. Thomas' girl friend, Lydia, was sitting beside Rosie, blushing and shy. She was not as pretty as some, but would probably make a good wife. They were both sincere Christians, the Lord be praised. Martha sat at the end where she could wait on the table. From the bottom of her heart Mom thanked God for her. What would they do without her these days? She wondered what God had in store for Martha; surely not just staying at home and taking care of them the rest of her life.

After the dishes were done came the climax of the day. How Mom did enjoy Johnny's shout of joy when he saw the red wagon, and Bethy's happy smile when she was presented with the doll buggy! Philip took the train in stride, although he proceeded to make a deafening racket with it at once. And the girls were all delighted with their dress material.

There were other presents, too. Thomas self-consciously handed a gift to each one. There was a soft, warm, dark shawl for Mom, just the thing to put around her shoulders when she sat up. For Pop there was a box of his favorite candy, which brought a chuckle from him. He immediately passed it around to the others, who nibbled at it with sated appetites. There were sewing baskets in different colors for Rosie, Mary, and Alice. Then there was a new purse for Martha. Her old one, Thomas explained, was wearing out from carrying all her money around.

When the last gift had been unwrapped, Mary and David had to leave for home to do their chores. Rosie and Joe, too, left for home, their arms heaped high with presents. Martha and Alice set about to bring order to the house, which was in a state of utter confusion. Mom surveyed it all with a contented sigh. It had been such a wonderful day. She was tired now, however, and Pop helped her to bed, where she was content to stay the rest of the day.

Much to the folks' disappointment, Ervin and Alice could stay only three days. Because of the great distance involved, over half of their vacation had to be spent on the road. Very little mention was made of Mom's illness, and Pop, seeing her up and around most of the time, kept on hoping that she might be all right after all. He pushed the doctor's verdict resolutely to the back of his mind. Only on the last day of Ervin's visit did he look at it squarely, and that was when Ervin bluntly asked him what her trouble was.

They were out in the barn, standing in the feed alley at the time. Pop picked up a piece of straw and sighed deeply. "Cancer," he answered slowly. All the cares and anxieties of the last months came back swiftly.

"Oh, no!" Erwin exclaimed in dismay.

Pop nodded without looking up from the straw.

"Didn't the operation help?"

There was a bale of hay behind him and Pop dropped down onto it. The thought of it made his legs weak and tired. "No, I guess not. It was too far gone by then.

You know how Mom is—won't go to the doctor until she has to."

"Did the doctor say how long she has to live?"

"Six months; a year at the most." Pop spoke dully. He was sitting with his head propped on one hand, the other aimlessly playing with the straw, his eyes downcast.

Ervin was silent for a moment, meditating. His heart went out to Pop, although he hid his emotion. "Does she know?"

Pop dropped the straw and buried his face in both hands. "I can't bring myself to tell her," he said brokenly. "I thought I would long before this, but I just can't." He broke down completely now, and his tall, broad frame shook with sobs. Ervin's eyes were wet, too.

After a moment, Pop's sobs subsided. "I know she is right with the Lord and ready to go," he said, putting his handkerchief back in his pocket. "That doesn't bother me. The thing that hurts me the most is the idea of what she is going to have to go through before death comes. You know how cancer patients suffer." Ervin nodded, speechless before such love and emotion. "I pray that God will give her grace and spiritual strength to endure, and that He might not allow it to be so painful. Or if it is, that He might be very near to her. I am praying most of the time, in my heart," Pop said simply.

For a long moment they were both silent, Ervin leaning against the manger, staring at the chaff-strewn ground, and Pop gazing at his hands, folding and refolding his fingers. The barn was silent, except for the sound of the horses munching hay. A little banty rooster, who made his home above the horses, crowed in triumphant well-being. Ervin smiled thinly, looking up at him roosting above Pop's faithful driving horse. He stooped down and picked up a corncob, and threw it with good aim. Banty gave a terrific squawk and flew to the other end of the barn, cackling and squawking as he went. Ervin laughed in spite of himself. Even Pop chuckled.

"Still like to tease my banty," he remarked amusedly.

"They are funny—always making a big fuss about nothing. Do you still have some around? You said Joe didn't like them."

"He doesn't. We only have this rooster. I kind of like to have him around, just to hear him crow."

Pop got up from the bale of hay. Maybe they should go back to the house again, he thought. Mom might be needing something. As he stepped forward, Ervin laid a hand on his shoulder, detaining him.

"Pop, you said you were praying for Mom. Well, I would like you to know that I'm going to be praying for the same things for her as you are."

They were looking deep into each other's eyes, not as father and son, but as man to man. "You know what the Bible says about prayer, Pop," Ervin went on earnestly, his hand still on Pop's shoulder. "I mean, where it says, 'If two of you shall agree on earth as touching any thing that they shall ask, it shall be done for them of my Father which is in heaven.'" Pop nodded. "Well, Pop, right here I want to say that those things you mentioned that you were praying for for Mom, such grace for her, and that God might be very near to her—well, I will be praying for them for her, too."

"Thank you," Pop said, his voice almost breaking again. "I will remember that." Involuntarily their hands clasped, their eyes bright with emotion. "And when you are praying for her, don't forget me," Pop said simply.

"I won't forget." Ervin gave his hand a hard squeeze and added, "You pray for us, too."

"I will. I always do anyway. My children's welfare, especially their spiritual welfare, is very precious to me."

Perhaps never again would these two be as close to each other as they were now. The common bond of the shared knowledge of Mom's illness, together with being brothers in Christ, drew them closer together than ever before.

"Have you told any of the others?" Ervin asked, as they started to the house.

"No, I haven't," Pop said heavily. "I want to tell Thomas before he leaves; then I guess I will tell the others, too. At times she seems to be getting along so good that I think maybe the doctor was mistaken after all. It is easy to believe she will be getting better."

"Didn't he give you any hope at all?"

Pop shook his head. They were at the gate now, and he put out his hand to lift the latch. "He said I might just as well face it, and not keep on looking for someone to help her. He said she had some of the best doctors in this part of the country look at her, and they said the same thing."

They were on the porch now and neither said any more about it. There was little in Ervin's leave-taking early the next morning to reveal his knowledge: only a suggestion of brightness in his eyes as he bade Mom good-by, and when he shook Pop's hand for the last time. Then they drove off in the early morning darkness.

30

AFTER THE CHRISTMAS SEASON was over, with the stimulation of the children's presence gone, Mom kept to her bed more. Besides, the pain was gradually getting worse. But she kept her pains to herself. It had always annoyed her to hear some people make a fuss about their aches and pains, real or imaginary, and she was determined not to be like them. But watching her as closely as they did, they noticed a more subdued spirit at times. It filled Pop with heaviness and dread, which told on him as time went on. He lost weight and his clothes hung loosely on his big broad-shouldered frame. The lines in his face deepened and that, coupled with his flowing gray beard, made him look like one of the patriarchs of old.

Martha noticed the gradual decline in Mom. It was impossible not to, with the daily care of her. Mom protested less and less about being taken care of. This in itself was an indication that something was wrong. In the old days she took care of herself and everybody else. Now to have her quietly submit to constant care, even if ever so lovingly given, just wasn't natural. Martha finally confided her feelings to Pop.

They were on their way to town, as they each had an appointment with the dentist. Rosie had volunteered to stay with Mom while they were gone. It was the week after New Year's Day and Pop wanted to get his income tax figured, too. They had been riding along in silence for a while, Martha vaguely troubled about Mom. At last she spoke. "Why doesn't Mom get any better? The week Ervin and Thomas were home she seemed so much improved, but since they are gone she seems to get worse instead of better. What's wrong?"

Pop sighed. He might just as well tell her; she had a right to know. But how he dreaded telling her! It seemed as if every time he told anyone, he had to relinquish his hold on Mom a little more. He blew his nose before replying. "Your mom has cancer," he answered at last.

"Oh, Pop, no!" Martha protested in shocked voice, lifting her eyes to his.

Pop nodded.

"Didn't the operation help?"

"She was too far gone, the doctor said. You know how Mom is—never goes to a doctor until she has to."

Martha's eyes filled with tears and she reached blindly into her purse for a handkerchief. "Isn't there any hope at all?" she asked through her tears. Pop shook his head. He felt like crying himself. He cleared his throat gruffly.

"The doctor said there isn't," he said in a husky voice.

"How much time did he give her to live?"

"He said six months or so; a year at the most."

Both were silent for a while, each with his own thoughts. Martha's mind was racing around like a squirrel, trying to convince herself it was all a dream. Why must God ask her to give up her loved ones? First Daniel, now Mom. She had just gotten to the place where she could look back on Daniel's death calmly, leaving it all in God's hands, and now she was being asked to give up another. It hardly seemed fair. For the first time in months, Martha felt a tinge of bitterness against the workings of God. Some people had so much and didn't appreciate it, while she was being compelled to give what

272

little she had. The realization of what Mom had done for her, had suffered for her and with her, came over her like a flood. If Pop hadn't been with her, she would have broken into a storm of weeping. Even so, she cried silently, heartbroken. Pop sat beside her in dumb suffering. Martha's nature was so like his own, he could understand a little how she felt. At her age, he would have taken such a thing just as hard. They rode in silence, the only sound being the squeak of the buggy wheels across the frozen snow. They came in sight of the town, nestled in the valley below them, before she spoke again. "Will she get worse and worse then, until the end?"

"I am afraid so."

"Oh, Pop, how can you stand it?"

"God helps me carry the load. I couldn't get along without Him."

* * *

Rosie's baby—a girl—was born the first week in February, and Rosie surprised Martha no end by naming her Martha Ann. Martha was touched; a namesake was nice to have. The care of the helpless little one was the sweetest joy Rosie had ever experienced. So jealous was she of its care that she would have no one help her. She kept it spotless, changing gowns two or three times a day. Usually, after the first few weeks, she brought it proudly over to the other house every day for Mom to see. Mom enjoyed it at first, but as the days passed into April and May and Martha Ann still took no notice of anyone, and made no progress beyond a very few aimless movements, Mom's heart began to be troubled. Was something wrong with the child? Her own children were so long grown she had forgotten about their development, but surely Mary's children hadn't been so passive and quiet at

273

that age. Johnny could sit up alone at the age of five months. Seeing the joy Rosie took in the baby, however, and hating to cause needless worry, Mom kept her thoughts to herself.

Then, too, life was becoming more of a burden every day. Pain was her constant companion, although at times it wasn't so bad. Some of the better days she teased and joked and laughed about everything, until those around her were on the brink of forgetting about her illness.

Pop had told all the family about her condition. Mary wept and resigned herself, but Rosie, in whom life was making itself felt so heavily, refused to believe it at first. How could one talk of death and Mom together? Mom wasn't old enough to die, being only in her fifties!

One night, a short time later, when sleep refused to come to Mom because of the pain, Pop told her. It all came about so naturally. He had been reading to her out of his well-worn Bible, a chapter here, a few verses there, when suddenly she said, "John, read the fourteenth chapter of John for me, about the mansions, please."

He turned to it and began reading in a steady voice: " 'Let not your heart be troubled: ye believe in God, believe also in me. In my Father's house are many mansions: if it were not so, I would have told you. I go to prepare a place for you. And if I go and prepare a place for you, I will come again, and receive you unto myself; that where I am, there ye may be also.' "

" 'That where I am, . . . ye may be also,' " Mom broke in softly. "John, I love those words. Where He is, I shall be also. I think that is going to be before too long." She said it quietly, almost dreamily.

Pop sat motionless, hardly breathing. Then she knew. He reached up and rubbed his hand over his eyes. "Then you know?" he asked huskily.

"Know what?" She turned toward him.

"That you have cancer and you can't expect to live long." He was almost breathless.

"Is that what's the matter with me? I should have known." She seemed almost indifferent about it. She lay with her eyes closed for so long Pop began to think she had fallen asleep. He stirred slightly and the rocker squeaked. She opened her eyes again and met his gaze, smiling tremulously. "It's quite a blow, isn't it?" she asked softly, lovingly.

Pop nodded mutely. She reached out her hand, and his own big one closed over it tightly. True to her nature, she was comforting him, he thought. And he should be the one to be doing the comforting.

"God will help you bear it," she said, her eyes looking deep into his. He nodded, tears in his eyes.

Summer came, and Mom, seeing it, perhaps for the last time, felt the bittersweet pangs of a godly person who knows his days are numbered. There was sadness in the thought of leaving loved ones behind, yet her soul longed for release from her earthly pain. "Someday," she thought, "my spirit will escape my body and there won't be any stopping it." Then, too, the longing to see her dear Saviour's face at last, the One whom she had loved so long without seeing, was like an ache. This was especially true when she suffered intense pain both day and night. If at all possible, she kept silent, for the sake of the family. Only when it was at its worst did a groan escape her lips. At such times the family listened, heartsick at their inability to help her. They went about the house on tiptoe, fearing the slightest jar would intensify the pain.

There were days when the pain subsided and they spent as much time as possible together. There were moments of ordinary life which carried them over the troubled times. There were friends who called and brought gifts, and every day brought a handful of cards and letters, which helped to pass the time. Evenings, after school, Paul came in and shared his bits of school news, something he had never done when good health kept her too busy to listen. They held their morning devotions every day around her bedside. The thought of her certain departure was always in the back of their minds; consequently the words of the Scripture leaped into life before them, in a way not possible in ordinary times. They comforted them and strengthened them in a way never possible when life was smooth.

Pop had long since ceased wondering what he would do without Mom. His constant prayer was for her, that she be comforted and given grace and strength for this ordeal. What did it matter what happened to him? If only he might, by sheer force of will, be able to transfer that pain to his own body, how gladly he would suffer it for her!

Seeing Mom suffer and grow thin and hollow-eyed awakened in Martha the old painful question. Why? Why must Mom suffer so? Why must she, Martha, be called upon to give up another loved one? Why did God do this? Daniel's death had been a shock, knocking her off her spiritual balance by the very suddenness of it, but this was different. On the worst days, Martha felt as if she were a piece of taffy being pulled apart and folded, pulled apart and folded, and for what reason? What was there in suffering and sorrow that God deemed it such a necessary part of His children's lives?

276

31

MARTHA GAVE the porch swing a shove with her foot and swung softly in the warm June dusk. It had been a hot day, the first one of the season, more miserable because they were not used to it. From the other house she heard the thin, fretful wail of little Martha Ann, who felt the heat and responded with heat rash. Martha sighed. Poor little thing! With all the other troubles she was beset with, heat rash seemed like the last straw. For unquestionably Rosie's baby was abnormal. Even Rosie had to admit that it was not as strong as other babies, although she refused to admit that it was abnormal. From the bedroom inside, Martha heard Pop's low voice speaking softly and Mom's higher voice reply.

Again Martha sighed. She wondered how much longer Mom could be with them. It was getting to the point where they were looking for death any day. Martha felt more like a piece of taffy than ever. Her spirit was weary and heartsick, trying to see the loving hand of God in this, and yet at the same time having a desperate, unanswerable cry in her heart. Why do we have to go through this? Why just especially us? Why? Why does a loving God twist our hearts and bruise our spirits? These last few days had been the worst Mom had gone through. Pain had fastened its dreadful, racking claws on her until she cried out in agony. All anyone could do was stand by and watch her suffer. Pop was as nearly skin and bones as Mom was, and Martha grew thin and pale with great hollows under her eyes. Even Paul had lost his appetite.

The headlights of a car came up the lane, the bright beam interrupting her thoughts. It was probably the neighbor, who had kindly offered to stay with Mom part of the night. Martha and Pop had been up the last two nights and the lack of sleep added to their weariness.

The car stopped before the gate and the neighbor lady got out and came up the walk. Martha was too tired to get up. The lady saw her there and asked in a kindly voice, "Cooling off after the heat?"

Martha smiled, "Yes, I guess so."

"How is your mother?"

"About the same," Martha answered wearily. The light from the kitchen shone on the porch, making soft squares of light. The neighbor stood for a moment with her hand on the screen door. Martha felt her sympathetic eyes on her.

"Martha, I wish I could make it easier for you some way."

Martha's eyes filled with tears. She was so heartsick that the least bit of sympathy could bring on a flood. "Thank you," she said in a muffled voice.

The lady opened the door and stepped inside, leaving Martha to herself again. She wiped her eyes and leaned over against the chains of the swing, her eyes closed. The lump in her throat was getting to be unbearable. She was beginning to feel nauseated with weariness and heartache. She wished she could go somewhere, where no one could hear her, and throw herself on the ground and cry until she could cry no more. This was getting to be too much!

Abruptly she got up from the swing and almost ran

278

off the porch and out into the yard. But there was no place to go! She ran to the end of the yard bordering the garden. Here was a bit of soft grass and she flung herself down on it, but the tears refused to come. Her face was hot and her eyes burned. Her hands were cold and clammy. She felt as if she were going to fly to pieces. For a long time she lay there fighting this thing—lay there until all at once she heard Pop's voice calling softly through the darkness, "Martha."

Martha sat up. "What?" she answered softly, her voice tight.

He came down the steps and peered in her direction. His eyes, unaccustomed to the darkness, searched for her. He was almost ready to call again when he saw her sitting there. He came toward her slowly, his gaunt frame stooped and stiff. There was a whitewashed tree stump a few feet from her; in the old days Mom kept a bucket of geraniums there. Pop sat down on it, took out his handkerchief, and wiped his face. "This heat makes it worse for Mom," he observed, putting his handkerchief back into his pocket.

Martha remained silent. What didn't make things worse for Mom? There seemed to be no power on earth to relieve her—only God; and God didn't choose to do so. Again Martha felt ready to fly to pieces.

"Your mother is pretty anxious about you," he began softly.

"Me!" Martha exclaimed in surprise, momentarily checked in her desperation.

"She is afraid you are having a hard time keeping faith in God," he said.

For a moment Martha remained silent, considering his

words. She plucked a blade of grass from the soft sod and began nervously to pull it apart.

"How does she know?" she asked, unknowingly revealing the truth by her question. The revelation added another layer to Pop's already burdened heart.

"From things you have said, I think. Then, too, she seems to sense it without words. She can't bear to think of it."

"But, Pop," Martha's voice rose desperately. "Pop, how can He be a loving God and make His children suffer so?"

"Martha, Martha!" his voice chided sadly. "Don't you know, the more He loves us, the more He tries us?"

"Well, but why? What is there about us that makes it so? Wouldn't it work just as well to have things going smoothly without any crying and tears and pain? Wouldn't it?"

"No. Don't ask me why, but it doesn't. Our nature is such that the best Christian character is developed only through trials and sorrow. Whom the Lord loves He rebukes and chastens, you know. Don't think that suffering is a sign of God's displeasure. Oh, I grant that it can be to someone who is not right with God, but for a child of God such as Mom is, and I am, and you, too—for such a one, the more we suffer, the more of God's love is revealed to us. Please believe this, Martha."

Martha plucked another blade of grass and pulled it nervously to pieces, considering his words. Pop remained silent, too, praying all the while that God would reveal His love to her through this. Finally Martha spoke.

"When Daniel was killed, it was so sudden it knocked the props out from under me all at once. It took me a long time to get over that, to get to the place where I could see God's loving hand in it. But this—this is the same thing, only before death. It's like being stretched out tight on a frame, then suddenly loosened again. Then stretched tight again. It's getting me down," she concluded wearily. Her hands were lying quietly in her lap now.

Pop's heart ached intolerably for her. He longed to put his arms around her and comfort her as he had when she was a little girl and came to him for solace in some small childish hurt. But he remained on the whitewashed stump.

"Is that ache healed then? I mean of Daniel's death."

"Mostly," Martha replied simply. "Oh, there are still times when I get lonesome for him, but like I said, I've gotten to the place where I can see God's loving hand in it."

"Can't you see the same thing in this case?" Pop asked softly, lovingly.

"Oh, Pop, I try, but to see her suffer so is like a knife twist in my heart! And there is nothing we can do to help her. I never realized that seeing someone you love suffer would be like this!"

Pop realized the truth of her words. In Daniel's case, death had been so sudden and swift that Martha had been spared the pain of seeing him suffer. There had been no dreary days, no weary endless nights of standing by, powerless to relieve a loved one.

"Listen, Martha," he began. "Listen. Mom says in those days when the pain is at its worst, that is when Christ is nearest to her. She wanted me to tell you."

Martha looked up quickly. It was too dark to see his face, but she felt the tenor of his voice—loving, kind, tenderly wanting her to see the brightness through the

281

clouds. There was a catch in her voice when she asked tremulously, "Is that how it works?"

"Yes, I have found it so myself. When she seems to be torn apart with pain, when nothing on earth can help, God's hand is clearly revealed. That is what makes it bearable."

Martha considered this for a moment. All at once the bittersweetness of its truth came over her, and those tears that had refused to come in her desperation came like a flood. She was powerless to stop them. She flung herself down on the grass again and cried and cried. Pop let her cry. He sensed that this was a healing flood and had best not be stopped.

At last she sat up and wiped her eyes. "I can see it now," she said simply, quietly. Pop, for all his heavy heart, felt a surge of quiet joy flow through him.

*   *   *

The end came quietly about a week later. Ervin and Alice were there, and Thomas also. Mom passed into a coma the last twenty-four hours, and the others tiptoed around the house, solemn in the face of death. Mary and David came over, too, to spend the last hours of the vigil. At the last, Mom opened her eyes and looked around her, as a child does when waking from a deep sleep. She didn't seem surprised to see them all there. Her eyes went around the bed noticing each one: Pop was on the old rocker, with Paul beside him, and Martha was standing behind the two. Ervin stood at the foot of the bed, his arm around Alice, and next to them was Thomas. On the other side were Mary and Rosie, with David behind them, and Joe off a little, sitting in a chair. All were solemn and watchful, sensing that the end was near. As her eyes took them all in, she gave them each a wordless, wonderful smile. The children returned the smile, too awestruck to say anything. Then she said weakly, gladly, the soul within her poised and ready for flight, "I'm going now. It's all over." Then her eyes closed again. The others were breathless, every eye riveted on the motionless figure on the bed. Once more she opened her eyes and whispered ever so softly, "Good-by." And it was over.

* * *

The joy, for Mom's sake, of having this sickness ended forever took most of the grief out of her departure. True, for Pop there was the deep sorrow of having a life companion removed from his side, and there would be many lonely hours ahead for him, but right now there was only a quiet relief in knowing that pain was over for Mom forever. He submitted humbly to it, finding peace in knowing that there would be no more standing by, unable to help the one he wanted most of all to help. For the others it was much the same. There would be sincere grief for her after the bustle of the funeral died away, but for now, a strange sweet peace carried them through.

Martha was especially glad she had had that talk with Pop. There was no desperate questioning why in her heart any more. And through the days of the funeral the presence of God was sweeter, more real than anything she had ever experienced before. It was worth going through the experiences of the last months to have this in return. For Martha had found out the eternal truth of God, that He takes nothing away but that He gives back a full measure in return, pressed down, and running over.

32

MARTHA SWUNG THE HOE cleanly, sharply, cutting off the weeds in a wide swath. They were a disgrace to her name. With the strawberries such a big crop and with Rosie's new baby, they had gotten out of hand. She stopped and wiped her face. It was hot—too hot to be out in the sun hoeing, but she was determined not to go in until she had finished. She looked to the end of the row. Only a few more yards and she would be finished. She wondered what time it was and resumed hoeing with renewed vigor, her mind busy with her thoughts.

It was a year now since Mom's death. How swiftly time flew! Quite a lot had happened in that year. Thomas had been married on Thanksgiving. Mary and David had another baby in April—another boy, whom they called Laverne. Just two weeks ago, Rosie had given birth to a boy, called Devon. He was a lusty, squalling, red-faced youngster, giving healthy evidence of fitness from the start. Even now, at two weeks of age, he was more active than Martha Ann. At the thought of Martha Ann, Martha sighed. Poor, weak, helpless child! Even Rosie admitted at last that Martha Ann was definitely abnormal. Now, at sixteen months, she was as helpless as she was at birth. Frail and nervous, she would probably be a baby as long as she lived. It was heartwarming to see Rosie care for her. With her natural love for little ones coupled with mother-love, she cared for Martha Ann with a tender, protective hand that warmed Martha even as it shamed her.

For shame her it did. Martha had a secret, undefined distaste for physical abnormality. It repelled her. When she was a child, there was a little boy in church like Martha Ann, and Martha never looked squarely at him if she could help it. It made her sick to do so and she usually avoided any encounter with him. With any baby, physically perfect and cute, Martha would play, but any suggestion of abnormality made her recoil in horror. So even now, much as she hated herself for it, she harbored the same horror. True, Martha Ann was perfect in her imperfection and appealing in her own way. She had lustrous curly hair, and smooth white skin with a faint pink tint in her cheeks, and Rosie kept her spotlessly clean.

Martha was at the end of the row now and she sighed in relief. She was glad to be done. Her back ached and her throat was dry and parched. Clutching her hoe with one hand, she took off her straw hat and fanned with the other as she made her way to the house to get dinner.

Rosie was doing light housework again and so was getting her own dinner now. At Baby Devon's arrival, Martha went over to the other house to do the work while Rosie was at the hospital. Pop and Paul ate dinner and supper over there, and the arrangement worked fairly well. But Rosie liked to be mistress of her own house and, as soon as she was able, she took over, except for Martha's help with the heavy work.

Martha washed her hot face and hands in the coolness of the washroom. Then, taking off her shoes, she washed her hot dusty feet wiggling her toes delightfully in the cool water.

Now what should she prepare for dinner? There were boiled potatoes to heat, some steak in the refrigerator, and a dish of string beans on the table that she had picked earlier in the day. Sinking into a chair, she began to clean the beans, her thoughts as busy as her swift, sure hands.

It was gratifying to see some flesh come back to Pop's gaunt frame. After Mom's death, he became quieter than ever. He missed her terribly after the first shock wore off, although he never mentioned it. Not that they had stopped speaking about Mom; they did that often, finding solace in talking of her. Things she had said or done, some saying or idiosyncrasy of hers brought quick laughter, while others brought silent, longing tears.

Lately Martha was growing restless, longing for something different. Although she loved Pop and Paul, the thought of spending the rest of her life taking care of them, or of Pop at least, made her vaguely dissatisfied. It wasn't that she expected to have a home of her own; she had put that idea away with her wedding dress in the old cedar chest. But she wanted something else—a change perhaps: travel or even work away from home for a while. It might look like shirking her duty to some, and, for the time being, she felt bound to stay at home, but after the summer's canning was over and the fall work was done, she might look for something else, she thought.

Paul took quite an interest in cooking, perhaps because of his great interest in eating and, with a little coaching and the help of prepared mixes, he could turn into a passable cook. Then, too, Pop could do a lot of Rosie's work and Rosie could lend a hand if needed. As the plan formulated in her mind, it brought a pleasing sense of anticipation. The thought of it carried her about on fly-

286

ing feet until dinner was ready. She decided to discuss it with Pop at the first opportunity.

There was no opportunity at noon, as both Paul and Pop were helping Joe with the haying, and they gulped down their food in a hurry and left for the field again, with only a few desultory remarks about the haying and the heat. But in the evening, when they were sitting on the porch cooling off with a dish of ice cream and the last of the strawberries, Martha opened up the subject.

"Pop, what would you say if I went on a trip this fall? After the fall work is over, I mean."

Pop took another bite of ice cream, savoring its delicious coolness, before replying. "Oh, I don't know. It would be all right, I guess. Are you getting tired of staying at home all the time?"

'Oh, no, don't think that," Martha assured him quickly. "It is just—well, I would like to have a change of scenery for a while. I have never been out of the state, you know, except for Ervin's wedding. I was just thinking—well—" her voice trailed off rather lamely. Now that she had put her idea into words, it sounded as if she was tired of staying at home. She was half ashamed of even thinking of going away.

"Well, I can't say that I blame you, Martha," Pop said in his slow, understanding way. "I have been glad to have you here with us just for your company, but I can see how it would be for you. Like you say, you have never been out of the state much; so if you want to go, I won't try to keep you. I want what is best for you."

"Do you and Paul think you could get along without me? I would hate to go and leave you if you couldn't."

"Well, now, we aren't that helpless." Pop said Martha could have seen a twinkle in his eye if darkness hadn't

287

blurred his face. "Are we, Paul?" he added, laying a hand on Paul, who was sitting beside him.

"We can get along without women around," Paul boasted teasingly, with all the nonchalance of ignorance.

Pop winced at his words. "I wouldn't want to go as far as to say that," he chided in a deep, quiet voice. "Women are pretty important in life, boy, as you'll find out in a couple of years. But I do think Paul and I could get along without you for the winter at least, Martha. We will just put an apron on Paul and make him cook his own meals. If he cooks as well as he eats, we will get along all right," he finished.

"Aw, Pop," Paul said, abashed. "I know I eat a lot, but I can't help it. I'm always hungry."

"No offense, no offense. I know growing boys do need a lot to eat. Like an old neighbor of ours said about us, when we were your age, that we had bottoms in our stomachs, but they were so far down. Go ahead and eat; you earn it," Pop said in a loving voice.

Paul got up and stretched, holding his empty saucer above his head. "Speaking of eating, is there any more ice cream, Martha?"

"Oh, you," Martha chided. "Yes, there is. Eat all you want."

Pop and Martha sat in silence for a while after he left. They heard him open the refrigerator and clatter around in its big interior. Then the door banged shut and Martha heard him go into the living room—probably to read; he was the worst bookworm she had ever seen. The heat of the living room would go unnoticed if he had his nose in a book.

"Do you ever think about wanting a home of your own?" Pop's voice came abruptly through the darkness.

Martha was half startled. "Not any more," she said quietly. "I gave that up when I submitted to God after Daniel died."

"Doesn't that hurt you any more, either?"

"I can't say it never does, but time has healed most of it," she answered. Time. How fast the years had gone in retrospect! In September, it would be five years since Daniel's death. Was it really five years since the world had almost stopped for her? Although she still cherished his memory as one does a lovely flower, yet all the sting and pain of it was gone. Martha considered herself richer by far to have been his, yet time had shown that life could go on. There could still be laughter and joy. One picked up the pieces and, if they were turned over to God, one found they could be cemented together again stronger than ever. Since the frail, human prop of Daniel's presence had been removed, good and kind as he was, she had learned to lean more heavily on God.

"I just wondered," Pop broke in on her thoughts. "You never say anything and you are not very often with people your age; so I wondered if you ever thought of anyone else to take Daniel's place."

"No, I haven't," she answered slowly. "There is a complete blank where that is concerned. I guess if God has someone in store for me, I will meet him when the right time comes. Until then, I am content as I am."

"I'm glad," Pop said quietly.

There was silence for a moment and then Martha said abruptly, "Pop, I am dissatisfied with the church, too. In fact, I have been thinking of changing my membership. I wanted to tell you first, though."

Pop sighed heavily. He'd been wondering how long she would be content to stay. One couldn't blame these spiritual-minded young folks if they left the old church in droves, as they had been doing lately. Even many of the older ones were leaving. But to have so many of the leaders and prominent members opposed to any spiritual growth made it bad. In losing these spiritual-minded young folks, they were losing their best members, if they could only see it. Conditions were getting worse and worse. Just last Sunday a visiting preacher had been in church services and severely criticized these "missionary-minded people," who weren't content with the traditions of the fathers. More than one of those missionary people had gone home heartsick and dissatisfied. Pop himself hadn't the heart to encourage Paul to become a member; consequently Paul had joined a more missionary-minded church, for which Pop had been severely criticized. Ervin had changed his membership before his marriage. And now Martha.

He was so long in replying that Martha wondered if he understood her. She was just ready to speak again when he spoke. "It hurts me, of course, Martha. If so many of you go, the church will be worse than ever."

"But, Pop, I can't go along with them any more and I don't think you can, either. You heard that preacher Sunday. Why, anyone who reads the Bible, even halfway wanting to see it, can see that the whole theme of the Gospel is the salvation of lost sinners!"

"I know, I know," Pop said in a heavy voice. "I didn't agree with him, either. It made me heartsick to hear him."

"It did me, too. I felt like crying after services, and I know some of the others did, too. The traditions of the fathers!" she mimicked. "As if the fathers had died for our sins!"

Pop chuckled. Who were the fathers but fallible people like him? Only as tradition is based on the sure Word of God can it endure. With the rejection of more light had come also a looseness in the morals of many of the young folks. Smoking was beginning to be quite common among the boys, a thing unheard of ten years ago. And whispers were going around that drunkenness was getting common at the Sunday evening sings. It was enough to make one weep. Even as the elders rejected the cure, they lamented the sickness.

Martha broke in on his thoughts. "So, Pop, I really think I will change membership. Maybe I will wait until winter, when I am gone. It might spare you some of the embarrassment of having one of your children make the change."

"Well, Martha, you are your own boss, I guess. I wish with all my heart that conditions were such that you would like to stay. If you go, it makes it all the harder for those like David."

At his words Martha grew very sober. Poor David! True, Bishop Fred shared his sentiments, but they were in the minority. Some of the most prominent members of the church were their bitterest enemies. And there was nothing they could do about it.

"I know," she admitted slowly. "But the thought of staying is almost abhorrent to me."

"Then if it's like that, go. I won't stand in your way. Do what you think God calls you to do. God bless you." He was standing now, ready to go in.

Martha got up, too. "Thank you, Pop," she said quietly. "I am so glad you understand."

33

NOW THAT SHE KNEW Pop approved of her plans, Martha set about making definite arrangements for her trip. She worked harder than ever to get all the work done so that there would be no extra load on the others. She canned innumerable jars of fruits and vegetables, knowing how handy they would be in her absence. She wrote Ervin and Alice about her plans as soon as they were made and received a prompt reply. Ervin wrote:

"If you are considering going on a trip and don't come to see us first thing off, I'll put a black mark after your name, for sure. We'd love to have you here with us all winter if you care to. We have a three-room ground-floor apartment with a dear little old widow, Sadie Good. It's a huge old house and she has another couple upstairs. I feel sure you could stay here.

"I love my teaching job here. I have the fifth and sixth grades in the parochial school. This is my first week. They begin earlier than the public school and I am sure we will get along fine. Teaching seems to be my lifework, I feel sure, and I praise God for His leading the last few years. Without His help it would have been impossible to keep up. Many is the time I would be discouraged and think of giving up, wondering what a clod-dirt farmer like me was doing studying to be a teacher. But He led me through those periods, I can thankfully say. Then, too, my good wife helped wonderfully. She has been so patient in doing without things, skimping and saving in those lean college years. I would like to make it all up to her if I can, although it seems an impossible thing; she was, and is, so wonderful.

"But to get back where I started, as I said, you could stay here and get a job in town. Girls like you are much in demand as domestic help; they can almost name their own salaries. Do you want me to inquire around for a job for you? I am positive I could get one.

"I forgot to tell you that we are attending a little mission about twenty miles from here, in Cleveland. We love it. It is run by a young couple, Fred and Betty Stoll. They seem to be fairly on fire for the Lord. To see them hover over their little flock is a pretty wonderful thing to see. They are short on help, though. Fred is Sunday school superintendent, usher, and secretary, besides being preacher, and they are so genuinely glad to have us come and help that it is heartwarming. It makes me humble, too; I'm so afraid I am not everything they take me to be.

"Here's hoping to hear from you in the near future, telling us you are going to come. Please do, Martha. I would appreciate it so! Love and prayers, Ervin."

Martha would have been hardhearted indeed to turn down such a plea. So now she made plans to leave for the eastern town, where Ervin was teaching, by the last week of October, at least. By that time the fall work should be over and there would be no qualms about unfinished work. She began teaching Paul to cook, and was gratified to see him take to it as a duck takes to water. The first time he served a meal, entirely cooked by himself, was a momentous occasion. It consisted of delicious fried, country-cured ham, mashed potatoes, and gravy, some of Martha's home-canned beans heated and seasoned with ham drippings, and cole slaw. To top it off, he brought in a luscious chocolate cake. True, it was made with a mix and frosted with one, but Paul's pride was evident.

There were mishaps, to be sure. Some of them were serious—like the time he dropped a tea towel on the gas burner and nearly set fire to the kitchen. Another time he broke Mom's cherished crockery mixing bowl, which had been in the family for years.

Some of his mistakes were comic, too—like the time when Martha set him to making pancakes and he forgot to add the baking powder. The leathery, brownish result almost discouraged him, but he eventually saw the humor of the situation and laughed with the rest of them. Then there was the time when Martha found him poring over the cookbook, looking for a recipe for gravy. She had a good laugh over that.

One day, while cleaning the upper cupboards in the washroom, she found a small stewpan, the inside of which was burned black. At first she was perplexed, but finally light dawned on her. Paul had made a cake one day while she was on a shopping trip, and served it without frosting. Come to think of it, the house had smelled peculiar when she returned, but in her haste to put her bundles away, she had forgotten about it. What would be the proper procedure now, she wondered. Should she present it to him as it was? No, a better idea flashed through her mind. Leaving the cupboards momentarily uncleaned, she set to work with a will and scoured it herself.

That evening she kept it under the table until grace was said. Then, pulling it out, she shoved it under Paul's nose before he had a chance to reach for food. Because he was thinking of the day's history lesson, he failed to comprehend the significance of it. For a moment he stared at it blankly, then a flush crept over his face to the roots of his well-combed brown hair. Martha never saw him so embarrassed before. It was too much for her, and she burst into helpless laughter, laughing until the tears ran down her cheeks. All the while Paul kept looking from her to the pan on his plate.

Pop watched the proceedings with a puzzled look. "Would you mind telling me the joke?" he asked Martha in a polite voice.

"Oh, Pop, it's so funny!" and she burst into laughter again.

Pop reached for the bread plate beside his glass of water, his eyes on Paul's red face. Martha reached over and took the pan off his plate. "Paul, I wish I could take a picture of your face," she said gayly as she wiped the tears from her eyes. The dull red slowly disappeared and he raised his eyes.

"Where did you find it?" he asked at last, reaching automatically for the plate of bread Pop was holding.

"Where you hid it. Whatever made you think I wouldn't find it? What were you going to do with it—clean it after I'm gone?"

"I don't know," he grinned.

"What is this all about, anyway?" Pop asked again, curious.

"Paul burned that pan black with something. What was it anyway?" Martha asked, turning to Paul.

"Frosting," Paul answered, abashed.

"For the cake, Saturday?"

Paul nodded.

"Well, anyway, he burned it as black as coal and then hid it out in the upper cupboards in the washroom, thinking I would never find it. Didn't you?" she asked, turning to Paul with a merry twinkle in her eyes.

Again Paul nodded, a disconcerted grin on his face. The humor of it hit Pop all at once and he burst into hearty laughter, quickly joined by Martha. Even Paul grinned until it looked as if his face would split, and he burst into a loud guffaw. At last Pop stopped laughing and, reaching over, gave Paul a light shake.

"Think you can get the best of a woman, boy? Well, I'll tell you, you can't. They will find you out every time!"

*   *   *

Martha picked up another big juicy pear from the dishpan in her lap and began peeling off the thin yellow skin with quick, skillful fingers. This was the last of the year's canning, she hoped. It was nice to go to the cellar in the winter and bring up the fruits of one's labors, but she did get tired of canning! She was helping Rosie with these, having done her own the day before. They were working in silence for a while, each busy with her own thoughts. Martha's thoughts were on her coming departure. She was leaving the following week and had most of her things packed and her train ticket bought already. She was as excited about it as a child, with little else on her mind.

Rosie said little about the whole thing. Of late she seemed like a different Rosie. She was quieter for one thing, and no longer so determined to have her own way in everything. Joe was firm with her. He wasn't one to be pushed around by a childish wife; neither was he unkind to her in any way.

Mom's death, coupled with fragile little Martha Ann, seemed to have a softening effect on Rosie. Martha wondered if she had fully yielded herself to God. Before her marriage, she always passed off such suggestions with a scornful air. For a long time now, Martha had said nothing about it; yet she wanted very much to know how Rosie felt about God, about having Christ in her heart. Dare she ask her?

Taking a deep breath, she began.

"Rosie, how is it with your soul? Have you ever given yourself to Christ?"

Rosie looked up quickly, rather startled. "What makes you ask that?" she inquired.

"Well, I just wondered, that's all. I would like very much to know. Have you?"

Rosie was silent for a moment, and Martha wondered if she had offended her by asking. Finally she answered in a slow, hesitant voice, "I don't know if you would call it that or not, but I know something has happened to me in the last few months—something I can't explain. I only know that having my own way doesn't seem so important any more."

Martha listened, breathless. Then she spoke again: "How—what—what happened, Rosie? Tell me, please; I so want to know!"

"Well, I hardly know where to begin," Rosie said. "Partly it was because of Mom's illness, I think. That and Martha Ann not being—not being so well, I think. But, anyway, those two things worked together to bring this change about. Especially Martha Ann. Oh, Martha, it almost broke my heart to have my own sweet baby not normal! If you only knew how much I looked forward to her! Before she was born, I used to lie awake nights planning for her. What she would look like, what she would wear, how she would talk—I felt sure it would be a girl—and things like that. Then to have her be like she is!" Rosie's voice broke in muffled sobs, and she groped in her apron pocket for a handkerchief. Martha swallowed an unbearable ache in her throat.

"Those last few weeks before Mom died were awful ones for me," Rosie began again. "Seeing her go through all that made me realize how much she really meant to me, I think. I know you can remember how I used to be so stubborn and hard to manage. Then, after Mom died, I used to think about it and wish with all my heart that I hadn't been like that. I finally decided that was why Martha Ann turned out to be like she is, because I was so mean to Mom. Then somewhere along the line—I really don't know when it was—I began to pray to God. That was something new for me; I'm sure you know that. I always felt before that I was capable of handling my own affairs—that I didn't need God. I can see now that I need Him worse than anyone else. At least, I told Him to come into my heart and manage me. Since I did that, everything seems to be so different."

"Oh, Rosie, you don't know how glad I am to hear that," Martha said in a voice choked with emotion, tears running down her cheeks.

Rosie's eyes met hers. "Does it mean so much to you?" she asked.

Martha nodded, the lump in her throat threatening to get out of hand. "I have been praying for you for a long time, Rosie. Ever since I yielded myself to God," she said simply.

Rosie picked up another pear and began to peel it. "You used to talk with me when I was younger, but you haven't said anything for a long time; so your question surprised me a little. I guess I thought you didn't care any more. Not that I could blame you, at that. I used to be pretty nasty about it, I know."

Martha smiled wryly. "Yes, you were," she admitted. "Although I never held it against you. I realized you did it because you didn't know better. I used to cry sometimes, because I was afraid you never would give up."

"But God finally got me, thanks be unto Him," Rosie said softly.

"Amen!" Martha echoed fervently.

34

A WEEK LATER found Martha situated, at last, with the little old widow lady, Sadie Good, pleased and excited with the novelty of it. True to his promise, Ervin had found a job for her. She was to be a part-time worker in the home of a well-to-do physician, Dr. Steven King, and his semi-invalid wife. As Ervin had said, girls like Martha were so much in demand that they could almost name their own salaries.

Not that she did. In fact, when they offered her twenty-five dollars a week, she had half a notion to refuse it, wondering what she would ever do with so much money. At first she was rather self-conscious, as she had never been around people other than those of her own culture. They did their best, however, to set her at ease. Big, restless Steve King, with his deep, booming voice, and Myra, his fragile, quiet wife, had had girls of Martha's kind before and valued them highly for their efficiency and dependability. The three children—Karen, fifteen; Billy, twelve; and Steven, Jr., seven—were friendly enough, too. So after the first few days, she got along fairly well.

Because they wanted only day help, Martha went back to her room in the evening. She usually ate breakfast with Ervin and Alice, and that, together with morning devotions, was the highlight of the day. How she did enjoy those times! There was something so refreshing and stimulating about Ervin and Alice, with their consecrated Christian outlook on life. Baby James was over a year old now, a perfect specimen of small boyishness. More than once Martha thought of Martha Ann when she looked at him. How great the contrast between the two! She usually gave him a hard hug when she compared them, causing James to give her a quizzical look. Why did Aunt Martha hold him so tightly, he wondered. More than once she wiped a tear on his curly brown hair.

From the first she attended the small mission church with Ervin and Alice. And to Martha, with her warm zeal for Christ and His work, it was wonderful. Fred and Betty were so friendly, so concerned about the lost souls around them, and so interested in their little flock of believers. They were only a few in number: Harry and Ernestine Jones and their four children, Grandma and Grandpa Bell, old Mrs. Akes (a widow), Miss Stearns (a maiden lady), and a dozen or so children who attended more or less regularly. These, together with Fred and Betty and their three lively youngsters, and Ervin and Alice, made up the Salem Mission Church. It had been going for a year when Martha came on the scene.

Martha plunged into the work immediately. Fred and Betty, who had the fringe of their enthusiasm worn off by now, what with the discouragements so common to city mission work, took fresh courage from her contagious enthusiasm and worked with renewed vigor.

Because of the scarcity of teachers, the nursery class and the first-grade class had been put together. As a result, the pupils were very hard to manage. When Martha came, they were divided again, and she was put in charge of the first-grade class.

In her youth she had taught the ABC class back home

in her old church, but aside from that, teaching was an entirely new experience for her. At first she felt rather self-conscious, but the friendliness of the class soon put her at ease. She had six pupils: Jeanie Bell, Grandma and Grandpa Bell's granddaughter; Carol Jane Stoll, Fred and Betty's eight-year-old daughter; Joey Shook; Tony Grimes; Blossom Smith, a little Negro girl; and Johnny Jones, the son of Harry and Ernestine Jones. Johnny was the only fly in Martha's ointment. To begin with, he was slightly retarded. This in itself would have been fairly easy to cope with. But, to make matters worse, he was spoiled. Since he was the only boy in the family and was five years younger than his youngest sister, he had been petted and pampered all his life. Consequently Martha realized from the beginning that he was going to require a strong hand and much prayer.

*   *   *

By the end of the third month Martha felt so much at ease and was so genuinely happy that the idea of going home seemed farfetched and dim. She began to wonder whether it was actually necessary for her to go home in the spring. Would it be possible for Pop and Paul to get along without her next summer? It would bear looking into at least. However, she mulled the idea over in her mind and prayed about it for a few weeks before writing.

She enjoyed her work at the King home, although, because of Mrs. King's increasing invalidism, more and more duties were heaped upon her shoulders. That made no difference to her, however, as she was used to hard work. She had been doing it ever since she finished the eighth grade in school. Karen helped a little at times, but generally she was too busy with her school activities to do more than run through the house on her way coming or going.

Finally Mrs. King stayed upstairs all the time. Martha wondered what her trouble was, but was too polite to ask. As the weeks passed, it seemed to her that there was an undercurrent of tragedy in Dr. King's manner—as if his booming voice and hearty guffaw were only a front for some unbearable ache. Once she came into the living room to find twelve-year-old Billy crying as if his heart were broken, and he refused to confide in her. This troubled Martha.

A week or so later, however, she discovered the reason. She was unusually busy all day making arrangements for Karen's birthday party the following day. Mrs. King seemed too weak to do more than plan and give orders. In the evening, just as she was ready to leave for home, a heavy rain came up. It would be only a matter of minutes until she would be thoroughly soaked if she started out in it; so she decided to wait a while. Just then Dr. King came through the hall, looking for a magazine. Seeing Martha, he said in his characteristic way, "Raining cats and dogs, isn't it?"

Martha smiled. "Something like that," she admitted. "I think I will wait and see if it lets up a bit."

Dr. King paused. "I'll drive you home. Not fit for a dog to be out, much less a woman."

Martha protested feebly. "Oh, really, I can wait. Should you leave Mrs. King?"

"She will be all right with Bill and Sonny till I get back. Won't take me but a minute."

Martha waited by the door while he went upstairs. In a minute he returned in raincoat and cap.

"Hadn't you better put something over your bonnet?"

he said kindly. "You will have that ruined before you get to the car. Here, take this," and he picked up Billy's raincoat and handed it to her. Martha took it self-consciously and draped it over her head as she followed him out on the porch. It was raining as hard as ever. Turning to her, he said, "Wait here till I get the car out."

Martha nodded. He dashed out into the downpour and disappeared around the corner of the house. She heard the roar of the motor as he backed the car out of the garage.

"Some rain," she commented, removing the dripping raincoat from her bonnet as she got into the car.

They drove in silence for a block, Dr. King peering intently into the darkness. "Myra loves rain," he spoke at last. "Before she became sick, we used to drive through town sometimes when it rained at night. She loved it."

"Too bad she can't do that tonight, if she likes rain so well," Martha observed.

A look of care came over his face. "Lots of things she can't do any more that she used to do," he said briefly.

Martha was silent for a moment. There must be something seriously wrong with Mrs. King, she thought. "What is her trouble anyway? Or would you rather not tell me?" she asked timidly.

"Mrs. King has leukemia," he said in a heavy voice.

Martha gasped softly. "Oh, that is serious!"

Dr. King nodded. There were heavy lines across his face, reminding her of Pop's careworn face. "We have done everything there is to do for her," he said wearily.

"I know what you mean," she said softly. "My mother died of cancer over a year ago."

He gave her a grateful look. "It is an awful thing to

go through, isn't it?" he said in a voice husky with emotion.

Martha nodded. Her eyes became moist as she recalled those heartbreaking weeks before Mom's death: the weary, pain-racked days; the endless, sleepless nights; the unbearable ache in one's throat! "The only thing that carried us through was the grace of God," she said.

Dr. King looked at her quickly. "I haven't been conscious of anything like that," he said. "Would it be worth-while?"

"Oh, but you must!" Martha faltered, rather startled at his words. "Why, nothing else could help. Only God can help you bear a burden like this!"

Dr. King sighed, almost wistfully. "We have never been religious people," he said after a pause. "I always thought I knew too much to be religious. But lately I have been wishing I didn't have to carry this alone. It seems more than I can do," he finished.

They were in front of Sadie's big house now. Martha fumbled slowly for the door latch, wishing with all her heart that she could point this man to Christ, the Only One who could help him. Turning to him, she said, "Dr. King, don't you know that Christ is ready to help you carry this burden if you come to Him in faith and say so?"

"I can't do that," he said wretchedly.

"Why not?"

He raised his head and said in a tired voice, "I have denied Him too long for one thing. So why should I come to Him now like a beaten pup? No, I will just have to carry it alone."

There was nothing to say to such unbelief; so Martha got out of the car, and Dr. King drove off into the darkness.

305

35

THE NEXT SUNDAY Martha had her first open encounter with Johnny Jones, who had been getting worse each time the class met. He kicked whoever sat beside him, giving that unlucky one black and blue spots on the shins; or he appropriated the crayons and kept them in his possession. He made loud noises when she was telling stories until it was impossible to get the undivided attention of the others. Martha dreaded the idea of complaining to Fred and Betty, feeling they had enough to worry about. Yet, if he kept getting worse, something definitely had to be done. She tried soft admonitions, gentle pleadings, and, finally, rather sharp warnings.

On this particular day he seemed determined to upset the whole class. He pinched Blossom Smith until she cried. When Martha scolded him, he just sat in sulky defiance. Then when coloring time came, he kept his arm around the box of crayons and would let none of the others have any. With a sinking heart and worried frown, Martha finally got them away from him. At story time, he took out a hidden safety pin and stuck Carol Jane Stoll, causing her to jump up and cry with pain. The others all looked at Martha with frightened, questioning faces. Was she going to let him get away with this?

For Martha this was the last straw. Plainly more was needed than verbal rebukes. Taking Johnny firmly by the shoulder, so suddenly it gave him no time for thought, without a word she took him to the rest room and gave him a sound spanking. She was almost crying herself when she finished, but she managed to keep her voice steady as she asked, "Are you going to behave now?"

Thoroughly quelled, Johnny looked up at her and nodded, his face tear-stained.

"Well, all right, we will go back to class, but remember, if you act naughty, I will do the same thing again. Remember!"

He looked at her in wordless, unmistakable respect and Martha led him back to the classroom. She kept him beside her, however, until the bell rang for worship services, at which time he made a beeline for his parents.

With a sinking heart Martha watched him go. She hated the idea of spanking him, but there just seemed to be no other way. All through the worship hour, she was heavyhearted, her ears deaf to Fred's excellent sermon. Only at the last, when Fred announced a series of meetings in the near future, did Martha rouse from her reverie.

After the services were over, in the flurry of handshaking and greetings, Betty came up behind her and invited her to stay for dinner. Ervin and Alice were staying, too.

At the dinner table, Martha resolutely pushed Johnny to the back of her mind and took part in the genial conversation, which turned naturally to the coming meetings.

"I surely was fortunate to get him," Fred said after requesting a second piece of his wife's delicious peach pie. "I wrote him back in January and asked him to come, but I didn't hear from him for so long I was afraid he wouldn't accept. Then just last week he wrote and said

307

that the Lord has definitely opened the way for him to come. I was really pleased."

"Who is he, anyway?" Martha asked.

"Gerald Roth. Haven't you ever heard of him?" Martha shook her head. "Well, he is the up-and-coming evangelist of the next few years, I think. He really can preach. He can almost bring you to your feet with the fire of it."

"Yes, but poor fellow, he has had a pretty rough time of it. He lost his wife about four or five years ago, wasn't it, Fred?" Betty remarked.

"Something like that, I think. After her death he had a nervous breakdown. But I guess the Lord had His hand in it all. At least you can't help seeing that, when you hear him preach," Fred said.

"What happened to his wife?" Martha asked, in sympathetic interest.

"She was killed in a car wreck, poor thing. It happened one Sunday night when they were on their way to church. Some drunken teen-age driver drove into them from the side, I think. It happened to be her side, and it killed her outright. Gerald was pretty bad, too, for a while. They had been married only a year or two at the time," Fred concluded in a sober voice.

Martha was silent. She could certainly sympathize with him. Had there been wells of grief for him, too? Dull, dreary days and tormented, sleepless nights? Had his faith almost faltered as hers had?

All at once a queer look came over Fred's face and he stared at Martha—stared at her so hard she became embarrassed. "Betty," he said in a hushed voice, "Betty, I just happened to think of something." All the while he kept his eyes on Martha.

"What is it?" Betty asked, her eyes following his gaze

until they rested on Martha. The others looked on, puzzled.

"She is just the girl for him," Fred said solemnly, more to Betty than to the others. "I can see the hand of God in this."

"Oh, isn't that right? With all she's gone through, she would be just the right one for him."

"Oh, you silly people!" Martha said, half vexed, half amused at their talk. "You will make me too embarrassed to even come to the meetings. Besides, I have never laid eyes on him."

"Now maybe you have something here," Alice chimed in. "If anyone deserves a good man, Martha does."

"Well, he would be the one for her," Fred assured her. "You know, I think I will have to get busy and work on this thing."

"Oh, stop!" Martha protested, thoroughly aroused by now. "As I am the one involved in this, I think I should have something to say about it!"

Fred and Betty laughed heartily at her disconcerted face, and Alice joined in, too. Only Ervin remained silent, regarding Martha with amused, quizzical eyes.

After dinner, while the men were in the living room listening to Fred's new records, the women helped Betty with the dishes. There was no more talk about the evangelist; for all their teasing at the dinner table, Fred and Betty respected Martha's feelings.

As Martha washed the dishes in the hot, sudsy water, her thoughts went back to Johnny Jones. Unconsciously she sighed heavily. The episode of the morning still rankled.

Betty heard the sigh from the cupboard where she was

putting away the dishes. "Having trouble, Martha?" she asked.

Martha looked up with a rueful smile. "How did you guess?"

"Well, a sigh like that, and you ask me how I guess?" Betty teased.

"It's Johnny Jones," Martha admitted.

"So you are having Johnny trouble, are you? I was hoping his good behavior would last."

"Good behavior!" Martha exclaimed. "I thought his behavior was trying all along."

"I suppose it looked like that to you, being new here, but Johnny has been the terror of the Sunday school ever since he started to come. What happened now?"

Martha recounted the tale of the morning's woes to Betty and Alice, who listened in sympathetic silence until she had finished.

"These things happen, Martha," Betty said gently. "I know how you feel about it. You can't let him disturb the whole class, but of course one hates the idea of punishing him. If it is any comfort to you, Fred has had his run-ins with him, too."

"He has! What does he do about it?" Martha asked, interested.

"Well, he makes him understand who is boss, first of all. Then he tells me about it, and we both pray for Johnny," Betty said with a smile.

Martha smiled, too. "Well, if it works for Fred, maybe it will for me, too! Why don't we all pray for him now?"

"No sooner said than done," Betty assured her, and the three women bowed their heads and prayed for Johnny.

*   *   *

Mrs. King continued to grow weaker and weaker, until the care Martha could give her was no longer sufficient, and a gray-haired nurse came on the scene. She was a kind, motherly sort of person, and Martha liked her from the beginning.

The atmosphere around the house became hushed and still. Karen stopped bringing her friends home to watch television. In fact, except for the news in the morning, when it was turned on ever so softly, the rest of the family ignored it. Martha found out from Mrs. Imes, the nurse, that loud noise was forbidden in the sickroom, as well as all through the house.

Usually in the morning, as soon as Martha arrived, she prepared breakfast for the family. While they ate in a haphazard, come-and-go fashion, she went upstairs to see Mrs. King and to receive her orders for the day. Again in the evening, just before leaving, she went up to bid her good night.

Every evening Martha came down with a burdened heart for Mrs. King's soul. How must it be, to be so near death and to have no provision made for eternity? Some might have said that Martha had no right to judge, but for her the facts were plain. Didn't God's Word say that he that believed on the Son had life; and that he that believed not the Son shouldn't see life? And as far as Martha could see, the Kings made no profession of believing. Not once in her four months there had the name of Christ been so much as mentioned. If they owned a Bible, Martha had never seen it. Plainly, Christ meant nothing to them. She shuddered for their sake. Couldn't someone show them the way? With a prayer for the right words to say, Martha resolved to speak to Dr. King the first chance she got.

Meanwhile the coming meetings had them feverishly busy every evening, canvassing the vicinity in which the mission was located. Ervin and Alice were one team, Fred and Betty another, and Miss Stearns and Martha paired off and worked remarkably well together. Grandma and Grandpa Bell helped by baby-sitting for the Stolls, and Harry and Ernestine helped, too.

Martha started out rather timidly, with a prayer in her heart for the right things to say. After the first evening, however, she found it was much easier than she had imagined. Miss Stearns helped a lot. Her job as saleslady in a dime store made her more or less used to meeting strangers; consequently, she was more at ease. The first evening she took the initiative, while Martha stood in the background and prayed silently for God's grace. Some people listened in a noncommittal way, while others seemed glad for the invitation. They had decided to give a salvation tract with each invitation card, praying that the tract might be a means of awakening someone. One family the first evening refused both the tract and the card, slamming the door in their faces when they mentioned the nature of their errand.

"Well, I guess they told us off," Miss Stearns said.

"Didn't they, though!" Martha agreed. "Some people don't know what they are missing."

"Oh, well, we did our duty," Miss Stearns said, resignedly.

The next evening Martha was a bit dismayed to hear Miss Stearns say as they started out, "Well, Martha, tonight it is your turn to do the talking."

"Do you think so? Couldn't you do that again tonight? You did so well last night, I thought."

"How am I going to find out how you do, if you don't

try?" Miss Stearns asked. "I think you should try. It will be good for you—really, it will."

Martha approached the first few houses timidly, but God was gracious to her. Everyone she talked with was friendly and courteous, and they willingly accepted the tracts and invitation cards. Later, however, the tide turned. One man threatened to run them off the property if they didn't get out; another told them curtly that they were a bunch of d—d fools; and a third slammed the door in their faces without a word. As a result, Martha was considerably discouraged.

"Don't you think we had better quit for tonight?" she asked Miss Stearns in a disconsolate voice. "No one seems to care to hear us in this neighborhood."

"Now, Martha," Miss Stearns said in gentle rebuke, "surely you can take more than that. Where is your Christian fortitude? We haven't taken anything yet that amounts to a hill of beans. Come, Martha, I thought better things of you than this."

Martha bit her lip, thoroughly ashamed. The rebuke was needed, she admitted. She looked at Miss Stearns with a rueful smile. "You win," she said half laughing. "I needed that, I know."

"Sure you did," Miss Stearns said. "Now, for all Christ has done for us, we can take a little abuse for His sake."

They trudged the half block to the next house in the sparsely settled district and, with a prayer on her lips for Christian fortitude, as Miss Stearns had called it, Martha knocked gently on the door. It was opened by a rotund middle-aged man in shirt sleeves. Martha handed him the tract and invitation card with a smile.

"Would you like to know how to be saved?" she asked kindly. "We are from the Salem Mission, and we are having an evangelist to hold meetings next week. I am sure he will have a message for you. Would you care to come?"

At Martha's words he broke into a wide smile and exclaimed happily, "Well, blessed be God, I am saved! Come in, come in! I want to talk with you."

He held the door wide open, and Martha and Miss Stearns entered the comfortable living room. "Mom, Mom, come in here and see these ladies. God bless them! They came to ask us if we want to be saved," and he laughed heartily.

A bustling, sweet-faced woman came into the living room, wiping her hands on her apron, a lovely smile on her face. "Want to be saved? Well, I am happy to say, we are saved."

"Oh, I am so glad," Martha said. "I—I mean, it's so refreshing to find someone who knows what we are talking about. Especially tonight."

"Well, I should say we do!" the genial man said heartily. "Here, sit down. I would like to talk with you. I always like to talk about the Lord."

It was impossible to resist such Christian hospitality, and Martha and Miss Stearns found themselves taking comfortable chairs. After all, they were tired. Miss Stearns had been on her feet all day at the store, and today had been cleaning day at the King residence.

"Well, now that we are here and settled, maybe we can find out who we all are," the man said warmly. "I'll begin with us. I'm Tod Smith and this is Lillie, my better half."

Martha introduced herself and Miss Stearns.

"Glad to meet you, glad to meet you! And so you know the Lord, too?"

"We certainly do," Miss Stearns answered emphatically. "I have known Him for the last two years and Martha has known Him longer than that."

"Is that right? Say, that sure sounds good to me. Well, Lillie and I have known Him for the last fifteen years and He's never failed us yet, has He, Lillie?" He turned to his quiet little spouse, who was sitting beside him.

"That is right, Tod," she assured him. "Sometimes He tried us pretty hard, but His goodness always shone through. He's been mighty good to us," and she smiled sweetly at the two women.

"You say you are having meetings?" the man asked.

"Yes, we are," Martha answered. "We would like very much to have you come if you can."

"Well, say, we sure will, if it's an evangelistic meeting."

Martha laughed, remembering how the last three persons they had talked with had so emphatically shown that they wanted nothing to do with the Lord.

"Are you ladies going around inviting people?" Mrs. Smith asked sweetly.

"Yes, we are. We have for the last two nights now. We don't get around as much as we would like to because it is usually late when we get started and then, too, we don't like to be out so long after dark," Miss Stearns explained.

"How are the people you talk to, pretty hard to convince?" Tod asked interestedly.

Martha and Miss Stearns exchanged glances, remembering their late encounters.

"Some of them are," Martha told him. "In fact, the last three were pretty nasty about it. One said he would run us off the property if we didn't get out. Another said

315

there was no God and we were a bunch of fools. And the last one before you slammed the door in our faces."

Tod clucked sympathetically. "Is that right? You know, some people just seem to be that way. It hurts to see it, doesn't it?"

"Yes, it does," Martha admitted. "For their sakes, it does. If they only realized what they were missing!"

"That is true," Tod acknowledged. "If you could just show some of them the predictions of things to come and convince them that God loves them and wants to save them from it. But I know what you mean. I meet lots of those, too. You see, I am a janitor in the high school of this district, and I meet many teachers who don't believe in God. Or, worse yet, if they do believe, they have a weak, watered-down version of Him. Brotherhood of man, and the fatherhood of God, and such stuff. It makes me want to cry at times."

Miss Stearns nodded vigorously. "I know how that is, too," she said when he had finished. "That is just the kind of people I meet so often in the dime store. You see, I have given out a lot of tracts in the last two years, and it's surprising how many people have the same attitude."

"Yet they call this Christian America," Lillie said soberly. "I wonder how many of them really are true Christians."

"I am afraid a very small percentage of them are, even of people who profess to be," Tod said gravely. "I guess it is just like the good Lord says in His Word; in the last days there won't be much faith on the earth."

"Maybe the Lord will be coming soon then," Miss Stearns said.

"That's true. But for me, I don't see anything to fear

316

in that. In fact, I'm hoping this is the year He comes. For I do want to see the Lord!" Tod said, a heavenly longing in his voice.

"Amen!" the others echoed fervently.

The clock on the wall suddenly struck ten and Martha jumped to her feet. "Oh, Miss Stearns, is it really that late? Hadn't we better be going? We told the others we would meet them at the mission at ten."

Miss Stearns got up quickly and said, "I think so. It will take us ten or fiteen minutes to walk over there."

"They will be worried about us if we don't get there soon. Well," turning to the Smiths, Martha smiled and continued, "I surely am glad that we met you and I really enjoyed our talk."

"Same here," Tod said heartily. "You know, it says in the Bible that God sees those people who talk about His name and He writes that down in His book. He has probably got this down now, don't you think?"

Miss Stearns and Martha laughed. He was such an engaging man.

"I hope so," Miss Stearns said. "We really must be going now."

"You will come to the meetings?" Martha asked.

"We sure will," Tod assured her.

They gave them the address and said good-bys all around. At last they were outside and going down the walk in the direction of the mission.

"My, that was nice, wasn't it?" Martha sighed.

"Yes, it was. Just like the dear Lord to have something good for us at the end."

"But we almost missed it," Martha said. "How glad I am for that pep talk you gave me!"

Miss Stearns patted her arm. "Well, you have learned

a pretty valuable lesson, Martha. So I think you will do better next time, by the grace of God."

"Thanks. I sure hope so," Martha said soberly.

36

IT WAS THE NEXT DAY that Martha got a letter from Pop, assuring her that if she was happy in her work, he felt that she should stay there. He wrote:

"It's been going better than I was expecting. Paul has turned out to be a pretty good cook. He will do for us men at least, and I have found out that cleaning and dusting aren't so bad. Rosie lends a hand now and then. I help her with the washing and she does our ironing. Then I've started keeping Martha Ann over here quite a lot. It helps to keep me from getting lonely. Do you know, she seems to enjoy being with her old granddad. She almost never cries with me. Rosie tells me she is pretty fretful at home at times.

"So, if you think the Lord can use you where you are, just stay there. Of course, we would be glad to see our Martha again, but I think we can manage the work here all right. Your letters interest me considerably. What you write about the Kings makes my heart ache for them. Like you say, what must it be to be looking death in the face without the assurance of the dear Saviour's presence? I shudder for them! But I have been praying for them. And I never forget to pray for my dear daughter Martha. God bless you. Pop."

The letter brought tears to Martha's eyes. She thanked God from the bottom of her heart for her wonderful, Christ-loving Pop. She ached with pity for him in his loneliness. If Martha Ann was company for him, perhaps the fragile, helpless little thing was a blessing after all.

About this time, in a last-ditch effort, Mrs. King was removed to the hospital. She was too weak when she went to speak more than a word or two to Martha. "Do what you think best," she faltered in a voice barely more than a whisper. "I know I am leaving the family in good hands." And then she was carried out to the waiting ambulance. Martha watched them until they were out of sight, the ambulance followed by Dr. King's big Buick. After they were gone, Martha went into the living room and dropped to her knees in front of the big, expensive couch and wept. The living room bespoke elegance, comfort, and wealth—everything money could buy, yet the one thing most needful was sadly lacking, making this beauty nothing but a mockery. The true riches had never seemed so precious to her as now.

The next morning at the breakfast table, Martha inquired anxiously about Mrs. King. Martha had left in the evening before Dr. King had returned home, and the thought of Mrs. King had been an ache in her heart whenever she had awakened during the night.

Big Steve King put down his coffee cup before replying. His face looked haggard and pale. "There's no change," he told her wearily, propping his chin in his hand. "I guess it really won't do any good to have her in the hospital, except make her last days a little easier."

"I am so sorry, Dr. King. If only—" Martha stopped, biting her lip.

"If only what?" He looked up interestedly. "Come on, what were you going to say?"

"If only she had Christ in her heart," Martha burst out passionately. "If only she was ready to die!"

Dr. King gave a wretched little laugh. "Oh, Martha, come now, you aren't going to start in on something like that, are you? Didn't I tell you that we weren't religious people?"

"Religious!" Martha scoffed. "I wasn't talking about religion; I was talking about having Christ in your heart."

"All the same difference," Dr. King said indifferently. "I admire you for your faith; it is all right if you want it. But I don't think I will try it this late in the game."

"Oh, but please, you must! Don't you realize that unless you ask Christ to come into your heart and cleanse you from sin, you will be lost in Hell forever?" It seemed to her that he must be moved by the very passion of her outburst.

"Listen, Martha," he said in a stern, terrible voice, "I admire you for your convictions and all that, but please don't be preaching to me like this again. I told you that we are not religious people. If you want to be, all right, we will leave you alone. So if we don't try to foist our ideas on you, the least you can do is not try to force your ideas on us. I hope this settles it once and for all." His face was terrible to behold.

Martha found herself trembling so much she had to grab the stove for support. How could anyone be so hardhearted? To her it seemed to be the voice of the devil himself.

She fought for self-control, turning to the sink with her back to him. The very atmosphere seemed to be charged with unbelief. For the first time since she had begun working here, a violent wave of homesickness swept over her. If only she were at home with Pop!

The meetings were to begin the following Sunday, and Martha found herself looking forward to them longingly.

The atmosphere of the King home was like a blight on her soul the last few days, although Dr. King was civil enough in the short periods he was at home. Martha was kind and solicitous even with the burden on her heart. But not once again did she mention the name of God to him.

It was with these thoughts heavy on her heart that Martha accompanied Ervin and Alice to the mission on Sunday morning. It was a beautiful spring day. The warm breezes were beginning to bring the promise of greenery in the near future. As Martha gazed on the quiet landscape between town and city, a bit of the burden was lifted. There was even a faint smile on her lips by the time they arrived at the mission. She had been thinking, the last few miles, of the thrill of seeing the Lord for the first time. How she longed to see Him! Unknown to her, a radiance glowed from her eyes as she entered the mission. Her dark blue eyes were clear and deep, her cheeks were pink, and her lips were red. Besides, she had an inner radiance that only the King's daughters possess.

That was the way Gerald Roth first met her. He was standing with Fred just inside the door, greeting each one as he came in. They had been laughing at some remark of Fred's when the door opened and Martha stepped inside, followed by Alice and Ervin. Fred, with a twinkle in his eye, pounced on Martha at once.

"Well, Martha," he said, smiling, "I would like to have you meet Gerald Roth, the evangelist." Martha saw his eyelid drop in a faint wink and felt like making a face at him. Turning to Gerald he said, smiling broadly, "Gerald, I would like to have you meet Martha Yoder."

Gerald shook her hand slowly, his eyes probing deep into hers. All at once, without warning, this tall, beautiful girl before him, with her radiantly glowing face, walked into the inner confines of his heart and took possession, all unconsciously on her part, with a suddenness that left him breathless. He had only confused impressions of Ervin and Alice, vaguely gathering that they were in some way connected with Martha. During the short period when the others were all talking at once, he was dazed and quiet, without a thought of what they were saying, conscious only of the presence of this wonderful girl opposite him. Martha was silent, too, although she was regarding him out of the corner of her eye. What she saw impressed her well. He was of medium height, only a few inches taller than she, with a thin, dark face, dark, wavy hair, and intense, dark eyes. He seemed rather quiet, she thought, totally unconscious of the reason for it.

Just then more people came in and Fred began introducing them to the still-dazed Gerald, and Martha turned to go up the aisle with Alice and Ervin.

By the time the worship service started, Gerald had recovered sufficiently to preach a wonderful sermon. Martha listened, thrilled with his words. Here was food for the soul! After it was over, while she was talking with some newcomers who had come as the result of their visitation work, Fred stole slyly up behind her. "Say, you really knocked him over," he whispered. "Doesn't look as if he needed my help at all."

Martha gave him a reproving look and a jab with her elbow and went on talking to the couple before her, and Fred went chuckling up the aisle. Although she knew he meant well, he embarrassed her terribly. She would be glad to get away from those intent black eyes that seemed to be regarding her every time she looked up.

But she wasn't going to get off as easily as that. Betty insisted that they all stay for dinner—to get acquainted with each other, she said, with an innocent look at Martha. When the confusion finally subsided, Martha found herself in the back seat of Ervin's car, wedged in between Miss Stearns and Gerald Roth.

She was reserved during the short drive to the Stoll home, mentally resolving to put the teasing Fred in his place at the first opportunity. She was sure he was the one who had brought all this to pass.

Gerald sat beside her, not seeming to notice her reticence. He was so taken up with the nearness of her presence that he was content just to sit beside her, wishing the ride were ten times as long.

In the afternoon, following dinner, it was impossible for Gerald to keep his eyes off her. Countless times Martha looked up to meet his gaze. At first, when their eyes met, he looked away, but as the afternoon passed, he no longer did so. Instead, he met her eyes and held them for long moments. Each encounter made Martha more confused. What was this? Was she actually becoming interested in this man? She had given up all thoughts of the opposite sex long ago. Hadn't all those dreams of a home of her own been put aside when Daniel was killed? Not that she missed him any more. The memory of him was faint and far away, she was startled to discover, and would grow more so, if she was around this man very long.

All this eye play was keenly noticed by the Stolls. Neither did it escape the scrutiny of Alice and Ervin. Even Miss Stearns noticed that Martha seemed to get more confused as the afternoon wore on, rarely speaking unless directly spoken to. Her face was flushed, with moist curls escaping from her usually immaculate coiffure. Whenever the Stolls met, they exchanged meaningful looks, with a wink from Fred and a giggle from Betty. Martha saw it and could have shaken them both.

In the evening, the Bells left, taking Miss Stearns with them, and Martha thought hopefully of going home and getting away from the intense gaze of Gerald and the mischievous looks of the Stolls. She didn't take the matchmaking Stolls into consideration, however, when she did so.

"Oh, you don't have to go home," Betty said. "Why waste all that gas driving home, then driving back again?"

"Sure," chimed in Fred with a grin at Martha. "Might as well stay here. No reason at all for going home."

Ervin joined in with the treachery and calmly consented to stay. Martha was beginning to be a little vexed with the whole thing. Everyone seemed to be in a conspiracy to throw her at Gerald's head and she resented having so little to say about it. It made her a bit short with them. Betty connived with Fred to have Martha and Gerald opposite each other at the supper table. Gerald by this time was so far gone that he looked at her freely, even calling her by her name. Martha found it all the more confusing. When they were all in the cars ready to drive back church, Martha was not surprised to find Gerald beside her. This time he talked freely, seemingly not disturbed by her stiff answers.

How glad she was to get off by herself in a corner of the basement before services began! She hid her face in her handkerchief, wishing she didn't have to go upstairs and meet those piercing black eyes again. She prayed for courage to meet them, but even God seemed to take on the teasing face of Fred. As there was nothing else to do, she resolutely squared her shoulders and marched upstairs.

*   *   *

Late that night, after all the rush of the evening was over and Gerald was alone in the privacy of the Stolls' guest room, he sat down on the edge of the bed with his chin in his hand. What a day this had been! Who would have thought that he, Gerald Roth, would ever be interested in a woman again? He had thought his heart so thoroughly buried in Amy's grave, five years ago, as to be beyond any awakening. Their life had been so happy, those two short years of their married life together, and the shock of losing her suddenly so great that never had he imagined he would get over it enough to look at another woman. But life seemed to lack completeness lately, as if there needed to be an addition to make it right. At the time he didn't realize what it was, but he did now. He needed a wife, that's what it was! A man wasn't made to stand alone.

And what a helpmeet she would make! A sincere, dedicated, conscientious Christian, who had the radiance that came of tested faith, coupled with the fact that, from the physical standpoint, she was beautiful! He started to undress in an agreeable glow. "Well, let it come," he thought. "I bet I could go far and look wide before I would find a better one." It was with this thought uppermost in his mind that he knelt in prayer. God seemed to smile as if He were pleased with the idea, too. When Gerald finally went to sleep, it was to dream of Martha.

37

A S THE MEETINGS PROGRESSED, Gerald and Martha were thrown more and more into each other's company. He graciously met her every evening at the door, his intense gaze making her blush as soon as she met it. Although he never let it come between himself and his message, he was aware of her clear eyes on him all evening. It gave a new depth to his preaching, he realized. One night his text was on Revelation 19:7: "Let us be glad and rejoice, and give honour to him: for the marriage of the Lamb is come, and his wife hath made herself ready." He held the audience spellbound as he described the wonderful bride of all brides, the Church, the Bride of Christ. It made Martha thrill to hear him.

It was a good thing she found food for her soul there, for when she went back to the King home in the morning, she found Dr. King's mother there. Myra King was so weak that Dr. King no longer came home at night, waiting instead by her bedside, in haggard weariness, for the end. And the terror of a Christless grave came over Martha afresh.

How her heart ached for the children! They all knew, of course, that their mother's death was near. Karen grew morose and sulky. Bill's face was thin and pale, reminding Martha of Paul's face in the heartbreaking days before Mom's death. Small Sonny wandered about the house like a ghost when he wasn't in school. Never were they to see their mother; Dr. King didn't want them to see her in her last hours of suffering.

There was nothing she could do about it—not with Dr. King's terrible face before her. So during the daytime she accumulated the burden, and in the evening, under Gerald's preaching, she found rest and comfort again. This went on until the last day of the meetings, when Dr. King came home with an ashen face and told her dully that it was all over. Myra King had died at three o'clock.

Martha was already starting out the door for home when she met him on the porch. She was leaving early, for with Grandma King there, it was no longer necessary for her to stay and prepare supper.

Although she had been expecting it, the news left her almost limp. She managed to stammer out a few words of sympathy—words Dr. King acknowledged even though he seemed not to hear them. He turned wearily toward the door and she proceeded down the street. It was a soft spring evening. The trees were sending forth feathery green leaves, and from the branches overhead came the cheerful trills of the birds.

"Cheer-up, cheer-up," came the call of the robin. And a noisy jay called out loudly at Martha's approach. Only instead of "Thief, thief," as it usually sounded to her ears, it was a cry of "Lost! Lost!"

Lost! Without hope and without God in the world! Martha's heart felt as if it would break. It was with weary feet that she finally ascended the steps of Sadie's big porch. She was too preoccupied to notice the strange car in front of the house. Usually she stopped in to see Ervin and Alice when she came home, but tonight she went straight to her room. As she stood in the center of the room, her mind went round and round. All at once she fell on her knees and cried as if her heart would break.

For a long time she remained so, crying and praying—short little sentences. At last she was aroused by a sharp knock on the door and Alice's voice calling, "Martha, are you home?"

Martha got up quickly and opened the door.

"I didn't know—Why, Martha, what is wrong?" Alice asked, alarmed at the sight of her tear-stained face.

"Mrs. King died today," Martha said dully.

"Oh, did she really!" Alice exclaimed in sympathy. "And without Christ."

Martha nodded. "It's terrible. I just can't get over it," she said tearfully, wiping her eyes again. "It seems such a tragedy. She was a nice person and all that, and went through all that suffering, and—" Words failed her.

"And now to die without Christ," Alice finished solemnly. It's terrible."

They stood in silence for a moment, then Alice said, pulling herself up sharply, "I came to tell you supper is ready. We have company."

"Company!" Martha echoed. "Who is it?"

"Gerald Roth." Alice smiled at her. "I asked him to come last night and he came soon after dinner. We have had a nice visit this afternoon." She beamed on Martha, her voice full of meaning. The "nice" visit had been mostly questions asked and answered about Martha. The implication was lost on her, however, taken up with Mrs. King as she was.

The idea of having him there filled her with confusion. Her hair was a mess, she was sure. Her dress was soiled and rumpled, hardly the thing in which to greet a visiting preacher—especially since the preacher was young and good-looking and quite obviously interested in her. She cast a hurried look at herself.

"Well, listen," she told Alice, "you go on and I will be there as soon as I change my clothes and clean up a bit."

"Okay." Alice laughed good-naturedly, departing for the kitchen.

After she was gone, Martha hurriedly splashed some cold water on her face and combed her hair. Then she went into the closet for a dress, deliberating for a moment, woman-fashion, which one to wear. She chose a lovely blue one, not admitting to herself that she was doing it for him. It would have made Betty laugh to see her.

When Martha came into Alice's cozy living room, she found Gerald on the couch with James on his lap, apparently engrossed in conversation with Ervin, his manner totally belying the fact that he had been listening intently for her footsteps. He arose at once when she came in, dumping James, without ceremony, on the floor.

"Hello, Martha," he said, unable to keep the gladness out of his voice. His piercing eyes regarded her intently, as usual, and she dropped her eyes and blushed as she returned the greeting. She was delivered by Alice, who came into the living room to announce supper.

Although the others talked freely and gaily while eating, Martha was silent for the most part. The thought of Myra was heavy on her heart. More than once she almost choked on her food as she thought of the blue jay's call on the way home. Lost! Lost! The food seemed as tasteless as sawdust.

Alice noticed her lack of appetite and commented on

330

it. "Martha, aren't you hungry? Don't you like my food? I did so want it to be nice."

"Oh, it is delicious Alice," Martha faltered. "I just don't seem to be hungry, that's all."

"Well, you aren't eating enough to keep a bird alive. I think you have been working too hard," Alice said reprovingly.

Martha blushed again and made a valiant attempt to eat more. Her lack of appetite had been noted by Gerald, too. In fact, she seemed to be unusually quiet tonight, almost downcast. With a pang he wondered what was wrong. Had he done something to offend her? He was more determined than ever to talk with her alone tonight, if at all possible. Would she consent to ride to church with him? He surely hoped so! Here he had known her for eight days, and known almost that long that she was going to be the girl for him, and not once in those eight days had he talked with her alone. He did want to do that before he left. As soon as supper was over and the saucy little cuckoo clock in the kitchen piped out the hour of six, he asked her directly, "Martha, would you care to ride to church with me?"

Martha looked up, startled. She felt Alice's eyes beam on her, and Ervin was grinning, she was sure.

"Oh, I—guess I could," she faltered, knowing her face was red again.

"Do you suppose we could start right away? I would like to be there early if possible; perhaps we had better start soon."

Martha looked at the dirty dishes on the table and then raised her eyes to him. "I was going to help with the dishes."

"Oh, no, Martha! Don't let these dishes keep you. Why, I will do them in no time," Alice exclaimed at once.

"Sure, go ahead," Ervin chimed in. "I'll help her get those done. Old Ervin, the dish towel, that's me!"

Alice gave him a playful dig with her elbow as she assured Martha, "You go right away. Don't worry, we'll get these things done."

So there was nothing else to do but get her coat, purse, and Bible; and after Gerald had thanked the young folks warmly for their hospitality and for the nice visit, they stepped out into the lovely spring evening. Alice ran shamelessly to the window and watched Gerald open the car door for Martha as if she were a queen. She giggled.

"Here, you shameless peeping Tom!" Ervin said in mock reproval. "Can't you leave them in peace? Suppose they saw you?"

"Oh, Ervin," Alice giggled again, "isn't it wonderful?"

"What?"

"Why, Gerald and Martha! Oh, they would make an ideal couple!"

Ervin came over beside her and slid his arm around her waist. "Do you think they will be as ideal as we are?" he asked, as he leaned over and rubbed his cheek over her soft blond hair. Alice turned around and grabbed him tightly, giving him such a hard squeeze he grunted.

"Here, you," he chided. "You're pretty hard on that good supper you fed me. Can't you go easy on a fellow?"

Alice dropped her arms abruptly and made a face at him. Then she turned to the window again. But Gerald and Martha were gone by now. She turned back and sighed a happy, contented sigh.

"Seriously though, Ervin," she began as she started

clearing the table, "what would you think if it were serious?"

"Be all right as far as I know," Ervin replied. "Say, will you look at this boy!" he ejaculated, his eyes falling on James, who had crawled up on a chair and helped himself to a piece of chocolate cake.

"Oh, Jamie!" Alice dissolved in helpless laughter at his chocolate-covered face. "Daddy, go get a washcloth and clean him up."

When Ervin came back bearing a cleaner little James on his arm, Alice had run the dishwater into the sink and was already washing dishes with deft, swift movements. Ervin picked up a towel to help.

"What did you talk about this afternoon?" he asked.

Alice giggled again. "Martha."

"You mean to tell me that you voluntarily told him her complete history?"

"Oh, Ervin, of course not!" Alice retorted indignantly. "Land sakes, he wasn't here fifteen minutes before he was asking questions about her. Where did she come from? What was her folks' reputation? How many brothers and sisters did she have besides you? When was she saved? How long had she been a member of our church? How long had she been here? How long was she going to stay? How old was she? And, last of all, why wasn't she married, a wonderful girl like her?"

"Did you tell him all?" Ervin asked soberly, his mind on Daniel. Even now, over five years after his death, remembering him brought a sigh to his lips. He had never found another friend like Daniel.

"Yes, of course."

"What did he say to that?"

Alice's hands were deftly clearing the plates. "He was

quiet for a while; then he said that he could sympathize with her because he had lost his wife five years ago. Then he asked if I knew of anyone else she might be interested in, and I told him that as far as I knew, she had never seen another man since Daniel was killed, until he came on the scene."

Ervin laughed softly. Alice was as avid a matchmaker as Betty Stoll. "So I expect if he knows all is clear, he will not let any grass grow under his feet," he commented wryly.

"He gave me that impression. Yes!"

* * *

Gerald Roth had driven about a mile through the clear spring evening, fragrant with the smell of warming earth, when he turned to Martha and asked in a kindly voice, "Martha, what seems to be troubling you? Is it anything I have done or said?"

Martha looked up quickly. Did her feelings show that plainly? "Oh, no, it is nothing you have done," she assured him. "Did you—I mean, did I act as if I were offended by you?"

"Well, you did have me wondering," he said in a relieved voice. "But if it is nothing I have done, what is bothering you? You see, I would like very much to know."

What else could she do? Before she knew it she was pouring the whole story of the Kings into his sympathetic ears. He listened with a grave face, without a word, until she finished. Even as he was silent, he was sending a prayer of thanksgiving heavenward to his wonderful heavenly Father for this girl beside him. How like Him to give him a woman for his heart who shared his feelings so completely! Then his thoughts were drawn back to Martha's story and he sighed heavily. The old story of

334

unbelief! He had heard it so often he should be hardened to it, but he wasn't. It made him want to cry at the frequency of it. After she told him all there was to tell, she felt strangely relieved.

"You have prayed about this, haven't you?" he asked gravely.

She looked up quickly. "Oh, yes," she assured him. "I have been praying about it all the time, mostly."

"I hoped so. Martha, your story is the same old story of unbelief that has been on my heart for a long time. How many people are just like the Kings! Thousands of them, I'm afraid. There seems so little we can do about it."

"I know. I don't expect I know as well as you do, but I certainly don't think the Kings are an isolated case. If you could only tell them what they are missing," Martha said fervently.

"But you can't. They seem to be determined to go to destruction at all costs. You can tell them and warn them and then stand back and see them go to Hell. It seems as if they couldn't get there fast enough."

Martha nodded.

"But then, when I remember how long I lived in self-righteousness and unbelief, I can only thank God from the bottom of my heart for bringing me to my senses," Gerald said soberly.

"Me, too!" echoed Martha.

They were at the mission already. The twenty miles had flown on silvery wings. Gerald looked at his watch. They would have another fifteen minutes, at least, before the Stolls arrived. And there was something very important he wanted to tell her. He took a deep breath and said abruptly, "Martha, we have known each other for over a week now, and I can't begin to tell you how much you mean to me. I was wondering, could you—would you—care for me?"

Martha must have shown her amazement, for he hastened on quickly. "Oh, I know it is sudden and all that, and I don't want to scare you, but surely you must have realized, at least a little, that you—that I like you awfully well!" he finished manfully.

A deep dimple showed in her cheek. This thing had been out of her hands all along, and now came the mischievous, womanly notion of setting him in his place. "Oh, you do!" she said in mock gravity. "What makes you think I should have known it?"

"Well, but surely—but, Martha, I thought—" He floundered helplessly, a clammy fear grabbing hold of his heart. Was he mistaken after all? Surely she had seen by his eyes that he was desperately in love with her.

Martha's heart was too soft to leave him in desperate uncertainty for long. She gave a soft laugh. "I did think you watched me a lot when we were together," she said playfully.

"Surely you must realize that you have come to mean a lot to me—especially after tonight, when I can see that you share my burden for lost souls. So—would you—I mean—could you care for me?" It was all out quickly.

Martha's face became very grave. She hardly knew what to say. Certainly she respected and admired him more than any man she had met since Daniel. He was completely yielded to the Lord, as she wanted to be. Also he was young and extremely good-looking, but after all, she had known him only a week. It seemed hardly long enough to make so important a decision. Martha had sense enough to realize that widowers don't usually court ladies for the pleasure of it, as teen-agers might do.

336

They invariably mean business. She was at a loss for the right words.

Some of her thoughts must have shown on her face, for he said rather awkwardly, "I am sorry. I suppose I rushed you too much, but—well, because I am leaving tomorrow, I wanted to tell you. You have come to mean very much to me, you see."

Martha lifted grave, serious eyes to him. His own met hers and held them—held them until she felt all her reservations begin to melt away. She wrenched her eyes away at last and laughed shakily. Then she bit her lip. What was she to say? After a silent moment she began slowly, "I hardly know what to say. It is true that I respect and admire you very much. As you say, we both love the Lord and share a common burden for souls. I— well, I expect I will probably learn to care for you. But it is all so sudden!"

He listened, mingled hope and despair in his face. When she had finished, he picked up her hand and held it in his own as if it were the most precious thing in the world.

"Then you think in time you could—could learn to care for me?"

Martha met his eyes again. And looking deeply into them she found herself saying gravely, quietly, "In time, yes."

He gave her hand a hard squeeze and said fervently, reverently, "Thank God."

At that moment they were rudely interrupted by a loud shout. "Hey, what's going on here?" came Fred's teasing voice. Martha jumped and turned red as a beet and Gerald dropped her hand quickly—not quickly enough, though. Fred saw it and grinned broadly, one eyebrow raised quizzically. Flustered, Martha began to gather up her purse and Bible. Gerald reached across and opened the door for her. She was thankful to get away, and she hoped Fred wouldn't detain her with silly talk. For once he didn't. He had sense enough to leave them alone, now that he felt his help wasn't needed any more.

Martha was descending the steps to the mission basement when she felt a hand on her elbow. Startled, she turned around to meet Gerald's eyes once more. How he had managed to shake Fred off as a mystery. He asked gravely, "Will you write to me after I'm gone, Martha?"

Martha nodded.

"Please let me know as soon as you are sure." Again she nodded, wordless, and left him.

* * *

There was a tiny room, just off the furnace room, in the mission basement, where the Stolls kept the cleaning supplies. The first evening of the meetings, Gerald had appropriated this for his own private prayer room. There was a five-gallon bucket, half filled with paint, that made an altar. And, because five years of keeping his own clothes clean had taught him the value of an ounce of prevention, he looked around for something to lay on the floor to protect his knees. There was a box of old newspapers in the room. One of those, spread out, did nicely. Here he had gone every evening to pray while the mission slowly filled upstairs. Only Fred and Betty knew about his private trysting place, and they highly respected him for it.

So here it was that Gerald poured out his heart to his heavenly Father after detaining Martha on the steps. There was, first of all, glad thanksgiving for Martha— thanks for her burden for souls; thanks for her love for

338

the Lord; and thanks for her soft words of respect and friendship, bordering on a far deeper relationship. So confident was he of her answer that he thanked the Father for it as if it were already given.

His thoughts returned to the message of the evening. He had spent a large part of the forenoon in study and prayer, his custom always when holding meetings. This morning he had been reading in the thirty-third chapter of Ezekiel, and that seemed to fit hand and glove with Martha's sad story of the Kings. As always, when the thought of lost humanity came to him, he groaned inwardly. Why will you die when there is everything you need to give you life, eternal life? Why be plunged into destruction if Christ died on the cross to make atonement for the sins of mankind?

He stayed there on his knees, oblivious of the steady thump of footsteps upstairs, until a glance at his watch told him it was time to begin. Then he arose, conscious of the Lord's presence, and made his way upstairs with firm, determined steps.

The building was packed that evening. Looking over the assembly, Martha was pleased to see some people whom she had invited in evening visitations. Tod and Lillie Smith were there again; they had been there almost every evening. The entire mission family was there, too, of course. Blossom Smith slipped in shyly beside Martha and was rewarded with a wonderful smile.

Martha was surprised to have Gerald use for his evening's theme the story of the Kings. He omitted names, of course, but the story was told in all its heartbreaking reality. He chose for his text Ezekiel 33:11: "Say unto them, As I live, saith the Lord God, I have no pleasure in the death of the wicked; but that the wicked turn from his way and live."

Martha listened, spellbound, as he brought forth the evening's message. God took no pleasure in seeing sinners die, he said. Rather than a cruel, hard despot who found satisfaction in condemning humanity to Hell, He was a loving, compassionate sovereign, who wanted to give salvation freely to all. He was not willing that any should perish, but that all should come. He opened the way to eternal life through His Son, Jesus Christ, and now through the Holy Spirit, they were pleading these nineteen hundred and more years, wanting souls to come and be saved, to be fed with the bread of life and clothed with the garment of His righteousness. And yet, their pleading was immeasurably sorrowful because so few heeded. "Turn; why will ye die? Come and live!"

Without knowing it, tears were running down Martha's cheeks—tears because what he said was so true. Why did so few respond? When there was all they needed with the Lord, why did so few believe? The ache of it finally made her weep openly.

At the close of the service, when Gerald gave the invitation. Martha's soul leaped for joy to see not one or two but no less than six people go forward to accept the Lord as their personal Saviour. While she was praying that more would respond, she felt a soft moist hand being slipped into her hand and she looked down to see Blossom's dark, tear-stained little face raised to hers.

"Martha, I want Jesus for my Saviour, too," she whimpered.

Why, bless her! "Do you want me to go forward with you?" Martha asked.

Blossom nodded. With Martha holding her hand tightly,

they went up the aisle to the altar, to kneel with the others, Blossom crying softly and Martha praying silently. At the close of the meeting, they both followed the others into a side room, and it was here that Martha showed Blossom just how to be saved. Blossom was ready to accept Christ and after Martha showed her John 3:16, a glad, happy smile broke over her face. " 'Whosoever,' that means me, doesn't it?" she asked.

"Yes, it does, Blossom."

"Then I'm saved now, am I not? Because I know Jesus died for me!"

Martha had tears of joy on her face. Some might have felt that Blossom was only a little girl, so why bother? But Martha knew she was just as important in God's sight as any adult.

"Shall we tell Jesus 'thank you' for saving you?" she asked Blossom, hardly able to take her eyes off the child's happy smiling face.

"Yes!" So they both thanked God for saving little Blossom, Martha asking God to guide and direct her from now on and to use her to His honor and glory. When they arose, Blossom surprised her by giving her a tremendous hug.

"I'm so glad you are my teacher," she said lovingly. "I think you must be about like Jesus yourself, you are so nice and kind!"

Martha was surprised and touched. She stooped down and kissed and hugged the child. "Thank you, Blossom," she said gravely. "You just pray for me that I can always be like Jesus, will you?"

"All right, I will," she replied, giving Martha's hand one last squeeze. "I expect I had better go now," and she skipped away happily.

38

THE NEXT FEW DAYS found Martha too busy to miss Gerald or the meetings. There were house guests at the King home—Myra's brother and his wife, and their sixteen-year-old son, and one of Steve King's sisters and her husband. They had come for the funeral. So with meals and bedmaking, cleaning and washing, Martha was working from morning till night. Especially did Myra's brother's wife try her patience by endless requests for pressing a suit or doing some laundry. Martha was taken back at first. Then as the demands increased with never a word of thanks, she began to be half vexed. Couldn't she at least say thank you? Who did she think she was? As there was nothing to do but comply, Martha did her bidding with what grace she could muster and in the end was rather ashamed of herself, for the lady pressed a generous tip into her hand when she departed for home.

After the funeral was over, Grandma King, a widow who lived a rather lonely life in a hotel apartment, announced her intention to stay. With Karen's help, she would be able to manage quite well; so Martha found part-time work elsewhere, returning to the King home only one day a week to do the cleaning.

She had written Pop about Gerald and the meetings and Gerald's interest in her, although she omitted any mention of his proposal.

"He seems to be a fine man," she wrote. "Fred thinks the world of him. Ervin was favorably impressed with him, too. And I must admit that what I saw of him makes me admire and respect him very much. Poor man, I guess he has had quite a time of it so far. His wife was killed in a terrible wreck about five years ago. They had been married only two years at the time. Fred said Gerald suffered a mental breakdown after that, but he is completely recovered from that now. I did notice that he seems to be the intense, hard-driving type. That is something so unusual for our family; we all seem rather slow and easygoing."

Her letter told Pop more than she intended, and he chuckled after he read it. It seemed to be quite full of Gerald, and obviously Martha was impressed with him. Was this, then, what God had in store for her? Was she to find, after all, happiness with a man she loved? He sincerely hoped so.

Although the people she worked for were friendly and kind, Martha was a bit dissatisfied with her present situation. As it was, she was cleaning lady at a different place every day, and she didn't especially care for the instability of it. She hoped to find a permanent job before long. To her great surprise and delight it came from an entirely unexpected source. One evening after prayer meeting, Betty Stoll cornered her in the basement and asked, dimpling, whether she would care to work for them in August to take care of a new baby. Martha gladly consented. As it was already the middle of June, she decided to keep on with her present schedule until then.

Gerald was writing regularly two and three times a week—sometmies just hurried little notes written before a meeting, at other times, long newsy letters describing his work in detail. Martha found his letters fascinating. He was on call for meetings continually and, as he wrote of souls being saved, she rejoiced with him and her admiration and respect for him grew and grew.

She prayed for him continually—prayed that God might use him for His honor and glory; prayed that he might be courageous and fearless in preaching the plain truths of the Word; prayed that, if it were God's will for them to marry, He would make her worthy of being a preacher's wife.

Before Martha knew it, it was August, and she went to work for the Stolls. As the baby was due any day, there was an atmosphere of tense expectancy in the household, relieved only by husky little Mark Anthony's arrival on the fifth day of the month.

As Martha took care of the helpless little baby and saw how happy Fred and Betty were, she was struck with an overwhelming desire for a home of her own, and Gerald's letters intensified it.

The week after little Mark was born, he wrote, "Can't you give me the answer I desire? I respect your idea of wanting to be sure, but please, Martha, couldn't you tell me yes? I've prayed about it all summer and I am more convinced than ever that you are the girl for me. We have so much in common to begin with. We both love the Lord and want to live for Him, which is the most important thing. Then another thing, we both know what it is to go through a crushing sorrow. Last of all, I love you, Martha. I love you more than words can tell. I haven't mentioned that since the last time I saw you, but I certainly have been thinking it. If you can't answer my question with yes, I don't know what I'll do."

Martha sat down and wrote before the day was over and told him, at last, what he longed to know. "You have come to mean a great deal to me," she wrote. "I respected and admired you from the first, but I realize at last that I also love you. So if you can take me as I am, yes, Gerald, I will marry you. May God bless you and make me a real helpmeet for you."

She was unprepared for his response. While she expected a letter in reply in record time, it was two days afterward, in the evening, when in response to the ringing of the Stolls' doorbell, Gerald accosted her on the steps. She had been washing dishes, with some help from Carol Jane, while Fred was rocking a screaming little Mark. He screamed so loudly at the first peal of the doorbell that it went unheeded. Again it rang, an insistent, imperious ring. Fred cast a helpless look at Martha while he asked above the baby's wails, "Can you answer it, Martha?" Martha wiped her hands on a dish towel while going toward the door, expecting it to be someone to see Fred.

"Gerald! Where on earth did you come from?"

Gerald smiled at her. "Surprised?" he asked.

"Well, I should say! I thought you were busy holding meetings."

"I am. Or I mean I was, but I got someone else to preach tonight. After your letter came I just had to see you!"

Martha smiled shyly. She felt self-conscious all of a sudden.

"Aren't you going to invite me in?" he asked tenderly. "After all, I drove three hundred and fifty miles to see you."

"Oh, excuse me," she stammered. "Come in, of course." She stepped aside so that he could pass into the living room.

A harried Fred looked up from his fatherly worries

and exclaimed in happy surprise, "Why, Gerald Roth! What brings you here?" He jumped up and extended his hand, clutching baby Mark with the other.

"To see this hired girl of yours," Gerald answered happily. "Hey, what have you got here?"

His glance rested on the baby, whose wails had diminished a bit. Fred laughed. "My little new bawl baby. Didn't you hear him? Sounds awful, doesn't he? But we like him just the same."

"I should think you would. What did you do—pinch him?"

The sound of their voices brought Betty from the bedroom to see what the excitement was about. "Why, Gerald Roth, what in the world!" she exclaimed as she caught sight of him. Taking the fretting baby from Fred she began hushing him in that wonderful way so peculiar to mothers. "This is some surprise!"

Gerald looked at Martha with a wonderful smile on his face. Then he reached over and took her hand in his. Turning to Fred and Betty, who were all eyes, of course, he said in a glad, solemn voice, "This young lady has done me the honor of saying she will be my wife."

Fred grabbed Gerald's hand in a viselike grip and pumped it up and down with enthusiastic vigor. "So you finally won her over, did you?" he asked happily. "Congratulations, fellow. You are getting a good wife, I can tell you."

"You sure are," chimed in Betty. She balanced the baby in one arm while she pressed Martha's hand with the other.

"I know it," Gerald said gladly. "If I can only be worthy of her!"

They all looked at Martha, who was blushing violently

by now. The suddenness of Gerald's appearance had taken her breath away, to begin with, and then to have his announcement so abruptly given had taken her poise away completely. Under their laughing, loving eyes she found herself stammering like a teen-ager. "Oh—Gerald—I'm not half so wonderful as you think!"

"Spoken like a lady in love," Fred laughed. "Well, anyway, I think you are both wonderful people. I just hope you will be as happy as Betty and I are." He reached over and took Betty's elbow in his big hand. All at once Mark broke out in loud wails again, at which they all laughed.

"He doesn't want to share the stage," Fred said. "He has been about the most important person around here for the last two weeks, and he is not giving way to any Gerald Roth."

*   *   *

Later on, when they were alone at last, Gerald turned to Martha, who was sitting beside him on the couch, and took her hand in his. He held it in a tight, hard grip as he looked deep into her eyes. Those eyes of his! They had caught and held her the first time she saw him and they did so now. Martha blushed and laughed softly.

"I'm so glad, Martha. Glad and thankful that God has answered my prayers at last. Martha, can we be married soon? A bachelor's life is a lonely one, I can tell you."

Martha laughed softly. "Well, I believe you. And about getting married soon, I thought you were booked solid for meetings until way in the fall."

"I am. But let's get married by Thanksgiving at the latest. Now that I know I am getting married, I can keep some time free for that. Believe me, I will tell them all now! I can't wait to show you off. Wonderful girl!"

Martha grew sober. A faint inkling of the responsibilities of a preacher's wife came to her. Was she qualified? She was afraid not. Only the grace of God could make her so. A little of what she was thinking showed on her face and Gerald noticed it at once.

"What is wrong, dear? Did I say something to offend you?" he asked anxiously.

"I was just thinking about being a preacher's wife," Martha said seriously. "I'm awfully afraid I will let you down on that. I never thought I would be called to be one."

"Listen, Martha," Gerald said simply, "don't have any fears on that line. The same God by whose grace I am made a preacher will also supply grace for the preacher's wife."

Martha was silent as she pondered his words. "Thank you, Gerald," she said quietly.

So it was decided that they would be married on Thanksgiving Day, and that Gerald would visit at Martha's home, to meet Pop and the rest of the family, the last of September, when he would be holding meetings near there. Martha would leave for home soon after the first of September to spend the remaining time before her marriage. With these plans made, Gerald left early the next morning for his current series of meetings. Just before he left, he held Martha to him tenderly and whispered, "Good-by, sweetheart. God keep you till we meet again." Then with a kiss, he was gone.

*　　*　　*

It was good to be at home again. Good to see Pop and Paul and exclaim over Paul's height and, incidentally, his

348

cooking. Good to see that fragile little Martha Ann could sit up, thanks to Pop's patient teaching. Good to see Mary and David and their children. Johnny was already in the second grade, and Bethy, as dainty and ladylike as ever, was close on his heels in the first grade. Philip was chubby as ever. Rosie was glad to see her. And Martha basked in all their love and best wishes, thanking God for her wonderful family. Just a bit of sadness came over her, however, when she thought of how little she would, in all probability, see them after her marriage. Yet she was looking forward to it. The thought of sharing the joys and responsibilities of married life with Gerald was intriguing. If only she could always be everything he needed in a wife. Gerald's assurances on this point gave her confidence.

After the first flurry of greetings was over, a few days after Martha's homecoming, Pop asked her rather hesitantly, "Martha, now that you have betrothed yourself to another; and are looking forward to life with him, can you look back and see God's purpose for you in taking Daniel away?"

Martha looked up from the sewing in her lap. "Why, what makes you ask me that?"

"Well, I was just thinking. We all thought so much of Daniel, and at the time I felt you just fitted together. I never dreamed that God had other plans for you."

Martha looked at him gravely while the sewing went unheeded in her lap. "That is a hard question to answer, Pop," she said after a moment's reflections. "I know that at the time of Daniel's death, I was pretty badly in need of chastisement. I guess God saw it and did the only thing that He could have done."

"What do you mean?" Pop asked.

"I don't know just how to explain it. For one thing, I realize now that I was too possessive in my love for Daniel. I was getting to the place where Daniel was God to me, I'm afraid."

Pop was regarding her intently, almost afraid to break in. But when Martha stopped for a moment, he said, "Go on. What then?"

Martha picked up her sewing and began plying her needle in fine, delicate stitches before replying. "I always was too possessive with anything that was especially mine, for one thing. I know now that one should never clutch one's loved ones too tightly. It took me a long time to find that out. Even losing Daniel didn't take that out of me completely. God had to take Mom away in the heartbreaking way He did, before I finally learned that lesson. But looking back, now that every bit of the pain of losing Daniel, and Mom too, is gone, I can see that all these things have just been steppingstones to a closer walk with God. When I realize that, I am thankful for every bit."

"Martha, your words make me think of that verse in Second Corinthians, the third chapter: 'But we all, with open face beholding as in a glass the glory of the Lord, are changed into the same image from glory to glory, even as by the Spirit of the Lord.'"

"That is a lovely verse, Pop." Martha gave him a radiant smile.

"Isn't it? And so true. I can see that this is the way it worked for you. Changed into the same image from glory to glory.' You have something precious there, Martha."

"Thank you, Pop. I know I do. I have Christ, and I

350

also have a dear father who has been praying for me all these years."

"Yes, I have. I still do. And I pray for all my children," Pop assured her quietly.

Again they were both silent for a moment, each with his separate thoughts. Then Pop quoted again very, very softly, " 'Changed into the same image from glory to glory, even as by the Spirit of the Lord.' "